# a collision of stars

georgia stone

All rights reserved.

No part of this book may be reproduced or used in any manner without written permission of the copyright owner, except for the use of quotations in a book review.

This is a work of fiction. Names, characters, places and incidents in this book either are the product of the author's imagination or are used fictitiously. Any resemblance to actual persons, living or dead, is entirely coincidental, and any portrayals of business establishments, events or locales should not be perceived as reality.

Without in any way limiting the author's (and publisher's) exclusive rights under copyright, any use of this publication to "train" generative artificial intelligence (AI) technologies to generate text is expressly prohibited. The author reserves all rights to license uses of this work for generative AI training and development of machine learning language models.

Print ISBN: 9798868057151

Ebook ASIN: B0CK4V32R2

Formatting by Meg Jones

Cover design by Georgia Stone

# content warning

This book contains content that may be troubling for some readers, including but not limited to: alcohol consumption, cancer (not resulting in death), explicit language (including blasphemy), illness of a sibling, marijuana use, mental health, parental abandonment and sexually explicit scenes. If you're sensitive to any of these topics, read *A Collision of Stars* at your own discretion. Please put yourself first.

# playlist

**English Girls** - The Maine
**There She Goes** - The La's
**hiccup** - Valley
**On A Night Like Tonight** - Niall Horan
**She's A God** - Neck Deep
**Friday Forever** - Trophy Eyes
**Another Night on Mars** - The Maine
**Hush Hush** - The Band CAMINO
**Motown** - Grayscale
**Oh shit... are we in love?** - Valley
**What Took You So Long?** - Neck Deep
**Take Me as You Please** - The Story So Far
**What If It Doesn't End Well** - chloe moriondo
**Midnight Rain** - Taylor Swift
**(what i wish just one person would say to me)** - LANY
**Live Again** - Grayscale
**Taxi** - The Maine
**ceilings** - Lizzy McAlpine
**You Are In Love** - Taylor Swift
**The Heart Never Lies** - McFly

## A COLLISION OF STARS

**Strawberry Wine** - Noah Kahan
**About You** - The 1975
**True Blue** - boygenius
**Till Forever Falls Apart** - Ashe, FINNEAS
**Our Time to Go** - State Champs
**Honey Moon** - Holding Absence
**I Can Feel It Calling** - Trophy Eyes
**Give Yourself A Try** - The 1975
**I Revolve (Around You)** - Neck Deep
**you!** - LANY

Find the Spotify playlist here:

*For anyone scared to take that leap.*
*Give yourself a chance. You're made of stardust, you know.*

# 1

## repeat after me: lying to men is not a hobby

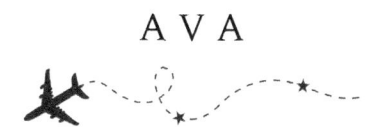

### AVA

It is fundamentally against my morals to tell a man he's funny.

For starters, he might believe it.

And if he does? He might take it upon himself to try stand-up comedy.

This is, incidentally, how I've found myself folded onto a too-small cracked plastic chair at a club in North London, watching a man I met on Hinge tell jokes into a microphone with the animated cadence of someone raised amidst the YouTube furore of 2013.

As always, there isn't enough space for my legs, which means I spend most of Harry-from-Hinge's set trying to rid myself of the pins and needles radiating from my toes to my left calf. When a violent squeak of microphone feedback jolts me to attention I look up to find Harry attempting a final bout of crowd work, before ending his set to lukewarm applause. Once the lights have come back on, we move to the bar for after-show drinks and I push my shoulders back, steeling myself to play an exhausting game where I pretend to care about this near-stranger's life.

Flirting, I've realised, is just small talk with an ulterior motive. I channel all my years of experience working in customer service; feigning enthusiasm when he mentions an obscure comedian I've never heard of and asking him questions that I try moderately hard to listen to the answers to.

'You have such a unique perspective,' I lie. He's an Australian living in Clapham. He has no such thing. And he has clammy hands, which is entirely unrelated, but on my mind nonetheless. But he's tall and hot (arguably the same thing) and if I go home with him tonight at least it won't be a long journey back to mine afterwards.

All I need from him is one night. One night to satisfy this urge, one night to stomp out the boredom without tipping the scales.

We sit there for a few moments, sipping wordlessly, the silence made even more glaring by the fact there's vibrant chatter at every other table in the vicinity. I'm not even two drinks in by the time Harry looks across the sticky table at me, apology written all over his face.

'Ava, I don't feel like I'm getting much from you. You seem kind of closed off.' His eyebrows draw together in earnest. 'I'm just not sure there's a spark, and I'm so sorry, I don't want to string you along. I think it'd be best if we called it a day.'

Damn, he took my line.

---

'Well that was a colossal waste of time,' I say, barrelling my way into the flat I share with my best friend, careful not to leave anything on the floor that she might trip on later.

'The show was good then?' Josie asks, pausing her podcast and twisting her copper hair up into a claw clip as if she knows I'm about to tire her out. True crime can wait—my dramatics cannot. Relaxing on the sofa in feather-trimmed silk pyjamas, silicone under-eye patches resting on her face, she's the picture of elegance.

Meanwhile, I don't need a mirror to know my eyeliner is smudged and my fringe is stuck to my forehead, and after a Tube journey in the almost-summer heat, sweat has made its perilous way down my back, snaking below the waistband of my skirt. I stomp over to my room, wading through the mess to find some semi-clean pyjamas, settling on a pair of shorts and a giant ratty t-shirt I got at a gig once.

'You know,' I raise my voice as I get changed so she can hear from the other room, 'I think I've been operating under the delusion that comedians are supposed to be funny.' When I rejoin her in the living room I hand her a plastic tub. 'I got you those fancy olives you like on my way home.'

'Ava Monroe, you are the love of my life,' she says, peeling back the plastic lid while I open my crisps. 'But stop stalling and tell me what happened.'

Josie managed to inherit both her lawyer father's charisma and her surgeon mother's no-nonsense attitude. Unfortunately, the only notable personality trait I inherited from my parents was an inability to be on time.

I bypass the sofa and sit on the rug with Josie's giant black Lab, Rudy, whose paws twitch as he chases squirrels in his sleep after a long day leading Josie around London.

'The man said he didn't think we had a *spark*. Do we really need a spark if all I'm going to do is join him on his lumpy mattress for one night of mediocre sex and then leave his life forever?' I grab a handful of crisps and shove a few too many in my mouth in one go. 'I made it very clear I'm not looking for anything serious. And by that, I mean, on my profile it literally says "I'm not looking for anything serious".'

'Maybe you're just so... alluring,' her mouth curls into a grin at the last word, 'that when he saw you he thought, "oh my god, if I impress this woman with my side-splitting comedy, she'll fall in love with me and we'll have one-night stands every night until we die".'

'Right.' My eyes water as one of the crisps pokes my windpipe and I have to wait for it to move before I speak again. 'And maybe he just ignored what I said.'

'I don't understand how you even find these people.'

She wouldn't, because she's been with Alina since before we moved into this flat, and consequently never once had to dip her toe in the piranha-infested waters of London's dating pool.

'Dating apps are dire right now.' I open my phone and start to lazily swipe to prove my point. 'Always have been, actually.'

'Read some profiles,' she says with a wave of her hand, settling back against the arm of the sofa as she waits for me to play our usual game.

'Right, okay. This guy rhymed "geezer" with "Bacardi Breezer".' I swipe left.

She shrugs. 'A wordsmith.'

'This one said he doesn't like Parmesan.' *Immediate* swipe left.

'Could be lactose intolerant.'

'This man,' I play a voice note aloud, 'is doing an impression of Shaggy from *Scooby Doo*. And it's not even a good impression of Shaggy from *Scooby Doo*.'

He's six-four though, so I swipe right.

Josie heaves a full-body sigh. Unfortunately, she's one of those hopeless romantics who's convinced there's someone for everyone, even me. But I've spent too long battening my heart's hatches to open them again for anyone, so headboardless one-night stands it is.

'Don't you think you could be judging them too harshly?' she asks. 'That maybe you're being a little too... pernickety?'

'Me? Pernickety?' I try for an indignant gasp but it comes out as a snort.

'We live in London. You could be living through an early-noughties romcom and you're not.' She leans forward, loose strands of hair swinging past her face. 'More importantly, I could be living vicariously through you, and to put it plainly, *I am not.*'

'I'm so sorry that me not wanting a relationship is ruining your fun.'

'Dating apps have killed romance,' she whines, and her head may as well be transparent, because I can practically see her imagination dropping me into a story where a young Hugh Grant comes into the coffee shop and immediately falls in love with me, floppy hair and boundless charm and all. 'Where's the courtship? Where's the tension?'

'You met Alina at a musical theatre-themed bottomless brunch. What tension?'

She narrows her eyes but her mouth twitches traitorously. 'The moment our voices mingled for the first time was *fraught* with it, actually.'

'The moment you met, you were singing *On My Own* from *Les Mis*,' I point out.

'Okay, technically, yes. But this isn't about me.' Her phone pings with a text and she's distracted for a second as the screen reader reads it aloud, too fast for me to understand as always.

Our relationship has always been like this. We were the only two girls in flat 1A in our first year of uni and stuck together amidst the chaos of the boys' endless drinking games and terrible kitchen etiquette. We'd have movie nights with Baileys hot chocolate and popcorn (she liked sweet, I liked salty, so naturally we both grew to love a mix) where we'd watch all the *Twilight* films in a row, reciting every line word for word.

Not much has changed in our living arrangements since that first term, except nowadays we live in her parents' so-called investment property in South London, and when we watch *Twilight* we fancy Carlisle and Charlie more than Edward and Alice.

'Have you ever considered meeting someone in real life? Off the apps?'

'And have *you* ever considered doing stand-up? I hear they let anyone in these days.' For someone so intelligent, this is an absurd thing for her to suggest.

'What? You could kill two birds with one stone. Get out more *and* meet someone new.'

I could hide my lack of a social life better while I was living with my parents back in Kent, but now we live together again it's impossible to ignore. It's not like I've ever had a massive circle of friends, but I used to get out of the house more, at least. Since Josie's been working long hours at the gallery recently, I've been left to my own devices. Devices that are, frankly, guided solely by my libido. Because there's no other type of socialising that I'm in need of.

'Ava, people do this all the time. It's really not that weird.' She lists the items on her fingers, 'All you need to do is go out, do something fun, a hobby or whatever, and find someone while you're there. It's simple.'

'But have you met me?'

'I believe so, yes.'

'Okay, well, we have two issues here. First, my only hobby is listening to mid-2000s pop punk while staring wistfully out of windows.'

'You could do something arty. See if you can get uni credits for evening classes on graphic design or something.' My stomach twists at her words but she continues, 'Or go pottery painting. I know you've always wanted to try it.'

'Pottery painting classes are exactly where I imagine the most torrid of love affairs to begin.' No one gives a disparaging eye roll quite like Josie and it's one of my favourite things about her. 'My second issue is that if any man out there is looking for a woman with the cheer of a tombstone and the emotional intelligence of a rock, he probably has some issues of his own that he should sort out first.'

She finishes her last olive and says, half fondly, half insultingly, 'You're not nearly as unpleasant as you think, you know.'

'Josephine, flattery will get you nowhere.'

'Oh my god, can we focus?' I am extremely aware of how I've interrupted her evening of relaxation. 'Please don't take this the wrong way—'

'This feels like something I'm going to take the wrong way.'

'—but can you tell me honestly if you have other friends?'

I splutter for a moment. 'I have you.'

'Sure. We live together.'

'But we were friends before we lived together,' I point out. She waits. 'And there's Max.'

'You shared a womb with him twenty-six years ago. I don't know if he counts either.'

'Yeah, well, let me tell you, you're a far better co-tenant. He took almost all the food and I ended up coming out looking like a scraggy little weasel.'

'I'm very sorry to hear that. Your wombmate and roommate aside... If we ever have a friend break-up, where would that leave you?'

From someone else this might be offensive, but I know it's coming from a place of care. Josie doesn't fully understand that having an easy life with a small circle of friends works for me. Though by "circle", I do mean "line", because she's the only other person in it. 'Why are you making contingency plans for the breakdown of our friendship? Are you trying to hint at something?'

'I'm a Virgo moon, I make contingency plans for *everything*.' She runs a hand along the textured pattern of a cushion before playing with the tassels at the corners. 'What happens when I'm gone?'

'God, we have at least a few more decades before we need to start worrying about that.' What she's referring to, of course, is not her departure from this mortal coil, but the period she'll be away from London next year while she tours with her exhibition. 'Josie, I'll be fine. You know I will.'

I'm not lonely. I'm happy with the way I live my life.

Yet, every so often my thoughts drift of their own accord and I wonder what might happen if I stopped staying still, if I let myself make leaps like Josie does, like my brother does. But then I remember how much there is to lose, and the thoughts weave themselves into the knot tightening in my stomach.

'Look, you were there for me in first year when I needed it, now I'm helping you.' She tucks her hair behind her ears and straightens her posture. 'We're in this incredible city, and it's time for you to get out there. You've spent too many years in the dark. Now's your time to learn to glow again.'

'Was that a quote from a Disney Channel Original Movie?'

She ignores me. 'I'm just saying, I am one of the lucky few to know the real you.' I find myself grimacing at her sincerity as she goes on, 'You should do it. Really make an effort to put yourself out there, meet new people. It doesn't have to be a *man*. Just a friend. I'm so busy at the moment and I don't want you to be by yourself, and—wait.' Her expression turns gleeful and I dread learning what she's about to say. 'You owe me. For the flat. You promised me when you moved in that in return for charging you what I can only assume is London's lowest rent, you would do something of my choosing. Well, this is it. This is what I'm choosing.'

Shit. I'd forgotten I'd said that. I drag myself up from the floor to sit on the sofa, pulling my knees up and tugging my shirt over them. 'That's low, Joey.'

'Don't call me Joey.'

'I'll call you Joey if you blackmail me.'

'Is the blackmail working?' Her green eyes glitter in mischief. Josie may be tiny, but everything about her is mighty. It's like every personality trait is concentrated into this barely-five-foot package.

'Of course it's working, that's why I'm annoyed.' If I agree, she might get off my back, so I clear my throat and tell her what she wants to hear. 'I'll do my best to put myself out there.'

She nods, though I'm not sure she believes me. Her phone buzzes, a reminder of the time, and she says, 'I need to go to bed. But I'm glad you left the house for the comedy show at least, even if it was distinctly lacking in comedy.'

'To be fair, the woman who went before my date was hilarious.'

Josie stands, brushing nonexistent crumbs from her pyjamas. 'Maybe you should've gone out with her instead.'

'I bet she wouldn't have had clammy hands.'

She sweeps over to her bedroom, Rudy devotedly trailing behind. Sometimes I think back to both of us huddled together in her uni room, and I realise I can't imagine her in such a small space now; no one else around to see her shine.

But I'm not Josie. I don't take risks, and I certainly don't intend to let go of the careful control I have over my life any time soon.

# 2

## latte art can be provocative, I guess?

### AVA

Every day I am pushed closer to the brink by our customers.

'I have a girlfriend,' the man in front of me says as I push his flat white across the counter. I glance up at him in confusion and the sliver of neck above his starched collar turns pink while he nervously shifts his weight to his other foot. I blink a few times until I catch him pointedly looking back towards the coffee now midway between both of our hands. I'd made a heart with steamed milk and the shape is just starting to shrivel as the bubbles deflate.

'Would you like another one?' I ask evenly, gesturing towards the drink.

'No,' he says, neck now an indignant shade of magenta. 'I'm very happy with her. We're going to get married one day.'

As he grabs the cup and storms away, a sigh rips through me. This is somehow not the first time a man has taken my innocuous latte art as some kind of sordid proposition. A few weeks ago, a customer asked for my number. I declined, because he was a regular and I'd never be able to execute my post-coital escape artist act if I had to keep seeing him once a week at the shop.

While the-one-that-got-away settles into one of the comfy armchairs in the corner, I grab a cloth to clean the surfaces just as something to do during the lull. I move around the shop, wiping reclaimed wood tables and tucking chairs back into place. The problem with working the same type of job for years is that you become so efficient you almost bring about your own boredom. The work isn't *fulfilling*, but I don't need fulfilling. I'm content enough working this job and not giving it a second thought after I walk through the door at the end of my shifts.

A surprisingly charming place for its location smack-bang in the concrete corporate catchment zone of the lawyers, accountants and wannabe finance bros of London, City Roast usually sees the bulk of its customers just before nine. Now late morning, the shop's scattered with laptop-laden students, parents with buggies, and our handful of retired regulars people-watching through the floor-to-ceiling windows that line two of the walls.

I swat a hanging vine out of my way as I head back to the counter. The plants trailing from light fixtures and shelves and sitting in heavy pots are all fake, after a rough patch when we realised a grand total of zero employees had any semblance of a green thumb. My manager thinks they're real though, which may or may not be because in moments of extreme boredom I water them anyway, and he's definitely watched me do it. While there are no new customers coming in to rudely interrupt my quiet time, I settle behind the counter to make myself a coffee, watching a single droplet of espresso trickle down the side of the machine.

'Ava!' a disembodied voice calls from the back room, knocking me out of my reverie. I catch eyes with my co-worker Mateo, who gives me a grimace in solidarity and takes my place by the coffee machine. I shuffle backwards, taking a deep breath before pushing against the door, preparing to defend myself against whatever affront to hospitality I have no doubt committed.

'Oh, there you are. I've been calling your name for ages,' my manager says, not even looking up as he peers at the shelves in confusion, a pen in one hand and a clipboard in the other.

Carl is, as always, immaculate, and as always, overcompensating for his height. His salt-and-pepper hair is slicked back with enough product to strike fear into firefighters everywhere, and sun-weathered skin pulls taut across features that were probably very handsome, twenty years ago. Nowadays he looks like someone with limited artistic talents tried to draw Mark Ruffalo from memory.

'I was serving a customer.' Desperately trying to mask the passive aggression I am instinctively drawn to expel whenever my manager is in the vicinity, my smile is as false as my excuse.

His chinos are just a fraction too short, exposing the "fun" socks he wears every day to let us know he is, in fact, fun, and anthropomorphic hamburgers peek out around his ankles from astonishingly reflective Oxfords. It'd be nice if he put as much time into helping out around the shop as he evidently does polishing his shoes, but such is life.

'Your apron's dirty,' he accuses, finally glancing up at me.

'Oh, is it?' We've been open for two hours and my apron is already covered in milk splatters, coffee grounds have migrated under my nails, and a single almond-shaped burn on my left wrist is still glowing after it touched the steam wand earlier.

'I'm doing the stocktake and have noticed we seem to be missing,' he pauses and glances down at his clipboard as if to check the numbers, even though I know he already knows what's written, 'seven KitKat Chunkies. Do you know why that might be?'

My mind darts back to last night. I'm glad he's technologically inept, because if he were to review yesterday's CCTV footage from outside the front of the shop he'd see clips of me cramming chocolate into my mouth with such gusto that a passerby had to stop and check if I was choking.

'No, no idea at all,' I say, a picture of innocence. His eyes narrow just slightly in a way that makes me think he doesn't quite believe me, but he doesn't push it. 'Was that everything, Carl? I think we have customers.' I push my way out of the room without waiting for a reply.

---

I'm crouching on the floor by the milk fridge organising bottles in order of expiry date when three men breeze through the door. I stifle a groan before getting up, joints creaking in that mid-twenties way. Who even comes into a coffee shop at four minutes to seven on a Friday evening?

The trio looks like a walking advert for their company's diversity and inclusion programme. Or maybe a corporate version of The Powerpuff Girls.

'Hi,' the tallest one says; dark suit, dark skin, all sharp lines and cheekbones and perfectly proportioned features that briefly make me think of golden ratios and Fibonacci sequences. He drops his voice and appeals to me through thick eyelashes. 'We would be obscenely grateful if you could serve us three double espressos.'

I've never been particularly receptive to male charm, but I force a closed-mouth smile and reply, 'Coming right up.'

Listening to gossip is one of the few perks of working in the service industry, so as the coffee extracts, I eavesdrop. From my recon, all I learn is that two of them are staying late in the office to work on a project, while the other is helping out as a favour, but their discussion is peppered with tech terms I don't fully understand. Frankly, it's nowhere near exciting enough to justify delaying my closing. I tap the till a few times while the final coffee is finishing up.

'Paying together or separately?' I ask, interrupting their chat.

'Together,' the first man says. 'Whose round is it? Rory, is it yours?'

'Nope, it's Finn's,' says Rory, a pale, gangly redhead with more freckles visible than skin and a mouth almost too big for his face, his collar half up and tie slightly askew. He grabs his coffee and knocks it back like it's tequila, before widening his eyes and panting the word "hot". Powerpuff Boy number one gives him a withering look that says *why are you like this?*

The third man comes to the till then—Finn, according to my unparalleled powers of deduction—taking out his phone. Dark curls fall over wire-framed glasses as he leans closer to the card reader to pay, and the slightest grin tugs at the corners of his mouth.

'You know the facial recognition doesn't require you to smile, right?' Powerpuff Boy number one says, sending a sideways glance at Finn.

Finn pockets his phone and takes his glasses off to clean them on his shirt; a baggy olive green number with the sleeves rolled up, more casually dressed than the other two. He's also the shortest of the lanky trio, probably just shy of six foot and an inch or so taller than me.

'I'm sure this isn't in your wheelhouse,' he retorts good-naturedly before pushing his glasses back up his nose, 'but have you ever considered that some of us are just happy to be here?'

He has an accent I can't quite place. It's as if an English accent has been sanded down at the edges; vaguely American in its cadence, the sounds softer and lazier.

'Sorry about this, by the way,' he says, looking across the counter at me. A bigger smile pulls all the way up to brown eyes that are unexpectedly warm as they catch mine. 'You've probably already cleaned everything, but the coffee machine in our office broke and we're working late, and Julien is a diva who categorically refuses to resort to instant coffee.'

The first man lifts his tiny mug in the air with a nod as if in a toast and says, 'Worth it, though.'

Ambiguously-accented Finn taps Julien's mug with his own and they sip their espressos, sensibly much slower than Rory, who's hovering impatiently by the door like a spaniel knowing it's about to go on a walk.

Finn makes a guttural noise not entirely appropriate for a public setting. 'Shit, I've missed good coffee.'

I'm emptying the coffee grounds for what I hope is the last time today when Rory starts talking. 'Are you two done? I would absolutely love it if we could finish work at a decent hour. I'm desperate to be home in time to watch The Chase.'

'Uh, I think it's a bit late for that,' Julien says, as he and Finn catch each other's eye and try not to laugh.

'Even on plus-one?' Rory asks, shoulders slumped, before forcefully pushing against the door once (it's a pull door), twice (still a pull door), then realising his mistake and yanking it open (there you go) and stepping outside.

'Sorry,' Finn says again, arranging the mugs into a triangle and pushing them towards me on the counter while Julien walks towards the door. Rory's already crossing the street, his posture still despondent even from a distance. Finn rubs a hand along his lower face, drawing my attention to the dark stubble covering what I can tell is a particularly defined jawline. 'Someone's coming to fix our machine on

Monday, so if you spot us in here at closing time again you are more than welcome to bar us.' I raise my eyebrows. I can only hope. His mouth twitches like he can read my mind, and his tone is somewhere between amused and apologetic when he says, 'Although, honestly, I can't promise I won't be back during actual sociable hours, because that was the best coffee I've had in a long, long while. I'm not just saying that because I feel bad about stopping you from leaving on time.'

This man has been in the shop for mere minutes and I can already tell he talks too much.

'Finlay O'Callaghan,' Julien calls out from the door he's now propping open with his foot, 'please stop flirting with this poor woman and let's go.'

A sheepish grin spreads across Finn's features and he mumbles, 'I was just being friendly,' before striding over to meet his colleague. Both men call out a loud goodbye before the slam of the door closes off the sounds of the street.

# 3

## notable skills: people pleasing and dog whispering

### FINN

I*n a moment of* impossible luck, I wake up ten seconds before my alarm. Five-fifty in the morning is marked by weak sunlight filtering through the gap in my blinds, accompanied by the rumbling of Brixton's near-constant traffic.

I find myself humming as I head into the kitchen, keeping an eye on my phone while I prepare a protein shake and resist my daily urge to reorganise my landlord's cupboards into a more logical layout. Because even though it absolutely would make more sense to have the mugs by the kettle and the knives by the chopping boards, I've been given strict instructions to keep things precisely as my landlord left them while I live here. Such is the price I'm willing to pay for a fully furnished apartment.

Six o'clock comes and goes and I get ready for the day, still listening out for my phone. I raise the blinds and open a few windows, breathing in the fresh South London air, which arguably isn't *super* fresh, but it does the job.

By the time it gets to six-fifteen, I type out a text. It takes me another few minutes to press send.

> Hey Dad, no worries if you're busy, but are you still free for a call?

A reply comes through quicker than I expect.

> Something came up at work, we'll try again another time.

He doesn't suggest an alternative day, so I make a mental note to contact his assistant to organise it. Protein shake in hand, I shake off the quiet pangs of disappointment and head out the door, aiming to get a quick swim in before work.

---

I was under the assumption that no one talks to each other in London. But on my walk, I say hi to the postman, promise the guy at the fruit and veg stand that I'll be back soon—their mangoes are infinitely better than anything you could get from Tesco—and have a *you-go-no-you-go* moment with a sweaty middle-aged man in the doorway of the leisure centre's changing room.

By the time I've dived into the water, my mind is settled. For years now, I've used swimming as a constant. Everywhere I've lived, the water wraps itself around me in a hug, the smell of chlorine so familiar it feels like a friend. There's something to be said about the sameness of moving myself through the water; arms, legs, breathe, arms, legs, breathe.

I let my brain make a tentative wander as I swim. I've only got a few more months left of my contract before I start preparing for my next move, and I fully intend to make the most of London while I'm here. I've left enough places half finished that I'm determined to change things this time around and do this city right. Or better than Paris, at least. Though I guess the bar's pretty low with that.

When my muscles start to protest, I push through a few more laps and then call it a day. I'm slapping wet footprints across the floor when someone calls my name.

Mia's another regular in the pool—and the weights, and the treadmill and the boxing ring, come to think of it. We've been out a few times to the pub as friends, and a little while ago I got a hunch she might want something more than I could give. There's not much I enjoy more than an easy flirt, but the guilt started to pull at me for inadvertently stringing her along, so I took matters into my own hands.

'I just wanted to say thank you,' she says, shifting her weight from one hip to the other. 'For setting Jack and me up the other week.'

Pink rises to her cheeks and I breathe a sigh of relief. 'It's going well?'

She drops her voice, excitement coating every word, and I lean in closer for the gossip. 'We've trained together for the pentathlon a few times, and we're going out for dinner this evening. You're basically Cupid.'

'I'll clear my calendar for your wedding,' I say with a wink.

She slaps my arm in mock reproach. 'Finn! It's way too earl—'

But at the sound of the changing room door opening behind me, her eyes light up and she never finishes her sentence. I turn around and see the man in question, in all his impossibly muscular glory. I'm pretty sure he's part-mountain.

'I'll leave you guys to it. Have a good session,' I say, shooting her a knowing smile and craning my neck to greet Jack as I pass. Jesus, the guy makes me feel like a cheese string.

I'm still grinning to myself as I get changed into my normal clothes. Because if I can't be the one people fight for, at least I can watch it blossom for others.

How long can you act like a tourist when you move somewhere? Because it's been months and I still feel like I'm in a movie every time I step on the Tube. Sure, in rush hour I occasionally fear for my life, and I've witnessed at least three people piss on the tracks at various times of day, but there's a *vibe*.

Plus, it has its own built-in hairdryer. I know this, because by the time I step off the train at Temple, my hair's completely dry and decidedly windswept. Hopefully in a cool way, but we'll see.

As I walk along the platform, I make a plan to stop off at the coffee shop opposite the office before I start work. I've spent the past few months whining to Julien about the lack of decent coffee in this city, but finally my prayers have been answered in the form of City Roast's espresso. I've been served by two different baristas on my three visits; a friendly Spanish man who managed to convince me to buy both a muffin and a cookie with my drink both times I've seen him, and a tall, beautiful woman who seems like she'd shoot daggers from her eyes before she'd ever give me the time of day.

By the time I get to the ticket barriers, I realise this very barista is at the gate next to me, presumably on her way to open the shop. She taps her phone twice against the reader with a scowl when it doesn't immediately register, lips pressed into a pout. True to form, the giant headphones she's wearing tell me—and everyone else at this station—to stay far, far away. When we exit she heads left, taking the quickest route to work, and I make a detour to the right that'll kill some time before the shop opens.

I start by walking through Victoria Embankment Gardens, where the flowers are in bloom and a handful of people are sitting on the benches, taking in the low thrum of the city before it wakes up. I sit for a bit too, enjoying the nice weather, before I text Julien.

> You still up for tonight?

He responds almost immediately, one message after the other.

> Shit, I'm so sorry

> Can we do it another time? Or something else?

> Promise promise promise I won't flake again

I'm not particularly surprised by this. I've known Julien since we went to the same school in not one, but two countries as kids, and he's never been great with following through on plans. But I don't want him to feel bad, so I brush off the remnants of disappointment for the second time today and type out my reply.

> No worries, see you in the office

I'd intended to visit a food truck in Shoreditch with him later. Knowing that my time here has an expiry date, I've been trying to cross items off my London bucket list before I go. Unfortunately, I'd envisioned most of this list to be completed with Julien, but I kind of forgot he had a life in London before I showed up, and this life wouldn't be disrupted the second I got here. He's a man of many hobbies, and even more whims. While he's a data analyst at the same company as me for most of the week, the rest of his time is currently spent training to become a florist at the London Flower Academy. It's a career change that is somehow both random and *incredibly* on-brand.

So for now, I'm adding items to my list whenever I come across something cool. Occasionally I cross off an activity or location alone, but it's just not as fun. I've never been great with my own company.

From the vantage point of my bench, the sights and sounds of pre-rush hour London wash over me like water in a pool, and I log them to memory, storing them in folders that I'll open in a few years when I want to feel nostalgic about this nomadic period of my life.

After twenty minutes or so I amble towards the park exit, where I befriend a particularly excitable beagle. My ego soars to outer space when she bounds over to me at the exact moment her owner says, 'Sorry, she's usually wary of men.'

I discover the dog is eight years old, named Sally, and often pees herself when she gets too excited. I learn the latter fact firsthand, which her owner unnecessarily over-apologises for before we part ways. Invigorated by post-swim endorphins, the early-morning sunshine beating down on my shoulders and the imminent prospect of drinking a decent coffee, I'm ready to face the day.

# 4

# hey Siri, how can I get someone to stop talking?

## AVA

'WHAT A BEAUTIFUL DAY!' a chirpy voice with far too much spirit for seven forty-three on a Wednesday morning interrupts my quiet restocking of the drinks fridge.

An unfortunate consequence of working in a coffee shop is that any time a customer walks through the door, I am overcome by a wave of potent rage. How dare they, a customer, approach me, an employee, requesting the service I am paid to provide?

The villain in question this morning is one of the three men who came into the shop late on Friday; the one with the unidentified accent. I cast my mind back to remember his name but come up empty.

'Morning,' I reply, trying in vain to summon even an iota of the energy he's exuding. He looks infinitely more alive than I feel; bright eyes behind his glasses, mustard-yellow shirt, a singular curl dropping so perfectly across his forehead I assume he must've styled it to fall that way. 'What can I get you?' The fake smile I've plastered on my face probably looks more like a grimace, but it doesn't seem to deter him.

'Three flat whites to take away, please.' He's practically bouncing already. I get the impression his enthusiasm level is at a constant state of Golden Retriever. The whirs of the machine punctuate the LoFi song playing over the speakers, the smell of fresh coffee grounds permeating the air as I make the shots. 'Did you have a good weekend?'

*Finn.* His name comes to me out of nowhere and it feels like I've scratched an itch.

'It was pretty uneventful. What about you?' I take this moment to pull three paper cups from a stack next to the coffee machine, while he replies to my question with a story I actually don't care enough to pay attention to. Customers love using me as a small-talk scratching post and I frankly do not have the energy to reciprocate with anything more than a few well-placed *ah, really*s and *that sounds fun*s.

'—So it makes sense I'm pretty wired already this morning,' he finishes, intently watching me steam the milk for his drinks. He spots the various snacks on display and analyses them one by one, finally holding up a pack of vanilla wafer biscuits. 'Have you tried these?'

'Yeah,' I reply. 'But go for the hazelnut. Unless you're allergic, in which case, uh, don't, I guess.'

He catches my eye and grins at me like I've said something funny, grabbing three of the hazelnut flavour instead.

I've learnt from my previous mistake of presenting suggestive steamed-milk-heart lattes to men, so I make a concerted effort to pour the milk into an innocuous leaf pattern this time. I can feel his eyes on me as I twist my wrist slightly to form the shape.

He smiles at his phone's facial recognition when he uses Apple Pay again this morning, and it's still just as unnecessary as it was the first time, before stacking his wafers in the one empty slot in the cardboard cup holder.

He tentatively reads my name badge. 'Thanks, uh, Monroe?'

The higher-ups decided our surnames should be on our name tags instead of our first names, because this makes us cool and trendy. Apparently it's a great way for people to *take us at face value* and *not judge based on our first name*. Never mind the fact Mateo is Spanish and only a third of his pentasyllabic surname fits on his badge.

But Finn doesn't need to know all this, so I simply say, 'Monroe's my surname. I'm Ava.'

'Hi Ava Monroe. I'm Finn.' The corners of his eyes wrinkle even when he's not smiling and I get the feeling he's the kind of person who's about a millisecond away from laughing at any given moment. He sips his flat white and keeps it close to his nose to inhale the smell. 'I've genuinely been dreaming of this. It reminds me of the coffee I used to get when I lived in Australia.' With a sigh, he adds, 'I think you'll be seeing a lot more of me, so sorry about that, I guess.'

He leaves the counter with his drinks tray, humming quietly and holding the door open for another customer he crosses paths with as he exits.

---

When the lunchtime buzz ends and Mateo and I are taking a moment to breathe and rest our vocal cords after hours of nonstop customer service-ing, Carl finally remembers we exist, and his voice carries across the shop. 'If you have time to lean, you have time to clean.'

I can't look at him for fear of what he might see in my eyes and instead start tidying the mess on the counter, and suggest Mateo goes to the back to "tidy the stockroom" because the expression on his face could curdle milk and I think he might be about to hit something.

Then, at two-fifteen, like clockwork, a woman with a scowl that should be paying rent on her face approaches the till. Like she does every day, she drops her reusable cup onto the counter and holds her card up to the reader in anticipation, without saying a word or looking at me at all. I ring up her regular order of a black Americano and start to prepare the drink.

Something about her sends my blood boiling. Maybe it's the fact she doesn't say please or thank you, and evidently thinks I am but a lowly barista with no other skills to offer. Maybe it's because she always looks like she's just smelled something rancid. Or maybe it's her kitten heels. Whatever the reason, I stew over her behaviour almost every time I see her.

She wordlessly takes her drink and I give a pointed, 'You're welcome.'

She doesn't even have the decency to look guilty, and she shuffles towards the sugar and napkin station, never fully lifting her feet from the ground. Without looking her way, I know she'll take two sugar packets, head to a table by the window, pour one sugar in, and leave the second packet on the table when she leaves. I know this, because she is a creature of habit, much like most of our customers.

City Roast is where people's routines converge. Favourite tables, Friday afternoon treats, eight o'clock espressos; the tributaries of their daily habits trickle into the delta of our shop. Routines and structure and unbreakable habits where I know what to expect and when to expect it. Where nothing can threaten the balance. For years, I've relished this consistency, back at my similar job when I lived with my parents, and now here. But while I used to wrap the mundanity of my days around myself like a blanket, familiar and warm, I can't help but notice that the wool's not as soft as it once was.

I'm on the customer side of the counter organising the snacks when the front door opens. I glance behind me out of instinct and immediately regret it. It's Finn again and his colleague from that first evening; Julien, or Powerpuff Boy with the cheekbones. After a busy day, the last thing I want is to handle Mr Chatty, but it's too late for me to go to the stockroom and ask Mateo to swap, so I reluctantly head back to the till.

'Hey Ava Monroe,' Finn says brightly as he holds the door for his colleague. His voice carries across the shop and other customers lift their heads from their tables to look at him, but he doesn't pay them any attention. The pair saunters towards me with the kind of insouciant confidence that only comes with being a tall, attractive man. I steel myself to greet them.

'I'm personally offended you never told me about this place. You know my thoughts on good coffee,' Finn says to Julien. 'I've decided it's my new spot.'

They're finally at the counter, both leaning their hips against it like its sole purpose is to support their weight. Julien quirks one corner of his mouth and looks at me with come-hither eyes. I am, once again, unperturbed. Though I'm starting to wonder if these are just his normal eyes.

'Finn's been going on and on about this coffee,' he says in a lazy drawl. 'He's looking for a new job, so if you've got any openings, I'm pretty sure he'd pay you to hire him.'

'I haven't been going *on and on*. Although,' Finn stops to think, eyes widening as an idea comes to him, 'do you and Mateo get free drinks?'

'We do,' I reply smoothly, 'one of the many perks of the job.'

'What are the others?' Finn asks, eagerly leaning forward, somehow defying the laws of physics and getting impossibly close to me even with a whole counter between us.

'Well,' I say, wracking my brain for a polite answer that doesn't come. 'I do really like that I don't work weekends.'

'The customers aren't a perk?' He looks carefully at me, like he's trying to gauge whether I'll play along.

Julien joins in too. 'I bet it's especially fun when they come in and interrupt your day by asking pointless questions you feel inclined to answer politely rather than truthfully.'

'Oh, definitely,' I say with a sharp nod. 'I also love asking people how their day's been eighty-seven times in the space of an hour. Small talk is my passion.'

'Okay.' Finn raises both hands in surrender, a short chuckle bursting out of him. My stomach dips—probably because I haven't gone on my lunch break yet. 'I promise I won't give you small talk. I'll give you big talk instead. What are your goals, Ava? Mine are eternal glory and to learn how to make balloon animals.'

'Could we get two flat whites please?' Julien interrupts, earning him an eye roll from Finn. 'Before he starts telling you about his greatest fears.'

'Abandonment and death, in that order.'

Julien puffs up his cheeks and blows the air out abruptly. 'He does grow on you, I promise. It's taken me almost twenty years but I think I'm finally warming to him.'

'Please, it took you eight at most,' Finn says. He looks back at me, lowering his voice conspiratorially, 'He acts like he's too cool, but he forgets I was there the day he opened a limited-edition Hot Wheels set when we were ten and was so excited he cried. Then cried every day that week at school whenever he remembered he had it.'

'I'm going to sit down so that I don't have to listen to you torching my reputation any more. And Ava,' Julien says my name as a question, not quite sure if he remembered it correctly, 'I wouldn't dream of telling you what to do, but I vehemently recommend you don't let him get started on dinosaurs. He genuinely will not shut up.'

He walks away, leaving me slightly thrown by the entire interaction. I grab their cups from the shelf and start making the coffees, multitasking by setting up the payment on the till for Finn as the espresso extracts.

And yet, he's still going. 'Would you consider me a regular?'

'Not yet,' I respond. By the decisive way he nods, I'm concerned he's taking that as a challenge.

I focus on listening to the milk aerate, and when the metal of the jug is too hot for me to touch, I start the process of swirling the liquid into latte art. Finn watches closely, just like last time.

'I'm adding that to my list,' he says with a dose of finality. He elaborates, unprompted, 'I have a London bucket list to complete and learning how to make those milk patterns is going on there.'

I finish the first drink and he pulls it towards him to take a photo of it from above, his full lips pursing as he concentrates.

'When I think of London, I do always think of latte art,' I say flatly, finishing the second cup.

He glances up from his phone to meet my eyes with a smile. 'I'm always on the hunt for new things to try. Do you think you could teach me?' My brain zooms through professional, not-awkward ways to say *absolutely the fuck not* but he saves me from answering by continuing, 'Maybe Julien will come to a class with me.'

After he's picked up the cups and thanked me, he goes to find his friend, who's chosen the table next to the grumpy customer from earlier. Unfortunately, Finn reaches the table at the precise moment she stands up, and when she bumps into him, it's only his fast reflexes that prevent him from spilling both drinks all over her. It was definitely her fault, and I expect her to snap a rude remark or shoot him a withering glare like she usually does to me. But to my utter consternation, after a few moments of Finn saying something I can't quite hear, she *beams* at him.

# 5
# work besties and future house guesties
## AVA

'So you really didn't know he was only eighteen?' Josie asks, shovelling her penultimate slice of pizza into her mouth in a rare moment of gracelessness.

I shudder as I cast my mind back to the disaster of last night's date. I went *bowling*. With a man who still lived with his mum. 'No, Josie, funnily enough, I did not.'

He was attractive in that artfully lazy, design-school boy way, and I'd planned on fuelling his ego by praising his bowling skills throughout the evening. And then, because there's nothing sexier than the stench of stale popcorn and the sight of a man in sweaty bowling shoes, the tension would rise in the heat of that intimate moment, and would inevitably lead to a bland but moderately pleasant fornication at his place, immediately followed by me getting an Uber home so I wouldn't have to sleep in his flat-pillowed, navy-sheeted bed.

Instead, in an impressive display of creativity, he managed to throw the ball in the gutter while the barriers were up. Then he told me he was eighteen. Unsurprisingly, this extinguished the fire in my loins.

Josie has the audacity to ask, 'And you just ran away?'

'You think I should have stayed until A Level results day? Saw if he got into the uni he wanted? Unfortunately, eighteen-year-olds aren't really my type.'

'Since when do you have a type?' Her eyebrows draw together in confusion. 'The only thing the men you've dated have had in common is that they could all breathe.'

'Not all of them,' I point out. 'Remember Congested Connor?'

'The guy who left all his used tissues on the table? With the... residue all over his hands?'

'That's the one,' I say, dipping a dough ball into a pot of garlic butter that now looks significantly less appetising. The patio of Il Pulcinella is packed with lunch-goers and we're squeezed onto a little table by the ivy-covered wall, Rudy tucked by Josie's feet on the floor. It's a little Italian place by Clapham North station that we found a couple of months ago, and our go-to spot when romantically-stable Josie wants some gossip about my shenanigans.

I move the pieces of pepperoni around my slice so they're more evenly spread. 'Believe it or not, I do have *some* things I care about when it comes to the men I go home with.' Josie snorts at this and I ask, 'Are you slut-shaming me?'

'No, I'm taste-shaming you, there's a difference.'

'There's nothing wrong with my taste,' I bite back, offended. Well, fine, not really offended, but I pretend to be for the sake of my own dignity.

'There's *everything* wrong with your taste. Look, you asked for my opinion—'

'I didn't, actually, you just gave it.'

'Oh. Yeah, you're right. Sorry.' She shrugs. 'Regardless, I'm giving it. You have terrible taste.'

'Well, my terrible taste has already found a new target, seeing as the last one was unsuccessful. And the one before. He's tall and he plays rugby and he works in military events planning or something.'

'He sounds like a Tory.'

'That's a stereotype. Anyway, it's fine, all I need from him is,' I lower my voice, 'moderately decent sex. Like, average is fine. I'm not expecting fireworks. So he's just a means to an end.'

She laughs at my ridiculous logic, 'You act like you're ordering something from Deliveroo.'

'What's the difference? My cards are on the table. I'm not gonna hook up with someone I *like*. That's dangerously close to a relationship.'

'A lot more goes into a relationship than sleeping with them and not completely hating their company,' she specifies. 'And I appreciate that you are a woman standing firm in her choice to have casual sex. But ugh, I want you to meet a nice boy. That's my dream.'

It's almost laughable to imagine. Me, in all my closed-off, snippy glory, with a *nice boy*. One who smiles at strangers and talks to his mum regularly, and not because he still lives with her.

'You know, it's actually all your fault,' I say, watching a waiter pass by with a tray of sizzling pizza and wishing I hadn't demolished my own in about twelve seconds flat. 'I'd never consider going home with strangers if I couldn't make my great escape straight after, and when there's no Night Tube running, I can only do that by getting an Uber, which I'd never be able to afford if you and your parents didn't charge me an obscenely low rent.'

Josie takes a few moments to decipher this. 'So the solution is to increase your rent?'

'Absolutely not. While both parties are agreeing to engage in a one-time thing, the solution is for me to continue what I'm doing.

Besides,' I grab another dough ball, 'I have a 4.96 rating on Uber now. Every cloud.'

'Okay. How's it going on your non-romantic quest to find people who'll care about you for more than one night?'

Our conversations keep coming back to this, so I attempt to brush it off. 'Bold of you to think those men care about me for even one night.'

'Ava.' She glares at me, her voice a growl. 'You promised.'

I've spent so long locked into a routine of work-hookup-home and I can't envision being able to break out of it. But I don't know how to get her off my back about the whole thing, because I feel like I owe her.

'I'm considering my options. And I will hang out with someone *platonically* soon,' I say. I'm sure I could find an acquaintance to go for a drink with. Probably.

Josie's appeased, at least for now. 'I'll still be your best friend, right? You won't get closer to them than me?'

'Depends what they can offer me. If their parents have a flat in Zone 1 that they'd let me live in for free, I may have to reconsider.'

'Shut up,' she says through a bite of her last slice of pizza. 'I'm sorry I've been so busy with work. I wish we could hang out more.'

'I've told you, I'm fine by myself.' I say with a flippant wave of my hand, happy to change the subject to more exciting things and ignore the weird feeling in my stomach. 'How's the planning going?'

Josie's been tied up for the past few months helping curate a new interactive art exhibition for a gallery set to open at the end of the year.

'It's going,' she says with a coy smile. I know the hours tire her out, but any time she talks about her work, her whole face lights up. I can't help but compare how my own work makes me feel. 'We think we've sorted most of the individual artists and their exhibits, but we're missing a large-scale centrepiece. There's an idea floating around for an exhibit where you experience all four seasons in one place, but there's a lot to do to make it happen.'

'Wait, that sounds so cool.' I try to imagine it. 'How involved are you?'

'Extremely. It's going to be a huge collaborative effort, but seeing as it was my idea, it's on my shoulders to get it right.'

I've never met someone so good at curating a style, whether that's her wardrobe or the decor in our flat. She *breathes* art. 'And you say you're not an artist.'

She shrugs, uncharacteristically modest. 'This is why I've been working such long hours. It's going to be expensive too, so I've been working on a pitch for a grant. But we'll manage. I know we will.'

I've always admired this about Josie. When she has an idea, she goes for it, full steam. She also always gives me her pizza crusts to finish, which I possibly admire even more, and she's sliding them over to my plate when we're interrupted by the woman at the table next to us, who's taken a sudden interest in Rudy.

'What a gorgeous boy, can I pet him?' she asks, her hand reaching down.

Josie simply says, 'No. He's working.' This is a common occurrence, so Josie continues talking to me, unbothered, 'Anyway, it's been fun, trying to figure out how to make this whole exhibition as accessible as possible. It's just really cool knowing how many Disabled artists and curators we're working with to get it right. It feels special.'

'I can't wait to be there on opening night. I'll be whooping from the crowd during your speech,' I say, chomping down on one of the crusts and sending pizza dust in all directions.

'Please, the day you even *think* about drawing attention to yourself in a public setting is the day I wear sweatpants out of the house.' She grins, adding, 'But I appreciate the support. I want you to have the full experience when you visit, so if you catch me sharing specific details about any of the pieces from now on, please tell me to shut up.'

'It would be my honour.' I dust the crumbs off my hands and stretch my legs out under Josie's chair, shifting my feet to avoid Rudy.

'Tell me about your job. I haven't heard a fun customer story in *ages*. Anyone interesting come in?'

Nothing exciting ever happens at work. It's the same people, the same conversations, the same stories every day. I wrack my brain for an anecdote. 'I did have these three men come in at closing the other day who were like some sort of hapless sitcom trio.' Josie raises her eyebrows in a question I refuse to entertain and I shut her down immediately. 'Nope, don't look at me like that. You know I don't shit where I eat.' She splutters out a laugh. 'Speaking of which, one of them has verbal diarrhoea. Literally does not stop talking.'

'Delicious. Tell me more.'

---

We're in between the early-morning chaos and the hectic lunchtime rush and the shop is mostly filled with our regulars. There's Belinda the eccentric octogenarian, soy-latte-Samantha, who will share intimate details of her life whether you ask for them or not, and Rufus, the man who comes in every day at ten o'clock in the morning and orders, to my constant consternation, a decaf espresso shot.

I'm refilling the coffee machine with beans when I receive a concerning text from Josie.

> SOS!!! CALL ASAP

Knowing her, she could either be letting me know she's fallen down the stairs and is currently in hospital in a full-body cast, or she wants to tell me she's decided to start making model aeroplanes and would like to know if I'd be interested in a trip to Hobbycraft to grab some supplies. There's no in between, and no way to know which one it'll be today unless I call.

Mateo's cleaning tables at the back of the shop, clearly trying to stay away from soy-latte-Samantha lest she tell him about her recent colonoscopy (I was not so lucky to avoid that particular topic), but I trust that he'll head to the till if another customer comes in.

I pull up Josie's number and duck into the stockroom.

'What's up?' I ask, when she picks up on the first ring.

'We're throwing a party.'

I guess that answers my question about which end of the scale her emergency would be. 'A what?'

'Par-ty. You know, those things we avoided like the plague at uni?'

'I thought that was boys?' I put my phone on speaker and place it on a shelf while I riffle through one of the boxes in front of me, on the hunt for a KitKat.

'That too, but you and I both know we avoided those for very different reasons.' Her girlfriend Alina laughs in the background and Josie takes a breath before adding, 'Anyway, you can't say no, because I've already invited Max.'

I freeze for a second. 'Max, as in, my brother Max?'

'No, as in, the guy in the corner shop who gives us good deals on loo roll.'

'His name is also Max, actually.'

'Really?'

'No.'

Josie huffs directly into the microphone. 'Well, your brother is coming to our housewarming.'

I decide to address the Max topic later. There are more important things to discuss. 'A housewarming?' I finally spot my chocolatey prize and grab it from the depths of the box. 'We've been in the flat for almost six months already. I think it's suitably heated up by now.'

'Let her do it, Ava,' Alina calls out, the vaguest remnants of her Colombian accent softening the sounds. 'She's already started making a playlist.'

Josie's voice returns. 'We live in an incredible home and we're wasting it! I want to show off.'

'That's unlike you,' I say under my breath, tearing open the packet with my teeth.

'Whatever,' she says, and I don't need to see her to know she's tucked her hair behind her ears. 'I'm a woman on a mission. All you need to do is show up, which won't be hard, because it'll be about five steps from your bedroom door.'

I pull my phone back up to my ear. 'Yeah, no, I'm busy.'

'Ha, nice try. I checked your calendar. Final weekend in August. You have no plans. You'll be there.'

'Bit early to be planning this, no?' I'm secretly pleased—that's three whole months for me to figure out an excuse not to go.

'Keep up, the number-one rule of party planning in your mid-twenties is to organise things at least six weeks in advance in order to optimise attendance. And you won't be wriggling out of this, so don't even consider trying to concoct an escape plan.' I roll my eyes like a petulant child, nibbling at my KitKat while Josie continues her spiel, talking about karaoke (we can sing *Misery Business* together, but only if we let people know we disagree with the anti-feminist message), snacks (she might order a pre-made cheese board) and guest lists (people she's working with at the gallery, plus a few friends from pilates). I'm too busy concentrating on separating the chocolate from the wafer to realise she's stopped talking, just about registering that she finished with, '—invite people too.'

'Sorry?' I ask, mid-chomp.

'I said, this is a great opportunity for you to test the waters and find someone to bring. A friend. Could be someone from the shop, even.'

There's a sense of camaraderie that comes with working in a coffee shop, but the staff turnover at City Roast doesn't allow for particularly deep friendships to be forged, which I've never been bothered by. My job is just a job, and my coworkers are just my coworkers. Everyone and everything sits neatly in its own box.

Maybe this is it. This is how I get Josie off my back about meeting people and trying new things. I open my mouth to indignantly spill my first lie of the day. 'I've made a friend at work, actually. Forgot to mention it.'

'You have?' I can hear the relief in those two words. 'This is amazing. It wasn't so difficult, was it?'

'Easy as pie,' I say, for perhaps the first time in my whole life. And likely the last.

'Invite them,' she says excitedly, 'I've never heard you talk about anyone. Are they new?'

'Yep. I'll mention the party the next time I see them.' I try to mimic some of the enthusiasm in her voice. I don't know if it's just because in her heart she knows I don't *really* have other friends, or if she just feels guilty that she's going to be leaving for a couple of months, no matter how many times I tell her I'll be fine. Either way, my dishonesty twists my gut.

'Okay, yes, love that. I knew you could do it. I'm proud of you for making a friend. I'm sorry, does that sound patronising? It does, shit.

But it's true. I just knew that as soon as other people saw the real you they'd like you too.'

If I didn't feel slimy for lying before, I'm now a glutinous little mollusc.

For a few moments the sound of traffic increases in volume from the other side of the stockroom door. I peek through the glass panel and sure enough, someone has just walked in, but Mateo's nowhere to be seen. 'Hey, Josie, there's a customer. I need to go.'

'Wait, wait! What's your friend's name?'

Just before I push open the door I register who the new customer is. I pluck his name out of the air in a final attempt to placate Josie. 'Finn. He's called Finn. I'll talk to you later.' I end the call before she has time to question me any more.

When I finally step out of the stockroom, I catch sight of Mateo, who's wielding a mop and dealing with a sticky chai spillage at the other end of the shop. Finn's now sitting opposite eighty-something Belinda, coffee order all but forgotten, and she's fluttering her eyelashes at him in a way that tells me she was a total siren in her heyday. He says something in a low voice and winks.

'Oh stop it,' she says, playfully slapping his arm, where his burgundy sleeves are pushed up to his elbows. 'A lovely boy like you will make a woman very happy one day.'

'Unfortunately, I'm not the settle-down type, Belinda.'

As he says this he notices I'm back behind the counter and stands up, adjusting a sleeve that's unravelled.

Belinda watches him with a twinkle in her eye and says, 'Well in that case, I wish you many a disreputable love affair.'

# 6

# no Mum, I have not yet sowed my seed

## FINN

THE WIFI'S SURPRISINGLY FAST in City Roast. I manage to finish off some work for my client, accompanied by the hum of fellow coffee-drinkers and the clatter of traffic on the other side of the window. I'm watching a young couple cross the street through the glass when my mum's face pops up on my phone, so I connect my headphones and swipe to accept her call.

'How are you, chick?' Her voice comes through my headphones slightly out of time with the video. Despite decades of moving around the world, the Irish lilt to her accent is almost as strong as it was on the day she left.

It's nine-thirty in the evening in Singapore, so she's illuminated by the big lamp in the corner of her office. She always holds the phone just below her chin and by now I've given up telling her to move it, so I know to expect that all I'll be able to see is the top half of her auburn head.

For the most part, we look nothing alike, save for the crow's feet at the corners of our eyes and freckles that show when I've been out in the sun. Much to her disgust, I'm sure, I take after my father almost entirely. On the rare occasion I go to Thessaloniki to visit his side of the family, I'm reminded that I come from a long line of off-puttingly similar-looking Greek men. Same unruly curls, same not-quite-six-foot build, same dark stubble that takes about four seconds to grow back after shaving.

I also inherited my dad's proclivity for running away to another country when the going gets tough, but that's neither here nor there.

'I'm good. Been in meetings with my client all morning and only just got the chance to sit down with a coffee and do some work on my laptop. How's work for you?'

She looks tired and I want to tell her to go to bed, but we've missed our last few scheduled calls because timings haven't worked out, so I'm determined to chat for a little while today.

'Hectic as ever. If I had a quiet day I'd be concerned.' It felt like my whole childhood my mum was desperately trying to catch up on the work she'd missed while she was on maternity leave with me, all while moving around because of her diplomat career. This wasn't made any easier when my dad left, and she became a single mum early in her career, with a needy baby who couldn't sleep without being held.

'You love it though,' I add. After she met my stepdad in Dakar, we were a trio for a while, until the twins came along. By the time they started school my parents agreed not to do any more moving around with three kids in tow, and Mum quit her job to start something new. She's been teaching at their international school in Singapore for years now, which means she's been around for pretty much every dance recital, every robotics competition, every Model UN debate.

'Have you spoken to your father recently?'

'No, he's, uh,' I clear my throat, 'been busy. I think he's coming to London soon though, so I'll see him then, at least.'

'That'll be nice,' she says primly, with a smile that hardly hits her cheeks, let alone her eyes. She's never been good at hiding her dislike for that man. Which is unfortunate, because I am genetically fifty percent him. It's no wonder she spent more time with the twins growing up than she did with me—they're half my stepdad instead.

'Did I tell you I've started looking around for other jobs? Just to see what's out there once this contract's over.' I settle my phone against my open laptop so I don't have to hold it.

'You could come back to Singapore,' she suggests. As much as I like being around my family, I've never felt like Singapore was home. I don't quite feel like I could slot back into their perfect foursome; the fifth wheel that makes everything a little off-balance.

'There's one in San Francisco I'm interested in.'

Her eyes widen. 'San Francisco?'

'It's where the opportunities are if I want another marketing role in tech.' It's also where my dad has lived since he started his business over two decades ago, which she's fully aware of. 'But I'm not sure yet if I'm gonna apply. I think the start date's sometime this autumn.'

I gulp my now-lukewarm drink, regretting that I got distracted people-watching earlier.

She sips from her own mug and I don't need to ask to know it's green tea. 'Is that an issue?'

'You know how I left Paris in a hurry? I've decided to do this thing,' I scratch my jaw as I search for the words, 'where I make sure I've "completed" my time here, if that makes sense? I want to feel like I've lived the city well.'

'I should've done something like that too when I was moving around at your age for work.'

'I've even made a bucket list,' I add with a grin, knowing how much she also loves a list. 'It's the most random combination of activities ever.'

She smiles and this one reaches her eyes. 'It sounds fun. It'll be a good way to make you stay put for a little while longer.' She tilts her head and adds, 'You know, I was always surprised you stayed in Australia for as long as you did.'

It was the closest I'd lived to that part of my family for a long time, though I still didn't get to see them as much as I might've liked. I didn't want to disrupt them when they were always so busy.

'If it wasn't for uni, I probably wouldn't have. Wait, actually,' I hold up my drink to the camera so she can see, 'I've finally found a place that does decent coffee. It reminds me of the stuff I used to get in that little indie shop near my apartment in Sydney. Remember when you came to visit that one time? I've practically been living here since I found it.'

'Can you flip the camera around? I want to see where you are.' I oblige, slowly panning the phone around the coffee shop, where plants trail from shelves and mismatched chairs cluster around wooden tables. She points at something she can see on her screen and I have no idea what she's looking at until she says, 'She's very pretty.'

'She is,' I reply, grateful I'm wearing headphones. I turn the camera back to my face and away from Ava, who's muttering to herself as she cleans a table nearby. She either hates my guts or is entirely apathetic and doesn't even remember my name, and I'm not sure which is worse.

But it's not like this is the first time I've noticed how pretty she is; the flush at the apples of her cheeks, dark hair tied back in a ponytail, soft bangs framing cautious blue eyes. Long legs, frustrating curves. Dangerous, for someone like me. As if she can feel my gaze, she glances my way, and I quickly avert my eyes.

Mum raises her eyebrows pointedly. 'It's been months since Léa. It's such a shame it didn't work out between you, but maybe it's time to try again?'

My mum doesn't know the truth about what happened in Paris. I haven't told her anything more than what she needs to know. Partly because even after everything, I don't want her to think badly of Léa. But partly because I don't want her to realise that I am exactly as easy to leave now as I was as a kid.

'I'm just enjoying my time here. I'm not looking for anything like that. Not until I'm settled. So maybe when I'm, like, forty.'

Her eyes bulge and she brings the phone even closer to her face. 'Forty? I'll practically be *dead* by then.' That math does not add up, but she's a diplomat-turned-teacher, not a statistician, so I'll cut her some slack. 'I want grandchildren before I'm senile, and if I have to wait until the twins are your age then I might as well just give up.' My younger brother and sister are twelve years younger than me and I don't have the heart to tell her she'll probably have better luck waiting for them to settle down than me. 'Don't you miss the touch of a woman?'

'Mum,' I say through a groan. I've been casually dating here and there, so if there's one thing I'm not missing, it's the touch of a woman, but we are also *absolutely* not the kind of family to discuss that type of thing.

'Do you use the apps? Tinder? Grindr?'

'I prefer to meet people in person. But as I said,' I over-enunciate my next words, 'not looking.'

'I don't want you to miss out on falling in love again. Just promise you'll give me grandchildren one day.'

Parents place a weird expectation on their kids to "give" them grandchildren, regardless of whether these kids actually want their own or not. The jury's still out for me. I love the idea of loving someone so hard it hurts, but only if I have someone to share it with. Like my mum and stepdad, more than my mum and my own dad.

Because I'm sure I'd be fun, just like my dad was. I'm sure I'd charm all the parents at the PTA, just like he did. But I'm also worried the permanence would stress me out, and I'd get itchy feet and need to move across the world, like he did, with or without my child. It's not outside the realms of possibility that I'd be exactly the same. I've spent my adult years locked in a similar system after all; move somewhere, make some loose connections, move again, start over.

'I promise I will let you know about any major changes in my life,' I reply noncommittally, refusing to bow to the pressure of being in your late twenties in a world that tells us we should be locked in already by this age. Mum's not satisfied with my response, but that's the best I'm going to give her.

I'm saved from further interrogation by the arrival of one of the twins. Unlike me, Aisha is the perfect mix of both Mum and my stepdad, and as the baby of the family—by seventeen minutes, sorry Ali—has managed to wrap both her parents around her finger. I used to think our ease with people was something we shared genetically, but I've since realised we both get it from our similarly charismatic dads. Clearly our mum has a type.

Our conversation moves to what the twins have been up to, and thankfully the topic of grandchildren and falling in love isn't broached again.

# 7

# I'd let Shrek do some very not-feminist things to me

## AVA

A LOT OF MEN seem to be under the impression that lying about their height will go unnoticed when you meet in real life. I guess they'd rather be a liar than short. Regrettably, many are both.

Rugby-boy Oscar didn't lie about his height. I notice this immediately when I step into the dingy, low-ceilinged Soho basement bar we're meeting in. As a woman who could never in any universe be described as *petite*, the Neanderthal in me raises her horny little head at the idea of feeling small next to this man.

'Who's your celebrity crush?' he asks, shoulders perpetually hunched, his frame too big for the bar stool.

'Shrek,' I reply, no hesitation.

His thrice-broken nose wrinkles. 'That's... an interesting choice.'

'Yeah?' I ask, eyebrows drawn. With a weak smile, I add, 'I also like men without donkey sidekicks.'

'I'm glad to hear it,' he says with a low chuckle.

Despite the evident confusion on his face, I know how to fluff a man's ego for my own gain, and I refuse to let tonight end the same way my last few dates have. So I soften my features, covertly tug the neck of my shirt down an inch or two and change the subject. When I ask him about his degree (an MA in Conflict, Security & Development in the War Studies department, concepts I have approximately zero understanding of) I realise this is a rookie error, because the topic is now firmly settled on something I'd rather avoid.

'What did you study at uni?' he asks, swirling the dregs of whiskey in his glass.

'I started doing graphic design but had to drop out in my second year.'

Then he asks the question I'd really hoped he wouldn't. 'Why'd you drop out?'

The boxes I taped shut long ago flex and pulse at the reminder, like their contents are alive and desperately trying to find a way to seep out and find something new to stain. But right now, while I'm sitting with a man I barely know, is not the time to let my brain go to that place I've spent years trying to get away from. So in the end, I say, 'Just family stuff.'

'Did you ever go back and finish your degree?'

I tear a corner off my napkin. 'I never got around to it.' If he notices the prickle of defensiveness in my words, he doesn't mention it. 'But I'm fine where I am now. I work a job I don't have to think about after I leave in the evening. It pays the bills and then some, and I live with my best friend in her parents' flat and they charge me an unbelievably low rent for London.'

'You're lucky,' he says, and I laugh to alleviate some of the tension. He doesn't know how true his statement is. After everything that happened, sometimes I feel like our family is the luckiest in the world. When I look down, I realise my napkin's been ripped to shreds.

## A COLLISION OF STARS

'I still can't believe you think Shrek's hot,' he says a while later, joining me on the sofa we've moved to with yet another round of shots.

Candlelight dances around the mason jar between us, and I'm distracted enough by the way the low light catches the angle of his jaw and the stubble that grows there that it takes me a while to register what he's said.

'And?' I scoff, swallowing my tequila. The drink warms my insides and tastes more and more like bad decisions with every second that passes. I rest a hand just above his knee as I ask, 'What about you? Who's your most obscure crush?'

The primitive, alcohol-soaked part of my brain glues its focus to how his shoulders stretch out his shirt, how his arms are slightly too big for his sleeves, how his thighs are wider than mine, for once. An image flashes across my mind of him picking me up and throwing me around, which in theory I want to hate, but in practice probably wouldn't hate at all. I let my leg press lightly against his.

After a moment's pause, where my heart thuds and the air grows thick, he replies, 'Margaret Thatcher.' I yelp and, startled, he leans back a little. Yeah, *he's* startled. One of our answers was a born leader who brought prosperity to a nation of underdogs. The other was Prime Minister of the United Kingdom. 'I know I shouldn't say that, and I'm not a Tory, but I really admire a formidable woman, you know?'

I'm of the opinion that if you ever have to justify your stance with *I'm not a Tory, but...* there's a high likelihood you are, in fact, a Tory. Unfortunately, in the presence of alcohol my moral compass is way off-kilter, and I don't think I could find true north right now if I tried.

## GEORGIA STONE

My brain is suitably fuzzy by the time we've bitten into our final lime wedges, my eyes squeezing shut against the bitterness. When I open them, Oscar's made a quick recovery and is looking at me with hungry eyes that send heat fizzing across my skin before pooling somewhere in my lower belly. I say the magic words. 'Should we get out of here?'

*Finally.* He nods and I grab my bag and lead the way up the stairs, his hand at my lower back as we step through the door. When we reach the surface, I blink at the unexpected light. The early-summer sun is making its way to the horizon, teasing a sunset I know I'm going to regret missing when I'm on the Tube.

'Are we going back to yours?' he asks, hand moving to my waist. I think about my flat. The one place I can just *be.* A sanctuary I refuse to contaminate with these kinds of hookups.

'Let's go to yours instead, it's closer.' I don't know if it is, but he seems to believe me.

As I'm in the Uber on the way home afterwards, already deleting his number from my phone, I wonder if I may have taken the phrase *fuck the Tories* a little too literally.

---

The work day's been going too smoothly, so when the door opens sometime in the afternoon, I should've known something was about to go down.

Rudy's in his harness, dutifully guiding Josie towards the counter where I'm refilling the snacks. I wring my hands, inexplicably apprehensive. 'I didn't know you were nearby. What's going on?'

'You're on the early shift today, right? I had a meeting up in Farringdon and thought I'd drop by so we can travel home together.' Her eyebrows wiggle like a cartoon villain's. 'I noticed you got in late last night.'

There is no way in hell I'm admitting who I went home with. Absolutely no way. Not when it turns out she was right about Oscar being, well, *right*. 'I was just at the pub with my friend. Date was a bust. You know how it is.'

She reaches the counter and lowers her voice, which, for someone whose two volume levels are "loud" and "louder", isn't actually very low at all. 'Is Finn in here?'

A wave of realisation rolls over me as I remember what I told her the other day to get her off my back about the party. At the mention of his name Finn glances up from the laptop he's been eagerly tapping away at for the past couple of hours, his face significantly closer to the screen than is probably recommended by most opticians.

'Who?' I hedge, hoping she won't elaborate.

She does. 'Your new friend at work? Your words, not mine.' There's no reason for the real Finn to come to the conclusion she's talking about him, because in reality this mysterious friend called Finn is a figment of my imagination. But she keeps prodding. 'Is he in here?'

I risk a quick glance in his direction. 'No… ?' Wrong move. I didn't say it with nearly enough conviction.

She turns, and whether due to her incredible instincts or my terrible luck, she faces the table to the right of the door, precisely where the man in question is sitting; glasses perched on his nose, curls in disarray from the number of times he's run his hand through them this afternoon. 'Finn?'

'Yes?' His voice is cautious, but his eyebrows lift slightly in curious amusement.

'Hi, I'm Josie, Ava's flatmate.' She reaches her hand out for him to shake, which is such a Josie thing to do that I'd laugh if not for the fact

I'm currently planning my own demise. He returns the handshake, a smile threatening to bloom. 'Has she invited you to the housewarming we're hosting yet or is she being habitually flakey with plans?'

'She,' his eyes flick towards me, 'is being habitually flakey.'

What does he know about my "habitual"? There's a moment of silence and suddenly I see a sliver of a chance to rectify the situation. I have three options.

One, I tell Josie I don't really have a friend called Finn and I made him up for the purposes of the party. She'll understand, but she'll feel sorry for me, and frankly, so will this unsuspecting man who's been pulled into this, because realistically I am a grown woman and there was absolutely no need for me to tell this stupid lie in the first place. I probably could've scrounged up an acquaintance instead of making someone up entirely like I'm seven years old and bragging about an imaginary friend.

Two, I let her know that I do have a work friend named Finn but he's not here today. Unfortunately, this option runs the risk of her coming to the shop another day and finding out then that he (still) doesn't exist.

Or, three, I engage in what is apparently my new favourite pastime, and drop another lie.

'No, no, I invited you, remember, you said you couldn't go?' I prompt.

To his credit, Finn barely skips a beat and replies evenly, 'I did say that, didn't I?'

'Yeah, especially when you found out it was a karaoke party.' I shudder to show him how utterly tragic that would be.

'When I—what?' At the final two words his whole face lights up and I realise I have made a hideous mistake. 'Uh, nope, I think I'd remember if you'd said it was a karaoke party.'

'No, I definitely told you and you definitely told me you were busy.'

His eyes are positively gleaming. Oh god, what have I done?

'Hey Josie, what date is it again?'

I don't move, my eyes frantically bouncing between them, watching their conversation unfold like I'm at a tennis match where it doesn't matter who wins, because I lose either way.

'It's the final Saturday in August,' she replies.

'Yep, just as I thought. I'm free.' He folds his arms across his chest and leans back in his chair. 'There must've been some miscommunication.'

'So you'll be there? Promise?' Josie's pitch rises with excitement.

'Wouldn't miss it.'

'Bring friends too, the more the merrier.'

'Of course. Where do you guys live again?'

'Stoc—'

'Stockwell,' he finishes for her, as if he knew all along. 'I remember now.'

'Wait,' Josie says, pointing at him accusingly. 'Were you the reason she got home at two in the morning?' Neither of us get a chance to answer before she continues. 'Thank god, because I thought she might've gone home with that Tory. I'm all for having fun in your twenties, but there's a line. You know what she's like.'

'Absolutely,' he replies earnestly.

Unfortunately, as much as I hope for it, the ground does not swallow me whole, so I snap back into action, saying as quietly as I can, 'You know, actually Josie, Finn and I don't really have the kind of friendship where we talk about that stuff.'

Realising she may have overshared, she clenches her teeth at me in an apologetic grimace that wouldn't be amiss on the face of Wallace and/or Gromit. 'I'll take a seat while I wait for you to finish up,' she says. 'Is my favourite table free?'

Reluctantly, I reply, 'Yep. Iced oat chai?'

'You're an angel. The best friend ever. *So* sorry. Uh, it was nice meeting you, Finn.' Josie sends us an impish smile and makes her way with Rudy to the table in the left corner by the window, where she moves a cushion out of the way and settles into one of the comfy armchairs.

'Have you been talking about me?' Finn asks at the same time I say, 'Thanks for covering for me there.'

I pointedly ignore his question, which is difficult when he's looking at me with the kind of mischievous eyes that I have a feeling could convince anyone to do anything. 'Thanks for covering for me there,' I repeat. 'I'll come up with an excuse for you not to come.'

'Why?'

'Why what?'

'Why am I not coming?'

I blink a few times in confusion. 'Because that entire situation was the result of some poor decision-making from me and I'd rather just figure out a way to pretend it never happened.'

'But I've given your friend my promise. Do you not want me there?'

My eyebrows pull together. 'Uh, not really? No offence.'

'None taken.' Amusement returns to his face, but he nods. 'Fine. We'll come up with an excuse. But I do love karaoke. And making friends.'

'I don't need any new friends,' I say, slightly sharper than I intended in order to cover the undercurrent of defensiveness.

Unbothered, he starts packing up his laptop. 'Clearly. You have plenty of people to keep you occupied.'

# 8

# I simply cannot pretend to be interested in bitcoin

## AVA

OUT OF SHEER EMBARRASSMENT I've managed to avoid serving Finn every time he's come into the shop since our awkward run-in with Josie last week. This hasn't been the easiest task, seeing as he appears to have taken it upon himself to become the world's most irregular regular; coming and going at different times each day and forcing me on more than one occasion to "check the deliveries" out back while a bewildered Mateo takes over at the till.

I'm sure he's not wasting his energy thinking about the time that one barista strong-armed him into trying to convince her best friend she had friends to invite to a party and wasn't a total lonely loser. But still, I'm avoiding him.

The day's swell of customers has left me tired and ready to collapse into my bed, which unfortunately isn't my plan for the evening, thanks to a date I reluctantly agreed to the other day. Now I'm left to close the shop, wiping down the surfaces and emptying the bins in preparation.

To my annoyance, there's one customer still here. And of course, it's Finn. I note that although I'm the one forced into a uniform every day, he seems to have his own. He must have an entire wardrobe of baggy button-ups. Today's shirt is pistachio green, tucked loosely into his trousers, its sleeves messily pushed to his elbows.

He doesn't look stressed, per se, because I get the impression he's the kind of person who waltzes through life without breaking a sweat over anything, but judging from the overgrown stubble on his jaw, the way he's dragged his hand through his hair three times in as many minutes, and how he's clicking his mouse like it's about to run away from him, I think this is his version of it.

I've been turning all the lights off around the shop for the past fifteen minutes, and now the only one left on is the one shining directly onto his table like a spotlight. But my passive aggression is futile, because it's still mostly daylight outside and he hasn't noticed a difference.

And unfortunately, while he's probably on a deadline, so am I. It's time to deliver the bad news. 'Hey, we're closing in less than ten minutes, by the way.'

He looks up at me, bleary eyes blinking, then stares around the room. 'Oh god. What's the time?' Before waiting for me to answer he glances at his phone and his eyes widen. 'Shit, I'm so sorry, I didn't realise. I've been trying to finalise this piece of work for my client and got caught up. I'll be five minutes, I just need to finish this off.'

I glance at his laptop screen and without thinking, say, 'You spelled accommodate wrong. It's two "m"s.'

He grins and deletes the extraneous letter with a flourish. 'Thanks.' He pulls the laptop closer and takes the paintbrush tool, painstakingly changing the colour of something in the background.

I *really* want to lock up, but I have to make another suggestion. If helping him out will make him leave sooner, I'll do it. 'There's an easier way to do that. Can I show you?'

As I'm clicking through the programme, he fills the silence with chatter. 'It's been a while since I used Illustrator. I'm usually a Canva guy for work. Don't often need anything fancier than that. Are you a designer or something?'

'Studied graphic design for a bit at uni,' I say distractedly, though my heart thrums with an emotion I can't name at his suggestion that I could be something more than someone in an apron.

When I turn his laptop back towards him, he clicks "undo" to see if he can do the sequence himself, the way I just showed him. He can. Fast learner, I guess. I'm about to go back to the counter when he calls my name.

'Ava?' I pause mid-turn. He's looking up at me from the table. 'Do you know your way around London?'

After a confused pause I reply, 'Kind of?'

'And do you know of any cool local places? Maybe some that you don't think tourists have heard about?'

My brain flips through the possibilities; places I've been on dates, fun spots Josie's told me about. 'A few, I suppose.'

'Remember I mentioned my London bucket list to you?' Not at all, to be honest. I refrain from telling him that. 'Well, I want to complete my list before I leave, and I think it'd be more fun to do it with someone.'

'Why me?'

'Why not you?' he says with a shrug. 'It'd be good to complete it with someone who knows the city better than I do. I'd hang out with Julien, but he's really busy at the moment.'

I refuse to believe this man has no other friends to spend time with. 'What if I'm busy too?'

He tilts his head, eyes amused behind his glasses. 'Are you?'

I'm not, ever, but it's presumptuous of him to think I could rearrange my whole social life around him. My system works as it is. For the most part. 'I'm sorry, I just don't know if I'm really in the mood to make friends.'

'No worries, seriously. Just thought it could be fun. Let me know if you change your mind.'

---

The Thistle and Thorn is the kind of place that's practically purpose-built for business meetings and after-work drinks that end with grey-suited people rushing to get home to the families they've neglected all week. It may be devoid of any real charm, but with an extensive gin menu and a front door only a few hundred yards from City Roast, it seemed the perfect spot for a few drinks with tonight's date.

Oliver is another finance boy, which was a mistake on my part, because by now it's been an hour since we met, and he spent the first forty minutes out in the smoking area, taking drags on his vape while talking at me about bitcoin.

He's one of those people who lives in Essex but says he's from East London. If we're still talking by the end of the night, I'm almost certain he'll ask to come back to mine; not necessarily because he wants me specifically, but because he's missed the last train back to Chelmsford and doesn't want to get a cab the whole way home.

And as attractive as this man is, with near-impossible bone structure and a hairline at a reasonable position on his forehead, I'm not sure I'll be able to tolerate him for much longer. I'm pleased to learn I do have some standards after all.

I could bail, but I'm thinking that if I stick it out for another hour until Josie's finished work, I can leave and go to the pub with her instead. His voice filters through my subconscious and I realise he's moved onto NFTs, a topic I have about as much interest in as I do bitcoin.

'Essentially, they're a way of owning art, without physically having to own the art, and no one else can own it.' He shows me a cartoon of a dog playing football and it takes everything in me not to laugh.

I noisily slurp the last of my drink through my straw, wondering if he'll pay for the next round after I paid for the first. And the second. 'So, it's like if I bought the concept of a gin and tonic, but never got to taste it?' He doesn't get the hint. 'And no one else would be able to order it from the menu either?'

'I mean, actually yeah, that's about right.' I'm slightly offended by his use of the word "actually".

Eventually he finishes his own drink, crunching on an ice cube before spitting it back into his glass. 'Should we get another? My shout.'

Better late than never.

'So, when did you start working in London?' I ask, leaning against the polished, sticky mahogany of the bar with Oliver at my right. There's deep laughter from somewhere behind me; that singular, unified laugh that groups of middle-aged men adopt when they're together.

'A few years ago, I was on a grad scheme straight after uni and then worked my way up.'

'Oh, nice. I fully intended to—'

'There are just nonstop opportunities here, you know? Entrepreneurs to be inspired by. Ideas in every corner. You can't beat it. If you're bored in London, you might as well be anywhere else. If you're *unemployed* in London, you clearly aren't trying hard enough.' He's brandishing his card at the bartender, who's ignoring him, whether intentionally or not, I can't tell.

'Sure, there's a lot of opportunity, but it's not always as simp—'

'All these companies, all these jobs, and some people do fuck all. Like, imagine going to uni and getting a degree and then becoming a waiter or something.'

'I went to uni and I'm a barista,' I interrupt, finally managing to get a full sentence in. It's not quite the burn I wanted it to be seeing as I dropped out in second year, but he doesn't need to know that.

'Schools should be pushing for economics and business degrees rather than fluffy subjects like arts and humanities,' he says in a drawl.

'Surely if everyone did economics and business degrees, you'd have a surplus of people with those degrees against the jobs they're applying for? As a Business graduate, you'd know all about supply and demand, right?' I finish innocently.

That's when the person on my left expels a soft snort, and I sneak a glance to see a familiar figure leaning against the bar as he waits to order. I snap my eyes away from him and try to listen to the man on my right, who's still going on about lazy people who don't take the opportunities in front of them.

I'm saved from more of his septic spewing when the bartender finally notices him and he leans across the bar to yell his order in her ear at a ridiculous volume.

## A COLLISION OF STARS

'I don't know if this is crossing a line,' the figure to my left says, amusement in his voice. 'But would you be offended if I told you that this guy seems like an asshole?'

I don't look at him at first, continuing to pretend I have a vested interest in the rows of spirits lined up on the wall in front of me. Oliver is still leaning into the bartender's ear, gesticulating wildly and over-pronouncing his "p"s. She surreptitiously wipes spit from her face before answering his question, and I stifle a grin when she yells into his ear just as loudly as he did, making him flinch.

I finally turn my head so that I'm eye-to-eye with Finn, watching his gaze quickly sweep over me, noting my non-uniformed self in a Never After band tee and midi skirt, presumably. I imagine it's similar to how you'd feel when you'd see a teacher out in public as a child. He looks a little less dishevelled than earlier, his posture more relaxed.

'Not offended, no,' I begin. 'This is just a hiccup. Because I'm generally an excellent judge of character. For instance, right now, I'm judging that your character should stay out of my business.'

'I don't think that's what that phrase means.'

A smirk pulls at his mouth as soon as Oliver starts to talk to me again. 'Ugh, this place is fucking ridiculous, they don't have my favourite IPA. Can you believe that?'

'Devastating,' I deadpan, confirming to myself that I am not, in fact, an excellent judge of character.

'So, uh, my card is playing up and I really need to take a slash. Could you cover me? You're a babe.'

I cringe at the pet name and just as he's turning his back to me I ask, 'Did you order for me too?'

He glances over his shoulder, not even slightly sheepish, before replying, 'I didn't realise you were thirsty.' I notice he doesn't apologise to any of the four people he bumps into as he makes his way towards the bathroom.

For a second I pause, and then catch Finn's eye to say, 'I can change him.'

He laughs then, a proper belly laugh that sends his whole body flinging backwards like one of those flailing inflatable tubes outside a car dealership. I want to remind him that what I said wasn't actually that funny, but he's got one of those laughs that seeps into your bones like a day out in the sun, and god knows I could do with a bit of sunshine.

'Please say that man is a business acquaintance and not a date.'

I squint at the bottles in front of me again, but I can feel Finn's gaze on me. 'He's a business acquaintance… from Hinge.'

'He seems like a delight.'

As much of a dickhead as Oliver is, I can't stop thinking about one thing he said. *If you're bored in London, you might as well be anywhere else.* I'm not bored. Am I? It sounds an awful lot like what Josie's been repeating over the past few weeks, trying to get me to make the most of this city.

The bartender puts a whiskey on the rocks onto the bar, condensation already dripping down the sides of the glass amidst the syrupy heat of the room. 'Where did he— oh. Did you guys want anything else?'

She eyes me warily and I consider the whiskey for a second before shaking my head and saying, 'That's all.'

She shrugs and keys in the order. Oliver has ordered one of their most expensive brands. A double, obviously. After I've paid, I pick up the glass, already recoiling at the smell.

'Is that mine?' Oliver's grating voice hits me before I see him, back far too soon. I bet he didn't even wash his hands. Manky boy.

'It *was*,' I say, before launching the drink to the back of my throat, trying in vain to avoid the ice cubes while the burn travels down to my stomach. I wipe the back of my hand across my mouth and mutter, 'I hate whiskey.'

'Did you just take that as a shot? That's vintage.' His eyes are wide.

The warmth of the whiskey has loosened my tongue just enough. 'Oliver.'

'You can call me Ollie.'

'Oliver. This isn't happening. I'm out.'

'What do y—'

'You are not nearly tall enough to have an ego this big. Have a good evening.'

I'm unsurprised to note it takes approximately twelve seconds for him to lose interest and head back to the smoking area, where he will no doubt find someone else to exhaust with fascinating stories of cryptocurrency and lazy graduates.

'Do you want anything?' Finn asks, his jaw working like he's chewing on a laugh to keep it from spilling out.

'No thanks.' He continues giving the bartender his extensive order. *If you're bored in London, you might as well be anywhere else.* 'Finn, what are you doing here?'

'Ordering a round... ?'

'No, I mean, here-here. Are you with a business acquaintance? Or, you know, a *business acquaintance*?'

The corners of his mouth twitch and he says, 'I'm here with the guys for work drinks.' He looks behind us at a group of people sitting at a table against the far wall, which includes Julien and the lanky redhead from the first night. He sighs when he catches sight of his friend. 'God, Julien's indecently handsome, isn't he? But why do you ask?'

I think about that rough wool of mundanity. I can be spontaneous. Tonight, I refuse to be bored.

'Show me your bucket list.' I remember to tack on a modicum of politeness at the end, 'Please.'

He slides his phone out of his pocket, pulling up his Notes app, and I skim it, not sure what I'm looking for. The items range from vague to extremely niche, with a whole lot of middle ground. Most aren't specific to London at all, which makes the list even weirder. *Eat at a local restaurant. Become a regular. See the dinosaurs.*

At the bottom of the list I spot a line that says: *Find a rooftop.*

'Fancy crossing something off the list?' I ask, handing back his phone and spitting the words out before I regret them.

'And leave my colleagues? I'm the life and soul of the party.'

I glance over to where the raucous sound of his coworkers' laughter is emanating. 'I'll be honest, I think they'll survive.'

'But Ava, won't they think we're doing something *salacious*?'

'We're going to Tesco.'

'Oh.' He frowns. 'I didn't know that was on my list.'

'It's not.' The pub is loud around us, and I have to lean towards him to be sure he'll hear me. 'Listen, I have an idea, but this is a one-time offer. Take it or leave it.'

His smile catches me off guard, bouncing across his face and up to his eyes the way sunlight hits a skyscraper; unexpectedly brightening an otherwise gloomy day. 'Of course I'm taking it. But let me get these drinks to the others first.'

Julien must've been keeping an eye on the beverage progress, because he appears at the bar just as the bartender finishes making the last drinks on Finn's order.

'Hey Ava,' he says, voice as velvety as ever. 'Please tell me you've figured out how loose this man is with his credit card. He'll *always* get you a double, even when you ask for a single to be polite. It's my favourite thing about him.' He slaps a hand on Finn's shoulder and plants a kiss on his hair.

'I'm actually leaving in a minute,' I clarify. 'But I'll bear that in mind.'

'There's always next time,' Julien says with a shrug. There's definitely *not* always next time, because there won't be a next time. I know that much.

'Wait, that's your favourite thing about me?' Finn asks. 'Not my eternal optimism or encyclopaedic knowledge of palaeontology?'

'I said what I said,' Julien replies smoothly.

'Ava's helping me with my bucket list.'

'I'm helping you with *one* item on your bucket list,' I correct.

'What did he promise you to get you to help?' Julien asks, picking up four glasses with a level of dexterity I envy. 'Did he offer any kind of payment?'

'I was thinking of requesting a vow of silence for any time he's in the coffee shop, but I'm open to ideas.'

Julien's pensive. 'Can you petition for that vow to extend to the office as well? I'd love some peace and quiet.'

'Absolutely, I'm sure we can come to an arrangement.'

'Hey, not sure if you two know, but I am right here,' Finn says, raising his hand. He spins around to tap his phone on the card reader to pay. 'And to think, Julien, I was gonna offer you my drink, seeing as it's now going to waste. Guess it'll have to go to Rory instead.'

For a split second I feel bad for pulling Finn away from his friends, but he doesn't seem too bothered.

'All Rory needs is half a pint and he's smashed, so I'm taking it. I accept your gesture of goodwill.'

'I'll just say bye,' Finn says to me, lightly tapping my arm before picking up the remaining drinks and heading over to the table with Julien, neither of them spilling a drop amidst the constant jostling of people in their path. Finn takes about five times as long to say his goodbyes as I would, all dramatic expressions and giant gestures that make him look like he's playing charades. Eventually he rejoins me by the bar and I motion him towards the door, which he holds open and makes me walk through first.

# 9

# we found love in a hopeless place (the drinks fridge at Tesco)

## AVA

ONCE WE'RE OUTSIDE IN the waning daylight, we turn right and weave through narrow, cobbled alleyways to make our way in the direction of the Thames.

To my horror, Finn does not stop talking for the entirety of the eternity-filled four minutes. 'Where are you taking me? Am I being kidnapped? I have 999 primed and ready.'

'I told you,' I say through slightly gritted teeth, wondering if I might come to regret my spontaneous decision. 'Tesco.'

Walking with Finn feels a lot like walking with an exceptionally long-legged toddler. We hit a busier road, and opposite the Royal Courts of Justice, right where Fleet Street morphs into the Strand, is a dragon statue he's taken an interest in, softly illuminated by the dregs of evening sunlight.

'What's this?' He cranes his neck to get a better look.

'It marks the entrance to the City of London from Westminster.'

His head whirls to face me. 'How do you know that?'

'I know a lot of things,' I say, waiting for a car to pass so that I can keep walking. 'But also, I Googled it once.'

He pulls himself away and follows me across the road to our destination; a tiny Tesco Express sewn into the patchwork of twentieth-century buildings lining the street.

As we cross the threshold, it strikes me that there's something innately intimate about being in a supermarket with someone, so I attempt to make the process as quick as possible, directing us to the drinks fridge.

'Take your pick. I owe you one after pulling you away from yours.'

He opens his mouth as if he wants to protest me paying, but sensibly, he stays quiet. I don't pay much attention to him while we analyse the selection. Unfortunately, it's Friday night and pickings are slim. All I can see are cans of whiskey and coke.

'Want to split some wine?' Finn asks from somewhere to my right.

'If you want?' a man's voice replies. 'I was going to get some beers, but if you're offering.'

My head shoots up and I find a man looking at Finn in total earnest. I'd suspect he were sober if not for the slight sway to his posture.

Half a second of confusion floods Finn's face before it splits into an easy smile. 'Unfortunately, I was asking my friend here. But on any other day, I promise I'd have said yes.'

I don't really know Finn, but I'm certain he's telling the truth.

'Oh,' the man says, looking at me with red-rimmed eyes. 'Yeah, no, definitely drink with her. I'm not nearly as pretty.'

Finn grabs the man's shoulder, a compliment rolling smoothly off his tongue. 'Don't say that. You're extremely pretty.'

'You think so?'

'I've seen many faces in my lifetime, and yours is one of the loveliest.' Who knew there was a Jane Austen novel set in a Tesco Express on Fleet Street?

'You promise?'

'Cross my heart,' Finn says.

'Well. Enjoy your bottle,' the man says, picking up a four-pack of beer. 'Think of me when you drink it.'

Finn nods sincerely and we watch his new friend walk to the crisps aisle, lightly bumping into the shelves as he goes.

'Was that a yes to the wine?' Finn asks, leaning against the edge of the fridge and holding up a bottle in the opposite hand, entirely unflustered by the interaction. I look back at the cans and the nauseating whiskey from earlier flashes across my memory.

'Yeah. Let's get wine. As long as it's not red.'

---

When he's not distracted by signs and statues, Finn matches my pace easily. We make a left off the Strand and head down a side street, the river just about visible in the distance. The buildings to our right cast the whole street in shadow, so as we approach the gate at the bottom, I can't quite tell if it's open, and I'm suddenly struck by the fear that this place I'm taking him to will be closed. But then, when we're a few metres away, relief washes over me.

'Tah dah,' I say, motioning towards the gate, which sits at the foot of a set of concrete steps, flanked by high stone walls.

'A staircase? Ava, you shouldn't have.'

I shake my head and make my way up the stairs. At one point, I turn to check he's following, and with the way his head suddenly whips to the side with a guilty smile, I wonder if he's following me a bit *too* attentively.

'You wanted a rooftop, here you go,' I say, walking backwards to gauge his reaction as he reaches the top of the stairs. 'We're not very high up, so I'm sure there are better ones with better views, but I think this works.'

In the golden hour light, Finn crests the top step and his eyes dart around, taking in the view, before focusing on me. 'This works.'

We lean over the far wall, looking down at the road below, which is still busy despite the bulk of rush hour traffic having dissipated. The sun sends beads of warm light dancing across the surface of the Thames beyond the road. In the distance the London Eye makes its lazy circuit, while Big Ben's gold plating glints in the final moments of daylight, and behind them both, the sky's an Impressionist's delight; sweeping strokes of yellows and oranges illuminating lilac clouds.

Finn takes photos and asks me obscure, unanswerable questions about landmarks and bridges, before we both drop onto the bench behind us. I take the wine out of my bag just as the sun dips below the horizon.

'I can empty my water bottle if you want to split it evenly,' he says.

I unscrew the cap and pass it to him. 'I don't mind sharing if you don't.'

'Fine with me.' He shrugs and takes a swig.

I can't stop thinking about what Oliver-from-Hinge said. Bored? Not me. I can be spontaneous. I can accost a man in a pub and be sitting on a bench drinking wine with him half an hour later. *And* I can tell Josie I did a platonic activity and it won't even be a lie.

'How have I never noticed this place? I come via Temple every day for work.'

His question's rhetorical, but upon hearing the indeterminate twang in the way he says the word "via", I have to ask my own question. 'Where are you from? If I listen for English, that's the accent I hear, but if I listen for American, I can hear that too.'

He takes another swig and hands the bottle back to me. 'Do you want the long answer or the short answer?'

'Long.'

'Are you sure?' He adjusts his sleeves. 'When I say it's long, I mean it's *very* long.'

'Heard that before and been extremely disappointed,' I say with a sigh, about to take another sip.

He looks at me shrewdly. 'I'm not known for disappointing people.' The bottle misses my mouth as he continues, 'So my Mum's Irish—'

'Never mind, give me the short version.'

'You're funny,' he says. He flashes me his lockscreen and I see a woman with auburn hair. 'This is my mum. She's Irish, while my dad's Greek but raised in the US. Add the fact that my mum was a diplomat and we moved around a lot throughout my childhood, and you have the perfect example of a third-culture kid.'

'What's that?'

'Someone who finds the *where are you from?* question difficult to answer.' I nod at him to elaborate and he says, 'It's basically anyone who grows up outside of their parents' home countries or cultures, or is raised in more than one country.'

'Look at you,' I say, taking one more sip before I pass the wine back to him, 'checking all the boxes.'

He lifts the bottle to his mouth but doesn't drink yet. 'Mum worked a lot so I spent more time with my dad back then, which was great for me. I idolised him. Basically just copied him for years. I even had a little American accent like he did. But he left when I was about five to start a company in Silicon Valley.' He takes a glug of the wine, and then another, before speeding through his next few sentences. 'He had to do it. He wouldn't be as successful today if he hadn't had a base in the US.' A curl drops into his eye and I get the inexplicable urge to push it back, but then he does it himself. 'Anyway, around that time, my mum was set to be stationed somewhere kind of volatile, so she sent me to an international boarding school here in the UK for a few years. She wanted to keep doing her job and know I'd be safe.'

It's difficult to imagine this, knowing that Max and I went to the same secondary school as most kids from our primary school, which also happened to be where our parents met, twenty years prior. 'Was it weird for you to be so far from your mum and dad?'

'A little, I guess, but I got used to it.' His eyebrows draw together for a fraction of a second, but then his expression relaxes into a smile. 'A few years later my mum met my stepdad in Dakar and soon after, they had the twins.' He smiles when he brings them up.

Instinctively I say, 'I'm a twin too. Me and Max.'

His eyes light up. 'Are you close? Do you see him a lot?'

'We're close. But he travels a lot for work, so sometimes I don't see him for months.' He opens his mouth to ask another question and I realise he's latched onto this tiny piece of personal information I've granted him, so I quickly add, 'Sorry. Carry on. Where'd you go next?'

He seems like he wants to keep the focus on me, but thankfully he continues with his own story. 'Between us we moved around a few more times,' he lists them on his fingers, 'to Brussels, Geneva and Singapore, which is where my family has been for about ten years now.'

'So your siblings haven't moved around as much as you?'

He shakes his head. 'Not as much, no. Mum's not a diplomat anymore; she became a teacher a while back. Her students have probably spent more time with her than I ever did as a kid, to be honest.' His smile freezes on his face for a split second, then he adds, 'Anyway, to answer your original accent question, loads of people at international schools have this very specific English-American hybrid accent, which I guess I picked up over the years too.'

I pretend I'm not fascinated hearing about this rootless life so different from mine and ask indifferently, 'Is that all?'

He gives a short laugh. 'Almost. I moved to Sydney for uni, stayed there an extra year after graduating, went back to Singapore for a bit, then Paris, and now here I am.'

'Here you are.' I take a drag from the bottle. 'What was the short answer?'

'I have a shit ton of passports and minimal need for visas.'

'Yeah, that probably would've sufficed.' A car beeps its horn below and it drowns out the sound of another laugh from him. 'Do you enjoy moving around so much?'

'It's what I've always done,' he says with a shrug, taking his glasses off to clean them on his shirt.

'That's not what I asked.'

The sun's disappeared by now, but it's not dark enough to miss the intensity in the gaze he fixes on me. He seems like he's weighing up how much to say. 'I start to feel kind of claustrophobic if I'm in the same place for too long. I try not to get too attached to any one place or person. It makes it easier to leave.' He reaches for the bottle and takes another pull. 'Plus, I own, like, two and a half suitcases' worth of belongings. I've got no space for emotional baggage too.'

'Makes sense,' I say gingerly. 'So why are you in London now and not Paris?'

His mouth opens and closes before he replies. 'I kind of had to leave Paris in a hurry. Didn't really know where to go. But I know Julien from school and he works at PaidUp—this fintech startup here in London—and told me they were looking for a marketing consultant on a six-month contract. It all fell into place. I hadn't lived in the UK since I was at boarding school, and six months felt like the perfect amount of time to experience London before I move again.'

'Do you and Julien work on the same team?' Alcohol, asking questions and avoiding divulging any information about myself? God, I feel like I'm on a date.

'Nah, he's a data analyst. And Rory's a lawyer.' At my evident surprise, he shouts a single loud 'ha!', flinging his head backwards as he does. 'No common sense whatsoever but incredibly smart when he needs to be. I mean, I've never required his services so can't confirm firsthand, but I assume he knows what he's doing.'

'I believe you.' I'm not sure I do, but I'm trying not to judge a book by its cover. 'So is that your thing? Fintech? And marketing?' I think about my horrific attempts at upselling, which I only ever do when Carl is in the vicinity. It feels fitting that Finn would know how to get people to buy things. He seems like the type of person who can talk his way into anything.

'I'm not exactly passionate about it. It's not *dinosaurs*.' He grins, his knee bobbing up and down. 'But it pays well, and I'm good at it.'

'Sounds like me.' My forehead creases. 'Except that being a barista doesn't pay well. So not like me at all, actually.'

He laughs and runs a hand through his hair. 'Forgive me if this is crossing a boundary, but you don't seem like you love your job.'

'Well.' I purse my lips. 'I'm not really a morning person. And I'm not exactly a people person either.'

'I hadn't noticed,' he says politely.

'But it's easy to get out of my head there. I enjoy some parts of it. The coffee and the organisation, mostly. Sometimes I get to be a bit creative with the menus too. That's usually enough to keep the boredom at bay.'

He swipes through his phone and shows me something I recognise. It's a photo of one of the menus I drew on our chalkboard a couple of weeks ago, and my heart squeezes a little in my chest. 'I always love the menus. Is art just a hobby for you? Or could it be a career?'

My insides coil at the thought. 'Years ago I wanted to be a graphic designer, but I just haven't got around to starting back up again. One day I will.' Probably. Maybe. 'So the coffee shop is fine for me, for now.'

We're inching far too close to something real, and I don't want to go near it.

'If it works, it works,' he says quietly.

I think it through for a moment and add, 'There's also a revolving door of employees, and I don't *hate* training them.'

'So what you're saying is, you're in the process of building your own personal barista army.' He drapes an arm on the back of the bench and angles his body towards mine. 'Who are you fighting?'

'Customers who give me exact change after I've already input a whole number in the till.' He barks out another laugh and my mouth threatens to betray me with a smile. 'I'm serious, I can't do the maths. I pretend the till won't let me add their change.'

'In that case, I vow to only ever pay with my card.'

'Setting an example to customers everywhere.'

I'm about to take another swig but he pulls the bottle back from me with a smirk. The caustic look I send his way doesn't even make a dent.

We face the river, where fragments of light dart across a slick of darkness, and I have to tip our bottle almost vertically by this point to get any liquid out. At least Finn's under no illusions about how classy I am.

My insides are warm and my eyelids are beginning to feel heavy, but I know myself after wine, and I know it's only a matter of time before tiredness turns into irritation, so I'm about to call it quits when Finn does it for me.

'Shit,' he says. 'I need to get going. My brother was mad he missed me on FaceTime the other day, so I said I'd call before he goes to school. He's a bit of a talker, so I'd rather be at home for it.'

I register that he has a habit of over-explaining everything he does.

'A bit of a talker,' I repeat. 'Wonder where he gets that from.'

'It's a mystery. But it's in my best interests to be sitting somewhere comfy if I'm gonna be attached to my phone for an hour.'

'Fine with me. Let's go.' Our shadows ripple down the stone steps as we head back to street level. I drop the bottle in a bin with a wince-inducing clatter. Sorry, recycling mafia. Maybe next time.

By this point, I'm ready for a quiet journey home. It's been a long week, I've done way too much talking, and my bed is waiting.

'I promise I'm not following you,' he says, as we both take a right.

'That sounds like something that someone who's following me would say.'

'I live in Brixton,' he says by way of explanation. A sigh escapes me at the realisation that I'll have a companion for the entirety of my Tube journey.

When we reach the platform, a train's just pulling away, and the board says the next one is in five minutes. I am an ardent supporter of the Tube, but any wait over three minutes feels like a personal affront.

'Oh, awesome. Five minutes,' Finn says happily, sitting down on one of the benches. I drop down too, leaving one empty seat between us.

We don't talk for a few moments. The tempo of Finn's foot tapping against the floor doesn't match the tune he's humming and I kind of wish he'd stop. I take a few deep breaths to soothe the fatigue-induced irritation I predicted would come.

'Isn't it nice when you can just sit in comfortable silence with someone?' he says, after no more than nine seconds.

'Is that what this is?' I ask tonelessly, watching a particularly robust mouse scurry along the platform and stop dangerously close to a middle-aged man in a suit, who, by all accounts, looks like he's about one surprise rodent away from crying.

Momentarily distracted, Finn follows my gaze to the end of the platform. The man eventually notices the mouse and reacts in stereotypical London fashion. Which is to say, his eyes widen and he feigns a nonchalance that fools nobody around him.

Finn's feet go back to tapping that discordant rhythm. 'Just sitting here quietly, watching the world go by.'

I *wish* he'd sit here quietly and watch the world go by, but he's clearly got a bee in his bonnet, and my patience is rapidly waning. Eventually, I say, 'Spit it out.'

'What?' He stops tapping, resting both hands on his knees.

'I think you're working up to something. What do you want to say?'

He's clearly been turning this over in his head, because there's no build-up when he starts to speak again. 'Why did your friend think we were close friends? That day she came in with her dog asking about the party?'

I try to read his expression; the tilt to his head, the tiniest furrow to his brow. He doesn't seem like he's making fun of me. I think he's just curious.

'It wasn't you specifically. I just needed to give her a name and you happened to walk in at the right moment.'

He nods slowly, taking it in, clearly still confused. 'But why did you need to pretend?'

Our train finally pulls in and I step on first, leaning into the alcove of the opposite doorway, while Finn stands a few feet away with his hand holding the bar above his head.

'Because Josie thinks I've been cooped up for too long and she's been trying to get me out of the house more. But she's busy with work at the moment, and she's leaving for a few months at the start of next year and I think she feels guilty about leaving me to fend for myself, for some reason.' I let out a long exhale. 'And she thinks making friends will help me, I guess.'

'Do *you* think you should be getting out more and making friends?'

I can't explain those desperate promises I made long ago. How I refuse to do anything to jeopardise the careful balance that's kept me content enough these past few years, that's kept life simple. How I switched off both the sun and the rain and turned my heart into the badlands, because if it's inhospitable, no one will even try to get in.

Instead of saying this, I reply, 'Whenever I want to get out of the flat, I find someone new, and then I spend time with them. A very small amount of time.' I square my shoulders and lock eyes with him, daring him to say anything. From experience, men either find this attitude off-putting, or take it as an opportunity to make a lewd comment.

Finn does neither. 'Sure. But on top of that, what about when you're bored and want to hang out with someone for a coffee? Or a walk?'

'I don't think I'm lacking in the coffee department,' I say drily. 'And I'm not really an outdoorsy person.'

He shifts his grip on the bar above his head as we pull away from the station. He looks like he wants to say something but changes his mind, and eventually he surprises me by moving the focus to him. 'I'm only asking because I'm in a similar boat. I don't have many close friends either.' I find this difficult to believe, and he registers something on my face that must tell him as such. 'Honestly. I told you, I move around too much to make good friends. Which is completely my decision, but still. Most people are just friendly acquaintances. Julien's the only one who's stuck around, and that's probably because our families know each other. His parents and my stepdad grew up together in Senegal.' He shrugs. 'Well, that, and the fact he knew me when I was a gangly nerd with braces, and you simply cannot unfriend someone like that. They have far too much ammunition against you.'

'Right.' I breathe again, letting my mind move away from the topic of my barren heart. 'And now you're a gangly nerd *without* braces.'

'Exactly. Although,' he peers at his own bicep, flexing slightly as if to check it's still there, the muscle expanding to fill out the space in his sleeve, 'maybe not *super* gangly anymore.'

I want to roll my eyes. But I'm a drunk, heterosexual woman and he's an objectively attractive man, so I still watch him do it. To my annoyance, he catches me looking. He raises his eyebrows in a question I'm not sure I want to answer, the hint of a smirk on his face, and I turn away as the doors open at Westminster.

The London Underground gods must be looking out for me, because an American couple grappling with approximately fifty-three bags gets on, positioning themselves directly between us. Almost immediately, Finn's drawn into their conversation, and I briefly think he'd do well in the US, where people are generally friendlier and more open to a chat with a stranger.

Friday and Saturday nights are arguably the only time that conversation on the Tube isn't completely frowned upon, which is good for Finn and his new friends, because all three of them seem to operate at a higher decibel level than the rest of us. I attempt to block out the noise by closing my eyes and testing myself to see if I can run through all the stations on the Circle line in my head without a map. Unfortunately this game doesn't last long, because with my eyes closed, my centre of gravity takes a nose-dive. I stumble to the side and Finn catches me mid-topple, warm hands wrapping tightly around my elbows and only letting go once I've regained my balance.

I glower at him as if it's his fault I fell. His mouth twitches at the corners but his voice is level when he asks, 'You good, Ava Monroe?'

When the doors open at Victoria we all get off, and Finn picks up two of the couple's suitcases and places them on the platform. He gives them directions to the coach station and they say goodbye, thanking him profusely.

'Look at that, I knew how to get them somewhere. Maybe I'm a real Londoner after all,' he says smugly. The further our feet take us underground, the higher that tiredness rises, threatening to breach the surface. 'Did you know the Victoria line is one of only two Tube lines that's entirely underground?' I don't think he even wants me to respond; he just can't handle the quiet. A few moments pass and he starts up again. 'I love the Underground. How each line has different colour fixtures and seats to match its colour on the map? *Extremely* satisfying to me.'

I make a grunt that might translate to *cool* but more than likely means *please stop talking*.

'I think we can help each other out,' he says at last, keeping up with the strides I'm taking through the station and ruining my efforts to outpace him.

'You know where I can find a gag?' I mutter. 'I'm on the hunt for one. Like, right now.'

'Hey, what you do behind closed doors is none of my business.' I stop mid-stride for just long enough that he has to swerve to avoid me. He answers my glare with an easy smile and steps onto the escalator before swivelling and looking up at me from a few steps below. 'But look, I have a proposition for you. What if we entered into a mutually beneficial friendship?'

'Aren't all friendships mutually beneficial?'

'Sure. But you're not looking to make friends, I know that. I, however, need company or I will likely go insane. So at the risk of sounding like I'm five, will you be my friend? My summer-bound, deliberately regimented friend?'

There's a group of drunk women behind us in a cloud of glitter and perfume, and one of them yells, 'Be his friend!'

I sigh. 'What would that entail?'

Bolstered by the fact my response wasn't an outright "no" as he—and I—probably expected, Finn's words flow out of him easily. 'Hardly anything, I promise. I'm low-maintenance. Just tell me I'm pretty and laugh at my jokes.'

'I'm unlikely to do either of those things,' I say quickly, stepping off the escalator behind him.

'Do it!' the women say. I feel like I'm at a panto, so I move down the platform away from our audience and wait for Finn to follow, a train pulling in as we walk.

'Sure. Logistics. I have a list of places I want to see and things I want to do before I leave London, which will probably end up being sometime this autumn, depending on the next job I get. You can accompany me to some of them.'

We step onto the train in single file and claim the two semi-standing benches at the end of the carriage.

I clutch the nearest handle to avoid falling off my perch as we pull out of the station and ask, 'What do I get out of this arrangement?'

Finn turns to face me, leaning against the partition. 'Aside from time spent with me?'

'I meant the benefits,' I say, which elicits a snort from him.

He cleans his glasses on the hem of his shirt before squinting through them to check for smears. When they're back on his face, he says, 'You can tell Josie you're hanging out with me and you can stop worrying about how *she's* worried about you being lonely or bored or whatever.' I don't love that he's managed to pinpoint the exact source of my concern, but I'm still not convinced. He continues, 'It's like... a friendship of convenience.'

For a little while, the Tube is too loud to be able to hear each other, so he waits for a quieter moment before he starts up again. 'But what I mean is, we get to know each other.' He sees my grimace and adds, 'In a friendly way. Just like tonight. I get to explore the city and not go mad in my own solitude for the next few months, and you get to test out all your cutting remarks on someone whose threshold for taking offence is somewhere in outer space. It's a win-win.'

I untie and retie my ponytail three times while I think it through.

Maybe this is the perfect solution. A sign from the universe. Because it's not just Josie who thinks I should be getting out more. The spiny fibres of boredom have been itching, and this could be a way to scratch.

He talks a lot. Enough that I see a purchase of earplugs in my future. But if tonight's been any indication, he's easy enough to be around, and I don't need to worry about keeping him at arm's length because he said himself he doesn't get close to people either, *and* he's leaving in a few months. What's the worst that could happen in one summer?

'What's the verdict?' he asks, peering at me.

'If I say yes, and that's a big "if", we would run through your list at my pace. I choose what we do and when.'

'Yes. Definitely.'

'And you'll let me do my job in peace next week if I agree. I don't want this to interfere with my daily life.'

The dam on his smile breaks and it spills across his face, deepening the laughter lines bracketing his eyes. 'I won't say a single word to you on Monday.'

Frankly, that's enough for me to concede. 'Fine.'

'So. Does this mean you're accepting my very inorganic offer of friendship?'

With a resigned nod, I reply, 'I am.'

'Friends,' he says, sticking out his little finger and preempting a pinkie promise.

I glance down and back up to meet his eyes, sure the warmth behind his must be a direct contrast to the ice behind mine. 'I am absolutely not doing that.'

He spreads his fingers and switches to holding out his hand for me to shake instead. I match his grip, momentarily relieved he doesn't have the kind of limp handshake that my mum always taught Max and me to be disparaging of.

He leans back against his side of the train, a gloating smirk on his face. 'For the record, telling your friend you'd invited me to a housewarming party was a really weird lie,' he says, closing his eyes for a few moments before adding, 'I hope I can say this to you, now we're pals.'

'Don't say pals.'

'Mates. Buddies. Amigos.' I scowl, but he continues, 'Comrades.'

'Alright Karl Marx, pipe down.'

We pull into Stockwell and I step in front of Finn, waiting for the door to open on his right.

'Chums,' he declares at last, accompanied by a click of his tongue and not one, but two finger-guns. A second later he adds, 'I actually don't think I've ever said that word in my life.'

'Yeah, there's a reason for that,' I bite back, stepping off the train.

I turn back to look at him leaning against the bench, neck bowed slightly to look down at me on the platform. Just before the door slides shut again, he says, 'I think you're gonna like me.'

It's accompanied by a smile, but it feels like a threat.

# 10

## are wine-drunk agreements legally binding?

### AVA

As I stick my final poster up by the till I desperately hope our new summer frappés are unpopular, because making any kind of blended drink is the unequivocal bane of my working life. I've just moved back behind the counter when Finn breezes into the coffee shop, propelled by invisible sails and lit by a sun I can't see. This is the first time I've seen him in the few days since the signing of our wine-fuelled treaty.

'Morning!' he says to no one in particular as he enters. Someone says it back.

'Flat white?' I hedge, when he reaches me. He seems to change his order depending on his mood, which is against everything I thought I knew about coffee lovers.

He leans his hip against the counter and peruses the poster before pointing at one of the new drinks. 'Can I try one of those?'

'Sure,' I say through gritted teeth. I get the ingredients together to throw in the blender and add, 'You know, most people have one or two favourite drinks and stick to them. Keeps it simple.'

'I don't like to pin myself down. Where's the fun in that?'

He makes a poor attempt at comedy while his drink is blending; pretending to be talking but making it seem like the noise of the blender is drowning him out.

'I said, when's our next mission?' he yells at the exact moment the blender cuts out. Oh. Not comedy.

'I've thought about it some more with a sober mind, and I've realised I'm all booked up.' I grab a cup and start to pour the sugary concoction.

'Ah, right. Until when?'

The snap of the lid clamping onto the cup makes me flinch. 'When are you leaving London again?'

He narrows his eyes like he can tell where I'm going with this. 'Sometime in the autumn, probably.'

'Then I'm booked up until sometime in the autumn.'

'You should stop thinking about me leaving, it'll only upset you. Need I remind you we made a deal?' He makes his way over to the straws while I ring up his order. When he rounds the corner again he smiles and waves at a middle-aged man sitting at one of the back tables.

'Friend of yours?' I ask, eyebrows raised.

'Why, you jealous?'

'Not in the slightest. Maybe he can take over from me and go with you on your *missions*.'

'Stan's a lovely man, but I don't think he likes to try new things.' Considering Stan has come into the coffee shop at the same time every day (nine-thirty), ordering the same drink (Earl Grey with hot milk) and same snack (a pack of ready salted crisps) ever since I've worked here, I'm inclined to agree. I don't want to think about the fact that without intervention from Josie, or Finn, frustratingly, I'm well on my way to becoming a Stan too.

'I don't think a drunken agreement would stand in a court of law,' I point out, grabbing a teabag for myself and pouring boiling water into a cup.

'Our handshake would.' He takes an appreciative sip of his drink. 'But do you remember anything from the list? What have you got planned for me next?'

Unfortunately, at this exact moment I see something through the floor-to-ceiling windows that sends me dropping to the floor out of sight.

'Fuck *me*,' I say under my breath.

'I usually take a woman to dinner first,' he responds. When I don't reply, he asks, 'Is there any particular reason you're on the floor?'

'Is there a tall blonde man by the window still?'

'Great beard? Yeah he's coming ins—' I dart into the back room before he can finish his sentence, leaving the door ajar. Finn greets the person who just walked in, cheerful as ever.

And then comes the rich, audiobook voice of a man I haven't seen in months. A man who proved to me that I should never hook up with men I meet in real life.

'Hello,' Jonas says on the other side of the door. 'When I was outside I'm sure I saw someone behind the counter that I knew.'

'Mateo?' Finn asks. 'Makes really good chai lattes?'

'Her name's Emily.'

I can't see Finn's face but I can imagine the calculated amusement in his eyes. 'Don't know if there's an Emily here.'

'She's tall, curvy, sort of like if Botticelli's Venus had dark hair and a fringe and was a bit emo.'

I won't lie, it's not a terrible analogy.

'Very specific,' Finn says. 'Though could you maybe give me some more details?'

'Well, not to be crass,' Jonas says, 'but she has an incredible ass. Great personality too, of course, so bright and warm, but, you know. The ass is... yeah.'

'Nah, there's definitely no one here who fits that description,' Finn replies coolly, raising his voice slightly. I think I should be offended, so I send him a glare he can't see.

After a few more painful moments of back-and-forth between them, eventually I grit my teeth and push the door open, where I'm met by two drastically different expressions on two drastically different men. As expected, Finn's mouth is curved into a smirk, while Jonas looks like he just won the lottery.

'It *was* you,' he says, eyes softening, moving towards me.

'Oh, you meant that Emily,' Finn says, scratching his jaw. 'I forgot about her.'

I wipe my sweaty palms on my apron. 'Jonas, it's been, what, two months?'

'Ninety-four days.' Finn's mouth drops open behind his blonde counterpart as he starts to piece it together, delight swimming in his eyes. He moves away but I know he's eavesdropping, because he's gone to the straws and he already *has* one.

'God, that long?' I ask, wringing my hands in front of me.

'I've thought about you every day since.' He looks in my eyes like he's trying to find the secrets of the universe in them. 'It must be fate that I walked past at this exact moment. How have you been?'

'Good, really good. Can I get you anything to drink?'

'Oh. Sorry, I'm overwhelmed. A latte please.'

The night we met, Jonas wrote me a limerick. I decided it would be the last time I met someone out in public instead of on an app, where I can at least vet my subjects first.

While I make his coffee, he peppers me with questions. 'Do you want to go for a drink later? I'd love to spend more time with you. When do you finish?' He drops his voice. 'I can't stop thinking about that evening we spent together on the boat. It was one of the best nights of my life.'

My face burns as memories resurface. I mean, I had a good time. Multiple good times, if we're being honest. But there was a reason I cut him off completely afterwards, and he's showing it now. Too emotional, too dramatic, too much. I don't see people again, and if I *did,* it definitely wouldn't be this extraordinarily intense man.

He watches me swirl the milk jug and whispers, 'You always were good with your hands.'

'Thanks.' I tap the till a few times to ring his total up, and then I lean against the back wall to keep away from wandering hands.

'So is that a yes to drinks tonight? I've written some poems I'd love to share with you,' he says eagerly.

This man has all the threatening energy of a slice of damp bread, but I'm concerned he won't give up. My brain reels through things to say that'll get him off my back.

'Emily can't come out for drinks,' Finn says, reappearing by the till, 'because she's married.'

My mouth drops open as Jonas's eyes widen in despair.

'Married? You didn't tell me.' To be fair, I didn't tell him anything at all. 'I thought we had something.'

'Yeah, I know,' Jonas replies. His shoulders slump and I make every effort not to catch Finn's eye, whose jaw is clenched with the effort to hold back a laugh at this ridiculous repetition. 'Is it serious?'

'It's uh, yeah. Quite serious. What with the marriage bit,' I reply.

'Who is he?' he asks in a whisper.

'It's me. I'm Emily's husband,' says Finn, fully inserting himself into a lie for me. For the *second time*. 'Nice to meet you. I'm Finn.'

While Jonas looks down at his feet, I finally meet Finn's eye, who shrugs and grins, evidently enjoying himself.

'I hope you know how fortunate you are,' Jonas continues, clutching his latte like he's adrift and the cup is his lifebuoy. 'She's a gift.'

'Oh, I'm thankful for her every day. Her positivity, her vibrant light. I'm so lucky.' He gazes at me longingly and I fight the urge to swear. 'Although, I would love to hear one of your poems. It'd be nice to hear from someone else who *gets* her.'

I give Finn The Eyes, which he has the gall to completely ignore.

'I've got one written down here. It's called *Angel on Earth*.' He reaches into his bag and pulls out a tiny notebook, ripping out a page and handing it to Finn. 'Here, it's my gift to you. I don't think I can be around to listen, so I'll get going now. Let me know if you ever... get a divorce.'

I nod and Finn waves enthusiastically as he leaves. The second the door closes, he clears his throat and starts to read aloud in a surprisingly sultry voice.

*'There was a woman; fair and divine*
*A beauty so classic, bound not to our time*
*A black dahlia amidst an ocean of roses*
*My heart opened to her as the Red Sea did to Moses*
*And when she left me I feared I was dead*
*For I never believed in God until she gave me h—'*

A strangled noise escapes me as I yank the paper out of his hand before he can finish.

Finn puts both hands on the counter and leans towards me, dropping his voice to ask, pure glee coating every word, 'What did you *do* to him?'

'I don't even know. I spent a single evening with him and that's what he turned into.' At my nonplussed expression, laughter finally tumbles from his mouth, and it melts into the cracks, sending a smile to my face too as I settle into the ridiculousness of the situation. 'That's not normal, right?'

'Serious question,' he collects himself enough to ask, 'who the fuck is Emily?'

'Do you not see why it might've been prudent for me to lie about my identity to that man?'

'Okay, fair.' He lets out another chuckle. 'I honestly thought he was about to carry you to a registry office. And he was built like a Viking, so I'd have stood no chance. I had to think on my feet.'

'I had it covered,' I grumble. Then I look up into the warmth of his eyes and say, 'But thanks for helping me, I guess. Again.' How is this the second time he's saved my ass in this very shop? First my fake friend, then my fake husband. What's next?

'To really show your thanks,' he twirls his straw around his cup, 'you could repay me by crossing another item off my bucket list.'

I catch sight of Stan in the corner. Am I too young to be so stagnant? It's just a summer. A trial run of living a life that's a little more exciting than it has been over the past few years. Not pushing the boundaries too much to draw attention, to remind the universe that I've already asked for too much, but enough that I can appease the discomforting boredom that's been simmering.

I tighten my ponytail. 'Fine. Let's get this over with. AirDrop me your list and I'll pick the option that sounds the least heinous.'

'You really know how to make a guy feel special.'

'Heard that many times.'

'From Jonas, apparently.' His mouth quirks up on one side.

I ignore him and skim the list he's just sent. 'You free around three tomorrow?'

He blinks a few times, somehow surprised I've suggested something, even though he did just semi-blackmail me into it. 'Yeah. You want to hang out tomorrow? Really?'

'*Want* is maybe overstating, but I didn't want to hurt your feelings.'

'You're considering my feelings? Sounds to me like you're being a good friend.'

I shake my head with a sigh and spot the tea I started making earlier, no doubt bitter and cold by now. I pour the stewed liquid down the sink and start making a fresh one. That's what I need, I think. Something new.

# 11

## London is just sky rats and living statues

### AVA

When I take off my apron and change into my own clothes at the end of each day, it's as if I'm peeling off sticky layers of a false identity. But coffee grounds burrow beneath my nails, steam wand burns mark my arms, and I can never quite get the smell of espresso out of my hair.

I don't bother waiting for Finn to arrive to find out what drink he wants, instead making him an iced latte and assuming that'll be fine. He steps into the shop at three o'clock on the dot, and I wonder if he's been hovering outside until now. Excitement rolls over him, brightening his eyes, loosening his smile, sending his hands fidgeting inside his pockets. You'd think I was taking him to Disneyland.

I hand one of the cups over to him and, impossibly, he lights up even more. 'For me? For free?'

'I've started a tab,' I tell him blandly, before letting Mateo know how I've left things and heading towards the door. Finn holds it open and I step outside, squinting in the light.

'So. What's the plan?' he asks from behind me.

I turn and have to cup my eyes to look at him. 'I've only got about an hour before I have to leave you. But do you trust me?'

'Absolutely.' I hunt for any sarcasm in the word, but it's pure, easy acquiescence.

'Then follow me,' I reply, about to step off the kerb.

In a flash, a linen-sleeved arm flings out across my front, milliseconds before a motorbike whizzes past, which would've no doubt promised me a particularly grizzly end.

'If that's how you move around, I'd rather not,' he says with a sharp exhale, looking me up and down to check I'm unharmed.

'Thanks,' I mumble, adrenaline coursing through me as we wait for the green man. We step onto the road, safe from rogue motorbikes and death sentences this time. 'But you shouldn't have saved me. That was intentional, actually. I just really, *really* didn't want to hang out with you this afternoon.'

'There are less messy ways to do it. You'd have got blood all over my favourite shirt.' I glance at the shirt in question. It's sage green, the sleeves rolled to his elbows, one button too many open at the neck for my liking. He catches me looking at his chest and beams, mistaking my distaste for something else. I snap my eyes away, but it's too late. He steps in front of me as we cross the street, walking backwards so we won't bump into each other. 'It matches my eyes.'

I frown. 'But your eyes are brown.'

'Don't tell me you've been looking into my eyes already, buddy. This is a business arrangement, remember?'

I let out a sigh to end all sighs in response. I'm not even going to *entertain* the idea of there being anything else with this walking, talking (really, so, so much talking) nuisance of a man.

It's not quite a summer's day just yet, but there's more blue sky than cloud, which is pretty much England's equivalent to the Maldives, and finally I remember to take my sunglasses out of my bag. Right on schedule, a red bus pulls up to the stop we've walked to, and Finn dutifully follows me up the stairs to the top deck.

'Where are we going?' he asks, settling into the righthand aisle seat at the front, while I take the one on the left.

*Take a tour of London* was one of the first items on his list.

'I'm not paying for an official London tour,' I reply. 'We have buses and feet.'

'You've completely hijacked my list,' he says halfheartedly, watching Fleet Street pass us at a snail's pace through the window. 'I'll be honest, this wasn't quite what I had in mind for that item.'

'I'm sitting at the front of the bus with you, which is against my personal code of conduct. The least you can do is say thank you.'

'Thank you.' He offers a saccharine smile that I return with vigour.

'Think of it as a private tour. I'll give you all my fun facts.'

Appeased, he leans forward. If the barrier weren't blocking the way, he'd have his face pressed up against the glass. 'Fine. But only if it's the *funnest* facts.'

We're close to the Tesco Express we visited the other day, but I already used up my fact quota when he asked about the statue. 'Uh, Fleet Street has been around since the Roman era.'

'Not fun enough.' He shakes his head, though is still interested enough to take a photo through the window. 'I've never been here before. Give me drama.'

I look around before pointing to the left. 'I tripped on a loose paving slab over there once and had the most horrifically slow-motion fall known to man.'

'Injured?'

'In mind and spirit only.'

'Sorry to hear that.'

'No you're not.' As I tighten my ponytail, I ask, 'Have you really never come down here?'

'Honestly, I've been terrible at doing the touristy stuff. Hence,' he waves his phone in the air, 'the bucket list.'

As the bus makes its slow procession along the Strand, I give Finn tidbits from my life, pointing out anything I remember. 'Saw *Mamma Mia* with my parents and brother there a few years ago and my mum cried during *Dancing Queen*.'

'It's an emotional song,' he says with a lift of his shoulder.

'Oh, and I got very drunk on a date in a cocktail bar up there,' I point up a side street, 'and went home with a man called Harold.'

His head swivels towards me, that single untameable curl flopping onto his forehead. '*Harold?* Was he on day release from an old people's home?'

'It was his retirement party,' I retort, accompanying it with the same sugary smile from earlier. 'God, you should've seen the way he moved those hips. Must've been a real hit with the ladies in the sixties.'

'Interesting. Is that your usual type? Geriatric?'

'Upset you wouldn't fit the bill?'

'I guess if the only reason you'd reject me is because I'm still paying into my pension, I can handle that.' His eyes meet mine as he sips his coffee.

'I love that you think that's the only reason I'd reject you,' I say, breaking eye contact to look out the windscreen. We're approaching Charing Cross now. 'I once sprinted halfway down the Strand to this McDonald's to get a sausage and egg McMuffin before breakfast ended. Haven't run since.'

'Just what Usain Bolt would've wanted.' There's a beat of silence. 'That makes it sound like he's dead. He's not dead. I don't think. Wait, *hey Siri, is Usain Bolt alive?*'

I suddenly notice where we are. 'Shit, we need to get off.' I scramble to my feet and inconsiderately hit the stop button a couple of times in a row, silently apologising to the driver for it. Luckily, he must be in a good mood, because he's willing to open the doors just after he closed them for the last passengers, and we spill out of the bus onto the pavement. 'Come on,' I say, heading towards the crossing, where our bus is currently waiting at a red light.

As we cross, I give the driver a tight-lipped smile, while Finn mimes a thank you and gives a thumbs up.

Finn's tone is playful when he restarts our conversation from the bus. 'If it's not my pension, why else would you reject me? Humble me, please. I'll relish it.' He almost bumps into someone as we hit the pavement on the other side and apologises about eight times more than necessary.

I don't think he needs to know the full truth here. 'Because,' I say, motioning my hand in his direction, 'you are entirely incapable of walking a single metre without engaging in intense conversation with someone.'

'You think I'm engaging?' He looks across at me with a grin so incandescent I almost want to squint.

'I'm not sure if you've noticed, but I typically function at a lower level of enthusiasm than you do.'

'And here I thought your deadpan delivery and stony exterior were just an act.'

'You're the human embodiment of pep.'

The gleam in his eyes makes it look like he's perpetually about three seconds away from either divulging a secret or breaking into song. 'You may be surprised to hear this is not the first time I have been described as "peppy".'

'I'm shocked,' I say, hand fluttering against my chest.

His arms swing by his sides as he walks, like they have to experience as much of the environment as possible. 'I also get "spirited" a lot. Sometimes "vivacious".' He's momentarily distracted by a red telephone box and points at it, expression hopeful. 'Should I get in?'

'Sure,' I suggest. 'If you're in the mood to contract every disease this city has ever known, all while inhaling the pungent odour of stale piss, by all means, step inside the phone box, Finn.'

'If it was *fresh* piss, I'd do it,' he says in a low voice as we pass, thankfully without opening the box and unleashing the horrors within. 'But what about you, what do people call you?'

'An ogre, probably?'

'I've always had a thing for Shrek,' he says absent-mindedly, reminding me of that date with the rugby boy. Before I can analyse what he said, I realise we're at our destination.

*Climb on the Trafalgar Square lions* was on Finn's list, and I figure we'll have just enough time to do it today before I have to leave.

'The lions. At your service.'

We squeeze through hordes of tourists down to where four bronze lions rest on massive stone plinths, a few metres above the ground.

'I have another fun fact for you,' I say, and Finn's attention pulls back to me. 'Legend says these lions will wake when Big Ben chimes thirteen times.'

'That's what I was looking for. *Fun* facts. But now I wanna...' He gestures towards the lion closest to us, where two kids are posing for a photo for their mum, who's standing with a baby in a buggy. We move closer and wait for them to finish.

## A COLLISION OF STARS

I think there's a photo of Max and me on these lions as children. It was from those halcyon days of the summer holidays, when the moment you open your eyes all you feel is the unfurling of possibility, soaked in sunshine and warmth and magic. Back when happiness came so easily it felt like a given.

The laughs of the two children jolt me out of my reverie; squeals in high-pitched French as they try to clamber off the lion. The older sister slides off effortlessly and runs back towards their mother, but the younger boy freezes, unsure where to put his hands and feet as he realises how high up he is. Before his mother even notices he's in distress, Finn approaches him.

'Tu veux un coup de main?' he asks softly in French, offering his arm and shoulder for the boy to hold onto as he climbs off.

Once the boy's reunited with his family, I ask, 'How many languages do you speak?'

'A few,' he says noncommittally, heading towards the back of the lion. Somehow detecting my dissatisfaction with his answer even with his back to me, he turns around and continues, 'I usually just say four. But I don't really know how many. My dad spoke Greek to me growing up, and Danish was one of my first languages but I'm not sure how much of it I remember. And then I lived in a few French-speaking countries, and other languages I sort of picked up over the years, mostly just from stuff I learned at school, but I dunno if those count either. Some of them are still in my brain somewhere and come out occasionally. Depends where I am. It's usually when I'm drunk. I speak, like, ten languages when I'm drunk.'

I mull this over. As someone with a B in GCSE German and not much else, I can't fathom the idea of speaking so many fragments of languages that you aren't sure how many of them you speak.

He approaches the statue from behind, using its tail as support before pulling himself up with far more grace than you'd expect from someone scaling a giant brass lion. He settles into place and sits there for a few moments, swinging his legs and looking across Trafalgar Square at the people milling about by the fountains and beyond.

'You know you're a child, right?' I call up to him.

'Men have two main passions in life: digging holes and climbing things. Don't take this one from me.'

I move closer. 'How do you feel?'

'Regal,' he replies, looking down at me with an imperious nod. He slides off elegantly and I briefly try to envision what I'd look like trying to get on and off that thing. Not like that, that's for sure.

'And was it worth its spot on the bucket list?'

He adjusts his sleeves and brushes down his trousers like he didn't just mount a statue. 'Absolutely.' He raises his eyebrows and points a thumb behind him. 'You getting up?'

'Good joke.' I step away from the lion, which is immediately overrun by a family who's been patiently waiting for our departure. Finn shrugs and falls into step beside me as we walk across the square, overconfident pigeons flying far too close to our heads, before perching on the stone wall encircling one of the fountains. I wouldn't like to know who or what has been in the water, but Finn bravely (or stupidly) dips his hand in regardless.

I watch his gaze glue to a mother and son as they walk past, both laughing hysterically. 'Are you close with your mum?'

'I try to be. But the fact we live on different continents means it's difficult to organise calls and visits. She's so busy all the time.' He pulls his eyes from the pair and clears his throat before adding, 'Always has been.'

'Does it bother you?' I prod.

'I'm used to it,' he says. He blinks a couple of times like he's surprised he said it, and his leg starts to bounce.

'And your dad?'

'I don't get to talk to him as often as I'd like either. But he's a really busy man too, so that's why. He does amazing work. He sold his first company and is now high up in this organisation that focuses on sustainability in tech.' I notice the way his words spill out when he talks about his dad, like he wants to say as much as he can to convince me. 'Both my parents have spent a lot of time on their careers. It's healthy, I think, for parents to live their own lives, without being around their children too much.'

'Yeah.' I don't really know why I lie, but it feels like that's what he wants to hear.

I have distinct memories of my dad coming into mine and Max's room late at night after a twelve-hour shift at the hospital while I was half asleep on the bottom bunk, brushing my hair from my face and whispering that he'd missed me. Or, years later, when I was at uni, FaceTiming me while I was mid-movie marathon with Josie just because he wanted to tell me about a band he thought I'd like on his way to a night shift. He's always made the effort.

'I've started looking for new jobs for when my contract ends here and there's one in San Francisco that I'm interested in. I've wanted to work at this company for years, and the role seems like it'd almost perfectly fit my skill set. If I get it, I might end up seeing my dad more often.'

'That'd be nice,' I say, though I have no idea if it would be. I barely know Finn, but a part of me feels like I should be careful with how I respond. It seems to be the right answer though, because his face lights up.

'He's really cool. Like, we're probably more like friends than father and son. He just doesn't give a fuck.' He tilts his head and says, 'Maybe a little like you.'

It sounds like a compliment, but something about it niggles at me. Both his knees are bouncing now, so I stand up, knowing he'll follow and can start walking off some of his restless energy.

'You're not like him?' I'm aware that the more I ask him, the less likely he is to ask me questions.

He inhales deeply and releases it even slower. 'In the way we live our lives, yeah I am. But I've always admired the way he knows who he is. When he moved away, he really found who he was meant to be. *Where* he was meant to be.' I don't think he knows I can hear the unspoken words. *And it was away from me.* 'I want that too. I want to find the thing that really speaks to me, you know?'

He runs a hand through his hair and I catch the way the sun reflects the red strands there. He must've got that from his mum.

'That's why you move around so much,' I discern. 'To find it.'

We amble around the fountain, already on our second loop.

'I suppose,' he says, shooting me a rueful smile.

I can't quite figure this man out. I'd expected him to be an entirely open book, but apparently there are some pages he's either not willing to share, or doesn't even want to read himself. Fine with me. It's not like I'm going to share every secret I'm harbouring either.

'Well, I hope you find what you're looking for.' I'm surprised by the earnestness and I immediately feel the urge to lighten the mood. 'Because when you do, you might actually leave me alone.'

He laughs and the sound hits somewhere deep inside me, but I'm soon distracted trying to dodge a loud group of neon orange-clad summer school kids that runs across our path.

'I'll be gone before you know it, and all you'll have to remember me by will be the cavernous hole in your heart where I used to live.'

'I think you'll need a full-blown military strategy to get anywhere close to my heart, but please, try your best.'

'You underestimate my capacity for stealth.' I raise my eyebrows and he points at my heart. 'I'll find a way in. Make friends with the people who live in there.'

Befriending the few people I care about seems like a surefire way to wedge himself into my daily life even more than he is already. I'm once again glad he's not in London for long.

We're close to the statues again and my brain unearths those memories of Max and me from that summer day, years ago. Even then, as he climbed the lions, I was worried for him. Worried he'd slip and hurt himself, worried our parents would tell him off. He told me to stop being a baby so I joined him, because at least we'd both get in trouble together. Or, if it came to it, at least we'd fall together. On equal footing forever, neither of us with better luck than the other.

Just as Finn and I finish another loop of the fountain, something stops me in my path.

'Oh my god. I thought that guy was about to propose.' I draw his attention to a couple over by the foot of the stairs. I shudder and mutter, 'Horrific.'

His mouth twitches. 'Grand gestures are fun. *Fun,* Ava Monroe.'

'They're embarrassing.' I make an effort to wipe the disgust off my face.

'You should let yourself be embarrassed every so often. It's not the worst thing in the world.' I roll my eyes and he's pensive for a while before saying, 'I don't even know if I could get embarrassed anymore. I've fucked up in almost every possible way, I really don't think there's much that could do it.'

'I'm sure we'll find something one day,' I say. 'But not for me. Thanks, though.'

He scrutinises me with laser focus and I can almost see the cogs turning in his brain as he mulls this over. It's off-putting enough that my skin prickles. Out of nowhere, he asks, 'What's your middle name?'

I'm thrown by the randomness of the question. 'Noelle. Why?'

He pauses and launches a dangerous half smile in my direction. I don't even have the chance to decipher it before he drops down on one knee in the middle of Trafalgar Square, his entire face straining as he fights a laugh.

'Ava Noelle Monroe, will you—'

'No!' My hands fly to my face and I spit out, 'Get the fuck up. *Right now.*' I receive a glare from a father walking past with his child and growl, 'Get up or I will never give you a free coffee ever again. Ever.'

'You wouldn't.' He's still looking up at me from the floor, a stupid smile pushing out of every crease of his face, and I'm well aware that people in the vicinity have stopped what they're doing to watch.

'Try me.' I force myself to lock eyes, my face a stony mask in comparison to his unadulterated joy.

He sighs and pretends to tie his shoelaces, effectively dispersing the bubble of nosy people waiting for me to respond. 'Does this mean I'm gonna have to cancel the blimp?'

I deserve a medal for resisting the urge to push him in the fountain, I really do. I don't know whether to be infuriated or impressed he's figured out so quickly exactly how to press my buttons.

We climb up the main staircase and his voice is chipper when he asks, 'Was that *embarrassing* for you?'

'Obviously.' I draw out every syllable, each one more venomous than the last.

'And did you survive the ordeal?'

'Finn, our "friendship" is hanging on by a hair's breadth of a thread right now, please don't push it. I am *this* close to breaking our agreement and telling Josie all about this stupid mess I've found myself in. At this stage, I will take barrels of her pity and figure out how to deal with it.'

'But you won't tell her, because you know she's right. That you do need, and, dare I say, *want* to get out more, and I come as a convenient, pre-packaged, limited-time-only summer activity provider.'

I stomp the next few stairs and pretend I haven't heard him. As we hit the top of the staircase we're greeted by various performers and artists; a man painted silver pretending to be a statue, another drawing a portrait in chalk on the paving slabs, and one of those levitating Yodas that always give me the creeps.

'Those are my least favourite things about London,' Finn says abruptly, glancing back at the floating Yoda, whose eyes have been following us as we pass.

'Don't get used to me telling you this,' I grumble, 'but you're actually so right.'

The way his mouth drops open in shock forces a laugh to tumble out of me before I can remember to keep it contained, which in turn generates yet another smile on his face that psychiatrists could probably bottle up as a cure for SAD. I clamp my mouth shut and walk in front of him so I don't have to look at it.

Past the main crowd at the foot of the National Gallery it eases up a bit, and we join a semicircle of people watching a young busker play a cover of *I Wanna Dance with Somebody*. Finn positions us right at the front and I stand slightly behind him, scared the singer's going to call upon volunteers. She's talented, so I feel kind of bad, because who carries cash anymore? Just as the thought enters my mind, Finn darts forward to drop a note into her open guitar case, and it makes me want to laugh again.

The French family from earlier is on the other side of the semicircle, and because the crowd is almost entirely made up of tourists, everyone's really into it. *Too* into it. One of the French kids steps forward to dance, and that's all it takes. Finn shoots me another grin over his shoulder and in a moment of what I can only describe as abject terror, he moves into the open space in the middle of the circle too.

And right there, at the foot of the National Gallery, Finn dances.

He's not good by any means, and I hope he's self-aware enough to know it, but his unbridled enthusiasm is infectious enough to convince a few more people to join—all tourists, I assume. All the while, I'm rooted to the spot, morbidly fascinated by the way this alternate London is unravelling in front of my eyes. I didn't even know this kind of thing was legal.

Finn cheers for the kids, belts out the words with far too much gusto, and dances with an old man hovering at the edge of the crowd, and everything inside me wants to sink into the ground. But the moment my horror-struck eyes lock with his, he winks, and I feel a smile threaten to unfurl. I still have a shred of dignity, so instead of allowing that to happen, I mouth, *I hate this.*

He gives a one-shouldered shrug as if to say, *I know.*

The flash-mob gods must be sprinkling some of their coercive magic on me, because for the briefest moment, I consider stepping forward to join him. Would it be so bad?

In the distance I spot Big Ben, and that's when reality hits. The clock face is too far away for me to read so I pull out my phone to check the time. Shit. I peel myself away from the crowd and fire off two texts.

> omg I'm actually the worst I'm so sorry

> I'll be there in 10 mins

I get Finn's attention and gesture behind me, trying to tell him I'm leaving. His smile drops a little and he wriggles his way through the crowd.

'What's up?'

'I completely lost track of time and just realised I was meant to leave twenty minutes ago.'

'Oh, right, yeah, no problem.' He shakes his head like he's coming out of a dream, and he's tentative for once when he asks, 'I'll see you tomorrow?'

'Yep,' I reply, already moving towards the Tube, too preoccupied to give him a longer goodbye, too worried about wasting another second. God, I need to get it together. I can't get distracted by ridiculous, fanciful daydreams again.

# 12

# Avraham Lincolin, at your service

## AVA

'Colin!' my brother's voice launches my longest-running nickname across the concourse of Waterloo station, turning a few heads in the process.

Max's nicknames for me have a habit of warping and evolving, picking up debris as they move through the years like a snowball tearing down a slope. I've lived under a myriad of names, including but not limited to; a bizarre stretch as Avanti West Coast, a brief stint simply as Van, and now? Avraham Lincolin.

'I'm so sorry.' I reach up on my tiptoes to hug him, inhaling the familiar citrusy smell on his plaid shirt that never seems to fade. Pretty sure he's been using the same shower gel since we were teenagers. He prolongs the hug by squeezing me and I duck out of his grip. 'I can't believe I'm late.'

His eyebrows raise behind messy hair. 'Really? I can.'

'Hilarious,' I say, rolling my eyes. I'm not exactly known for my punctuality, and frankly, neither is he, but I hate that I missed him arriving. I made a promise to myself to be there whenever he needed me. As we walk I notice he's not putting his full weight on his right leg, which I haven't seen him do in a long while. But it's barely perceptible, and I know him well enough to know he won't want to talk about it. Instead, I shield my eyes as if I'm looking up at the sun. 'Were you always this tall?'

'Were you always this short?'

'Stop, you know I have a complex about that.' I spent years taller than him, shooting up to five-ten and a half (the half is important) before most other kids at school had figured out the truth about Santa. But then at fifteen I swear Max came out of his room one day and suddenly he was six-five.

As we walk through the station, I wonder if strangers can tell we're related. We have the same colouring; same blue eyes, same dark hair that never quite lies right. But the rest of Max's features are sharp and angular like our mum's, while I take after our dad's side of the family, with fuller cheeks and a rounded chin.

I lead us towards the lifts to take the more accessible route for his bad leg, but the scowl he gives me makes him look like Mum when she tells us off, so we head to the escalators instead. Someone passes us on the left as I look up at Max on the step behind to ask, 'How was the train?'

It's about an hour by train back to the nondescript Kent town we grew up in, with its dilapidated high street, nosy neighbours and multiple Spoons in a mile radius. Max always seems too big for it, which is probably why he spends so much time in other places.

'Dead, thank *god*. Got a table seat all to myself and managed to finish a video I was editing.' He swerves out of the way of a man shooting past to get his train and looks down at me. 'Mum and Dad send their love, by the way. But you knew that. And Dad wanted me to tell you that he's finally figured out Spotify so can you please send him that playlist you were talking about.'

Max is a travel content creator, and after a couple of years paying rent on a flat he hardly ever spent time in, followed by some health issues, he moved back in with our parents. This means that any of his free time between trips is spent eating Mum's vegan bolognese and listening to Dad's one-hit wonders from the eighties.

We catch up on the Tube. Any time he moves the conversation over to me, I push it back his way, reminding him that I am essentially a hermit and nothing about my life has changed since we last saw each other.

As always, I eat up his stories, just like I did when we were younger, when he'd bring me on his adventures to imaginary kingdoms. In his imagined worlds, I'd be as bold and brave as him. In real life, he's just come back from a road trip around Scotland and is raving about the beaches. Because only he would go swimming in the near-Arctic water.

'Got this to commemorate it,' he shows me, rolling up his sleeve to show me yet another tattoo; the tiny head of a Highland cow near his elbow. It joins a selection of entirely random images he's inked onto his skin. 'Honestly, it's so underrated. I'm gonna tell everyone to go.'

'Isn't that what you were paid for?'

'Yeah well, I'm gonna influence the *fuck* out of this one. Seriously, I wanna bring the whole family back. With Spud, obviously.' Our mother loves the dog more than she loves the two of us combined; a fact we've begrudgingly accepted over the years. 'Do you have any trips planned? I can probably get you included on one of mine if you want.'

Now it's my turn to give him a Mum-inspired look. 'Can you imagine me backpacking? Going to new places every day? Using a sleeping bag?'

He peers at me like he's trying to read my mind, but instead says, 'I was thinking earlier about when we used to go camping with Mum and Dad.'

'Shit, remember that one time with the sheep?'

'And the wheelbarrow?'

'I genuinely thought we were going to die.'

We speak our own language, coded by a nonsensical concoction of joint memories and inside jokes and references to niche pop culture quotes that no one else would ever remember. When it's just the two of us, I could almost believe we're back in the sticker-adorned bunk bed of our childhood room; the wooden planks on the top bunk dented with teeth marks because for some inexplicable reason he liked biting them. It feels like nothing's changed since those days, though of course, everything has.

We reminisce about the numerous ridiculous experiences we had as children in our parents' very lax care all the way home. I expect him to have given up on trying to get me out of London, but he brings it up again as we're leaving Stockwell station.

'You wouldn't have to come on one of the backpacking trips, you know. I'm often offered other types of trips too.' We make our way across the road. 'I can imagine you on a city break somewhere. I think you'd like it more than you'd expect.'

'I wholeheartedly disagree.' I'm on a proverbial no-fly list. My name'll flag on the system the second I do something fun like go on holiday, and I'm sure fate will come my way to take what I owe. Max groans at my response and I try to shift the topic of conversation to someone else. 'I reckon Josie would take you up on the offer, if you've got any luxury hotels on the cards.'

'I'll convince you one day, Col. But wait, speak of the devil.' He points at a figure slightly ahead of us on the pavement, accompanied by a canine-shaped shadow. He calls Josie's name, yet again drawing the attention of everyone around us. I really need to start hanging out with quieter people.

A smile spreads across her face as she turns and her free arm moves around Max in a hug. 'God, I've missed my favourite Monroe sibling.'

'I love that we can be so honest with each other,' I say, stepping onto the road so the three of them can take up the whole width of the pavement.

'Me too. But in the spirit of honesty, please don't tell me how hideous this outfit is,' Josie says, motioning towards her bottom half. 'I spilled coffee all over my *cream trousers*. Had to borrow these sweatpants from Alina's gym bag.'

'Looks horrific,' I say, marvelling at how she's made a pair of trackies look like an intentional part of her outfit.

---

'How were the Highlands, Max?' Josie asks as she pours one, two, three, fo—oh god, how many more—shots' worth of rum into a tall glass vessel that I'm wholly convinced is a vase, but she's dubbed The Cocktail Carafe.

'Some of us have work tomorrow, Josie. Including you.'

She ignores me and adds more rum.

'Amazing, it's one of my new favourite places.' Max is sitting on one of the stools, leaning his elbows on the breakfast bar. 'I was telling Ava she should come with me someday.'

Josie erupts into laughter at this. 'On a trip to the *countryside*? Your sister?' She actually has to stop what she's doing to dab at her eyes.

'Pot, kettle, Josephine?' I grab three glasses from a cupboard and go to the freezer for ice. 'Can you even remember the last time you stayed anywhere that wasn't a five-star hotel?'

'Please, I could rough it if I wanted.' She opens the next bottle. I don't even know what spirit it is and at this point I'm too scared to ask. 'I just have a very extensive skincare regime that I simply could not perform out in the wilderness.'

'Oh, well in *that* case,' I mumble, rummaging through a drawer. 'Where are the straws?'

'If they're not at the back of the cutlery drawer, they're in the one with the measuring cups,' Josie replies. 'Actually, can you grab those for me?'

I hand her the measuring cups and she uses them to measure out the remainder of the liquids for her concoction. Over the years I've learnt Josie's drinks are not for the fainthearted. For someone so small, the woman sure can hold her alcohol.

'How's Alina?' Max asks, flattening the pizza boxes to his left and bringing them to the recycling bin.

'She's really good,' Josie says, a smile playing on her lips. Most of her and Alina's relationship has been long-distance, and they're only now living in the same city. She dips a straw into the vase-stroke-carafe and tries the drink, nodding appreciatively, not a wince in sight. 'We're working together at the moment, which is kind of weird, but fun? I'd never worked with her in person before and it's unbelievable how talented she is. But what about you, how's your love life? Weren't you seeing that woman from Leeds?'

My ears prick up at the question. We aren't those TV-show siblings who share every minute detail of their love lives. We have an unspoken agreement that started as teenagers to not bring it up, and I guess it stuck. But I'm well aware of his dating style. We went to the same school, after all. And he's not exactly quiet on social media.

He grimaces when he replies, 'Yeah, no. That didn't end great. Messy. My fault, obviously.' We pour out our drinks and head to the living area. 'I told myself it was because I'm too busy for anything serious, but realistically it's probably due to the fact I am fundamentally emotionally unavailable.'

'Must be genetic,' Josie says, taking a delicate sip of her drink.

'Twins,' Max sings. He holds his hand out for a fist bump, which I return with a nod.

'The two of you need therapy.'

She's joking, but even if the NHS waiting list weren't seven years long, there's no way I could take resources away from someone else who actually needs it.

I take a giant gulp of my drink as Max settles in the armchair and replies, 'Already on it, Josie. But there's just so much to go through that I'm not even close to touching on romance yet. I'm saving that for a slow day.'

A few hours later, I'm more than a little drunk, but my stomach hurts from laughing. 'And then,' Max says, 'when he finally got out of the water he was like, "guys, guys, I think I've got amnesia". He meant *hypothermia*.'

Tears stream down mine and Josie's cheeks as Max regales us with stories of the wild mishaps on his trips. He's been drinking water for a while but somehow maintains the energy of someone seven drinks in; a trait I am particularly envious of.

Josie falls into another fit of giggles, but when she checks the time on her phone she releases a groan. 'We should probably go to bed.'

I want to stay up for five more hours. It's so easy with these two. There's no pretending.

But she's right; we all need to be up in the morning. So between us, we carry the glasses and empty crisp packets to the kitchen, and then Josie leaves Max and me alone.

'Is your spare bedding in the airing cupboard? Let's set up the sofa bed.' He leaves the room and returns a few moments later laden with pillows and blankets. Now it's just the two of us, my focus is drawn back to his slight limp.

'You okay?' I ask, watching him pull out the sofa.

'Huh?' He straightens and looks at me, so I nod towards his leg. 'Col, I'm fine.'

We slip into a tried-and-tested routine, putting the sheet onto the mattress together and prepping the rest of his bedding in the order we've always done it.

When he finds a dirty glass on a side table and walks to the kitchen with it I can't help but ask again. 'You're sure?'

'I'm sure. Seriously. I've just been overdoing it recently.'

I wring my hands as he grabs a tea towel from the handle of the oven. 'You'd tell me if there was anything to tell me, right?'

'Of course.' He smiles, but I don't fully trust it. 'Come on. You wash, I dry.'

I don't bother telling him we have a dishwasher. So I wash up and he dries, just like we did when we were kids.

# 13

## you could say my type has always been people who hate me a little

### FINN

'I SENT THIS REPORT to you and Greg earlier.' I move my cursor over the table I'm sharing on the projector. 'If I were you, I'd focus on fixing the easy stuff first, even though it probably won't make as big of a dent in the overall ranking. But it's your choice.'

'I trust your judgement,' says Miranda, glancing at her watch. 'And I appreciate you going the extra mile with this. I know it's not specifically what we hired you for, but it's been really helpful.' She closes the notebook she's been scribbling in, slowly moving everything in front of her into a neat pile.

'No worries,' I say with a shrug, disconnecting my laptop from the projector and closing it with a snap. 'I get that it's chaos for you guys at the moment.'

She chuckles brightly. 'You can say that again. But seriously, thank you. You do too much for us. You'll be receiving nothing but glowing compliments in my testimonial.' I grin and hold the door open for her to pass through, and we walk side by side down the hallway to the elevator. 'Any update on the San Francisco job?'

The doors open with a clank in front of us and we step inside. 'Nothing yet, I'm still only at the first stage. I haven't actually applied to a full-time job in so long, I'd kind of forgotten what it's like.'

'You'll get it, I'm sure,' Miranda says. The doors open again and we shift to one side to make space for the people getting on. 'How long have you been consulting?'

'On and off for about four years. So this'll be a nice change, I think.'

'Well, we'll miss you when your contract's up. Although you're more than welcome to stay on. You'll have to let me know if there's anyone you recommend to take over.' The elevator makes a jovial ping and with that, she adds, 'This is me. Enjoy the rest of your day, Finn.'

She heads off to another of her hundred consecutive meetings as I make small talk with the people who step in after her. I get off a couple of floors after she does, making my way to the building's common area on the ground floor, which is packed with rock-hard sofas, standing desks and plug sockets, and is where I occasionally sit and work. But today it's unusually loud. Rory's over in the kitchen, leaning against the counter in a daydream as the coffee machine churns out its unappetising liquid.

'Hey,' I say, interrupting his reverie. 'What's up?'

'Oh, hey. You looking for Julien? He just ran off to a meeting.' He takes his cup and sniffs it before taking a sip.

'Nah, it's fine.' I eye the machine, which I've been avoiding as often as possible ever since I discovered good coffee is available just across the street. Much to the distress of my bank account, unfortunately. I have to raise my voice to be heard above the din. 'Do you know why it's so busy in here today?'

'I think there's some event later for the design agency on the fourth floor? But I also might've just made that up.'

I look around and realise that with everyone milling about, there are no free seats available, which is the minimal incentive I needed to head to City Roast for the rest of the afternoon.

'I'm gonna head over the road to finish some work. I assume you won't be joining?' I look at his sad coffee and my stomach silently screams at me in response.

'I'm alright. I have a meeting in a bit anyway.' He takes a sip and eyes me over the lip of his cup. 'Julien mentioned you've been spending a lot of time over there recently. You must really like the ambience.' His mouth bends into a smirk.

'They do great coffee.' I narrow my eyes. 'And tell him to stop gossiping about me.'

'But you're just so easy to gossip about,' he says, pushing himself off the counter. 'Well, have fun. Say hi to the cute barista for me.'

'I—'

'I meant that Spanish guy.' He laughs as he passes, like he's just made the funniest joke known to man.

I'm not stupid. This isn't the first time I've developed the tiniest, most minuscule crush on a beautiful, intelligent woman who'd never give me the time of day. I think back to Léa and how good it felt to be around her before it went wrong. You could, in fact, say this is the *exact* type of woman I'm drawn to.

Luckily, Ava could not be clearer about how little she wants me. Or anyone, really. I've seen customers flirt with her so brazenly, and I can't tell if she intentionally ignores them or just doesn't even notice.

It's not my business, but I assume she ran off to meet someone yesterday. I thought we were having fun, but she scurried off like she was Cinderella and the Tube was moments away from turning into a pumpkin. She seemed distraught that she was gonna be late for him. But, you know, the heart wants what it wants.

So while she's happy helping me out with the bucket list, I'll make sure this is yet another amicable, surface-level thing that'll be easy to leave. That's how these things are supposed to go.

On my way out I read one of the leaflets laid on the tables around the room. *Atrium Design Services: creative graphic design solutions.* An idea comes to me and I approach a woman in yellow overalls who I know from various elevator chats.

'Hey Amber,' I say, 'do you guys ever hire interns?'

'Oh, yeah, sometimes. Hold on, let me check something.' She taps a colleague on the shoulder and brings her into the circle. 'Finn's asking if we hire interns. Aren't applications for the summer cohort open now?'

'They are, but they're closing pretty soon. Are you interested?'

'I'm asking for a friend actually, but where can I direct her?'

'Here, take a card and get her to check out the jobs page on our website. All the info should be there.'

I thank her and grab a business card from her outstretched hand, pocketing it as I hit the automatic doors that lead me outside.

An hour later I have to swerve with superhuman instincts to avoid colliding with Ava, who's just left the back room and isn't watching where she's walking, a waft of vanilla hitting me as she moves.

'Sorr— oh. It's you,' she says, tying her apron around her waist. Her hair's messy in its ponytail, her face like thunder. I think she's hungover.

'Your sunny disposition always brightens my day.' We walk in the same direction and at her scowl, I realise I'm in the mood to be annoying. 'Are you stalking me?'

'This is literally my place of work,' she retorts—which of course only encourages me. Nice to know she's just as surly hungover as she is well rested. A creature of habit.

'I'm glad you're finally here,' I begin, and when her gaze falls on me, tired as it may be, I have to look away for fear she'll ensnare me in it. 'Mateo's out back so your manager made me a latte and it was really shit. Sorry, I shouldn't say that. I'm sure he tried his best.' I scrunch my nose as I remember. 'No, but it was shit.'

'I'm sorry to hear that. I'll make sure to send you my rota so you can plan your visits around my hours.'

'That'd be a dream, thanks.' Another customer approaches behind me and I do my usual snack perusal while Ava rings up their order, curt and professional as always.

'Why are you lurking, Finn?' she asks, the moment they leave the counter. 'If you're not buying anything, can you sit down? You're scaring away the customers.'

At that moment, I spot Belinda at her usual table, who waves to me with her typical enthusiasm. I wave back with a smile but direct my question at Ava. 'Has anyone ever told you how incredible your customer service skills are?'

'I do get that a lot, actually.'

I wait for her to finish chugging an entire cup of water, and then another—in what I can only assume is a post-alcohol rehydration tactic—before my curiosity peaks and I broach the subject of last night. I make sure my tone is casual when I ask, 'Had a good evening, I take it?'

'Yeah, it was fun. Sorry I had to run off.' She glances at me and her eyes widen slightly in apology. I get the feeling she doesn't often hand genuine apologies out, so I lap up the moment while she continues. 'I ended up staying up way too late. Didn't even drink that much, but Josie's cocktails are borderline-toxic waste.'

'The best kind of cocktail.' At the mention of her spending the night with Josie, something inside me relaxes.

'My brother was over too.' She avoids eye contact. 'I had to meet him at the station.'

'How was he?'

'Good.' She shifts on her heels, uncomfortable, like she's reluctant to part with any more information.

I try not to laugh at the strange way she's behaving and instead look around the shop to see if any of my favourites are in. I'm meant to have a chat with Samantha but we keep missing each other, and as far as I can tell, she's not in here at the moment either. When I spot a man in a green plaid shirt at a table in the back corner, I almost do a double-take.

'Ava,' I say carefully. 'Could that vaguely intimidating man in the corner possibly be your brother?'

It *has* to be. His legs are stretched out under the table as he lazily scrolls his phone, dark hair falling into his face no matter how many times he pushes it away. Even from this distance I can see they share the same eyes, same furrow between the brows as they concentrate. Strong, beautiful genes, clearly.

She shrugs when I look back at her for confirmation. I remember she mentioned he travels around a lot, which makes him the perfect companion for an activity, and the perfect person from whom to extract vital Ava information. For platonic reasons, obviously. 'What's he doing today? Would he want to help with the list?'

'He probably would, actually,' she mumbles. She looks over at him and her expression softens infinitesimally. 'But he can't. He has plans.'

I nod, fingers tapping the counter. I want to find out how similar they are; if they share the same mannerisms, the same constant flow of dry rebuttals, but before I even finish the thought, she cuts in. 'Don't you dare accost him.'

'I wasn't going to *accost* him.' My shirt tightens across my torso as I cross my arms. I can't be sure, but I swear her eyes drop to my biceps for a split second.

'I expressly forbid you to communicate with him in any way.'

'But—'

'This includes flirting with him.'

I roll my eyes. 'Is it your mission to ruin all my fun? Someone as good-looking as that needs to be told.'

'Trust me, he's been told often enough. Please don't give his ego any more fuel.'

I analyse him again, tilting my head. 'You'd make an incredibly attractive man.'

'Appreciate that.'

'And you don't want me to talk to him. Why?'

'Because,' she says, turning away from me to load some mugs into the dishwasher against the back wall, 'you've already met my best friend, weaselled your way into both my work and free time, and have generally become an incredibly talkative, frenetic addition to my very quiet life. I don't need you to scoop Max up in your whirlwind too.'

'If we're getting technical, me meeting Josie was mostly your fault,' I reason.

'A series of events I have regretted setting in motion every day since.'

She closes the dishwasher with a slam. Fortunately for me, it's at this exact moment her brother stands up and heads towards us. This guy is *tall*. He hovers for a few moments, clearly unsure if Ava's in the middle of serving a customer.

'Go ahead,' I say to him, which Ava answers with a glower. I take her moment of distraction to add, 'Ava and I are friends. But she's forbidden me to talk to you.'

'Finn,' she says slowly, 'did you misunderstand what "forbidden to talk to him" means?'

Max's eyes glitter. 'I've learnt the hard way what happens when you don't listen to her.'

'Do *you* want to find out what happens?' Her smile is sickly sweet.

Before I can answer, Max stretches out his hand for me to shake. 'I'm Max, Ava's brother. Twin. Not identical, in case you couldn't tell.'

From afar, they looked deceptively similar, but up close, I'm able to see the differences. Ava's face is fuller, while Max's is defined by diamond-cutting cheekbones and a sharp chin. He's also more tanned than she is, a fading sunburn across the bridge of his nose. Their smiles are different, too.

'She's told me so much about you.' I pointedly ignore what I can imagine are pure laser beams shooting from Ava's eyes.

'And she's told me absolutely nothing about you,' Max replies matter-of-factly.

'Can't say I'm surprised,' I say. 'We've only hung out a few times. I think she's embarrassed to be my friend. Right, Ava?'

'Oh, so you *do* understand subtext,' she says drily from behind the counter. She turns her attention back to Max. 'You're leaving?'

'Yeah. My appointment's at twelve,' he replies. He elaborates for me, 'I've got to be at the Australian embassy for a visa interview.'

'You're going to Australia? We could swap numbers if you want, I used to live there so I—'

'*Finlay*, I swear to god,' Ava says through gritted teeth, and I trail off. I mime zipping my lips closed and twisting a key. She leans over the counter to aggressively grab the invisible key before pretending to drop it in the bin.

Max watches the entire silent exchange in amusement. 'Right. Well, I'm gonna go, I think.'

One of Ava's hands is outstretched towards a takeaway cup when she says to him, 'Do you want a drink for your journey? Or some food?'

He shakes his head. 'Nah, I'm good, thanks.'

'And you're sure you don't want to stay at mine tonight as well? It might be easier.' She walks to the front of the counter to hug him goodbye and my chest tightens. I'm watching an entirely different Ava appear before my eyes and for some reason it feels like I'm intruding.

'You sound like Dad. I'm fine.' He looks at something on his phone and says, 'I'm booked up for the next month or so but I'll see you in August for the housewarming?'

I've been trying—not very hard, admittedly—not to eavesdrop, but at the mention of the infamous housewarming party I can't help but meet Ava's gaze. I hold back a smile while she screams *don't you fucking dare say anything* with her eyes.

Max asks the question anyway. 'Are you coming to that, Finn?' When Ava's jaw clenches, he says, 'Shit, sorry. Did I just make it awkward? Did I invite you to someone else's party?'

'Not awkward at all,' I reply breezily. 'I've been invited.'

'Cool, so you'll be there?'

'I've been invited,' I repeat, which only makes him more confused.

'Finn's not sure yet if he's free,' Ava offers. 'He's a very busy man.'

'Sure. Well, hopefully I'll see you there. It was nice to meet you,' he says, definitely still baffled.

As soon as the door rattles closed behind him, Ava shakes her head at me, moving back to her spot at the till. 'I have never met someone so terrible at following the most basic instructions.'

'Weird, that's exactly what all my report cards said at school.' I grab a packet of hazelnut wafers from the display and place it on the counter. Knowing I can rile her up makes my life infinitely more interesting.

'I can't believe you've now met Josie *and* Max,' she says, almost to herself. As she prepares the card reader for me, she mumbles, 'Should I get my parents on FaceTime too? Might as well go the whole hog.'

'I love mums,' I say, tapping the machine with my phone. 'So feel free.'

She narrows her eyes slightly at me for a second, her expression unreadable. 'Mould. That's what you are.'

'You should consider a career in poetry.'

'Wiggling your way into every crevice of my life.'

'Did you really need to use the word "crevice"?'

'Everywhere I turn, you're there.' A look of horror crosses her face. 'Oh my god. I'm really not getting rid of you, am I? Not until you move away?'

'Nope,' I reply, popping the "p". 'Lucky you.'

# 14

## London in a heatwave or the inside of an industrial oven?

### AVA

I'VE WEDGED OPEN THE front door of the coffee shop in the vain hope that the weather gods will take pity on us with a breeze to cut through the stagnant air, but it's not enough. I wipe the back of my hand across my sweaty forehead, profoundly regretting my decision to have a fringe.

'Iced latte with oat milk, just needs a shot,' I say to Mateo, handing him a cup of ice and clumsily filling it with milk before bringing my attention back to the till, where a queue of customers snakes along one edge of the counter. In typical British fashion, it's a great queue; not blocking the front door, strategically-placed spaces for people to pass through once they've got their drinks, but it is nonetheless filled with grumpy, sweaty people in search of some respite from the heat. I turn my attention to the next customer and try to ignore the single droplet of sweat trickling down my back. 'What can I get you?'

We course through customers at military-level efficiency, the perfect assembly line churning out cold drink after cold drink.

'Fucking lazy man,' Mateo mutters under his breath at regular intervals, hurling poisonous looks at Carl, who gets up every few minutes to straighten the displays but never actually comes behind the counter to help us, or even clear the ever-growing piles of empty cups from the tables.

As the queue begins to wane, I spot Finn, who must've come in during the height of the rush. He's inexplicably tidying the tables, collecting plates and cups and stacking them neatly on trays. I step away from the till for a moment to prep the ingredients for my millionth frappé of the day and as soon he's in earshot, I get his attention. 'Psst. Stop that.'

He brings a tray piled with plates to the end of the counter and tucks it as far out of the way as he can. 'Stop what?'

'Clearing stuff away! You're not allowed.'

'I'm not allowed to move some tableware?'

'No!' I press the button on the blender and set up the customer's payment on the till before wiping up the milk spill I just made. 'It's not your job. You're not being paid.'

He grabs another tray that he appears to have dedicated to wrappers and dirty napkins. 'I'm just clearing the table so I have space to sit.'

'You need to clear every table?'

'I'm considering my options. Lots of good choices.' He tips the contents of the tray into the bin. 'You know, most people would just say thank you.'

The blender's beep lets me know it's finished.

'Iced Americano for Stephen!' Mateo yells over the din. 'Stephen?' He inspects the tiny woman who's expectantly hovering nearby, before glancing back at the cup. 'Stephanie!'

I reach behind Mateo to grab a lid for my customer's drink and catch Finn's eye as I do. 'Thank you.'

'Here. A gift for you, to say thanks.' I place a cup on Finn's table, where he must've been waiting for the queue to die down before ordering. His gaze lifts to me and I feel it radiate across my whole body. Probably just the heat.

He takes a sip and his eyes close briefly in satisfaction. 'No one makes iced lattes quite like you, Ava Monroe.'

'I've made enough of them today to last a lifetime.' I slide onto the spare seat at his table, my first moment off my feet in hours, and slug my own coffee noisily through a straw. Work must've been too exhausting for Carl, because he left the shop five minutes ago in a hurry. Poor guy.

'This weather is divine,' Finn says with a sigh, not a hair out of place on his head, not even a hint of sweat anywhere on his short-sleeved ivory shirt. He doesn't have his laptop with him, so I assume he just dropped in for a drink.

'I feel like I'm wading through one of the putrid cesspits of hell.' I blow air upwards but my fringe is too slicked to my forehead to move. 'I can't wait to get out of here.'

It's cooled down a bit now the sun's not directly shining into the shop, but the air is still far more syrupy than I'd like.

'Well, on that note, I'd like to take you out.' He takes another sip of his coffee as he gauges my reaction.

'Take me out, as in, kill me? Join the back of the line. There's a bouncer with a clipboard and everything.' I lower my voice as I lean closer and gesture to one corner of the shop. 'That man over there has first dibs, though. I apparently put "too much ice" in his drink. He was livid.'

'Ha, no. Like, take you out after work. A bucket list item of my choice this time. You, me, somewhere that's not the dullest area of London.'

I sweep my arm towards the windows. 'I, for one, love the soulless skyscrapers and post-apocalyptic ambience of the City.'

'You're avoiding my request.' There's a smile in his voice and I act like I can't hear it.

'Have you tried the chocolate wafers yet, by the way? They taste like someone whispered the word "chocolate" over them during the manufacturing process.'

'Gripping. Is that a no? My ego can take it.'

'I doubt it can, actually. But okay, listen, I have an amazing idea.' He nods at me to continue. 'At the end of my shift, I will get changed out of my uniform, because frankly, I'm sweating. I'll take my hair down in an attempt to alleviate the headache my ponytail's been giving me, before inevitably retying it thirty seconds later because I simply cannot handle the feeling of loose hair on my neck in this heat. And then—'

'And then?'

'I'll get the Tube all the way down to South London and walk to my flat, where I will remain until Monday, save for a snack run to the corner shop probably sometime between eight and nine this evening.'

He leans forward, dropping his chin onto his fist, and the movement pushes his bottom lip into a pout. 'Do I feature in this plan at any point?'

'I would rather shit in my hands and clap than be around people for much longer this afternoon.'

'Is that code for "it's not you, it's me"?'

'Oh no, it's definitely you.'

He grins. 'I have somewhere in mind and I think you'll like it too. It'll be quiet. Serene. *I'll* be quiet.' When I don't reply, he takes it as an invitation to continue, echoing the question I asked him a couple of weeks ago. 'Do you trust me?'

'Not even a little.'

---

All this to say, of course, I find myself stepping into the Barbican Conservatory with Finn less than an hour later. When we got lost trying to find the entrance, it occurred to me that if I were alone I would've just left at that point. It took Finn asking multiple members of staff for help, but we made it. It's not as air-conditioned as I'd like, but it's temperature controlled, so it'll have to do.

'Welcome,' he says, 'to London's *second*-biggest botanical garden.'

The Barbican complex itself is all grey concrete slabs and hard edges, but here in the Conservatory, we've stepped into another world. A greenhouse seemingly dropped onto this building at random, it's packed with dense foliage across multiple levels. I imagine this is what the city would look like after a major catastrophe; nature reclaiming her home with frond curtains and grass carpeting, blankets of greenery draped over the back of a concrete sofa.

Tiny plants line the walkways, and endless multi-storey palm trees fill the space between the floor and the steel-beamed glass ceiling. There's something triumphant about how blatantly green has won the battle against grey in this space.

We follow the gentle sound of trickling water to a pond filled with koi fish. It is, annoyingly, as serene as Finn promised it would be. And, for his part, he peruses a leaflet he picked up and stays quiet as we meander along the pathways, letting the stress of the day lift from my body and float away.

Out of the corner of my eye I catch his lips parting to say something, before he pushes them together like he's holding something hostage in his mouth. After a while, I put him out of his misery. 'Come on, hit me with a fact. I know you have one.'

He adjusts his glasses, no further instruction required. 'Okay. Did you know the Barbican has won the Ugliest Building in London award?'

'I did not.' I think of the stark lines, blocky shapes and dreary tones. 'But I can see why it would. Feels a bit, you know... Communist.'

'Well, I think it's misunderstood. It's kind of intimidating, but then you get to know it and there's something special beneath all the harshness.' His eyes flick over to me and then straight ahead as he continues, 'Regardless, in an attempt to make it seem less bleak, they started planting stuff here. Then a couple of plants became ten plants, which became a hundred plants, and now there are thousands of species from all over the world. Right here, in this tiny pocket of London. A mini rainforest.'

'I think I like the mini rainforest. So thanks for bringing me.' The corners of his eyes wrinkle behind his glasses at my admission. 'Yet another thing I can experience without having to leave London.'

We walk to a bridge crossing another pond, this one filled with terrapins. A not-insignificant part of me wishes I were a terrapin lazily floating around a pond right about now.

'Do you not like to travel?' Finn asks, as both of us lean over the railing to get a better view of the animals.

'Not really.' I have some money saved that most twenty-somethings would spend on a flight or two, but I can't bring myself to use it. I don't want to be thousands of miles away if someone needs me. 'I like it here. I know what to expect. It's easy.'

He turns to face me, head tilted. 'You should try it. It's fun to see new things.'

'You sound like my brother. And Josie. But I'm seeing new things today, aren't I?' I watch a terrapin climb out of the pond. 'It's easy for you to say, anyway. You probably came out of the womb a frequent flyer.'

'I was almost born on a plane.'

My head snaps around. 'What?'

He lets out a low chuckle. 'Honestly. My mum flew a bit later than she should've and I ended up arriving way earlier than my due date. I was born nine hours after she stepped on solid ground.'

I consider this information. 'You showed up a few weeks early because you were just so excited to be here. I came out hungry and dragging my feet.'

'Start as you mean to go on, I guess.'

I let out a laugh and he bites down a smile. As we make our way across the bridge, Finn touches the plants we cross like he's in a clothes shop feeling every item on the rails. We pass through an archway into a secluded area of the garden, beneath a trailing plant that sheds tiny white flowers I have to brush from my shoulders. Taller plants encircle us and the sunlight filters through palm leaves, light and shadows trapped here with us. It is, by all accounts, the perfect spot for a date, which is probably why the only two other people in the vicinity look so sickeningly in love, whispering to each other and giggling, much closer to each other than I'd ever like to be on a hot day like this.

'What's that expression?' Finn asks, apparently noticing my wrinkled nose and grimace as we sit on a bench. 'You look nauseous.'

'I think that's just my face.'

'Hm, no. Your face is usually sullen. Disdainful, maybe. Not nauseous.' I smooth my features as the couple wanders closer to us, though they're so caught up in each other they hardly notice we're there. He barely holds back his smirk. 'You don't like PDA.'

It's a statement, not a question, but I confirm it anyway. 'Feels gratuitous. You're already together at home, I don't need to see you mounting each other in public too.'

'I feel there's a happy medium between public fornication and only going near each other when you're alone,' he points out, lightly fanning himself with his leaflet as I lift my ponytail away from my neck and twist it up into a bun.

'They're one and the same to me.'

The pair walks past and one of them mutters, 'I love your heart.'

'I love *your* heart.'

'You're so good to me.'

Finn lets out a quiet snort at my reaction. 'If it's any consolation, I don't think anyone's gonna be saying that to you any time soon. You're the least amenable person I know.'

'Are you *trying* to turn me on?' His laugh wraps around me like cool silk. I like how it feels. Jesus, this heat is getting to me. I shake my head to clear the thought away and eye his leaflet. 'Fan me?'

He turns it onto me and the breeze is sweet against my skin. After a minute or so he frowns and stops fanning, looking at me in confusion as if he's only just realised what he's doing. He blinks and fans himself instead, and I mourn the loss of my personal air con.

With no warning, he launches out a non sequitur that throws me completely off balance. 'Do you believe in love?'

'Of course.' His eyes widen like he's surprised, but the truth is, my parents have been married for decades, and I see Josie and Alina's quiet, considerate love play out on a regular basis. I clear my throat and add, 'Just not for me. It's messy.'

'And you don't like anything to upset your equilibrium.' I shrug and he halts his fanning, eyes fixed on me. My breath stutters at the intensity of his gaze. 'You've never felt that spark with anyone?'

'Why would I want to?' I hope he doesn't notice I've answered his question with a question. 'Sparks grow into flames. And nothing good can come of fire.'

As much as I try to keep my life level and calm, sometimes I'll laugh too loud or dream too vividly and it feels like I'm flirting with chaos. Like I'm dry brush in the desert just one spark away from an inferno. I don't want to know what would be left after it's burnt down to ashes.

Finn nods slowly, leaning one elbow on the back of the bench. 'I get it. My last relationship started with a spark and ended like a fucking firework. Went out with a bang.' He clicks his tongue. 'In more ways than one.'

'What happened?' I have a hunch, but I hope I'm wrong.

He rubs his hand along his jaw and my eyes draw to the dark stubble there. Then I feel guilty about looking at his jaw and thinking about what a good one it is, because he's about to tell me an emotional story and my horny little overheated brain has apparently decided that now is the time to devolve.

After a while he says, 'Her name was Léa. She's French but we met in Singapore and were together for a while. When her visa ran out I was adamant we'd be fine; her in Paris, me in Singapore. But she needed me—emotionally, physically, whatever—and I wasn't there. So I guess,' his knee starts to bob as his words speed up, 'she found someone else who *could* be there for her. By the time I moved to France, the damage had been done.' His face crumples into a grimace as he adds, 'Didn't *love* walking in on them, I'm not gonna lie. Not one of my favourite memories.'

'She cheated?' He winces at the word and shakes his head like he disagrees. The faintest wisp of anger curls up the inside of my chest on his behalf. Does he think he's to blame for his ex's actions?

'It was for the best, in the end. She was amazing, but I was too swept up in her. It wasn't healthy.' He looks ahead and squints at nothing in particular, pulling at the hem of his sleeve. 'Long-distance is rough at the best of times, and I move around too much to put in the effort my partner deserves. It's not fair on anyone. So, right now, experiencing new places, progressing in my career, those are my goals. Nothing else.'

'I could never do long-distance either.' I replay my own words and realise I need to elaborate. 'Just to be clear, I also couldn't do short-distance. Any distance, really.'

He laughs to himself and the sound seeps into my skin. And I don't know if it's because in this moment I'm so sweaty that I can't imagine a fire ever being able to do damage here, but the smallest part of me wonders if I should rethink my stance on sparks. Because crackling in the space between us on this bench, something simmers. I just don't know what.

Or maybe it's just a hot day, and on days like these I essentially turn into a wild animal on heat and can't control my thoughts.

So I swallow and say, 'Here's to not getting involved with anyone, ever.'

He reaches his hand out so we can shake on it, and I hate that I notice the muscles in his forearm, hate that his grip somehow squeezes my stomach, too.

'I'm so sorry to interrupt, but could you take a photo of us?' A woman's voice cuts through the heavy air and Finn releases my hand immediately. She gestures towards the archway we entered through and Finn leaps to his feet, taking her phone and barking out directions while making sure to get every angle; at one point squatting almost completely to the ground. I don't *not* look at his ass when he does this. I am but a hot-blooded woman, after all.

'Let me know if you want any more,' he says as he hands the phone back. 'Sorry, I might've gone a bit overboard.' He looks back at me with a grin, entirely unaware of the strange intensity generated within my brain during the last two minutes.

'No they're fab, thank you so much.' The woman scrolls through the photos, her eyes alight. 'Do you want pictures too?'

I say 'no thanks' at the precise moment Finn's much louder voice says 'absolutely', so I begrudgingly walk over to the arch to stand next to him, as close as I can get without touching.

'You have petals in your hair, by the way,' the lady says to Finn as she takes his phone from him.

'Yep. You do,' I confirm with a glance, arms settling by my sides.

'Could you perhaps,' he speaks with the easy patience of someone teaching a preschooler two plus two, 'take them out, please?'

I sigh and he dips his head for me. The humidity's defined his curls and I reluctantly pick out the white flowers from the soft mass of hair, streaked with shades of auburn and gold amidst the brown, willing myself not to give in to the overwhelming urge to run my fingers through it.

Unwelcome foliage removed, he stands up straight. We're back to not touching, but he turns to me, our eyes level, and asks, 'Can I?'

I nod and he rests a tentative arm around my shoulder like we're just two platonic buds hanging out on our platonic afternoon in a platonic date spot. Because that's what we are. But still, my brain is whirling with confusing thoughts at his proximity.

'Wiggle a bit closer together.' The lady motions with her hand, evidently taking her photographer duties extremely seriously.

I shift into him and delicately place my hand on his back, feeling the soft linen of his shirt. A waft of musky cologne washes over me as he shifts position, and I tighten my hold on the fabric. I'm keenly aware of the moment his hand drifts down to my waist and he pulls me infinitesimally closer, long fingers searing through my t-shirt as they splay across my ribcage.

Am I okay? It's his fucking *hand*, Ava, chill out. I really need to work on allowing physical touch in non-sexual settings.

'Oh you guys are so cute!' I have no idea what's going on with my face, but she seems to approve, so I pull the same expression the whole time, my mind in hazy disarray behind the eyes. 'Okay, I'm done. Incredible work, if I say so myself.'

We thank her and I head through the arch first, eager to escape the confined space and reenter the real world, where I can collect my thoughts.

'Do you want to see the photos?' Finn asks as we walk back across the bridge over the koi pond.

'I'm good. I'm sure they're great.' I wonder how to put some distance between us. We get stuck behind a group of school kids looking at the terrapins and Finn takes the moment of pause to step in front of me, eyebrows raised, an infuriating smirk pulling at one side of his mouth.

'You okay there? You seem a bit, I dunno. Weird.'

'I'm fine.' The heat is doing something to my brain. I need to remember why I keep people at arm's length. Why I'm not allowed to lean into volatile things like sparks and potential. And while we're at it, I need to remember how to not act like a teenager who's never so much as held hands with a boy before. I didn't spend countless nights with men from dating apps to fall at the barest touch from a Finn-shaped hurdle. It's embarrassing. What I really need is to spend another uncomplicated night on an easy, insignificant date. While my thoughts whirl, Finn waits, so I add, 'Just a bit thirsty.'

Immediately his eyebrows draw together. 'Want me to fill up your bottle?'

As he hunts for a fountain, I watch one of the gardeners work. He sweeps fallen foliage to the edge of the path, only for more leaves to fall in its place the second he's finished. As hard as he tries to keep everything contained, there's always mess to clean up.

# 15

## looking for someone who does, actually, take themselves too seriously

### AVA

A BOOMING VOICE SOUNDS across the pub. 'For a total of four points, what are the four official languages of Switzerland?'

'German, French, Italian and Romansh. Write it down,' my date says under his breath. I struggle to hear him over the murmurs around us as people try to come up with their own answers. He grabs the pen out of my hand to write the answer himself. 'No, that's not how you spell it. It's "sh", not "ch".'

Sam-from-Hinge is, apparently, an ultimate quizzer. I'm usually attracted to intelligence, so figured he was as good a person as any to go on a date with. Unfortunately, he is extremely intense, and somehow, *impossibly*, appears to have even worse interpersonal skills than I do.

'Excuse me,' he says, shooting his hand in the air like we're in year three, stretching in his seat to raise it high enough to grab the quizmaster's attention.

'Would you like me to repeat the question?' the man asks into his microphone. I down my second drink of the evening in preparation for whatever Sam is about to say.

'I wanted to let you know that this team,' he points at the table to our right, 'just searched the answer on one of their phones.'

The entire room stifles a laugh as everyone looks in our direction.

'Sam, I'm sure they were just checking the time,' I say quietly, hoping to divert attention.

He looks at me like I've suggested we wrangle a snake right here in the pub and continues, volume rising over the growing hubbub, 'No, they should be disqualified.'

'The prize is a £20 bar tab,' I reason, 'it's not that deep.' The glare he sends my way confirms that he believes it is, in fact, that deep. To him, it is the Mariana fucking Trench.

'Thanks for letting us know. We'll, uh, look into it,' the quizmaster continues, evidently lying. 'But that's round three complete. We'll take a ten-minute break before the fourth round.'

I take my phone from where I'd stashed it in my skirt's waistband and Sam almost yanks it from my hand.

'What are you *doing*?' he hisses. 'We could be disqualified too.'

'Right,' I say, keeping my phone out of his reach. 'I'm just going to pop to the ladies'.'

I weave through the tables to the bathroom. Leaning against the tiled wall, my fingers hover over my screen. I think about texting Josie, but she's working late as usual, and probably far too busy to care about any of this. I open up a fresh text thread.

> I am STRUGGLING on this date

> Who is this? Please delete my number

I roll my eyes and send a response.

> do you have plans tonight?

You can't expect me to hang out with you any time a date goes sour

I won't be your little bitch boy

Within seconds, two more texts come through.

But no, I don't — little bitch boy at your service

What are you thinking?

> you wanted to go on a boat right?

Is this gonna be another thing like the bus tour where you completely ignore my wishes and change the plan to something you want to do instead?

> if the little bitch boy is scared just say so

A few moments pass.

Where do you wanna meet?

Round four has already begun by the time I return to the table and whisper a hurried goodbye to Sam, who barely notices I'm leaving.

'In what year did rock band Blink-182 officially release their album Enema of the State?' The voice rumbles through the room and Sam furiously scribbles a number on our answer sheet.

'I'm pretty sure it's 1999,' I tell him. 'And the demo version was 1998.'

He looks up at me, pupils dilated, drunk on the power of being a grass, I assume.

'It's 2000,' he says with a roll of his eyes, turning away from me so he can pay better attention to the next question. The answer was definitely 1999.

---

Finn leans against the wall outside Vauxhall station with the same nonchalance of the early evening shadows sprawling across the ground between us. Under the golden-hour sun the blue of his shirt pops against his skin, and I realise he's more tanned than he was when we first met. As soon as he spots me, he pushes off against the wall, Cheshire Cat grin making a home on his face.

'Nice of you to show up.' He saunters forward and for a split second I wonder if he's about to give me a hug, but then he shoves his hands in his pockets, a picture of ease. The light has turned his brown eyes to amber, somehow making them even warmer than usual.

'Sorry,' I reply, 'the bus took longer than I expected.'

While the sun's been blazing all day, there's a static threatening to lift the hairs on my arms, a heaviness in the air that hopefully means the heat is going to break soon.

'It's fine,' he shrugs, following my lead as I take us across the street, once again trusting I'm taking him to a bucket list activity and not anything sinister. 'I was enjoying people-watching.'

'Did I pull you away from anything when I texted?'

'Nothing interesting,' he waves a hand flippantly. 'I was having a beer at home. Do you want to talk about your date?'

'Not particularly. He was a smartass, and not in a cute way.'

He pushes his sleeves up his arms and asks, 'What's the cute way?'

'My way, obviously.' We hit the riverside pathway. 'I'm extremely cute and sweet, as you are well aware.'

He raises his eyebrows but has the sense to keep quiet. In a rare few moments of silence, we meander along the river.

As the days get longer and the sky gets bluer, the city smoulders with pure magic. The unparalleled joy on the first day you don't have to wear a jacket. How the atmosphere when England wins a match could set the world on fire. The way people spill out of pubs after work like liquid, chatting and laughing and pooling in puddles along the pavements.

'Shit, London in the summer is something else,' Finn says at last. 'I feel like I was sold a lie. I was expecting grey sky and rain, and instead we get this?'

We've definitely had uncharacteristically good weather over the past few months; more iced coffees made than hot drinks, sunglasses required more often than my umbrella. It's probably because of global warming. Still, when Finn turns to me, glowing in the sun like he was born from it, I wonder if it could be something else.

I clear my throat to say, 'If Paris is the City of Love, London is the City of Unreliable Weather.'

Finn purses his lips as he thinks. 'I prefer City of Pigeons With Mangled Feet.'

'City of Declaring Your Allegiance to North, South, East or West and Sticking to it Forevermore.'

'City of Temperatures That Get So High on the Central Line, They Border on a Human Rights Violation.'

'The City of Standing on the Right of all Escalators and Never Ever on the Left, or So Help Me God.'

Just as our laughter merges into one homogenous sound, I notice we're walking perfectly in sync too, so I intentionally slow my steps to get out of it.

'Paris isn't the City of Love, though,' he says quietly. He chuckles at my raised eyebrows and adds, 'I realise this makes me sound bitter because of what happened there with my last relationship. But even before that I felt this way.'

We step out of the way for someone to rollerblade past, and I say, 'Okay. Make your case.'

'I will die on this hill, just so we're clear,' he says. 'It's an incredible place, obviously, don't get me wrong. And it has a ton of positive attributes. The history, the food, the art—'

'Finn, Paris can't hear you. You can talk shit about it if you want. I won't tell.'

He barks out a laugh that brings a smile to my own face, and for once I let it sit there.

'Okay, okay. Basically, if Paris is really the City of Love, it's like, the Hallmark movie version. Does that make sense?'

'I've never been,' I admit, aware that the train takes less than three hours from London, that flying takes half of that. 'But I don't think it'd be on my list even if I were someone who liked to travel. Its reputation for being the place couples hang out would probably deter me. Not really my thing.'

'Well, exactly. But other French cities are more romantic anyway. Friendlier, more beautiful, just as much culture.' I stumble over my own feet, not looking where I'm going, and Finn eyes me warily, like he's not sure if I'm capable of being a functioning human. Which is fair, honestly. 'I liked Paris well enough, but the whole world seems to pretend it's this perfect picturesque city when in reality it's actually kind of dirty.'

'So do you think London should be the real bearer of the nickname?'

He's quiet for a few seconds as he mulls it over. 'You can't just *dub* somewhere the City of Love. It has to earn it. So yeah, maybe London could be, in time.' Those liquid gold eyes settle on me. 'It doesn't rely on appearances. It's romantic in a way that's not so obvious.'

'It's fast-paced and loud,' I say. Right on cue, a police car passes, siren blaring.

'Don't people want a love like that? Something exciting and unapologetic?'

'Some people do.' I think harder, wondering how he'll spin the next thing I suggest. 'People here can be guarded. They aren't always warm.'

'Sure, but it's not a bad thing to guard yourself.' He scratches his jaw and upon seeing his profile; messy curls, strong nose, I feel like I'm walking alongside a living version of one of those ancient statues at the British Museum. Which tracks, because his dad is Greek. Maybe he's distantly related to one of the aforementioned hot statues. 'I think this place is accepting. You can be who you want here. To me, that's *extremely* romantic.'

London's the one place that I've felt a connection to, so I'm not sure why I'm trying to fight against Finn's romantic notions on this. 'Everyone knows London can chew you up and spit you out before you even realised it was hungry.'

'But before it does, it'll make you feel special. I think I'd take a few moments on top of the world, even if I knew it was only temporary, just to be able to say that I'd done it.'

We pass an elderly couple on a bench looking out at the river, their heads and hands together; two souls intertwined on the bank of the Thames.

'And it's old as fuck,' I say eventually. 'Steadfast.'

'Loyal. Keeps all your secrets.' Finn looks across at me, that ever-present smile lighting up his face. 'Do you see what I mean now?' Before I get the chance to answer, his eyes widen and, haloed by the sun, I know I've struck gold. 'What is *that*?'

'That, Finn, is the boat you wanted.'

*Go on a boat.* Number four on Finn's list.

Even in the dying daylight, the floating bar of Tamesis Dock is a vibrant pop of colour nestled on the riverbank. Permanently moored in its home between Lambeth and Vauxhall Bridge, the boat is painted blue and yellow, adorned by eclectic décor and fairy lights across its open upper deck. At low tide, it sits on a bed of stones and river debris, but this evening, it bobs slightly on the water.

'Okay,' Finn says, ducking his head as he steps inside and raising his voice over the buzz of activity, 'this is way better than the bus tour. No offence.'

The ceiling's low and so are the lights, which hang and sway with the gentle rocking of the boat, and the wood-panelled walls are festooned with rope and anchors and fishing nets. When we approach a gap in the small crowd at the bar, Finn gestures at me to go first as a lanky bartender waits expectantly for our order.

'Could I have an Aperol Spritz?' I ask.

He smiles and nods before looking at Finn, who fixes his eyes on him as he says, 'A gin martini, please.'

'Dirty?'

'Filthy,' Finn replies in a deep rumble. The bartender's eyes widen and he scurries off to the other end of the bar, no doubt intending to replay that single word in his mind for eternity.

I lean towards Finn so that he can hear me over the noise. 'You shouldn't do that.'

'Do what?' he asks, his body inching even closer to mine in response, a smile tugging at his mouth even though neither of us has said anything funny.

'That poor, unsuspecting man just wanted to take your order and you practically seduced him.'

'Everyone likes to be seduced, don't they?' He quirks an eyebrow and waits for me to respond.

I narrow my eyes and take a step backwards. Drunk Ava is not known for making intelligent decisions when men are involved, and right now I'm sober enough to have a speck of common sense.

'For the record,' he says easily, 'Aperol tastes like cough medicine and cheap perfume.'

'That should be its new slogan.'

'I think perhaps it's an acquired taste,' he suggests.

'Acquire some taste, then.'

'Ouch.' His eyes catch mine in the low light from the bar and I take a long inhale in an attempt to compose myself. I'm increasingly aware that most of the brown of his eyes has been taken over by pupil, that heat radiates off him even from this distance.

I really should've stayed at the pub with the grass. At least he didn't make the inside of my head feel like a cursed frappé whizzing around a blender.

'You can talk; a martini?' I try to ignore whatever is going on in my brain. My rapidly thumping heart has other ideas, however. 'Like someone shoved hand sanitiser and a packet of Monster Munch in a cocktail shaker and thought "hmm, you know what would make this better? An olive!"'

The bartender comes over with our drinks, placing them delicately on the bar and stealing a quick glance at Finn and his perpetual half grin before handing us the card reader. Finn taps his phone before I get the chance to protest. He has a few missed calls on his home screen and I briefly wonder who he's avoiding.

The bar is packed, but I want to show Finn the deck, so I move back to the main door.

'How'd you find out about this place?' he asks as we step outside, floorboards creaking beneath our feet. I inhale the fresh air and it refocuses my tipsy brain somewhat. I lead the way, walking up to the bow of the boat in search of a free table.

'One of my dates,' I reply, sipping my Aperol. 'Thank you, Chris the quantity surveyor. Not a great lover in the end, but he had wonderful taste in bars.'

In reality, I know Tamesis Dock is a well-known spot, but it's small and secluded enough to still feel like a secret. As we near the front of the boat we come to an incredible vantage point of London's skyline. From here, the London Eye, Big Ben and the Houses of Parliament are silhouetted against a dusty pink and purple sky as the sun says its final goodbye.

By some miracle, a couple is packing up their stuff, and in an uncharacteristic bout of speed, I claim their spot within seconds of them vacating it. There's a spillage on the surface of the metal table but it's a price I'm willing to pay for its prime location. One seat faces the skyline while the other faces the back of the boat. I reluctantly take the one facing backwards so Finn can have the better view.

Once we've sat down and Finn's investigated the sun-bleached life preserver attached to the railing next to us, he slides his martini towards me.

I take a sip and pull the kind of face a toddler would make before they've learnt it's polite to neutralise your expression sometimes. 'Foul, as expected.'

I push it back across the table, making a trail through the spillage from me to him.

'That's perfectly fine, you're entitled to your wrong opinion,' he says breezily, noticing at the same moment I do that his phone has lit up with a call, before flipping it over on the table. He looks over my shoulder at the sunset. 'This is my favourite bar, I've decided.'

'It might be mine too.' I gulp my radioactive-looking drink and wash away the taste of the martini. A few drops slide down the outside of the glass and I lick them without thinking, catching Finn's eye as I do. 'What's your favourite place you've lived?'

He leans back in his chair with a stretch. 'It changes. But you know what? London's making a case for itself right now.'

'Because of this bar,' I offer, meeting his gaze over my glass.

He nods slowly, eyes boring into me. 'Sure. Because of this bar.'

His phone buzzes again, and the light peeks out even though it's flipped over.

'You should get that,' I suggest.

'It's fine.' His dark eyebrows furrow into a frown. It doesn't look right on his face.

'Could be important.'

'It's not.'

'How do you know?'

He grimaces. 'It's my mum, who's clearly up extremely early. Or late. She's congratulating me on getting a job interview. I've been applying for a bunch of them recently and just heard back from one today.'

A smile hits my cheeks, though there's something else under the surface. 'Anything exciting?'

'It could be.' His voice is clipped and I get a glimpse into how people must feel when they ask me questions and my replies are cagey. But I always appreciate when people respect when I'm reluctant to give answers, so I try to do the same for him. He sighs and says, 'I was waiting for my dad to get back to me before I told anyone else. I can see he's read the message, he must've just forgotten to reply.'

'Well, congratulations,' I say, touching my glass to his. 'To new opportunities.'

I can't help it; the bitter lick of envy paints my insides. Because as much as I want to be fine doing what I'm doing, I wish more than anything that I had even an inkling of a plan, that I could find a way to move forward without disrupting the balance I've so carefully constructed.

'Wait, that reminds me. I picked this up for you the other day.' He reaches into his wallet and hands me a business card. I meet his eyes and he explains, 'It's for the design agency in my building. They're taking interns. I remember you saying you did graphic design at uni and thought you might be interested.'

I stare at the card for a few moments, and then, under the fairy-light glow of the deck, a truth I've been avoiding is illuminated. At school, I chose design subjects because I was good at them, minimal effort required. Then at uni, I hoped skill could take the place of passion. Now, I draw on our menus at work to minimise boredom. There's never been any passion.

I don't want to be an intern, or take a course, or finish a degree. I don't want to do this thing I'm vaguely good at. The realisation makes me feel like I've been dropped into a dunk tank, the cold water forcing the truth out of me, and I scramble to get out, to determine how to answer the deluge of questions crashing over me.

At my lack of response, Finn backtracks, words spilling over each other in his rush to get them out. 'Seriously, no pressure, I just know you're not a huge fan of your job and found out these guys were hiring and thought of you. I didn't make them any promises or anything. Sorry if I overstepped.'

'No, that was really nice of you. Thank you. I might look into it.' Perhaps it's because I know he's only a temporary feature in my life that I don't feel the same pressure as I would telling Josie or Max, but I grant him a fraction of the truth. 'Actually, maybe I won't. I don't know if it's for me, anymore. I'm not sure it ever was.'

Part of me wonders if it's wrong to feel like I'm already too late. I know I'm young, I know I shouldn't feel like this, but when everyone around me is taking every exciting step forward, it feels like this is the universe telling me that this is it for me. If the simple *idea* of stepping towards something I'm good at, lack of passion aside, is making my blood freeze, this is proof that the best decision is to just stay back here where it's safe and comfortable and easy.

Even so, I'm grateful he at least saw something in me, some version of me that doesn't have coffee grounds under her nails or wear an apron every day.

He appraises me for a moment. 'You know Belinda from the coffee shop? She started an English degree last year and she's eighty-two. Take as long as you need to figure things out. You're allowed to.'

It seems he's developed an astounding talent for reading my mind.

His phone buzzes once more and he mutters, 'Sorry, I'm gonna ask my mum to call me back tomorrow.' Once he's put his phone in his pocket, he visibly relaxes, and I do too. He leans forward, bracing his elbows against the table and resting his chin on one hand, his usual grin returning to his face.

'What do you think she's thinking about?' he asks, nodding his head at a table to my left.

One of the women is practically inhaling her partner and I ignore the PDA to reply tonelessly, 'The particle accelerator at CERN.' I shift to the edge of my seat and look for someone else to analyse. 'And that guy?'

'The fact sharks are just dolphins with bad PR.'

'What about those two?'

He follows my line of sight to another table and thinks for a moment before replying, 'How much pressure you feel when you're filling up a bottle at a water fountain while someone's behind you.'

'And you only fill it up halfway because you can't handle the tension?' I mirror his position, pressing my cheek into my fist.

'Exactly. What nightmares are made of.' He sips his martini and I look at him with a tilt of my head.

'I can't imagine you being someone who reacts to stuff like that.'

His shoulders lift. 'Sometimes. Filling up a water bottle, bringing food to a party, any situation where someone's relying on me, I guess. I don't like how it feels.'

I turn this over in my mind for a few moments. 'It's not quite the same for me. I just get embarrassed by it. It feels like people are watching me and willing me to mess up. And I'll probably deserve it, because I've already used the water fountain and had a perfectly good drink today and it's greedy to want more.'

I'm not sure we're still talking about filling up water bottles.

'My therapist would love this conversation,' Finn says, echoing my thoughts. He eyes me carefully. 'My mum sent me to one when I lived with her but I haven't found one that's a good fit since then. It's been a while.'

'What's the verdict? What do they say about you?' If this is too personal a question, he doesn't flinch.

He tips more of his drink into his mouth before replying. 'Chronic abandonment issues from various people and parts of my life that have led to a desire to control my situation by running away before I can get properly close to anyone and risk them abandoning me first.'

He takes a breath at the end of his impossibly long sentence and, entirely unhelpfully, I offer, 'It's character building.'

A surprised laugh spills out of him, and its effervescence pops up and down my bare skin. 'It is. It's also led me to develop some more favourable traits, so it's not all bad. I'm alright.'

'If you're hoping for me to open up too, you'll have to wait a lot longer.'

I expect him to laugh again but he looks at me shrewdly and says, 'I'll be here when you want to.'

Despite everything, I want to believe him.

Aware he finished his drink a little while ago, I knock back the last of my Aperol before grabbing his empty glass to bring back to the bar. 'Round two?'

---

We take it in turns to get a round, no longer sticking to our martinis and Aperol Spritzes and instead mixing drinks in a very uni-student way. As usual, the alcohol's dissolved my filter, but Finn's loosened up too, so we go through question after question like we're in the quick-fire round of a quiz show.

'Fuck, marry, kill: Mario, Bowser, Toad,' I ask as he arrives at the table with two pints of cider, one of which I immediately lay claim to. 'There is a correct answer, by the way.'

Without a moment's hesitation, he replies, 'Fuck Bowser, marry Mario, kill Toad.'

When he drops into his chair, our knees touch under the table. I don't pull away, and neither does he. 'You're killing Toad?'

He looks at me like I'm being dense and leans closer to say, 'Sorry, you think he'd be good in bed?'

Even in the dim light, I still catch the way his eyes flash. I ponder his response while I dig around the slush in a long-since finished jug of Pimm's, spearing a piece of cucumber with a straw. 'Fine. What's your favourite chore?'

Still close, his voice is low when he says, 'Vacuuming. Is there any other option?' I'm not sure why him talking about hoovering has slowed my heartbeat to a sluggish thump, but I assume it's something to do with the alcohol and the air that's so muggy I can almost hold it in my hand. Finn twists his body away and attempts to take a photo of the skyline, so I take the moment of distraction to look at him.

He's so... *kinetic.* Always moving. That lone curl dropping distractedly across his forehead, a hand pushing his glasses up his nose or tapping the table, the way the corners of his mouth constantly twitch like there's always a smile on the verge of escape. His unsteady hands mess up the shot, so he grunts in frustration and gives up, eyes snagging mine for a beat. When he moves back into position, his legs end up bracketing mine. Which is helpful, actually, because for an entirely unrelated reason I'm feeling the urge to squeeze my thighs together anyway. He licks his lips before asking, '*Least* favourite chore?'

I clear my throat and drag my eyes away from his face. I try not to pay too much attention to people's mouths. Don't want them getting the wrong idea. 'Putting the duvet back in the cover after I've washed it.'

He nods sagely, like he's logging the information for future use, and for a while longer we continue this silent competition where he pretends he's not sending sparks up the length of my body any time his thighs press against mine, and I pretend I'm unaware he's doing so. In a bid to bring us back to normality, I blurt the first thing that comes to mind. 'The more I get to know you, the more you seem like the kind of man who should be blonde.'

He studies me, eyebrows hitching higher. 'Thank you?'

'I don't know if it's a compliment.'

'Right,' he draws his cider to his mouth and the glass hovers there as he says, 'we wouldn't want anyone overhearing you saying something nice.'

'It'd destroy my reputation.' I'm finding his gaze exceptionally unnerving, so I decide to scrutinise the design on my glass instead. It's nothing special, but my inebriated brain thinks it's the best thing I've ever seen. 'Do you think I could buy this? It'd be the *perfect* glass for when I go through my biannual phase of trying to drink more water.'

'Take it,' he says with a grin and a gentle slur, hand stilling on his own glass. 'I dare you.'

I look at him, affronted. 'I'm not a *thief*, Finlay.'

'KitKat Chunkies?'

'They don't count. I'm not going to steal this.'

He hunches forward, and I notice a dark freckle on his cheekbone that I hadn't seen before. 'Then you'll be forever wondering what your life would've been like with a floral Rekorderlig pint glass in your possession.'

'I think that's a risk I'm willing to take.' Through the stuffy air come the chimes of Big Ben as it strikes the hour, eleven loud clangs that jerk me out of my own head. I can't help but swivel in my seat to look at the skyline in all its illuminated brilliance. 'Fuck, this *view*.'

When I turn back around I assume I'll catch Finn analysing the skyline too. A jolt runs through me when I realise he's looking directly at me, the slightest groove between his brows like I'm a puzzle he's trying to solve. Holding my gaze, he says simply, 'It's a great view.'

Goosebumps prick along my arms despite the balmy air. A foggy part of my brain knows it could make a decision that could make a mess of everything, but before I get the chance to either listen to it or tell it to shut up, my bladder informs me with utmost urgency that it requires imminent emptying.

'I need to pee,' I announce, snapping the tension like a rubber band and pushing back my chair to walk gingerly to the bathroom. It's marked by two signs reading *buoys* and *gulls,* which take me far longer to decipher than I'd care to admit. By some miracle there's an empty stall and I lumber in, a fumbling hand sliding the lock as I try to reacquaint myself with gravity.

It's not until I sit on the toilet that I have the epiphany. I am *extraordinarily* drunk. I put my head in my hands as I sit there and feel the world move around me, half convinced the boat has detached from its mooring and we're currently hurtling along the Thames.

It's the best pee of my life. Or like, at least top ten. I'm not super confident my arms are attached to my torso anymore, so I let them flop down on either side of my knees, resting my chin on my legs.

I take a few deep breaths and contemplate my evening. It feels like three years ago that I was sat in a pub quiz with that guy. Fuck, what was his name? I wonder if he won by himself in the end. And then Finn showed up and didn't bat an eyelid when I asked ridiculous questions like which of the Super Mario characters he'd sleep with. I mean, he doesn't seem to bat an eyelid at *anything*.

My mind flashes back to the way he looked at me just before my bladder almost exploded. Surely I have no business dissecting a single look when I know we both agreed to our very specific, strangely regimented rules of friendship. He flirts with everyone he comes across. And it's not like I'm not used to men looking at me. So why did the way *he* looked at me feel like he was crawling into my brain and making his own pathways between the neurones?

Nope, I need to sober up. I'll just rest here for a while. I *am* enjoying not using my arms.

'Ava?' a voice I don't recognise calls from somewhere on the other side of the door. What a coincidence there are two Avas here at the same time. Maybe I'm peeing next to her. The disembodied voice speaks again. 'Is there an Ava in here?'

There's a knock on my door and it occurs to me that she may be talking to me. Through a tiny hole in the wooden door I see someone walk past, so I flush the toilet and collect myself before sliding the lock. There's a woman standing at the sinks and I pull myself together enough to reply to her. 'Hey, that's me. What's up?'

'There's a guy outside asking for you. If you don't want to be found I'll tell him you're not here.'

Bless women and their camaraderie. 'What does he look like?' I assume I know who she's referring to, but considering an old hook-up recently stumbled upon my place of work and dedicated poetry to me, it's worth double-checking.

'Glasses, blue shirt, curly brown hair. Fit, to be honest.'

'Simultaneously looks like he could spout Star Trek trivia but also would've been the lifeguard you fancied at the hotel pool when you went to Spain with your family in year nine?'

The woman's mouth opens and closes in bewilderment before she answers. 'I mean, yeah. Just like that.'

Water splashes all over my top when I wash my hands. 'Yeah, I know him, thank you. He's just impatient. I'll get to him in a sec.'

'If a man who looked like that was asking after me, I'd be right there. Unless he's, like, your brother or something. In which case, sorry to make these comments about your brother, but do you want a sister-in-law?'

I shudder. 'He is *definitely* not my brother. He's my friend. My very antsy friend, apparently.' I wipe my hands on my skirt and pull my phone from my bra, looking past the holographic boob sweat on the screen to see a string of texts from Finn asking if I'm okay. I look up at the woman one more time. 'Thanks for letting me know.'

She heads into the stall I just vacated and I glance at my reflection in the mirror, fixing my skirt, which has somehow drifted halfway in the wrong direction around my waist.

When I yank open the main door, I'm surprised to find Finn sprawled across the sofa at a table nearby, chatting to the two women at the table next to him. Something flickers over his face the moment he spots me. Relief? Then his mouth curves into a smile.

'Is this Ava?' one of the women asks, looking between us.

'Have you been talking about me?' I accuse, mustering every ounce of energy I have to separate my slurring words.

'I would never do that,' he replies smoothly, winking at the women, who laugh and turn away. I don't have the brain capacity to analyse that. He moves up, giving me space to sit next to him on the cracked leather sofa.

'I don't want to think about what has taken place on this couch,' I say, lip curling in disgust.

'Thanks for that image.' And then, 'Are you good?'

'I'm dandy,' I reply. For some reason.

'I'm glad to hear it.' He looks me up and down and, seemingly satisfied with my state, he asks, 'Can I make a request that you check your phone every so often?'

'Who are you, my mother?'

'Forgive me for being concerned for your whereabouts when you drunkenly stumble away and disappear for almost half an hour.' He's trying to be flippant but it's ruined somewhat by the slur to his words. At least we're matching.

'Almos— what?' I look at my phone, taking a moment to focus my eyes, and check the times of all of Finn's texts, which seem to be clustered to the final ten minutes of my bathroom visit and prove his point. 'What if I was taking a particularly hearty shit and didn't want to be disturbed?'

'Wait, women shit?'

'Absolutely not, don't be vulgar.'

'Ava.' I look at him and his expression is earnest. 'Sorry if that felt overbearing. I was just worried.'

I lean my head against the back of the sofa and avert my eyes, unwilling to look at him while I say what I'm about to say. 'It's fine. It wasn't overbearing. It's kind of nice knowing you care.'

'I do care.' He leans back too, arms folded behind his head as he stretches his legs out beneath the low table. 'I thought you might've drowned in the toilet, and I still have a bucket list to complete, so that would've been a shame.' He clears his throat. 'And the other option was that you'd run away.'

'If I'd wanted to run away, I probably would've taken my bag with me.' Oh shit. Where is my bag? Before I get the chance to fully panic about its whereabouts, he wordlessly hands it to me. 'Thanks,' I say sheepishly.

I bite down a yawn and think I've done a great job of hiding it until Finn sends me a sideways glance and says, 'Are you ready to go? I am *fucked.*'

# 16

## thunderstorms and aeroplane wishes

### AVA

WHERE THE SUNSET EARLIER painted the sky with vibrant streaks of pink and orange, now it's the colour of the pot of water you use to rinse the paintbrushes.

'London's so radiant at night.'

'I think that's light pollution, Finn.' We make our way along the river again, heading back the way we came towards Vauxhall station.

'But knowing the stars are there. It's comforting,' Finn says distractedly, his face turned upwards in the direction of a twinkling light.

'And that's an aeroplane.' A droplet of something that's either rain or *eau de city* hits my cheek, but there's no more after that so I keep walking.

'I'm trying to muse and you're ruining it. If you're not going to say anything profound, be quiet.' His mouth twitches as I laugh, and he adds, 'Where's your imagination, Ava Monroe?'

'Probably tucked away with my zest for life.'

'You're missing out. It's fun to dream.'

'Yeah, well, my dream right now is to get home. So I'm walking,' I say in response, running across the road while the traffic light's still green and bypassing the Tube station entirely, with the intention to walk all the way home. I'm granted a few moments of quiet before Finn catches up.

'And I'm accompanying you.'

'This feels like stalking.'

'I'm not letting you travel home alone. If you don't want me to join you, that's fine. Tell me to leave and I'll call you an Uber instead.' My face scrunches into a scowl and he shoots me a self-satisfied smirk when I don't reply. I dart across another road and the smirk turns into a sigh. 'Why do you have no regard for your life?'

'What can I say? I like to walk on the wild side.'

'I've literally never heard a less true statement.' He removes his glasses and cleans them on his shirt before returning them to his face, and I can tell he's about to spill yet more Finn fun facts. 'Did you know the crescent moon sits at a different angle depending on where you are in the world?' As usual, he doesn't wait for me to answer. I know by now that his did-you-knows come with immediate follow-ups. 'Here it's vertical, like a letter C, but in some places it's more like a U. I think it's cool.'

'Are nerds allowed multiple specialist subjects? I thought dinosaurs were your thing.'

He shrugs. 'Dinosaurs are *one* of my things. But I fucking love space. For almost the same reasons. Millions of years packed into a single fossil? Infinite galaxies stretching further than we can even fathom? Sign me up. Remind me of my meagre significance.'

Dust motes cloud my brain, as if a door has just been opened in a room long since abandoned. I don't need any more reminding that I'm just a speck in the universe, at the mercy of its every whim. Don't need reminding how grateful I am that it listened to me when I begged, can never forget that I owe it something, everything, even now.

I attempt to pull myself back. 'Aren't space and dinosaurs kind of a conflict of interests? The asteroid, et cetera.'

'Too soon, Ava. Too soon.' We walk quickly towards Stockwell and I'm glad that for the most part it's too dark for him to be distracted by much of our surroundings, and that he can't see my face. 'By the time my mum met my stepdad I was already a walking dinosaur encyclopaedia and needed a new interest. So my stepdad taught me about the solar system. He has this massive telescope that I think has now lived on almost every continent.' He looks up again at the beige, starless sky. 'I know it sounds trite, but I just like knowing that when I look up, it's the same sky. Especially because my family is on different continents. All of us, all over the world, watched by the same stars.'

There it is. The open door. It disturbs a memory I'd forgotten about, tucked away in a box I don't open anymore. It tumbles out of me, overflowing before I get the chance to slam it back inside. 'When my brother was in hospital a few years ago after some complications with his cancer treatment, we weren't allowed to visit overnight. So I'd always tell him to look outside and find the moon, because chances are, I was looking at it too.' Out of habit, I search the sky, but the moon's hiding tonight. At Finn's silence, it occurs to me that I've shared a piece of information I hadn't intended to.

He gives me a long, searching look. 'I bet he's glad he has you.'

My eyebrows pull together. 'I'm glad to have *him*.' Finn goes to interject but stops himself, then nods at me to continue. 'I mean, sometimes I think that if he weren't my brother, I'd probably kind of hate him. He can be a little arrogant and almost always gets what he wants. But I guess, after everything he's been through, maybe he has the right to believe in himself more than the average human.' My eyes dart around the sky, searching for even a sliver of moon. 'He's probably a better person than me in almost every way. The world would be a much darker place without him.'

The last sentence comes out like a hiccup, surprising even me. It's been a while since I've even let the concept of Max's absence enter my consciousness. I shake my head to dislodge the thought, but it gets caught on my brain's edges, just like it always used to. The thought ricochets, one crack on a sheet of ice echoing its threat across a lake. I take a few breaths, avoiding eye contact to mumble, 'He's okay now, though. You met him. You saw that.'

Max deserves every moment of *okay* he's been given. He's alive and happy and the gratitude I feel for that is so visceral it hurts almost as much as the fear of losing him did. But still, occasionally, if I'm not paying sharp enough attention, the thoughts seep in. The awful what-ifs that kept me up at night all those years ago.

As if he can see inside my brain, see the swirling wisps of smoke darkening through the window, Finn stops on the pavement. 'Hey.' He waits a long time for my eyes to lock onto his. 'Are *you* okay?'

'I'm fine,' I say instinctively. I *am* fine. I am. We're all okay now that Max is too. But something in the way Finn waits for me to elaborate lets me know he doesn't believe me. 'I promise. I know how to handle myself.'

I look ahead, aware of how deeply I'm breathing, how I'm clenching my hands into fists in an attempt to stop them shaking, fiercely hoping the wound in my heart doesn't reopen at the mere memory. My life has been blissfully uneventful over the past few years, and with that, there's been nothing to complain about. Nothing to worry about.

In reality, it wasn't until the dust settled after everything happened that I realised that maybe I needed some comfort too. That I'd spent so long trying not to need it so I could be the one my heartbroken parents relied on, that by the time I realised I did need it, there was no point. It was selfish to want. Because what should I need comforting about now, if I got my brother back in the end, just like I begged?

By the time I meet Finn's eyes again, warm and dark under the glow of the street lights, the old need rises to the surface. He unzips me with that single look.

And then a car drives past, its headlights illuminating his whole face, and before I have time to register what he's doing, he pulls me against him. For a split second I don't react. But I realise that some of the weight pressing on my skull is lifting at the feel of the warmth of his body against mine, so I wrap my arms around him and breathe him in, a weirdly reassuring concoction of swimming pools and spicy cologne that shouldn't make sense but somehow does. I'm allowed to take the comfort for tonight, I think.

'I'm sorry,' he whispers into my hair. I don't know if he's apologising for how I feel, or for the fact he's broken our unspoken no-direct-contact rule, but I don't mind. Partly because we're both drunk, and I've done far less wholesome activities with men while drunk. But mostly I don't mind because, briefly, I remember what it felt like to be a child, when a hug was enough to make everything okay.

And with every inhale, each corresponding exhale pushes the coils of smoke clear from my vision. In, out, in, out, until the fog has lifted entirely. For now, at least.

I don't know how long we stand there. It's long enough for me to realise he's sturdier than I expected; broad shoulders that I'd thought were just an optical illusion from the baggy shirts he always wears, strong arms clutching me as if he's scared I'm going to float away. It's long enough for me to register that it's been a long time, to the point where I'm sure I should pull away. And it's long enough to notice something else, a decidedly solid *something* pushing against me.

'Finn,' I murmur into his shoulder. 'Please tell me that isn't your penis.'

I feel him laugh more than hear him, and he steps back, severing whatever force was keeping us together and bringing me back to reality. 'I forgot, I have a present for you.' He reaches into his trouser pocket—why are men's pockets so impossibly large?—and pulls out a familiar-looking item. The cider glass from the bar.

Something twists in my stomach. Maybe it's the alcohol. Maybe not. 'You took it? For me?'

'For you,' he confirms, handing it to me with a flourish as we slowly start walking again. The likelihood of me dropping a glass is high at the best of times, let alone when I've had a few too many drinks, so I clutch my contraband against my chest as we inch closer to Stockwell.

'Thank you.' For the glass, for not making a big deal out of the few pieces of information I shared, for taking away some of the weight without even knowing. But still, this isn't what he signed up for. I set out to lighten the mood. 'Didn't know you were such a bad boy.'

There's a pause, until he replies, 'There's a lot you don't know about me, Ava.'

I raise my eyebrows in disbelief. 'Tell me something else I don't know then.'

'That,' he runs his hand through his hair and looks up, like he's searching for answers in the sky, 'would defeat the purpose of there being things you don't know about me.'

A huff escapes me and we keep walking, and my inhibition-less self asks a question, hopefully one that doesn't send me crushed against his chest again. 'Do you think I spend too much time alone?'

'I think we could all do with being a little more selective when it comes to choosing who we spend time with.'

'When you said earlier that you got a job interview, was it at the UN by any chance? Because that was a lesson in diplomacy. And complete bullshit.'

'I just mean,' his head tips back on a laugh, 'that we should be focusing on quality over quantity.'

'And yet, here I am, with you.' I shoot him a grin.

'Hey, you asked me to join you tonight.' He raises a hand in surrender. 'I initiated nothing.'

I purse my lips. 'God, how much have you had to drink? I'd never do that.'

'Admit it, you like spending time with me.'

'Perhaps *like* isn't the word,' I stomp my way along the pavement and he follows, 'but I don't dread it as much as I expected to.'

'Was that... a compliment?' He steps in front of me briefly and even in the dark, I can see his eyes are alight.

'It was compliment-adjacent. And if you tell anyone, I'll deny it.' We keep walking, and every time we pass under a street light's glow, I catch him glancing in my direction. 'Why are you looking at me like that?'

'Like what?' He snaps his head forward, the corner of his mouth lifting.

'With those eyes.'

'Sorry. I'll try to look at you without my eyes next time.'

For a while, all I can hear is our steady muffled footsteps, until a different sound joins the mix; the quiet pitter patter of rain, barely even a drizzle.

But the moment Stockwell Tube station comes into view, the heavens open with a roar, the long-brewing rain finally tumbling from the sky in sheets and breaking the suffocating heat. We scoot to stand under the station's overhang with fellow late-night rain-avoiders and watch as people open up umbrellas and lift hoods or, in most cases, continue walking down the street unfazed.

'How far do you live from here?' Finn calls over the din of cars splashing along the road, their lights bouncing off the wet tarmac like neon signs.

'A six-and-a-half-minute walk.'

'Thank god, thought it might be seven.'

'Well, I'm walking. My bed is calling.'

I step out into the downpour and immediately regret it, but it's too late to go back. Within a minute, it's soaked me through, every step accompanied by a squelch of my boots. A car comes dangerously close to driving through a puddle and coating me in dirty road water, but I manage to avoid it. Or rather, Finn pulls me out of the way, somehow more aware of me than I am. By the time we hit mine and Josie's street, the rain's slowed back down to a drizzle, and I realise that if I hadn't been so impatient, I probably could've avoided getting drenched. I snort at the thought, and then I look at Finn and even more laughter bubbles out of me.

'Sorry, did you *drown*?' I manage to squeeze out between splutters.

This is not the same ironed-shirted man who strode into the coffee shop with Julien and Rory that first evening. He puts his hands on his hips, glasses tucked in one fist in a futile attempt to keep them dry, rainwater dripping from his head to his shoulders, shirt slicked to his chest. He looks like he's just emerged from the sewer. But the surlier his expression, the more I laugh, and eventually his face splits into a grin, his own laughter forcing itself out in sharp bursts.

'Remember when I ranted about London's unjust rainy reputation earlier?' he says. 'I fear I may have unlocked something.'

He shakes his head to dislodge some water and I notice the rain's brought out the texture in his hair, curls collecting droplets like dew in a forest.

'Oh my fucking *god*,' I say, leaning one arm against a garden wall to keep myself upright as the torrent of laughter rolls through me. 'You look ridiculous.'

He feels around his torso for any piece of fabric that might be dry. Eventually he lifts his shirt to ineffectively dry his glasses on the waistband of his boxers, and my drunken eyes cling to the strip of skin it reveals. When he returns his glasses to his face he takes a step back to look me up and down. 'I look ridiculous? *I am the one* who looks ridiculous? I cannot wait for you to get to a mirror, you bedraggled little gremlin.'

'Fuck off,' I say, noting how my hair is plastered to my head, fringe devoid of any kind of volume, skirt entirely stuck to my legs as we start walking again. We make it to my building's entrance and I turn to him. 'I'm sorry you got drenched while you were trying to be nice walking me home. It was kind of you.'

'Your standards for basic decency are extraordinarily low,' he replies, swiping away a droplet making its way down my forehead to my eye, so fast I almost miss it. But I feel the contact long after he's put his hand back in his pocket. Before I have the chance to decipher it, out of the corner of my eye I spot something.

'Look,' I say, pointing to the sky, where a red light flashes; the last flight of the day coming into Heathrow. 'Shooting star?'

'You're learning,' he replies, a smile pulling at his cheeks. 'What are you gonna wish for?'

'I can't tell you, obviously.' We both look up and close our eyes. Or at least, I close them for a second, because I soon realise I need them open if I want to stay upright. I take an inadvertent step to the side when I try to right myself. 'Done.'

I realise with sudden clarity just how close we now are. Two Finns swim through my blurred vision, an unreadable expression on both of his faces. But I can see his chest rising and falling, see the bob of his Adam's apple, see the trails of rainwater dripping from his hair down his face.

My eyes refocus and then there's only one Finn, wordlessly waiting, eyes dark and careful, supercharging the air simply by being this close. Static crackles between us and every cell in my body is set alight under his gaze.

There's thunder, too. It rumbles through me; its weighty roar pounding in my ears and drowning out every coherent thought. I don't know if it's the alcohol pulsing through my veins or some other force at play, but one of my hands finds its way around his bicep. My eyes drop to his lips. They're close, too. My breath catches as I incline my head, and I dimly register that he tilts his too, and the static frenzies as we draw closer together, millimetre by torturous millimetre.

But then, the lightning strikes.

'No,' he whispers, warm breath hitting me before the meaning of his word does.

It's amazing what two letters can do to your self esteem, even amidst the stormy depths of intoxication, and I blink a few times and take a startled step backwards.

'Oh.' Nothing more intelligent comes out, and my cheeks flame with embarrassment.

He looks at me, pleading. 'I'm sorry, I just— I don't think it's a good idea right now.'

I try to push the storm clouds away, feigning a brightness I know sounds fake to both of us. 'It's fine, don't worry. *I'm* sorry. That was—

yeah. I'll be okay from here.' I gesture vaguely back the way we came. 'You should go home before the rain starts up again.'

'Are you sure?' His brow furrows from behind his rain-streaked glasses.

'I'm sure. Thanks for walking me. Sorry, I know I already said that.'

He nods, and I'm inside my building before he's even started walking away.

---

I blearily open my eyes and in my half-conscious state conclude that if I don't extract myself from my duvet's sweltering heat within the next three seconds I may actually die. I ungracefully free my desiccated self from the twisted covers before getting out of bed, tripping on a pile of clothes on the floor and stepping out into the great unknown.

'Morning, sunshine!' Josie calls brightly from the sofa, where she's listening to what sounds like a self-help podcast on nurturing healthy habits. When I don't respond, she says, 'Been reminded you're not twenty-one anymore?'

'Get a hobby,' I bite back, and her snort accompanies the rest of my perilous walk to the kitchen. No one has ever been as dehydrated as I am right now. I'm sure of it.

'I didn't hear you come home. Thought it meant the date with the quizzing guy had gone well. Which, I'll be honest, was unexpected, because from what you told me about him, he seemed like a bit of a wet blanket. But maybe he was a dark horse.' After multiple futile attempts to figure out where to press on the handle-less doors, I open the dishwasher instead, grabbing the first vessel I can find to pour myself some water; a mug with "hot" embossed in braille. There's no sound for a while apart from that loud, echoey, breathless gulping that kids do when they come inside for a drink after playing in the garden. Except it's not a child, it's me, rejuvenating my dried-up prune of a body after a night of mixing drinks. I fill up the mug once more and head towards Josie and Rudy on the sofa, where I'm hoping some canine energy will revive me.

'The date?' she prods. I try to stay as still as possible, the comforting feel of Rudy's fur under my hand.

'The date was...' I wrack my brain for details to give her but everything's a blur that I need to reorganise into something that makes sense. 'It wasn't great. He was kind of intense. But I ended up bumping into Finn.' She sits up and the sudden movement makes my hand fly to my stomach, as if that'll help settle it in any way. I notice I'm still wearing my outfit from yesterday, and it feels weird. Almost crispy, like it dried funny. 'He has this list of things he wants to do in London, and going on a boat was one of them. Remember the boat bar by Vauxhall I went to with that guy I was sure secretly worked for MI5? Finn and I went there and hung out for a bit. I have him to thank for my current state.'

Her eyebrows raise a fraction of an inch and she asks, a picture of nonchalance, 'And you stayed out late with just Finn? Again?'

'Is that news?' I reply, at the exact same moment a murky memory of what happened at the end of the night flashes across my brain. The rain, the electricity, and the violent embarrassment when it became apparent we were both reading the situation very differently. Shit. He was being a good friend and I was ready to fall all over him. What *was* that? I need to lie down again. 'I'm going back to bed.'

'But we haven't finished this conversation,' Josie whines, and I can't tell if it's disappointment or glee in her voice, but I'm too hungover to figure it out.

'Have fun finishing it by yourself.' My snappy response doesn't generate the same impact when my feeble voice breaks halfway through.

Desperate to hunker down under my duvet and hide from the consequences of my own actions, I grab my phone from the bedside table to check for notifications—it has a full battery; good to know that even drunk me is technologically dependent enough to put it on charge—and lie down. Between the hangover and the raging carousel of my turbulent thoughts, being horizontal helps.

On my screen is a single text from Finn.

> Alive?

I stare at it for what could be a few moments or ten minutes before replying.

> negative

Three dots appear on my screen straight away, and a beat later a message comes through.

> On a scale of 1-10, how fresh do you feel?

> can the scale be 0-10?

> Sure

> then 0

The three dots appear again, before disappearing and reappearing three more times. Finally, they stop.

> Can we talk about last night?

We probably should talk about it. It's the adult thing to do. I put on my big girl pants and type out my suitably grown-up response.

> nope x

To my unimaginable horror, when a notification for a FaceTime appears on my screen, my clumsy, hungover fingers accept it. Finn's face fills the frame and I pull my duvet up so that only my eyes are visible, peeking out from the bottom of the box. He, on the other hand, looks fresh as a daisy; crisp white t-shirt, hair damp from the shower. Wasn't he drinking as much as me all night? Life isn't fair.

'Why not?' he says straight away, no time for pleasantries, leaning his phone against something on his kitchen counter. I watch him move around to make a coffee, opening cupboards and taking milk from the fridge.

'I'm embarrassed.' My reluctance to admit it coats every syllable.

'Why?' he persists, before muting the microphone as his coffee machine extracts.

I take the time to think of a response. I'm not used to people wanting to get to know me, or me wanting to get to know them. He listened to me and showed me he cared, and I don't have much experience of a good friendship that isn't Josie, so I misinterpreted the signals. *And* I was drunk.

Besides, I can't afford to take risks. I can't tempt fate when it's already given me so much. I refuse to let this set me off course.

He unmutes himself, picking up his phone and mug and bringing them both over to what must be the living area, which gives me a pixellated glimpse at the upper half of his flat as he walks. It occurs to me that seeing Finn in his own space is strangely jarring. Until now, it had never crossed my mind to imagine him existing anywhere other than the work-bucket-list bubble I'd placed him in. Schrödinger's flat, if you will.

'Because,' I begin, choosing my words delicately, 'we're friends. I'd never act like that sober, I promise. I'm not about to start throwing myself all over you at every opportunity.'

A strange expression crosses his face but it's gone before I can decode it, and then he says, 'Okay. Let's just forget about it. But before we do, I just wanted you to know that it wasn't like I didn't— it's not that I don't think you're—' he pauses and a cleft forms between his brows as he tries and fails to come up with an ending to his sentence.

I didn't know he was capable of being this awkward and I can't help but laugh. 'Finn, I was drunk. So were you. Nothing happened. I do things like that when I'm drunk. And worse. It's really not a big deal.'

Because imagine we'd kissed. Imagine we'd done more than kiss. And then imagine still seeing him every day at work. Messy, problematic, difficult.

'Right. I know that. But I want to tell you something. You know I mentioned I'd got a job interview? The one my mum kept trying to call me about? It's for the job in San Francisco.'

My heart seems to skip a beat, but my brain convinces my mouth to say, 'That's amazing. Are you excited?'

At my enthusiasm, his cautious expression is overtaken by the easy smile I'm familiar with. He tells me about how much he wants this job; the company, the role itself, the fact he's only ever been to San Francisco once on a short trip and really liked it but didn't have the chance to explore properly.

Suddenly I'm even more glad he had the sense to pull away last night. I'd almost forgotten he's intending to leave in a few months. And I could've ruined this tenuous friendship we have, all because he flirts with everyone and I was feeling weird and drunk and hormonal.

He finishes talking about everything he wants to do in San Francisco and sips his coffee patiently for a few moments before adding, 'I really like being your friend.'

The comfort of his honesty curls around me, much softer than I expect it to be. And maybe having a screen between us makes me bolder, because I admit, 'I like being your friend too.'

I don't think this thing has been fake since the day we decided to form our strange alliance, however much I've pretended it was. But the air feels heavy, like there's too much static lining the airwaves between us, left over from last night's storm.

I'm grateful when he breaks into a chuckle and says, 'Was that another compliment? I need to start stacking them up. They'll be worth something some day.'

'You deserve it after last night. Hanging out with drunk me is probably the worst thing ever.'

A smile tugs at his mouth when he speaks again, setting his coffee down. 'Don't be so hard on yourself, it's just as bad when you're sober. Like when you're the world's grumpiest barista at seven-thirty in the morning.'

'Kick a woman while she's down, why don't you?'

'And obscenely pessimistic in mundane situations that don't affect you whatsoever.'

'Been holding that in for a while?' I ask, eyes wide, and his phone shakes in his hand as he erupts into laughter. As the sound spills through my speaker, it unlocks something inside me and I can't help but join in. By the time we stop, he takes his glasses off to rub his eyes, and they're still creased at the sides when he looks at me.

'Oh Ava,' he picks up his drink and takes another slow drag, 'there's a lot more that I've been holding in, trust me.'

I don't know what to make of that, so I simply say, 'I miss when you spent your days only being nice to me.'

He analyses me over the top of his mug. 'No, you don't.'

I wiggle under my duvet and sigh in agreement. 'No, I don't.'

# 17

## who knew I was capable of thinking with my head?

### FINN

SHOVELLING A FEW SLICES of toast into my mouth and downing almost a litre of water before I went to bed last night saved me this morning. Thank you, drunk Finn, for being smart.

After I've spoken to Ava and let my heart rate settle, I call my mum on my walk to the leisure centre, letting her congratulate me on my job interview.

'It's still only early in the process,' I say. 'I might not even get it.'

'You will.' There's a pause before she asks, 'Does your dad know?'

'I told him I got an interview but I haven't told him specifically what for yet. Or where.'

Another pause. 'And this is definitely something you want?'

We always gloss over the fact she doesn't like my dad, and for the most part it's not an issue. But I wonder if she's worried that being closer to him will take me figuratively further from her. I'm my dad's only child, so we both know that his attention doesn't have to be split three ways.

'You know I've always wanted to try living in San Francisco,' I tell her, avoiding a pile of fried chicken on the pavement. For years, San Francisco has always felt like a distant dream. Something was holding me back and I could never quite bite the bullet to apply for jobs there until now. Maybe it's because I finally feel like I have enough experience to go for a role that feels *right*. 'The position seems like it was made for me. It was one of those job ads where I could check off every single item on their requirements list and then some.'

'Of course it was, you're so—' her voice is muffled for a moment and I can hear someone else in the room before the sound sharpens again, 'I'm sorry chick, I've just realised I should've left to drop Ali at robotics five minutes ago, can we chat later?'

I push down the heaviness in my chest. 'Yeah, of course. Tell him I say hi.'

The twins have so much going on all the time and she's there for all of it. It makes me feel like it's a good idea to focus on my relationship with my dad for the next few years, knowing she'll be focused on Aisha and Ali for a bit longer.

Just before I slam my locker closed in the changing room, I notice I've received an email from my dad's assistant. He's having a hectic time at work, so I don't expect much direct contact at the moment. I haven't mentioned anything specific about the job yet, but I can't *wait* to tell him I'll be moving closer to him soon, if it all works out.

Now, in the pool, choppy water tumbles around me the way thoughts crash against the inside of my skull and my brain goes somewhere else entirely. To that same place it's been going a lot, recently, any time I'm alone.

It goes to a beautiful woman with a near-constant scowl.

When Ava answered my FaceTime earlier, sleep-deprived and hungover and prettier than anyone should be in that state, I didn't wish I was next to her instead of a screen away.

When I gave her the glass I stole from the bar and her face lit up, I didn't almost blurt out that I felt like I was standing alongside living, breathing moonlight.

And when there was lightning in the air and she was looking at me like I might be able to answer every question she's ever had, if only I closed the distance, I didn't want to kiss her.

Okay. I didn't want to kiss her *like that*, after she'd just shown a vulnerable side of herself, still reeling emotionally from telling me about her brother being sick.

I almost fucked it up last night. Almost.

I think she's beginning to trust me, and I won't jeopardise that. There's also the glaringly obvious fact that she as good as told me that whatever that moment was last night, that almost-something we almost had, was an embarrassing, alcohol-fuelled mistake. So thank god I listened to my brain, especially when other parts of my body were begging for attention.

I was never quite enough for what Léa needed, and I doubt I could be for Ava, either. Even if she *were* looking for something else, I know I won't be around for much longer. I refuse to start things I know I won't finish. The simpler, the cleaner, the better.

What I can get from her as a friend is far more valuable than a drunken night that ends with her never talking to me again. Because I know what she does with the men she hangs out with, and I don't want to be discarded with them.

As much as I tried to push against it, before Ava came along I was beginning to feel the brushes of loneliness, the special kind that only exists in a city like this one. So many people, so many lives, yet you can't quite touch any of them. But since starting the bucket list, London's felt a little more welcoming, a little more familiar, a little more liveable. That's too important to lose.

So I'll stomp out these unnamed emotions, no one will know, and we'll continue exactly as we were. I'm not going to let my feelings make a mess. We started with a handshake and a verbal contract, and I can't let it get any more complicated than that.

# 18

## the lady doth protest too much, methinks

### AVA

Drunken encounter very much ignored, Finn and I get into a loose routine with his bucket list. Some weeks we squeeze in two items, other weeks one of us is too busy and we have to skip. We hit a pop-up vintage shop in Dalston, have a pint at London's oldest pub, and I reluctantly agree to take Boris bikes out for the shortest possible ride around West London. Apparently you can, in fact, forget how to ride a bike.

One day we go to Greenwich with Julien and Finn crosses off two items in one fell swoop. First, we visit the Prime Meridian, where Finn takes an impossible amount of joy standing on both sides of the line and being in both the eastern and western hemispheres at once.

Then I leave the pair of them to it, letting Julien be Finn's companion when they climb the O2. Heights haven't agreed with me since a particularly painful experience when Max and I were seven involving a wall and, soon after, the pavement.

As I'm walking back to the flat from the station, Finn texts me a selfie from the top, eyes scrunched up in a smile with the satisfaction of someone who's just summited Everest. His joy is infectious and I have to make a conscious effort to press my lips together so that I don't turn into the idiot grinning at her phone. That is *categorically* not the kind of person I am.

This is swiftly followed by a photo of Julien, who looks more like a model than anyone should in this situation, and an accompanying text.

> My favourite view <3 <3 <3

> get a room

> You would have loved this

> let's not lie to each other Finn

> Fine fine

> I just wanted you to be jealous

> impossible

> Julien's upset he couldn't be your knight in shining armour

> He was hoping to protect you from the big scary heights

> Your height knight

> unless Julien has a substantial supply of Xanax he may need to put his chivalric dreams aside

He sends a photo of the actual view then. London sparkles under the sun, the Thames a ribbon of pale grey running through the city, the few skyscrapers poking out of the ground like they were dropped there by aliens. I'm not mad I skipped out; I'd have been embarrassing up there, and I have a stoic reputation to maintain. But my heart swells just seeing the whole city from above. The more time I've spent exploring it recently, the more it's felt like the place I could build something. The place I can really live.

I swipe back through the photos and land on the selfie Finn sent, and I'm sure it's just some weird secondhand vertigo that makes my stomach fill with butterflies.

---

Somehow, even as we cross items off the list, I notice it isn't getting any smaller.

'This is new,' I'd said to him as I was closing up yesterday, half putting things away, half looking at the list.

He grinned and in that moment I realised he was definitely one of those kids at school who the teacher said had "a lot of potential, but distracts others". 'I know, I know, but I've had two dreams about bagels recently and then someone mentioned that shop in the office yesterday and it just felt like fate. I have to believe the universe was sending me a sign.'

So, this morning we squeezed in a visit to the Beigel Bake Brick Lane Bakery before I had to be at work. As expected, Finn made appreciative noises with every bite of his bagel, and as expected, I had to politely ask him to shut the fuck up.

Somehow, just hours later, Finn's ready for another item already. 'What about *eat at a popular local restaurant?* When can we do that?'

'I have an idea. There's this restaurant in Covent Garden I went to once when I third-wheeled a date with Josie and Alina. But we need to wait for a day I'm on an early finish, because if you don't get there early enough you end up at the shitty tables crammed against the wall. You want the window booths. They look across the whole piazza, which means you can people-watch.' A new customer steps through the door and I say in a low voice, 'And you're nosy as fuck, so you'd love it.'

His eyes light up in confirmation, before he steps aside to let the other customer place his order; a young guy who's barely out of uni and always shifts on his feet while he's talking to me.

Unfortunately for him, after I've pushed his drink across the counter, he stumbles over his words; starting to say "lovely", but switching to "thank you" at the last second. So, as he picks up his cup, he gives me an enthusiastic, 'Love you,' instead.

His eyes widen and he goes beet red before scurrying away to the straws, and I press my lips together in a futile attempt to hold back a laugh.

Finn approaches the till again, shaking his head. 'Poor guy. But I don't blame him, you look good today.'

'Shut up,' I say, fully aware the ponytail I've been sporting for hours is very much askew.

'What?' He narrows his eyes and I realise he's being serious. Why do men have no idea what looks good? 'I'm not in the business of denying myself the simple pleasure of telling someone they look pretty. Watch.' He calls over to the other end of the counter, 'Mateo, te ves bien!'

My coworker turns his face to hide a smile and a playful glint reflects in Finn's eyes when he looks back at me. This man is a menace. It's no wonder my alcohol-soaked brain thought he was into me the other week.

'Okay, well, you're not allowed to say stuff like that to me.' I don't need any more ammunition for the next time we're drunk in each other's presence.

'Your ever-increasing list of arbitrary rules is tiring me out.'

'Your ever-increasing presence in my place of work is tiring me out, so I guess we're even.'

This isn't entirely true. I'd never admit it to him, but I've come to relish the way he breaks up the monotony of my time. He's in the shop most days, sometimes in and out for a quick drink, but more often staying for hours, occasionally until closing. He claims it's because the WiFi's fast and the LoFi playlist is soothing, but I imagine it's because I've started to slip him free snacks and drinks.

But it's been kind of nice having someone around who doesn't have ulterior motives. We set out our agreement and we're following it. I know his time in London is temporary, so maybe that's why I care less about making a good impression. Maybe it's because nothing seems to get under his skin, and I'm beginning to wonder if anything ever could.

---

'I quit.'

My head snaps up to find Mateo facing Carl; hands on his hips, power pose very much in play. I want to eavesdrop, but a customer comes in and completely ruins my fun. By the time I've finished serving them, Mateo's back behind the counter with me, sharing the details. Predictably, Carl has left the shop to supposedly run an errand.

'What's the plan?' I ask, refilling the coffee machine with beans and already dreading the fact I'm probably going to work extra hours while they find a replacement for him.

'I leave at the end of this week. You know that really hot day when it was super busy and we had all the extra customers? It made me want to pull all of my hair out. So I found something better.' I'm impressed by how quickly he got the ball rolling. 'I'm twenty-three; I'm too young to feel so angry at work all the time.'

All I can do is laugh. He might have a point.

He wipes the counter and continues, 'You know, I'll miss working with you. Especially when you say things to customers and they don't know if you're joking or serious. It's always funny to me. I hope my new coworkers play angry music on the speakers at the end of the day when the manager leaves, too.'

I blink a few times, taken aback. We've never chatted much, just worked alongside each other in efficient, civil harmony. I never really thought we took any notice of each other. I wonder if I could've made more of an effort, if perhaps we could've been friends. 'Oh. Thanks. I'll miss working with you too.'

He shrugs. 'I hope they find a good person to work with you. Or that you find a better job than this.' He lifts his head to the door, which has just opened with a new customer. 'It's your friend with the dog. We can swap lunch breaks and you can take yours if you want to talk with her.'

He goes to clean a table with a smile. If I'm not mistaken, he's in a better mood than I've ever seen him. Amazing what leaving a job you don't like can do.

'What are you doing here?' I ask as Josie approaches, Rudy leading her on the usual route to the counter. 'You had a talk nearby?'

She's looking peak Josie today; a seventies-print satin shirt tucked into a pair of high-waisted trousers, half her hair pulled back with a claw clip. She's even given Rudy a matching bandana in the same pattern as her top.

'A meeting, but not yet, it's in an hour or so. I thought I'd drop in and see my favourite flatmate.' She reaches down to Rudy's level and whispers, 'Don't worry, she doesn't need to know the truth.'

'Well, speaking of favourites, your table's taken, but the one to the right of it is empty. I'll bring your drink over in a sec.'

---

Ten minutes later we're settled at the table, me finishing off my panini and Josie dabbing her finger on her plate to pick up any remaining pastry crumbs from her cinnamon swirl.

'My co-worker Mateo is leaving.' I lean forward and lower my voice in case someone happens to be listening.

'Was there drama? Please tell me there was drama.'

'Kind of. He basically told Carl he's a shit manager. Which is entirely true. I'm just really hoping whoever they bring in to replace him is decent, because I'm gonna end up having to train them.'

'But you're good at that stuff,' she says, finally establishing there are no crumbs left on her plate to pick at. I huff and she says, 'You are! You're good at explaining things, and you're always really patient whenever you're showing me how to do something new. Which, to be quite frank, is completely at odds with the rest of your personality. *Patient* isn't a word I would expect to use to describe you.'

'Yeah, but you're a competent person. It's not a chore to teach you.'

'What about when you let those kids from our building practise their face paint on you?'

'I honestly just think kids flock to me because they know that they kind of freak me out.'

'Or that time I was in here and you left me for half an hour to talk an elderly customer through emojis?' She drops her voice at the end in case he's nearby.

I'd forgotten about that day. I'd shown Stan-with-the-routine how to use emojis, taught him what some of them meant, explained when it was and wasn't appropriate to use them, all because a little piece of my stubborn heart had throbbed when he'd told me he wanted to seem cool when he texted his grandchildren. Josie continues, 'I'm just saying, you're good at that kind of thing. Explaining stuff to others.'

I've never thought about it before but I suppose I see where she's coming from. I do kind of enjoy the satisfaction when someone picks up something I've taught them. The tiniest bud of an idea takes root in my head, but I don't know what to do with it right now, so I box it up alongside the rest of my fanciful notions. 'Yeah, maybe you're right.'

'As I usually am.' She starts to yawn, covering her mouth with her hand as she does, always polite.

'You've been working too hard.' I take a sip of my drink and watch as she bites down a second yawn.

'It doesn't feel like work, that's the problem. Consulting, doing talks, sitting on panels, *that* feels like a job. Sometimes it's fun, sometimes it's draining. But it's what pays the bills. Doing this work at the gallery is a passion project. I mean, they pay me actual *pennies,* but somehow it's the most fulfilling.'

'I'm not just saying this because you're my best friend, but I really can't wait to see what you've been working on.'

'Wait!' she exclaims, making both Rudy and me jump. 'I completely forgot to tell you, we found out yesterday that we've been approved for the grant for the central piece in our exhibition.'

'Seriously? The installation you came up with about the seasons?'

'Yep. My little baby.' She grins, eyes bright, the nerves she had when she first mentioned it seemingly out the window.

'Josie, that's amazing!' I lean forward and ask, 'I know you told me not to ask you for details, but how's it going?'

'If you find me wailing on the sofa one day, it's gone terribly wrong. But for now, it's looking good, and we're set to be ready with it way before the opening in December. I reckon it'll be your favourite part of the whole exhibition, actually.' Her smile drops and she narrows her eyes. 'But don't ask me any more about it. I'm bad at secrets.'

'My lips are sealed.'

'Speaking of lips—'

'Terrible segue.'

'Thank you.' She takes a single, dainty sip of her drink. 'How are things with Finn?'

'There are no lips involved when it comes to Finn.'

I should've known she wouldn't let this go. Truthfully, I've done pretty well at reconfiguring my brain back to how it used to be before I drunkenly propositioned him the other week. Everything seems normal. If anything, he's been more irritatingly unflappable than ever, pushing back against every borderline-disrespectful thing I say with nothing but a cheerful quip and a smirk. 'And there never will be any lips involved, for the record. That's not what's going on here.'

'I believe you.'

'It's not like that at all. I have a separate cohort of men for that kind of thing. Don't pull that face. You're thinking the lady doth protest too much. But you're wrong, because the lady doth protest a perfectly adequate amount for the situation in question, which, as it stands, requires a certain level of protestation.'

Josie doesn't move a muscle during my monologue. You know, in hindsight, maybe the lady doth actually protest too much.

She nods slowly. 'I said I believe you.'

'You do?' I rein in my surprise. 'I mean, yeah, obviously you do. Because it's true.' It's true. It *is*.

'Sure. As long as he's being a good friend to you?' She tilts her head, the worry I've been scared of etched in the crease between her eyes.

I sigh, remembering how he walked me home in the rain, how he took me to the Barbican when I was grumpy and stressed, how he tried to set me up for an internship that sent me into a moderately-sized spiral, but was overall a very nice thing of him to do. 'Yeah. He's being a really good friend, to be honest.' Another reason I'm glad nothing ended up happening that night. Sure, sometimes my brain fills with a what-if or two, but I've always had an overactive imagination.

'Good. He'd have me to answer to if he was being a dick.' My heart pangs at her protectiveness. 'You're spending more time with him than me recently. I'm sorry I'm working so much. I'm being kind of a shit flatmate. A shit friend, even.'

While I'd definitely envisioned a lot more singalongs and movie marathons in the flat this year, I'm not going to tell Josie that. I don't want her to feel like she's disappointed me in any way. I'm not sure she could disappoint me if she tried.

'You could never be a shit friend. You've been working hard being such a *girlboss*.' My mouth twitches at the last word.

'Please never say that again.'

'What, girlboss? But you're such a girlboss. The girliest girlboss.'

'I hate it so much. Like, it's a visceral thing, I feel it in my bones.' I can't hold my laughter in, and she eventually joins, swirling her straw around her cup and shaking her head. 'You're ridiculous. I hope more people get to see the Ava I know. She's my favourite.'

If you'd asked me six months ago if anyone but Max and Josie would ever know this version of me, it would've been a vehement no. But now, something's loosened in my chest, and I'm not so sure it's the same answer.

'I'm working on it.'

# 19

## someone remind me to go to the opticians

### FINN

'I'VE LOOKED THIS OVER a hundred times and I feel like I'm going in circles,' I say to Julien.

We're sitting on stools at one of the high tables in the common area of the office and I'm decidedly uncomfortable. It's no City Roast armchair, that's for sure.

'You need to step away from it for a bit. You can't make it any better if you're staring at it from three centimetres away. Speaking of which, you need new glasses. You're always squinting.'

He's probably right. I've been staring at this document for hours, fuelled by gross coffee after gross coffee.

'Finn, if it's meant to happen, it'll happen. You've still got a couple of weeks to sort it. You might have one of those faces that looks like it clocked out in primary school, but you're deceptively smart.'

'You're making me blush.'

'You're welcome.' He flashes a smile. 'They'll hire you. You've got this.'

'I'll look at it again later.' I snap my laptop closed, giving up. 'You know, I wasn't even sure if I was going to apply at first. But I know I'd be good at it, and it just seemed like something I couldn't pass up, you know?'

'Yeah.' He looks shifty, as if he's considering his words. 'And it's got nothing to do with the fact it's the same company your dad works at?'

'It's a *branch* of the same company. Which is a massive organisation. So no, it's not related.' I draw my finger through the ring of coffee my cup has left on the table and am glad for the tan from my aforementioned father that covers the heat rising to my cheeks.

'Okay,' Julien nods and starts peeling a clementine he seems to have appropriated from thin air. 'Why, um, are you here, by the way?'

'What do you mean?'

'You're just usually in the coffee shop over the road. I feel like I never see you in the office anymore.'

I'm not entirely sure why I've avoided City Roast today. I think I wanted to get this work done away from Ava. It's not that she's intentionally distracting, I just sometimes find myself spending hours there and writing about five words. And maybe a tiny part of me doesn't want her to see me and ask questions about what I'm working on.

'I was in the mood for a change of scenery.' I lean back and nearly give myself a heart attack when the stool goes off balance, catching myself just in time. 'But the coffee here is shit. Really, really bad.'

'Oh yeah I know, it's hideous. But it's also free, so...'

'If Ava's in a good mood—which, fine, isn't often—she gives me free coffee. So it's not as ba— oh!' My gaze lands on someone in the lobby and I slide off my stool, much to the confusion of Julien. 'Sorry, I'll be right back.'

I wind through the tables to where a red-haired woman and her dog have just stepped out of an elevator. 'Josie?' I call out her name tentatively as I get closer and she looks in my direction, expression unreadable. 'Hey, sorry, I don't know if you remember me. It's Finn, Ava's friend. We met in the coffee shop a little while back?'

'Oh my god, Finn, hey!' Her face splits into a smile and she stretches her arms out for a hug. Clearly she and Ava have very different ideas about personal space. 'Of course I remember you. You're coming to the housewarming.'

I'd almost forgotten about the party, even though it was the basis of getting to know Ava in the first place. It feels like a lifetime ago. 'I've been warming up my vocal cords for karaoke. I'll be ready for any and all requests.'

'As you should be. You know, we'll probably need to tag-team convincing Ava to sing, but once she's got a few drinks down her, that's it. Performances you'll never forget, I promise.'

Josie rolls up one of her cuffs that's unfolded; a move I am all too familiar with. I can't help but point it out. 'Your outfit is really fucking cool, by the way. Is that weird to say?'

'Not weird at all, you clearly have good taste. In all areas.' She leans a hand on one of her hips before she speaks again. 'She talks about you a lot, you know.'

'Oh yeah?' I feel something squeeze in my chest and try to ignore it. I'm distinctly aware that Ava will despise the fact Josie has told me this. 'Good things?'

Something shimmers in her eyes. I think it's mischief. 'Mostly.'

I can't tell for sure, and I don't know what battle I'm fighting yet, but I think I may have an ally in Josie.

'Do you work in this building? Why have I never seen you around?'

She blinks a few times and the glimmer disappears. She tucks her hair behind her ears and says, 'No, I just had a meeting on the top floor with an accountancy firm to work on their equality, diversity and inclusion strategy. On my side, I consult mostly on disability and accessibility, LGBTQ+ matters, stuff like that. Ways to make companies do more than the bare minimum for minority groups.'

'Did it go well?'

She shrugs. 'I think so. It's hard to tell. Whether they decide to do anything with what I told them is up in the air. We'll see, I guess.' She expels a quick breath, then says, 'It was lovely chatting with you Finn, but I've got another meeting in a bit so I should probably shoot off.'

'I can walk you out if you want?'

'I'm alright, but thanks. I'll see you at the party.'

'Can't wait.' She walks away and I wander back to Julien, who's standing by the table with his stuff packed away, scrolling on his phone. 'Sorry, I spotted Ava's flatmate and just wanted to say hi. Are you heading off?'

'No worries. And yeah, I've got to head back upstairs. How was she? The flatmate?'

'No worries. And yeah, I've got to head back upstairs. How was she? The flatmate?'

'Fine, I think. I have a feeling I might be in her good books.'

I slide my laptop into my bag and we wind through tables back towards the lobby.

Julien looks at me shrewdly. 'I'm going to join you in the coffee shop this week. I need to decide if I should stage an intervention.'

'What's that supposed to mean?'

He shakes his head with a chuckle and steps into the waiting elevator without answering, before my feet take me across the road.

## A COLLISION OF STARS

True to his word, Julien starts joining me at City Roast, and it's as if I'm being watched over by a particularly suave bodyguard. He's managed to talk his boss into letting him work here, under the stipulation he bring a coffee back for him whenever he goes back to the office.

Some days, he doesn't let me go up to the till to order, and I can't even complain, because then he'd know I'm still at the mercy of that tiny *something* I swore to get rid of. The thing that somehow lets me know where Ava is without looking. The thing that feeds on every morsel of attention she gives me, as platonic as it may be. But it's surely only a matter of time before it fades. And if it doesn't, I'm leaving in a few months anyway, so distance will do the job for me.

Today is one of those days, and Julien's leaning against the counter as he orders, his perfectly tailored back to me. I don't need to see his face to know he's quirking a half smile, molten eyes switched on. Likewise, I don't need to see Ava's to know she is entirely unaffected by this.

I type some nonsense on my computer when I notice him coming back to the table with our coffees.

'She's tough to crack,' Julien says, settling into his chair and opening his laptop. I bite down a laugh. He's never had issues charming anyone. When he cranks it up to full volume, it rolls off him in waves and I almost want to propose to him myself. So it never fails to make me laugh when someone resists him.

'Maybe she sees right through you. You just want free drinks and she's decided to make you work for them.' My mouth presses into a smirk. 'And you could've avoided having to pay full price, had you let me go up instead.'

'Nope.' He wiggles his finger from side to side. 'You're not off the hook. I don't trust your motives. You don't think I've noticed you're typing random shit on your laptop?'

I flip him off and slide down lower in my chair, making a concerted effort this time to type real words. I'm successful for a while, until my phone pings with a text.

> tell Julien he's trying too hard

I look up and meet Ava's eyes briefly over the counter as she slides her phone into her back pocket, the echo of a smile on her face as her manager and a young woman approach her. It sends my heart into a flurry.

It's at this moment that Julien punches me on the arm.

'What was that for?' I clutch where he hit me. The guy has force, I'll give him that.

'*Putain*,' he curses under his breath. 'I was right. Do you know what you're doing?'

I wave a hand in the vicinity of my laptop. 'Putting together a deck?'

'With Ava.'

At the mention of her name, I have to forcibly keep my eyes from flicking over to her. I'm leaving. She doesn't see me that way. Neither of us is looking for a relationship. There's nothing else to it. 'We're friends.'

'And I'm Michael Bublé.'

'Get back in the freezer, Mike, it's far too early in the year for you to be here.'

He ignores me. 'I just hope you've thought this through.'

'There's nothing to think through.' I look back at my screen, wondering if I'll be able to find a believable answer in there. We had a moment a few weeks ago when we were drunk, but that's all it was. It wasn't even a moment. It was an *almost*-moment.

'Tell that to the grin on your face.' He switches to French, an old habit from when we were kids and trying to talk secretly at school. His voice is low when he says, 'I don't want you to get hurt. From what you've told me, I'm pretty sure she eats men like you for breakfast.'

'And?' My voice raises slightly and the person at the table next to us glances in our direction. I don't know why I'm so protective all of a sudden. It's not like me to get so defensive, and it's not like he's wrong.

'And even if she didn't, you never stay in one place for long. Between the two of you, that's not exactly a healthy recipe.'

'Which is why it's great we are solely platonic.' I'm trying to keep my tone light, but an unfamiliar wave of annoyance passes through me. 'Why are you being so weird about seeing me having fun?'

'Hey, that's not fair. I love seeing you happy, you know I do. I want that more than anything. But there's more.' Concern weaves across his face, into the downturn of his mouth, along the frown lines on his forehead. 'You're filling your days with her. I've seen you like this before.'

I meet his eyes as the defensiveness pushes its way out of every pore. 'She's nothing like Léa. We're nothing like me and Léa.'

He expels a long breath. 'Does she know you're leaving?'

'She knows it's on the cards.' But there's a twinge in my gut, and taking a drag of coffee does nothing to appease the churning there. I told her the other day I'd got to the second stage of the process for the San Francisco job and I couldn't quite figure out what she was thinking. I was excited to tell her, she was excited for me, and yet, it felt like both of us were lying somehow. That confusion hasn't really settled since. 'We're friends, like I said. And I'm not going to be the one to destroy that.'

Julien and I go back to our work but I can tell we're both still chewing over the conversation.

Even if I wanted to disrupt our friendship, Ava as good as told me she'd never come near me sober. And since she told me that, I feel like I've done a good job of pushing any potential feelings down. At least outwardly.

After a minute or two, Julien clears his throat and his lips turn up in a rueful smile. 'For the record, friends don't typically look at friends like they're the brightest star in the sky. But maybe I'm old-fashioned.'

I don't really know what to say to that.

By the time I've finished making my presentation—a surprisingly productive afternoon—Julien's packing away his stuff.

'Finn, I'm sorry if I sounded like a dick earlier. I like her, and I like that you're friends.' He nudges me with his elbow. 'It's about time someone else shared the burden of your undying affection.'

'Oh, I get it now.' I cross my arms. 'You were just jealous of the fact someone might come and steal your crown.'

He flings his head back and laughs. While everything else about him is controlled and smooth, his laugh is all-encompassing, so loud it always sounds like there are two of him in a room.

'Ava and I may share many notable characteristics,' he begins, nodding towards her cleaning a table in the far corner, 'as in, we're both tall, hot and have a sadistic interest in making fun of you. But if it comes down to a case of who knows you better, there's no contest. I can't be jealous of someone who's not even my competition.'

'Exactly,' I close my laptop too, pointedly ignoring the fact he called her hot and instead thinking about how we've hardly spent any time together outside of work recently. 'Are you free tonight? That Senegalese pop-up you like is back in Brixton Market.'

He closes his eyes and hums his approval. 'For you, I'm always free.' I raise an eyebrow and he amends, 'Fine, that's not true. But for Little Baobab, I definitely am.'

# 20

## there's nothing sexier than a good piece of masonry

### AVA

JUST AS I FINISH serving another customer, soy-latte-Samantha stops by the counter. She talked my ear off about her daughter for five minutes straight earlier and I brace myself for another onslaught of information.

Instead, she asks, 'Could you do me a favour?'

'I can try.' I'm careful not to promise anything.

'I was hoping I'd spot that young man Finn who's often in here today, because I'm going away for a few weeks tomorrow so won't see him. I've mentioned Alexandra to him before and keep forgetting to give him her number. Would you be able to give this to him the next time he comes in?'

She hands me a slip of paper and I stare at it between us. I've never explicitly asked Finn if he's dating, and he's never brought it up. He, like a well-adjusted person, probably keeps his exploits to himself. I'm not entitled to know everything about him. God knows he hears enough about my own dating life to make up for it.

Still, I say, 'I'm not sure if he's single.'

Samantha has a strange expression on her face and says, 'I'd really appreciate if you could give it to him. He knows I was going to put them in contact.'

I weigh up what to do with it. Maybe he is dating, and from what I've heard about Alexandra, they'd probably be a good match.

There's a pause, but eventually I say, 'Sure. I'll give it to him.'

After she leaves, the paper sits untouched for an hour, until I'm overcome by the unexpected, inexplicable urge to get rid of it. So I throw it away.

Unfortunately, I regret this almost immediately. Which is why, when the front door opens, I'm sure whoever just walked into City Roast will be bewildered to find me elbows deep in the bin.

'Am I interrupting something?'

Finn appears on the other side of the counter, eyes showing all the amusement his twitching mouth is struggling to contain.

I straighten, my hair dishevelled, coffee grounds as far as the eye can see, but in my hand is my prize: a crumpled piece of paper.

'This is for you,' I say, handing it to him.

He takes it gingerly between his thumb and index finger. 'Fantastic,' he says flatly, 'just what I've always wanted.'

I seize it back, wiping it on my apron to get rid of most of the gunk before placing it back in his outstretched hand. 'Soy-la— uh, Samantha gave me her number to give to you.'

'But I already have Sam's number.' This is not surprising in the slightest, though it does make me wonder why she couldn't have just texted him her daughter's contact info.

'Her daughter. She gave me her daughter's number to give to you. So you can ask her out.' I don't know what I expected from Finn. Maybe a heartfelt thank you, or some sort of celebration. I didn't expect him to look at me like I've just suggested he chop off his own hand. 'You never know, she could be the love of your life.'

'I feel that's unlikely,' he says, clearing his throat. 'What do we know about her?'

This is my time to shine. I talk to him over the sound of the coffee grinding. 'She's called Alexandra, Alex for short, is twenty-five, got an economics degree at Durham, did a master's in marketing at LSE, and now lives in Maida Vale.'

'Not much, then.'

'She's also an equestrian.'

'My favourite star sign.'

I glare at him as I tamp the coffee grounds in their basket. 'She travels the world competing and has won tons of awards. Samantha's very proud of her. I think you'd work well with someone who travels a lot.'

It's true. If he's going to be with anyone, it'll be someone who won't make him feel claustrophobic and glued to one place. Especially knowing he's further into the process of getting the San Francisco job.

'Sure. But no thanks,' he replies with a shrug.

My hands freeze. 'What do you mean, "no thanks"?'

'There's really only one definition, Ava.' He drops his voice to a whisper. 'No.'

'But I saw photos. She's beautiful *and* talented. She sounds kind of incredible.'

'What do you want me to say? I'm sure she's great. And I'll take her number, but I'm not going on a date with her.'

'Why not?' I'm not entirely sure why this comes out as a whine. Or why I'm so desperate for him to go on this date. I brush loose hair away from my face and wait for him to explain.

'Don't want to,' he says simply. He reaches towards me, but at the last second closes his fist and pulls back, murmuring, 'You have coffee grounds on your cheek.'

I guess my brain must've prepared itself for the touch of his fingertips against my skin, because I feel a little like I just missed a step. I rub the back of my hand across my face and steel myself to ask, 'But why not? You've already got enough women on the cards?'

His hand flexes on the counter, and for the briefest moment, something like frustration passes across his face, a muscle pulsing in his jaw. 'Sure. Something like that.' And then he exhales and looks askance between the bin and the dirty paper. 'Why was the paper in the bin?'

'Oh,' I say, scooping ice into a cup. 'I dropped it in there. By accident. Not intentionally.'

'Right. Well, I appreciate the effort. Thanks for diving through coffee grounds for me.' He quirks an eyebrow. 'I probably could've just asked Samantha for the number the next time I saw her, though.'

I hope he feels the fire emanating from my eyes. 'To make up for plunging into the bin for you, you should go out with her.'

He blinks slowly. 'Have you always been this pushy?'

'Have you only just noticed?'

The cogs turn in his brain, and then one half of his mouth pulls up. 'I'll go out with Alex-the-twenty-five-year-old-equestrian-who-lives-in-Maida-Vale on one condition.' I narrow my eyes and he continues, 'You agree to go out with someone of my choosing.'

My instinct is to say no, maybe this is all it'll take to make me feel normal again, to quieten the weird emotions that have been swirling around my chest cavity. Maybe it'll take my mind off the what-ifs. 'Deal.'

'I'm so sorry I'm late,' Henry says to me as we cross the threshold of the restaurant. He's the lanky blonde from the office Finn set me up with, and while blonde men are decidedly hit or miss for me, at least he's cute. Perhaps dating apps are where I've been going wrong and this whole time I should've been set up with mutual acquaintances. I'm hoping the evening ends the way I want it to, in large part so I can rub it in Finn's face.

The clatter of cutlery against plates and the low hum of chatter greets us just before the Maître d' does. 'Table for two?'

I'd initially set this restaurant aside for a bucket list item, but when Henry proposed we meet in Covent Garden after work, I panicked and suggested it. It's already rammed in here, as I expected it would be, but I'm holding out for a miracle. 'Please. Are there any window booths available?'

A wall of windows stretches to the left, with comfy booths perfect for people-watching, warm lightbulbs swinging over every table. To our right is a line of small tables and rickety chairs against the wall, so close together I'm concerned they defy fire safety regulations.

Her face twists in apology. 'I'm sorry, we're really busy tonight. We have one table free over there, otherwise it'll be at least an hour's wait for a booth, likely closer to two.'

She points to the single free table closest to the door and I say weakly, 'That table will be great.'

There's a tint on the windows, so the restaurant is darker than it should be, and we cast an eye over the menu by the light of our table's single tea light. At least it's romantic, I guess. Might get us in the mood.

Romance aside, I give up squinting and use my phone's torch to see properly. By the time I turn the flashlight off I look up to find Henry staring at me with an expression I can't quite read. It's either confusion or lust. I lean into the latter; that's what I'm here for, after all.

'What are you thinking?' I ask, nodding towards the menu and shifting onto one elbow, chin in my hand. The move doesn't *not* emphasise my chest.

'Not sure yet.' He licks his lips but avoids dropping his gaze. 'I just know I need to save room for dessert.'

'See anything you like?' I still can't tell what's going on in his head. I lower my voice, 'Something that isn't on the menu?'

Cornier lines have worked on men in the past, so I don't even have it in me to cringe. I'd argue a lot of men are boring enough that they *enjoy* these lines.

He purses his lips and gestures to the leather booklet open on the table. 'The main menu looks pretty good, to be honest.' He points at something on the page and his eyes light up. 'There's baklava.'

---

I soon realise Henry and I are not compatible, and just as quickly begin to wonder if Finn set us up as some kind of joke. And yet, I'm determined to stick it out, out of spite.

'And it was funny because of the reputation he has for being a player,' Henry says with a chuckle, graciously explaining the punchline of my own funny story back to me.

Someone leaves the restaurant and, for the millionth time this evening, the door sticks, noise and air from outside flooding in. Neither Henry nor I are quite close enough to shut it without getting up, so it invariably stays wedged open for longer than necessary.

I flag the waiter down for another drink, hoping it'll make me less irritable, but just as they walk away, I hear a noise that sends me reeling even further. A laugh I know all too well.

My head whips around to find the source, and then I spot him. Sprawled across the window booth in the corner is Finn O'Callaghan, wearing the same blue shirt he wore the night we went to Tamesis Dock. When the woman he's with leans forward as she laughs, hand slapping the table, I see it's Alex the equestrian. For some inexplicable reason, rage bubbles underneath my skin.

And after hearing his laugh once, I can't unhear it. He and Alex are having a wonderful time apparently, while I'm stuck with Henry, who's taken to explaining the merits of stone masonry over brick walls for the second time this evening. Every time I think we've found common ground, he says something else I either don't understand or have no interest in. But I'd be able to pay much better attention if I weren't hearing that fucking *noise* every ten seconds.

As time progresses, the annoyance threatens to boil over. How could Finn choose someone so bad for me when I found him someone he's actually having a good time with?

It's not until Henry's most surprising proclamation of the night that I realise I *need* to talk to Finn. So when Finn stands up to go to the bathroom, I follow thirty seconds later and wait in the corridor for him, tapping my fingers against my leg to a frenetic beat. When he comes back through the door, dragging a hand through his hair, he barely has time to breathe before I've backed him against the wall.

'This is entirely your fault,' I grit out, no more than two feet between us.

His eyebrows raise in aggravating amusement, eyes just the right side of tipsy. 'Nice to see you too, Ava Monroe. What a delightful coincidence.'

He doesn't seem surprised to see me. He must've already noticed I was here. 'Of all the restaurants in London you're here at the same one as me, at exactly the same time I am?'

'I'd heard good things about this place.' The corridor's low-lit, but there's enough light to see he's enjoying this reaction from me.

'I *told* you about this restaurant. And when to come.'

'And you're annoyed I... listened to you?' He folds his arms and leans back just slightly, appraising me with the kind of languid look that would make weaker women than me blush. To clarify; not me.

'You need to leave. It's not fair. You're...' I pull my eyes away from his arms, because he's quite obviously folded them to make them look better in that stupid blue shirt. 'You're distracting me.'

He barks out a laugh. 'Says the person keeping me away from my table by surprise-attacking me on my way out of the bathroom.'

'I'm distracted by how obnoxiously loud your laugh is. I can hear it from all the way over by the door.'

'Oh, you're sitting by the door?' His face fills with mock pity, eyebrows drawing together, lips moving into a pout. 'You should try the window booths, they're great.'

If looks could kill, he'd be worm food by now. 'If I have to hear you roar with laughter one more time I'm going to—'

'To what?' That stupid telltale mouth twitch. He drops his voice, 'If I didn't know better, I'd think you were jealous.'

'Why would I be jealous?'

He watches me steadily. 'You tell me.'

Fuck, he's right. Maybe I am jealous. Jealous he's having a good time. Not jealous of anything else. *Definitely* not of Alex the equestrian. Still, the air feels different in this hallway, somehow thicker and lighter at the same time, and it's making it difficult for me to fully catch my breath.

'Dinner with Henry is going well, I take it?' he asks. His biceps flex when he tightens his folded arms. 'I thought you'd like him. He looks like Milo from *Atlantis*, and I know you have a penchant for male cartoon characters.'

'He's lovely.'

'Agreed. A bit eccentric, but lovely.'

My eyes are slits. I can barely see but I'm hoping I at least look menacing. 'Eccentric is one word for it. Do you know what he just told me?'

'No?'

'Guess.'

He frowns. 'That's... Ava, that's quite a broad question.'

'Fucking guess.' I'm about four seconds from stomping on his head, and I'm wearing my Docs tonight, so I really feel like I could do some damage.

He looks at me, from my shoulders down to my toes, slow and deliberate, and my skin flushes under his gaze. 'He told you he likes your outfit?'

'No,' the frustration rises, a rumble in my stomach threatening to erupt into a growl, 'guess again.'

His eyes glint in the flickering light from the bulb above our heads. 'That blue biros are better than black biros?'

'No. But they are.'

'They absolutely are not.'

Someone comes out of the bathroom door behind me and I step closer to Finn to give them space. Neither of us moves after they've passed. Blood rushes to my head and my jaw clenches in determination to win this standoff. 'Try again.'

'He told you he believed Gareth Gates should've been crowned the winner of Pop Idol in 2002, not Will Young?'

'That,' I exhale through my nose as slowly as I can, that irritatingly perfect curl of his shifting on his forehead with my breath, 'was arguably too niche.'

'I've been spending too much time with you.'

'I know *that*.'

The glee in his eyes is unmistakable. 'Come on, the suspense is killing me. What did he tell you?'

'You are an insufferable man.' I heave a sigh. 'He just informed me of the reason his last relationship ended. Said he cheated on his ex-girlfriend. Do you know who his ex-girlfriend was?'

'You keep asking me questions that I have no way of knowing the answer to.'

'The Berlin fucking Wall, Finn,' I groan. 'A wall. He regularly took trips to Germany to see her. It.'

'So he's a history buff. Nice.' I was expecting at least a modicum of surprise at this reveal but his expression is entirely unchanged, arms still folded against his chest.

'He emotionally cheated on her with Hadrian's Wall.'

'The Ancient Roman one? That's a MILF of a wall, to be fair.'

His ease makes me want to scream. Maybe he already knew this about Henry. Or maybe he's calm because I set him up with someone who could at least like him back. The man Finn set me up with isn't even into *people*. 'How are you so unfazed by this information?'

'You're being very judgemental, did you know? To each his own.' His tone is flat, but when he shifts his weight and moves an inch closer, his chest starts to rise and fall quicker than normal.

'He can fancy a fucking helter skelter for all I care, but forgive me for being under the impression you'd set me up on a date that could actually *go somewhere*.'

He snorts. 'You won't believe me, but I honestly didn't know about this side of him. So I'm sorry about this, but,' he scrunches his nose before a smile splits his entire face open; the least apologetic any person has ever looked, 'I'm also not. It's funny. You have to admit that.'

'I think I'm too sentient for him,' I say under my breath.

'Must be nice. Bet you've never been told you have too many feelings before.'

I huff and the angry puff of air makes him blink. 'He said I'm "okay".'

'What every woman wants to hear.'

'But he'd prefer someone more positive.'

'You're less positive than the Berlin Wall? That's rough, actually, I'm sorry.' I glare at him some more and he meets it with a grin. 'I don't know why he'd agree to go out with you.'

'Because I'm that bad of a catch?'

His smile fades as his gaze trails over me again, and his voice rumbles between us. 'No, Ava.'

When he meets my eyes, his are liquid heat, and I'm trying to make sense of the pressure in my chest, of the way the atmosphere is pure friction scratching against me and searing my skin.

But then he claps his hands together and I suck in a breath and step backwards.

'While you're lamenting,' he declares, 'I have someone to get back to. So if you don't mind, I'd love to squeeze past.' His hand grazes the small of my back as he moves past, his voice coarse in my ear as he says, 'Enjoy the rest of your evening.'

For a few seconds I stand there, blinking, and then I remember it's his fault I'm here. Loath to go back to the table just yet, I storm into the bathroom to empty my bladder in a rage.

I'm not mad at Henry. Finn's right, he's not hurting anyone. But Finn? Whether he knew about Henry's proclivity for inanimate objects or not, he knows me well enough to know we'd be a bad match regardless. He knew I'd go into this with my guard down. I bet he's laughing about it with his date now.

I hear someone come into the sink area and try to quieten the sound of my pee, but it's one of those times where the quieter you try to be, the longer it goes on, so I have to finish what is quite possibly the world's longest piss knowing I have an audience on the other side of the door.

When I open the door I find a woman leaning against the sink looking directly at me, and for some reason it makes me jump, so I gasp, and then she apologises, and puts both hands out like I'm a skittish animal she's coaxing to safety.

'Hi,' she says, her expression concerned. It's Finn's date, Alex, I realise. 'Sorry, I didn't mean to scare you.'

'Oh, uh, no, you didn't,' I lie, heading to the sink. She shifts away from me so I can reach the soap.

'I love your dress,' she says, and I'm searching for any hint of malice or sarcasm in her voice but come up empty.

'Thank you,' I reply, soapy water splashing all over the clothing she just complimented.

'Sorry if this is weird, but when I was at my table I saw you talking to the guy I'm here with. He said you know each other, but it looked like you were angry when you were talking, so I was wondering if there's anything I should know.'

'Anything you should know?' My mind spirals. What does that even mean?

'You seemed upset, so if there's a reason I should tell him to fuck off then please let me know. He seems great but if he's really just a master actor then I'd rather just cut my losses now. His endorsement isn't worth it.'

Something about her choice of words is odd but I'm too distracted to think too much about it. I place my hands in the dryer, mesmerised by the way my skin aggressively ripples under the air. I almost messed this up for Finn by not giving him her number before. I won't do it again. Even though he doesn't *deserve* me being nice to him.

'No, honestly. He's a good guy, I promise,' I say eventually, as someone else comes out of another cubicle and starts to wash their hands.

'Okay, phew. Thanks.' She's visibly relieved, a small smile on her face.

'You're free to enjoy your date,' I say, returning the smile.

An odd expression crosses her face. 'It's actually—' I don't particularly want to hear the details, so I'm relieved when the other person at the sink blocks out the sound with the hand dryer. When the noise stops, Alex says, 'Anyway, thanks for letting me know. It was nice to meet you.'

As she moves into a cubicle I look at myself in the mirror. I don't recognise jealousy, but I think it's settled into the hard set of my mouth. I take a deep breath and try to release the tension with my exhale. I think I've got so used to hanging out with Finn that it's strange to me that someone else might take up his time now. But it's not my place to decide how he spends his time, and with who. I can't stand in the way of Finn starting something with someone who could keep up with him, whose lifestyle could match his. Someone who compliments women in bathrooms for no reason. Realistically, *that's* the sort of person he deserves.

And so, over the rest of the evening I try to lean into Henry's eccentricities. It sort of works. I'm still very aware we'd be a terrible fit, but while Old Ava would've left within fifteen minutes, New Ava sticks it out, because she knows that sometimes people surprise you. He's interesting, if a bit odd. It's probably a more enlightening way to spend my Friday than usual, at least.

At one point I glance over to the window booths and I'm not sure if it's the light glinting across his glasses, but I swear Finn winks at me. I avert my eyes and dig into my baklava, which is incredible, to be honest. If nothing else, Henry has great taste in desserts.

On my way back to the table after another trip to the bathroom—because I have the bladder of a goldfish at the best of times, let alone when I consume any quantity of alcohol—I cross paths with Finn and Alex leaving.

'Hey Henry,' Finn says brightly, making the man in question jump. 'Hope you've been enjoying the company of my wonderful friend.'

'Oh yeah, it's been great,' he says. We both know this is a lie, but there's a camaraderie between us about it.

I have to slide behind Finn to get back to my seat, and he leans his face towards my ear as I do, making me freeze.

'Ava.' I'm sure he can hear my heartbeat pounding through my head. He is far, *far* too close. He whispers, 'You have toilet paper on your shoe.' Sure enough, there's a trail of tissue at my feet. 'Have a good night,' he says with a grin, opening the door for Alex and following closely behind.

# 21

## cause of death: men leaning

### AVA

It is a truth universally acknowledged that every man looks fitter when he leans; against walls, counters, or, god forbid, doorframes. So when a familiar voice reaches me and the curly-haired man it belongs to props himself against the coffee bar, I'm embarrassed to admit that my eyes draw straight to him. But this reaction isn't a *crime*. I'm allowed to acknowledge these things.

Likewise, it was not a crime for me to have a particularly inappropriate dream about Finn the night after the catastrophic restaurant date. That was out of my control. I'd argue it was a cry for help, actually. It's one of many things I'd never tell Finn. Another is that my lingering anger over that ridiculous date is cooling to amusement, but I refuse to give him the satisfaction of hearing me admit that.

'Good morning to the coffee industry's most cheerful employee.' His eyes slide to my right, where my new coworker stands patiently. 'Unless your new colleague is intending to give you a run for your money.'

Dylan smiles but she's clearly not sure how else to react. Mateo's replacement isn't bad so far; she seems competent, which is more than

I can say for the man who did a trial shift the other day. She hasn't said much, and I don't know if it's because she has first-week nerves, or if she intends to have the kind of silently efficient working relationship her predecessor and I had. I make a mental note to try to find out which one it is.

'Dylan, this is Finn. He's kind of like the City Roast stray cat. You get used to him.'

'I'll bear that in mind.' She laughs quietly and tucks the chunk of hair behind her ear that keeps falling out of her tiny blonde ponytail. 'Do you want me to go and clean the tables?'

'That'd be great, thank you.' Once she's out of earshot, I lean across the counter. 'She's pretty, isn't she?'

Dylan's taller than me, with delicate features and thick-lashed hazel eyes as yet unburdened by the woes of working under Carl's management.

'Sure, but there's only one barista for me.' His eyes flash and my stomach squeezes. Jesus, this man flirts more than he breathes. 'And he just quit. Broke my heart.'

I let out an exasperated sigh and rest one hand on the machine, the other on a bottle of milk. 'What do you want to drink? A surprise?' Recently, he's been showing up at the till and saying "surprise me, Monroe" like he's the main character in a TV show.

'Please. But, as much as it pains me to say, can today's be decaf?' I grab the tin of decaf grounds and he continues, 'I've had three coffees in the office already today and I fear I'll spend the rest of the afternoon in the bathroom if I add one more.'

'What a visual. Thanks for that.' As I steam the milk and wrinkle my nose at the colour of the decaf, he scrolls his phone, distracted. I raise my voice over the bubbling. 'Everything okay?'

He rubs the back of his neck and exhales slowly. 'Yeah. Just trying to make plans with someone.'

It's rare he doesn't overshare (see: bowel movements), so there's a tiny twinge in my gut at his evasiveness. But he doesn't have to tell me everything. He's probably texting Alex; they were clearly having a great time at the restaurant. I log his order on the till and only the faintest smile pulls at his mouth today as he taps his phone against the reader.

Dylan's back behind the counter by this point, putting clean mugs away from the dishwasher. Before I even realise what's happening, Finn reaches out to grab his drink at the exact moment a mug slips from her hand and onto his arm, which knocks his drink all over the counter and his shirt.

'Oh my god, I'm so sorry!' Her cheeks and neck flush magenta as she frantically searches for paper towels.

'It's fine, I promise,' Finn says, unbothered as ever. But Dylan doesn't know she couldn't have chosen a better customer to spill a drink over. She hands me the roll and I tear off a wad for Finn to dab at his shirt while I wipe the counter.

'Dylan,' I turn to her, 'there's a mop in the cleaning cupboard. Could you grab it and— wait, hey, don't stress. Seriously, I can't count the number of times I've knocked something over. In my first week I broke four mugs. Who breaks *four* mugs?'

Finn leans forward. 'A few years ago I was working in a restaurant, and on my first day I dropped a bowl of French onion soup over a customer. Not my finest hour.'

I catch his eye, grateful he's trying to ease her worry. I think she's going to be good to work with, and this is such a minor incident; I don't want it to scare her away. Sure, Carl might ultimately drive her to the brink, but so far we've avoided him.

'Okay. I'll get the mop. I'm so sorry, again, really.'

She scurries to the cleaning cupboard and I turn back to Finn. 'Sorry about that. Go and sit down, I'll bring your drink over.'

---

'I could get used to this,' Finn says, putting his phone on the table as I place a new mug next to his laptop.

'Don't.' I take a hazelnut wafer bar out of my apron pocket and add, 'But thank you for being nice to Dylan.'

'I'm always nice.' His eyes glitter from behind his glasses. 'And I'm also wearing the right colour for a coffee spill today,' he motions towards the chocolate brown shirt, 'so it worked out.'

He links his hands together and raises his arms above his head, making that weird grunting noise that only comes out when you stretch, his shirt lifting on one side to reveal a band of tanned hip.

I blink and nod my head towards his screen. 'What are you working on that's had you stuck in the office drinking their shitty coffee today?'

'I started the day with a few meetings and then somehow I just lost track of time.' Gingerly, he adds, 'I got to the final stage of the process for the San Francisco job. Who knew I'd be able to convince them I could do my job?'

In my head, I say *I knew*. He could convince anyone of anything. But the corporate world is so alien to me; I'm not sure I could handle months of being in the middle of the application process.

He continues with a sigh, 'I need to prepare a pitch and it's taking forever. It's essentially preparing and presenting an entire long-term marketing campaign. I think I'm feeling the pressure more than usual because it's a company I've always wanted to work for.'

For all that we talk, any time San Francisco comes up, however briefly, part of me wants to yell *slow down, summer's not over yet*. I realise it's ridiculous; I knew this was coming. But the fact he's one step closer now puts it into stark perspective.

Finn's phone pings and he glances down at it instantly, before disappointment tugs at his mouth. I can't tell if it's the job application that's doing it or whatever has glued him to his phone, but tension pulls at his shoulders and lands in the set of his jaw. It looks alien on him.

'What's in your way?' I ask, wiping the tables around him.

'I've been looking at the pitch for so long that I'm just not sure if it even makes sense. There are two parts; a presentation and a handout that I'll email them, for them to reference afterwards. The verbal side of things is fine—'

'Because you can talk out of your ass.'

A short laugh puffs out of him. 'Well, yeah, exactly. But I want the handout to be good too, and I have to make sure I can actually read everything during the presentation. I want it to be perfect.' He scratches his neck and continues. 'Sometimes the words swim around a bit on the page, you know?'

I'm transported back to helping Max with his homework after school, going through line after line with him to make sure the words were sinking in. 'Are you dyslexic?'

He shrugs. 'Maybe? I've never been tested.'

I tuck a chair under a nearby table. 'I can look over it if you want.'

It takes every ounce of effort not to take it back when I realise this thing could be twenty pages long, could take me hours to check over. But I don't. The offer sits out there like a wayward ball in a game of catch.

'Really? Would you?' His gratitude glows bright and hopeful; sunshine warming a pavement, drawing out the weeds from the cracks.

'I'm not exactly busy.' I gesture to the near-empty coffee shop around us before untying and retying my ponytail as I reiterate, 'I'll do it.'

'You're an angel, thank you.' Something loosens from his posture, a single knot pulled from the tangle. 'Dunno what I'd do without you, Ava Monroe.'

I try to brush off his words like I always do, but some part of them takes root.

And then his phone flashes with a text, and his eyes light up as he reads it, and his full smile returns in all its blazing glory. I don't know who's texting him, but whoever's on the other end of the phone has untangled the remaining knots and released the weight from his shoulders.

I shake my head and the root dislodges. My heart's grown accustomed to a lack of sunlight. Nothing can bloom there.

'I'm studying part-time at the moment,' Dylan tells me one afternoon while I help her carry a few boxes to the stockroom, her short hair falling out of her ponytail as usual. 'But I'm hoping to squeeze in a bit of travel before my career properly starts.'

'Have you done much travelling before?'

'None,' she says. 'I've barely even left London.'

'Where would you go?'

I grab a KitKat while we're here in the back room and her eyebrows raise. One thing I've learnt about Dylan: she's a stickler for rules. She starts emptying her box and filling the shelves with its contents while I flatten cardboard and chomp on my chocolate bar.

'I love the ocean. I've lived in London my whole life, so the sea has always felt like the perfect place to refresh. I've been trying to convince my boyfriend to go somewhere but he doesn't think it's worth it right now. Thinks we should travel when we've retired and all our ch—' She grimaces and clears her throat before she continues, 'When we have more free time.'

'A few weeks here and there isn't going to destroy your career,' I say.

'It's fine. I'm kind of nervous anyway, so it's probably for the best. I'm not even sure if I'd enjoy it.' She says this, but her expression's still wistful.

'My brother works in travel. When it comes to it, I can put you guys in contact if you want. He'd probably— ugh.' I crane my neck to peek through the glass and see Carl walk in with a woman I don't recognise. 'Sorry, Carl's here. I should go and do my job.'

I wipe my hands on my apron and swallow my final bite as I push open the door. Our manager has seated the power-suited woman at his table and reaches me at the till with superhuman speed.

'We have Nadia from head office in this morning.' He's smiling as he talks, but it's entirely fake and he doesn't blink once. I'm reminded of Madame Tussauds waxworks, only less lifelike. 'She's going to observe and give feedback, so please put your best foot forward.'

He looks down at my shoes as he says this. I'm wearing my Docs, which aren't *technically* part of our uniform, but I'm going out after work and didn't want to lug them around with me on this morning's commute.

'Will do,' I reply evenly, resisting the urge to tap my heels together like I'm on my way to the Yellow Brick Road.

'Could you make her an oat latte? Make sure the milk is perfect.' I start to prepare the shot and he adds, 'And while you're there, can I have a flat white?'

I comply, and over the next hour or so, I'm on my best behaviour. From our short interactions, I get the impression Nadia sees right through Carl's smarmy exterior. She talks separately to both Dylan and me about how it is to work here, and of course, while I don't expressly say anything bad about Carl, I'm not exactly subtle either. I'd never claim to be good at his job, nor would I even want it, but he proves every day that some people are entirely unsuited to managing a team.

Nadia nods a lot when I speak, listening when I tell her what my favourite elements of working here are. I give her a more professional version of what I told Finn that first night we hung out; I like the structure and organisation and the satisfaction of knowing how things work and how to share that with people.

'Of course, we love when people stick with us for a long time,' she says, handing me her empty mug. An image floats across my vision of me, middle-aged, still working in this shop, and a shudder rolls through me. 'But it's important to us that everyone is working to their strengths, whether that's front of house or elsewhere. Your perfect role might not be behind this counter.'

Carl appears then and says, 'Dylan's new, so we'll be working on finessing her coffee skills as soon as possible.'

'She's doing great so far,' I tell them, and Dylan gives me a small smile in thanks. 'And we're already on it—we've planned a training session for later.'

'Oh, that's good,' Carl says. He turns to Nadia, 'Didn't I say Ava was on top of things?'

I *have* to be on top of things when he doesn't help, but that's neither here nor there.

'Well, this has been a lovely afternoon. It was good to meet you both,' Nadia says.

A few minutes after Carl sees Nadia out, he packs up his stuff and comes to the till to say, 'Sorry, I need to run. You'll be fine closing up, won't you?'

'We'll be fine,' I reply. As the door slams shut behind him I hear Nadia's words in my head. *It's important to us that everyone is working to their strengths, whether that's front of house or elsewhere. Your perfect role might not be behind this counter.* Something spreads through my chest. It takes me a long time to realise it might be hope.

---

When I open the dishwasher I'm accosted by a blast of heat straight from the underworld itself. As I turn my head to avoid it, I give a halfhearted wave goodbye to the final two customers in the shop as they leave. Well, final two apart from Finn, who's at the table closest to the till, having recently taken it upon himself to be the last customer to leave the shop every single day.

'Honestly, you should go home,' I suggest. 'You'll just be watching me painstakingly turn forty-four mugs around until all the logos face the same way.'

'Don't threaten me with a good time,' he says without looking up. He's squinting at his laptop, too close to the screen as usual. 'But are you free this evening for a bucket list activity?'

I'm in dire need of a physical and mental distraction, which is why I spent yesterday evening scrolling through Hinge matches and acquiring a new target. 'Nope, sorry. I have plans. A date.'

I pick up a spoon and immediately drop it back on the dishwasher tray when the metal scalds me. I go for the mugs instead, collecting a couple in my apron like it's a kangaroo pouch.

'A date, huh?' Finn's tapping increases in fervour and it makes me wonder how many keyboards he's burnt through. I somehow manage to transport the mugs to the counter without further calamity. 'What's he like?'

'He,' I gingerly stack the clean mugs in their home above the coffee machine, 'is six foot four.'

He's still only half paying attention, brow furrowed as he squints at his laptop. 'Happy for you. Any particular personality traits of note?'

'When you're six foot four, that *is* your personality trait.' I finish stacking my mugs before adding, 'But then, you wouldn't know anything about that, as a short king.'

The frenzied tapping of fingers on keys stops abruptly as I turn to the dishwasher to hide my smirk. I take my time collecting more mugs in my pouch, and by the time I turn back around, Finn's hauled his face from his screen and is eyeing me incredulously. 'Did you just call me a "short king"?'

'It's fine, don't worry. People love that now. You don't need to be insecure about it.'

'I'm not insecure, I'm *confused*. I'm literally— no. I'm not telling you how tall I am.'

I recoil at the noise as I drop the next batch of mugs onto the counter. 'Adorable that you think I don't know how tall you are.'

His eyes narrow and he folds his arms across his chest. 'Oh yeah?'

'Tall women have a preternatural perception of height, so I can say with absolute certainty that you are five-eleven and a half. Although,' I place the mugs one by one on top of the machine, 'I think you usually round down to five-eleven, because you'd rather pleasantly surprise someone than disappoint them. And you know what? I respect that. It's nice when short men embrace their height.'

'You're unhinged.'

'And you're not six foot,' I say, my stacking complete. 'Every inch matters.'

'So I've been told.' His eyes flash dangerously, so fast I almost miss it, and then he's back to normal, stretching his legs under the table with a yawn, a rumpled prince bored on his throne. 'No brickwork predilection?'

'Not as far as I know.'

'Ava?' I spin around to find Dylan in the doorway to the stockroom, where she's been tidying the shelves for the past forty-five minutes. If I'm honest, she's so quietly productive I'd kind of forgotten she was still here. 'Are we still doing the training?'

I glance at the time. I'm not meeting Aiden until later, so I'm struck by an idea. 'Today's your lucky day, Finn. Didn't you tell me ages ago you wanted to learn how to do latte art?'

He sits up straight. 'Now? You're not kicking me out?'

It's a few minutes before closing time, but fuck it. I stalk to the door and flip the sign to "closed". 'I'm showing Dylan anyway, so you can try too.'

'Do I get an apron and a badge?'

'No. And you're not technically allowed back here, so if you break anything I will tell Carl you forced your way behind the counter and intentionally caused mayhem, and Dylan and I were simply two damsels in distress too distraught to resist.'

She shrugs, tucking that loose strand of hair behind her ear. 'That sounds fair.'

Finn packs his stuff neatly in his bag, leaving it on the table before taking tentative steps towards Dylan and me. 'Literally no one would believe you could be a damsel in distress.' He mutters something that sounds a lot like, 'You're causing *me* distress.'

'Well, let's hope we don't have to test that theory,' I reply. He waits with one hand at the end of the counter, pretending to be casual but ultimately coming off extremely suspicious. 'You a vampire or something? I hereby grant you permission to come back here. But wash your hands first. With soap.'

I catch the tail end of an eye roll.

Once my students have both washed their hands, they stand to attention slightly to my right. In the five seconds it took for me to pluck a bottle of milk from the fridge, Finn somehow procured and tied the old apron that Mateo had haphazardly stashed in the cubby under the till on his last day. I can't be bothered to fight him on it.

'This milk expires today so I don't care about using it for practice, but I'd rather not waste coffee beans so I'm going to reuse some old grounds and hope for the best.'

'Secondhand coffee.' Finn nods sagely. 'Put that on the menu.'

I tamp some used grounds and brew a few shots in preparation. 'Right, so, different drinks require different types of milk, but we're going to focus on latte milk today.' I pour milk into the jug, just below where the metal protrudes at the spout. 'This is usually the amount of liquid you need. Some milks make better microfoam than others. Whole milk is the easiest to work with, while something like almond milk is kind of a bitch to steam properly.' I open my mouth to keep going but Finn has raised his hand like we're in class. 'Yes, Finlay?'

'Why is whole milk easier to work with?'

'It has a higher fat content. The chemical composition is better balanced to make the shiny foam we're aiming for. Generally, the creamier it is, the less finicky it is to use.' I turn my head to meet his eyes. 'Does that answer your question?'

'Yep. Thanks.' He gives me a thumbs up and I have to try extremely hard not to make fun of him for it.

I settle back into position. 'What we're doing is adding air to the milk, and in doing so, heating it up. Let me show you.' I go to turn a knob on the machine so that it'll release a burst of steam but feel Finn leaning over my shoulder to watch. 'Finn, I can practically hear your heartbeat. Back up a bit.'

He mumbles an apology and I start steaming the milk, talking them through the difference between the sharp tearing sounds at the start and the lower rumble as the wand moves deeper into the milk, telling them to pay less attention to how it looks and more attention to how it sounds and feels.

I tap the jug on the counter to release any bigger air bubbles, swirl it a few times and then lift it to my swamp-water espresso. I explain each step, every flick of the wrist and, even with the secondhand espresso, the art isn't bad. 'Who wants to try?'

Turns out this is not a skill you can perfect in one evening. On the plus side, Dylan's now made not one, but two near-perfect cappuccinos. We're meant to be making lattes, but a win is a win.

A few attempts later, the three of us stand over her and Finn's most recent cups, peering at the shapes in the milk.

'I feel like I'm cloud-gazing.' Finn turns his mug to look at it from a new angle.

'That's a really good hippo, if it's any consolation,' Dylan says helpfully.

'You know what,' he lifts the cup to inspect it up close, 'that *is* consolation, actually.'

'I'm going to wash some mugs up,' Dylan says, picking up as many as she can carry to the sink without spilling the contents all over the floor. 'There's no point running the dishwasher just for these.'

I look back at the few remaining latte attempts. Two of them are essentially just a mass of indeterminate foam, but the third contains an unintentionally intricate design. It's almost impressive how perfect the shape is.

'That's—' Finn starts to say, grabbing my forearm and pointing at the mug.

'Don't.' I put a finger up to silence him, wriggling out of his grip. I refuse to laugh at something like this. I am not twelve.

'I'm not completely depraved, you see it too, right?'

I bite my lip, avoiding eye contact as best I can. This isn't funny.

'See what?' Dylan asks as she comes to collect the final cups. She puts a hand to her mouth, eyes wide. 'Oh my god. That belongs in an anatomy book.'

That's all it takes for a snort to squeeze through the dam I've built, and then the branches give way entirely and Finn and I are snickering like school kids at the back of the classroom after finding illicit graffiti on the table. Apparently we are, in fact, twelve.

Once Dylan's back at the sink and the dregs of our laughter spill out of us in quiet chuckles, I say, 'I thought you were meant to be the mature one.'

'When did we decide that?' He wiggles his nose to adjust his glasses as he shoves his sleeves higher up his arms.

'When you were a fully functioning adult while I just flailed about in the shallow end.' I press my hip against the counter. 'I bet you even know how to do your taxes.'

'I do, actually,' he says after a pause. He wipes his hands on his stolen apron, tightens it, then adds, 'Okay, I'm gonna try one more.'

'I believe in you,' I lie.

He shoots me a mistrustful glance that makes my mouth twitch upwards and then takes his position at the steam wand, clutching the metal jug like a baby who's only recently discovered the use of their hands. 'I feel like I'm holding this wrong.'

'You are, you need to turn it a bit.' He turns it the wrong way. 'No, the other— let me help you.' I step between him and the counter to lean across his torso and carefully prise his fingers from the jug to reposition them. If my hands feel cold on his, he doesn't flinch. In fact, he's perfectly still, sending flames licking up my entire left side at every spot his body touches mine, solid and scorching. My voice catches in my throat as I say, 'Okay, now stay like that.'

When I turn the dial to release some steam, his hands immediately revert to their original position, so I instinctively place mine over his and hold everything where it should be. I feel his breath at my ear and I turn my head instinctively, my nose barely missing scraping against the dense stubble at his jaw. And yet, it's only when I smell that familiar body-warmed cologne and leftover chlorine on his skin that I really register just how close he is. Close enough to count the trace of freckles scattered across his nose and cheekbones like tiny fairy footprints. Close enough to see his pupils have dilated, the easy warmth of his eyes replaced by wildfire. Close enough to catch the way those eyes drop to my mouth once. Then twice.

'Shit,' he rasps, as hot milk churns up and over the lip of the jug and across the counter. In a whirl he rushes to the sink to run water over his hands while I leap back and look for some paper towels, ready to clean up the mess I was hoping to avoid.

'Woah, what happened here?' Dylan asks, drying her hands on her apron.

Brilliant question. I'm wondering the same.

As the door bangs shut behind Dylan ten minutes later, I hurriedly finish the rest of my tasks, desperate to be out of the shop and away from Finn and his confusingly magnetic presence. 'You can go too. I need to get changed in the back for my date.'

'Sure. I'll put these mugs away and then I'll leave.'

I give him a quick smile to say thanks but avoid his eyes, before I head behind the counter to the back room. My mind reels as I tear off my layers in our employee bathroom, replacing my t-shirt for a strappy corset-style top. I can't tell if the lace-edged sweetheart neckline makes me look too booby, or if I simply just exist, with boobs. Still, I reach into my top and rearrange them, because I know exactly what I want from my audience tonight.

I apply a red lip stain and smack my lips together a few times until I'm satisfied with the colour. Sure, Finn looked at my mouth, and I might've looked at his, but it's hard *not* to look when you're that close. I haven't had any action in a while, so the slightest contact with a man is sending my mind into a frenzy. Especially one with arms like that. And eyes like that. And a smile and— whatever. It makes perfect sense that I reacted the way I did.

By the time I take down my hair, I'm feeling much calmer. It's time to get horizontally distracted tonight with a giant man with a beard and a proclivity for putting three "x"s at the end of every text he sends. That's what I need.

I take my phone from its perch on the sink and read my texts. There's a message from Aiden.

> Can't wait for tonight, just leaving now xxx

I fire back a text that's probably more flirtatious than I'd usually go for, but I'm a woman on a mission. Then I spot three messages from Max.

> As IF you didn't remember what today is, I'm offended
>
> How dare you have a life
>
> (This is a joke, I'm glad you're busy)

Shit, shit, shit. My heart twists as my fingers fly over my screen to reply. This is the first year I've forgotten.

I slip my phone into my back pocket and take one last look in the mirror. The person staring back at me doesn't try for permanence. She gets her fill, and then she leaves. That's the way it works best. The way it's worked for years.

So why does it feel like I'm suddenly wearing clothes that aren't mine?

When I step back into the shop I expect to find it empty. Instead, Finn's leaning in that perpetually casual way of his on the other side of the counter, wearing the same coy smile from the other day while he texts.

As he glances up from his screen, something moves across his face. My heart betrays me with a stutter when his eyes train on mine. I push my shoulders back and stand tall, reminding myself that we are friends, and that I have a goal for tonight that he is categorically not involved in. I stride over to the till to make sure it's turned off.

He seems like he's weighing up what to say, his mouth opening and closing just slightly. 'Your date's a lucky man.'

'I'll let you know tomorrow,' I reply with a shrug, and he expels a soft laugh.

After a few moments of silence, he says quietly, 'I didn't mean it like that, though.'

I can't look at him. My efforts to forget the hunger in his eyes or the heat of him pressed against my side are futile when his words seem to have a similar effect on my weak-willed body. God, I need to get away from him. I need to release some of this tension with someone who won't leave a mess in my life.

'I hope he's not lying about his height,' I say, attempting some levity.

He matches my tone. 'It'd be terrible if he were only six-three.'

'Right? I'm so glad you understand me.' His gaze burns into my back as I walk around the shop unnecessarily, doing the final checks that I know I've already completed. I move back in his direction and wonder aloud, 'What do you think might disappoint him about me?'

He scratches his jaw and releases a long exhale. 'I can't think of a single thing that's disappointing about you.'

It makes my breath catch, but then I remember that Finn's like this with everyone. I mean, I've seen him give bedroom eyes to Belinda, for god's sake. But we're not like *that*. We can't be. He was dropped into my life at the exact moment I needed a scapegoat, and I have to keep him in that friend-shaped box for however long he stays in London. Nothing else would work. Nothing else would make sense.

I head towards the front door but he reaches it first and holds it open. For a few moments, we're in a standoff. I refuse to move, scowling at him for being, well, him, I guess.

His eyebrows raise in amusement. 'Just walk through the door, Ava.'

'Don't tell me what to do,' I challenge.

He folds his arms and leans against the door. Stop *leaning,* you bitch. It's not helpful. 'Did I do something wrong?'

'No.' I close my eyes and my exhale mixes with the evening air between us. 'I'm just in my head about something. Thank you for being the delightfully chivalrous, door-opening man that you are.'

'You have a real talent for making compliments sound like insults.'

I slide past him and he follows close behind. 'And you have an affinity for receiving insults as compliments, so I guess that's why the universe stuck us together.' I lock the door in three places, pulling the handle to triple-check. 'That, and a perverse desire to challenge me.'

The easy demeanour is back, and he cocks his head to one side. 'Challenge you how?'

'To see how long it'll take for me to get so exasperated by your facts and endless chatting that I bar you from the shop.'

'There's gotta be a part of you that loves it, because so far, I haven't even been kicked out once.'

'There's always time, Finn. But not tonight, because I have plans.'

I need this date, and at least five accompanying shots. My phone lights up with two more texts from Max.

> Officially six years old

> They (I) grow up so fast

Six years since wordless bargains with the universe that I'd make all over again if I had to. Since enough tears were shed to fill one side of the scales and tip the balance in our favour. And yet, as triumphant as today should be, familiar wisps of smoke skulk around the edges of my brain at the memory of our family being in that dark place.

'You're wrong, anyway,' Finn says, lightly bumping his shoulder against mine. His uneven smile is morning light burning through fog, and miraculously, the shadows retreat, and my head feels a little lighter. 'The universe stuck us together so that we could laugh at frighteningly anatomically-correct frothy milk dicks together.'

A laugh flurries out of me. 'How does it feel knowing you just said a sentence that no one in the world has ever said before?' I can't help but groan at the memory of that ridiculous latte art. 'Fuck, I hate that I laughed at that. It was a one-off. I'm actually an extremely delicate lady.'

'No it wasn't, and no you're not.' His gaze sweeps across my face, then slowly moves down my neck, then even lower, lingering on the lace-edged neckline of my corset. My pulse flutters wildly in response. His jaw tightens when he meets my eyes again. 'You are completely indecent.'

He says it like a prayer.

The silence lasts a second too long. My body's on high alert, so I clear my throat. 'What I am is someone who has to leave. I only have twenty minutes to psych myself up for an evening of pretending I enjoy the company of men.'

If there was any tension between us, it drifts into the night with the sound of his laugh, and it reminds me that he can snap out of this like it's nothing, like he didn't just send my stomach tumbling out into the ether. He is not for me. I'd do well to remember that.

'Look, it's okay if you still find dicks funny,' he says. 'Happens to the best of us.' I scowl at him before marching away. I can hear the smile in his voice when he calls out behind me, 'This is a no-judgement zone!'

# 22

## turns out honesty is not, in fact, the best policy

## AVA

'Can you feel how much I want you? How much my cock *needs* you?' Aiden breathes into my ear, mattress squeaking as he shifts position. He pulls me onto his chino-covered groin with a huff and I note that I can, in fact, feel how much he wants me. Quite aggressively, actually.

I assume his question is rhetorical, so I put my lips to his in the hope it'll make him stop talking, and it works for a while. The kiss is a bit sloppy, and by that I mean his tongue is so far inside my mouth I'm convinced I just felt it hit my small intestine, but it's been a while since I've had any action and I'm willing to overlook a lack of finesse this time. It'll be fine.

'Tell me how much you want this cock.'

I'm thrown off by his repeated use of the word "cock", but he's looking at me with eager eyes, and I get the impression he wants an answer to this one. I'm not quite sure how to respond, though. I wanted it a lot, when I was knocking back shots in the low light of the bar. I wanted it even more when we got back to his flat and I was intoxicated simply by the feeling of a man's hands on me. And now?

'Oh, uh, yeah. I want it so much. Your... dick.' It's a weak ending, but he seems unfazed.

'Such a good girl,' he says, voice gravelly.

I pause for a moment, blinking at him, heart pounding from the confusing desire and displeasure running through me simultaneously. I hold back a grimace and say, 'I'm not really into that, to be honest. Not my thing.'

I don't know why he'd assume it was, considering we've literally just met and had not discussed it until now, but he recoils like I've said something wildly offensive and inexplicably asks, 'Would you prefer "naughty girl"?'

'We don't need to talk,' I suggest. 'You can use your mouth in other ways.' Now it's his turn to stare blankly at me, so I say, 'Like kissing. That's what I meant.'

'Oh,' he says with a *silly me* chuckle. We give each other the kind of polite smile you offer your neighbour when you bump into them on the street, and he gets back to work, clumsily kissing my neck. But, well, I'm a simple woman; that's enough to get the ball rolling again. His hands run along my collarbone, then across my chest. Turns out my top offers just the right amount of boob. I know this, because Aiden's eyes were permanently glued to my chest the entire time we were at the bar. Sober, this might've made me feel dirty, but through tequila goggles I lapped up every moment of attention. Because I can still do this. I can still do the casual thing.

My jeans press into my stomach uncomfortably when I straddle his hips, and I tug at his hair and sigh into his mouth as I let my mind wander.

At least Aiden has a bedframe, which is a rarity when it comes to dating men. Now I'm thinking about it, I bet Finn has one. In fact, I can almost guarantee it.

I instantly pull back in surprise and Aiden asks, 'Is something wrong?'

What was that? Finn has no business being in my head. Not now. Not while I'm doing this. I smile and lean back in, reminding myself why I'm here. I peek at the headboard while he plants kisses up my neck. It's quilted leather, which tells me everything I need to know about this man, but he's decently attractive and I'm ovulating, so my judgement is skewed.

And yet, this situation feels weird for some reason. I've had this kind of mediocre, sloppy sex before. I've enjoyed it well enough. But a niggling voice in my head tells me I'm done. For all my talk about needing to distract myself, apparently this is not the way to do it right now.

He pulls away with a vigorous slurp that, frankly, makes me feel like I'm listening to dentist ASMR, and I know it's time to admit defeat. I wipe the wetness he's left around my mouth and gingerly remove myself from his lap to sit next to him; lower-belly heat rapidly cooling with every passing second.

I don't have time to tell Aiden there's no need for him to continue. To my surprise, he locks his gaze with mine, pulls at his waistband, and, like a magician pulling a rabbit out of a hat, there it is. Abra-ca-fuckin'-dabra, lads.

I'm unsure if it's the eagerness in his eyes, the unexpected deluge of saliva, or the way he keeps saying the word "cock" without a fraction of irony, but by this point my entire reproductive system has shrivelled up.

And yet, when he next opens his mouth, my insides somehow find new ways to close in on themselves. 'Will your tight little pussy be able to take me?'

I tilt my head as I peer at his crotch. 'I mean, probably?'

This stops him in his tracks. He clears his throat. 'What do you mean, "probably"?'

A strap slides down my shoulder as I shrug. 'I reckon I'd be fine with,' I gesture in front of me, 'that.'

His bravado is gone as quickly as my libido, voice half an octave higher than it was a moment ago. 'It's, like, okay though, right?'

I look down. It's still bouncing around in that slightly unsettling way that penises do. My mind goes back to lying on the carpet and playing with those springy metal doorstops attached to skirting boards as a kid, flicking them to get them to make that *boing* sound.

'Yeah!' Our eyes meet, much to my regret, and silence wraps its weighty limbs around us. I blink twice. Aiden's nostrils flare. His dick still moves in my peripheral vision. *Boing*. After twenty seconds or an eternity, I break the hold. 'Should I leave?'

'I think that would be a good idea.'

Josie almost screams when she finds me at the dining room table the next morning, hunched over my laptop and crunching loudly on the last of my toast, blinds still drawn to protect the sun-phobic demon I house within my body.

'Holy Mother of God,' she says, hand at her chest, the soft rollers in her hair and green silk pyjamas really heightening the whole Old Hollywood thing she's got going on.

'Nope, just me.' I peer into my mug to find it empty. When did that happen?

'At nine in the morning on a weekend. Who are you and what have you done with Ava?' She approaches the table and shakes my shoulders roughly from behind. 'Where have you taken her?'

'Ha.' I duck out of her grasp and push my chair back, peeling my bare legs from the wooden chair with a wince. 'Tea?'

'Always. Can you make one for Alina too? She's in the shower.'

By the time she's returned from taking Rudy out to the courtyard, I'm adding milk to our mugs.

'Are you going to explain why you're up?' She leans against the breakfast bar and eyes me suspiciously. 'Wait, have you even gone to bed?'

'I have in fact had a *delightful* night's sleep. I came home earlier than I expected and decided to be a grown-up by eating a banana and downing a few pints of water before bed so I wouldn't feel disgusting this morning.'

'Proud of you.' Josie leans on the counter and rests her chin on her linked hands. 'Why'd you come home earlier than you expected?'

I'm reminded of my response to Aiden last night. It was like my body was yelling *stop, this isn't for you anymore!* I don't know what *is* for me, but it categorically cannot be Finn, despite his inopportune appearance in my head mid-makeout.

The sound of the shower stops and I reply, 'Just wasn't feeling it.'

She's pensive, moving her pouted lips from side to side. 'And may I ask why you've decided to change a decades-long personality trait and wake up early on a Saturday?'

'I'm doing some work on my laptop and wanted to get it finished as soon as possible.' It's taken me a couple of hours to go through Finn's presentation. He's good with words so I didn't need to do much. I figure if I help him with his pitch, he'll get the San Francisco job, he'll leave as planned, and everything can go back to normal. No chaos. Because I don't want chaos. I want easy. 'Speaking of which, do you know of a printing shop nearby?'

Alina sweeps into the room, short dark curls dripping onto her t-shirt as she kisses Josie on the head. 'Morning. I didn't expect to see you out of your hovel yet, Ava.' I fake-smile at her and she snorts. 'And sorry to eavesdrop, but I've used a printing shop down by Clapham North before. Or there's the library?'

'I think a shop'll be better.' I hand her a tea before picking up the other two, and we all make our way to the living area, Alina's hand at the small of her girlfriend's back.

They're not one of those couples that falls all over each other at all times, but sometimes it feels like I'm intruding on the tiny moments they share; Alina moving something out of the way before Josie sits on it, Josie detangling Alina's hair as they sit on the sofa listening to a podcast, the pair of them facing each other talking about art and music like it's their religion.

'Ava's working on something mysterious,' Josie explains, 'on a Saturday.'

Alina opens the blinds and sunlight hits my vampire skin at last. I refrain from hissing.

'It's not mysterious,' I argue, curling into my spot on the right end of the sofa and pulling my massive t-shirt over me as far as it'll go. 'I'm helping Finn with a task he needs to complete for a job he's interviewing for.'

Alina's eyebrows raise and I can just tell Josie's told her every tidbit she knows about this man. 'If he gets a new job, he won't be around the coffee shop as much anymore, right?'

I don't know how to explain that he won't be around the *country* as much anymore, but I still haven't actually told Josie about the fact he was only ever a temporary step in my London life. 'He'll be here for a little while longer. It's a long application process.'

'Hm,' Josie says. I can't read what's going on behind her eyes, but then she says, 'How's your own job hunt going?'

'Oh.' My eyes water as I take a sip of too-hot tea. 'I never really started.'

'I thought you were going to apply to that internship Finn mentioned to you.'

Damn Josie and her impossible memory. 'I didn't get around to it before applications closed. And I'm not sure what else to try, so I figured I'll just stay at City Roast for now.' My drink scalds my tongue at the same moment the image of me working there in twenty years sears across my brain again.

'Ava come on, you hate that place.'

'I don't hate it. Not all of it, anyway.'

'It's not your passion,' she says, momentarily distracted by Rudy nudging her hand with a toy in his mouth, which she tugs absentmindedly.

'Tell me, when have you ever known me to be passionate about anything?' I pull my fingers through a knot in my ponytail. 'I'm walking apathy.'

'That's not true,' Alina butts in from where she's sitting on the floor. 'You have a real enthusiasm for masculine, anthropomorphic cartoon characters.'

'The Beast could get it,' I reply sagely.

'Stop encouraging her,' Josie says, frowning in Alina's direction. Alina and I share a grin, and Josie doesn't need to see it to know we're trying not to laugh. 'There's more for you out there. You're allowed to go and look for it, you know.'

I look over at the dining table, morning sunshine reflecting off the glass Finn took from Tamesis Dock. Would it be tempting fate to be a little brave in the hopes of being happy? Or would it be a disaster?

I make a noncommittal noise and drink my tea.

'Let's go to the common today,' Alina declares, now completely horizontal and soaking up the sun like a cat. 'Ava, you're coming too.'

'I don't wanna get all hot and sticky and see all the bugs.'

'Maybe the bugs don't want to see you either,' Josie argues.

'That was mean.'

She shrugs. 'You're coming. And we can go to the printing shop on the way.'

# 23

## and the Academy Award goes to... me

### FINN

When my eighth-grade crush Helena Karlsson wore a purple dress to our school dance I dribbled my drink all over my chin. Nowadays, I am metaphorically dribbling every time I see Ava. Frankly, it's probably only a matter of time before I do it for real.

I can't lie and say it was a perfect performance, but pretending like my heart wasn't flip-flopping around my chest last night when she came through the door looking the way she did should be studied in drama schools. She doesn't even have to try and all I want is to say something that'll make her laugh, or think I'm smart, or just give me a millisecond of attention.

I groan into my pillow. For the first time in a long while, I get the urge to text the woman I was casually seeing during my first few months in London, in the vain hope it'll solve my little problem. Fuck, *no*. I can't contact this poor woman when my mind's on someone else.

Someone who is committed to our original plan; be friends, hang out, complete the bucket list. I should be committed to the plan too, but it's difficult when she occupies every square centimetre of headspace. I'm the one who's leaving soon, I'm the one who suggested we be friends, yet I'm the one who can't help wondering about all the maybes.

Maybe I'm a fool for letting myself get too close. Even more of a fool for refusing to step away until the last possible moment, knowing full well it'll make it harder in the long run.

Maybe I'm imagining the moments where I swear she feels the magnetism too. Where, for a second, her lips part and her heartbeat thunders in the spot just below her jaw, and she's so perfectly legible I want to tell her, *we're speaking the same language, Ava. Please let me in.*

Or maybe I should get a grip, let her date random men whose entire personality is that they're six foot four, and continue giving Oscar-worthy performances where I act like she doesn't make me burn up with a single glance. I won't be at the mercy of someone who'd probably get bored of me within weeks. I'll get this new job and before we know it I'll be gone before any trouble really starts. It's not too late.

Someone yells on the street below and it's loud enough to snap me out of my self-indulgent whining. It reminds me to let some fresh air in, and when I open the blinds I find the sky is an entirely cloudless blue. I need to spend some time outside, feel the sun on my face, get my heart pumping. I'll ask Julien if he wants to go to the park and I can put Ava out of my mind until Monday.

I pick up my phone to text him, but, because the gods are laughing at me today, I receive a message from Ava the second I do. She's sent a picture of herself next to her laptop and my heart flutters. She's not exactly smiling, but I know her well enough to spot the slight lift of her cheeks that gives her good mood away.

With a sigh I fling myself back onto my bed and look at the photo. I zoom in and see my work on her laptop screen. I don't know why, but some part of me didn't expect her to actually look over it, and my little heart flutter turns into a whole flock of birds taking off.

> How was my presentation?

I wanna tell you it was shit

but it was actually quite good

> Not sure how to feel about the 'actually' you used there

I want to ask her how her date went. If she tells me she had a terrible time, I'll feel bad for manifesting it. And if she tells me it was a success, I'll feel even worse.

> what are you doing right now?

I open up my camera without thinking and send her a selfie in return. It's only after I've pressed send that uncharacteristic nerves fill my stomach. My hair's a mess, I forgot to check for any post-sleep grossness in my eyes, and it's just occurred to me that I haven't shaved in days.

nice beard

> Can we really call that a beard?

> I feel like it's heavy-duty stubble at best

whatever you say Santa

you should keep it

> It's honestly kind of itchy

the ladies love stubble

My fingers hover over my screen for a few moments while I decide what to say.

> In that case, I'll keep it
>
> Just for you

And then I tuck my phone under my pillow and speedwalk to the shower, because I don't want to see her response.

---

Julien meets me outside my building, bulky tote bag on his shoulder, and the second he sees me, laughter ripples through him. 'You look distraught.'

A weak laugh puffs out of me too. 'Don't. I'm having a moment.'

'Any particular reason?' I meet his eye guiltily and he whoops as he falls into step beside me, drawing the attention of a family waiting at the bus stop over the road. 'I fucking *knew* it.'

He chews his gum nonchalantly and waits for me to tell him some juicy gossip that doesn't even exist.

'Nothing has happened.' He raises his eyebrows like he doesn't believe me. 'I'm just...'

I trail off with a grumble and Julien switches to French in his excitement. 'I *told* you and you were adamant you'd never go there. Don't ever say I don't know you.'

My brain resolutely sticks to English. 'I still haven't gone there and *won't* go there. I'm not an idiot.'

'I know I wasn't entirely on board with it before, but I dunno. Seeing you interact over the past few months, in a weird way, it makes sense. The two of you together.'

'We're not together, Jesus. My point still stands. Maybe even more than before. There's a strong chance I'll get this job in San Francisco, and she's got her life here in London—it makes sense to keep this to myself. I'll be gone soon, and we can just forget about it.' Before he can butt in again, I add, 'She's dating other people. If that's not proof enough she's not interested, I don't know what is.'

For a while, I was under the impression Ava had stopped dating. My naïve subconscious thought it could've been because of me. But recently, she's started up again and there's absolutely nothing I can do about it.

It started with that guy I set her up with from the office, who, in my defence, I didn't know a lot about. Specifically, the wall thing. But I knew enough about him that I could predict it would not go well between them. I can admit that. Why did I set her up with someone I knew she was fundamentally incompatible with in the first place? The potential for some funny anecdotes? Hope that maybe after a disaster she'd just give up dating entirely?

'Or,' he reasons, 'maybe she's dating other people because *you* suggested the two of you be friends.'

His smile is bright on his face while I scratch at the scruff on my jaw. Because yes, it's itchy, but obviously I'm keeping it. 'Can we just move on?'

'Fine.' We wait at a crossing, stepping out when the coast is clear. After a few moments, Julien asks, 'How did your meeting go with that woman's daughter the other day?'

'It was good,' I say, eager for the distraction. 'I passed her information over to Miranda so hopefully she'll be able to replace me when I go.'

Sure, I could've told Ava that my so-called date with Alex at the restaurant was actually just an informal business meeting, but then I wouldn't have witnessed a new version of her. I'm *sure* she was jealous. Not enough to admit it to herself, and certainly not to me, but enough to make her so frustrated she popped her own bubble of personal space to get in mine. Not correcting her misunderstanding about my intentions with Alex felt like a rare situation where I had any semblance of control.

'It's weird that you're leaving,' Julien sighs. 'I've only just got used to having you around again. You sure you don't want to stay?'

The truth is, even if I hadn't got so much as an interview for this San Francisco job, I'd be leaving anyway. It won't be long before I've outstayed my welcome in London and I'll need to leave, whether it's for this job or another consulting gig somewhere else. That's the way it always goes.

'You'll just have to miss me.' I slap a hand on his shoulder, careful to avoid his bag. It's filled with what I can only assume are bottles of wine from the sommelier course he started and stopped a few months ago. I'm in the mood to drink at least three. 'Think you can remember how to do that?'

Julien throws his head back for one of his giant laughs, and says, 'I have more than enough experience.' While moving around so much as a child turned into a lifelong habit for me, it had the opposite effect on Julien. 'You're always welcome on my couch. Well, no. Not always. Two weeks, max. Three, if you're willing to clean.'

'You say this as if cleaning isn't one of my all-time favourite activities.' My apartment is spotless, but I can't wait to move into a new place and hopefully, maybe, finally be allowed to move the fucking mugs around.

'I mean this in the kindest way, but you need to get laid.'

'Oh my god, fuck off. I don't see your love life thriving at the moment either.'

'Yeah but I'm also not *moping*. Remember when we used to go on dates to the same bars and meet in the bathroom halfway through?' He takes longer strides along the pavement and I force myself to keep up. 'Nowadays, all you do is clean your flat, gallivant around London and pine.'

I pretend I didn't hear the final part of his sentence. 'Tidy apartment, tidy mind.'

'How's that working out for you?'

'Wonderfully,' I lie, chaos still tearing through my brain like a tornado.

# 24

## distinctly lacking in Vitamin D, in every way

### AVA

THE SUN BEATS DOWN onto Clapham Common with a ferocity that guarantees a burn, despite the layers of suncream I repeatedly slather on myself. It's the kind of weather we pretend is unusual, while deep in the knowledge we've actually had summers like this every single year for the past two decades, thanks to global warming.

Josie and I lie on our stomachs on opposite ends of the picnic blanket; Josie listening to an audiobook while I pick at the grass, her face obscured by the brim of her massive hat, her lesser-used cane folded up next to her since she left Rudy at home in our slightly-cooler flat.

'Does anyone fancy a walk?' Alina starts putting her shoes on from where she's been basking in the sun a few metres away. When we decline, she gets to her feet and walks away, whipping out her phone to talk to someone in unintelligibly fast Spanish. I'd naïvely assumed my intermittent use of Duolingo had improved my language skills until the first time I overheard Alina speaking to her Colombian mother on the phone. But don't worry, I can say "where are the eggs?".

Even in the shade, I'm cooking from the inside; my jumpsuit saturating with sweat any time I stay in one position for too long. After rooting around my tote for my water, I drink half of it in one go, ignoring the sensible part of my brain that tells me I should ration it.

Watching Alina's retreating form, a thought comes to me. 'Can I ask you a question?'

Josie frowns, taking out her earbuds to say, 'Did you say something?'

'Yeah. Sorry.' She places them in her case and props her chin on her palm when I start again. 'Am I the reason you and Alina don't live together? Are you scared to kick me out?'

She's silent for a few moments and then bursts out laughing. 'Oh god, no. If I wanted to live with Alina right now, I would. But she loves her flat and I love mine. *Ours.*'

'But you'll live together someday, right?'

'I assume so,' she shrugs. 'But independence is really important for both of us. We have so much to do individually that we intentionally put a lot of time into working on ourselves. Because then we'll be the best for each other too, you know?'

God, that's emotionally mature, isn't it? I'm out here knocking back shots with a stranger to get in his pants and then proceed to run away when he says the word "cock" one too many times. As if she's read my mind, she continues. 'Your way isn't wrong, by the way. It's just different from mine. It works for you.'

We're silent until the truth slips out of me, so quiet it's almost lost amongst the breeze that rustles the leaves above us. 'I don't know if it is working, actually. I've been feeling kind of weird about it recently. I think I might be done with one-night stands.'

Josie nods and, the way she always does, patiently waits for me to elaborate. I look out across the common, squinting in the sun. I can just about see a group of boys playing football, and it reminds me of how my parents used to drag me to watch Max play for the local team every Sunday as kids.

'Did you know it's been six years since everything happened with Max? He texted me last night. It's the first year I've forgotten.' She lets me turn my thoughts over before I speak again. 'I just can't believe I had to be reminded.'

'Was he upset with you for forgetting?' She knows the answer already.

'No. He's always wanted us to move on.' I relish the next breeze that passes. 'It's taken six years for things to stop feeling so precarious. I feel like I can trust my footing again.'

'So maybe it's a good sign you forgot. Your brain is telling you to move forward.'

'I think that's it. And I think, maybe, if I'm done with one-night stands, it's because I want to try something a little more permanent.' Embarrassment turns my cheeks pink at this admission, but Josie doesn't laugh, or tell me I'm ridiculous. Of course she doesn't.

'What would that look like for you?'

'To start with,' I say, plucking at the grass, 'I'm going to try something simple. Just meet a guy and hang out more than once and see how it goes. It doesn't have to be anything more than that.'

'What if there's someone in your life already?'

I know who she's talking about, obviously. 'That wouldn't work, Josie. For a multitude of reasons. Starting with my cardinal rule. No mess.'

She shifts up onto her elbows. 'Explain the other reasons to me.' She takes a family bag of crisps out of her bag and holds it open in my direction.

'Because...' I take a few crisps and gesture vaguely into the air as I think it through.

Because he's probably leaving soon.

Because I keep people out in order to preserve what little control I have.

Because in my heart, I know I'm not enough for someone like him. I'm not warm or loving or kind, and he deserves someone who can give him everything; no caveats. I hope he finds that one day.

I let my lungs empty before I tell her the most important reason. 'Because we really are friends. And I don't have many of those. I don't want to ruin that.'

Like she's done many times in my presence, with those eyes pooled with ever-flowing wisdom, she says simply, 'Okay.' She grabs a crisp and nibbles the edges. 'You've been happier than I've seen you in a while. Getting out more. I think having Finn in your life is good for you.'

I don't have the heart to tell her that this job he's trying to get is on the other side of the world. She's finally stopped worrying about me. It's probably nice for her that I'm not draining the joy out of the room anymore. 'He's successfully done what you've been trying to do since we moved here.'

'Right? The minute I get too busy after work, you find someone else to spend all your free time with. Maybe you just never wanted to hang out with me.'

'I will always want to hang out with you.' Through a crisp-filled mouth, I add, 'Even if you're someone who willingly chooses ready salted crisps as opposed to literally any other, better flavour.'

She grabs the bag back from me with a laugh just as Alina returns.

'What did I miss?' she asks, flopping down on Josie's other side.

'Ava's on the hunt for someone to date. Like, actually date-date.'

Alina digs her hand in the crisp bag and, like a normal person, grabs a fistful and launches them into her mouth in one go. 'Any candidates?'

'I was chatting to a guy on Hinge this morning.' I take out my phone to find him. He's not my usual type, but that could work in my favour. I need to try something new. 'He's a climber. Very into… climbing things, I guess. Big fan of adventure.'

'Sounds just like you,' Alina deadpans.

'I'll have you know I like adventure. I *live* for it.'

'Going to big Tesco instead of Aldi is not an adventure,' Josie points out.

I flick a beetle off my leg with a barely-concealed squeal. 'I can be outdoorsy too. I've been doing the same kinds of dates on repeat, so when he suggested I join him for a climbing session soon, I agreed.' Josie looks wary, which is made worse when I add, 'I might have told him I am also a big climbing fan.'

She sighs. I've noticed she sighs a lot before starting her sentences to me. 'Why would you tell him that?'

'How hard can it be? Everyone's doing it nowadays.' Maybe if I say it enough times, I'll believe it.

'You're a very capable woman, Ava.'

'I sense a "but" coming.'

'But I wouldn't necessarily say you have the best hand-eye coordination. In fact, I'm pretty confident in saying you have the worst coordination of anyone I know.'

'Please, tell me how you really feel.'

Max is sporty, so surely there's *some* hint of athleticism coded in my genes too.

Suddenly the boys playing football yell, 'Heads!'

A fraction of a second later a football comes flying our way.

While Josie does the sensible thing and clutches her head like she's in the brace position on an aeroplane, I try to catch the ball, but it slides past my fingertips to land just behind our blanket. By the time I've picked it up to throw it back to them, the person it belongs to has already started to jog over to our spot in the shade.

The moment he spots me, his mouth drops open in a perfect "o".

Whenever Finn stands in direct sunshine, I wonder if it grew him. I can almost imagine him, incubated by a warm glow, growing into a human from the tiniest seed of light.

I sent my last text to him this morning and proceeded to mute notifications because I didn't want to read his reply. For some reason I said "the ladies love stubble". Looking at him now, backlit by the sun, hair tousled from playing football, I can confirm that yeah, it's me, I'm ladies. God, it should be illegal to look put-together on a day as hot as this.

'Hi,' I say, launching the ball back to him. Even though it was the throw of a dizzy three-year-old, he catches it smoothly.

'Hey,' he says quietly. He's not wearing his glasses, so I can better see the way his smile illuminates his whole face, stretching upwards into the wrinkles around his eyes. Then, noticing Josie and Alina, he adds, voice clearer and brighter, 'Josie! It's so good to see you.'

Josie sits up and says, 'We have to stop meeting like this. First the office, now here?'

'The office? Why did I not know this?' I ask, looking at Josie for answers while Finn throws the ball to the group behind him with decidedly better aim than me.

Finn grins and says, 'We coordinated an illicit rendezvous to talk about you behind your back.'

'I had a meeting in his building a few weeks ago and we bumped into each other,' Josie amends with a laugh, taking a sip from her can. 'Didn't I tell you?'

'No,' my eyes flit between them, 'you did not.'

I wonder what they really spoke about. The universe apparently isn't satisfied with shoving Finn and me in situations together, it's also dragged my best friend into the fray as well.

Josie doesn't notice my suspicion and says, 'Finn, this is my girlfriend Alina. Alina, this is Ava's Finn. I mean, Ava's...'

'Friend?' I suggest as she trails off.

'Nice to meet you,' he replies, dragging a hand through his hair to get it off his forehead. 'Do you mind if I sit?'

'Go ahead,' I say, offering him a small smile of my own.

Someone calls his name and he looks over his shoulder to yell, 'I'm done! I'll melt if I play for any longer.'

There's a chorus of boos behind him and he shakes his head with a chuckle before folding onto the grass opposite me, legs outstretched and bent at the knee. I slide back down into a lying position and am briefly aware of his eyes dropping to the neckline of my jumpsuit.

I make the mistake of glancing over at Alina, whose mouth is twitching, and I resume my mindless picking of the grass.

'Hey, you guys are matching,' she points out. I look down at myself and then at Finn, both in a khaki green linen. Although, while I'm about five minutes away from sweating through mine, his shirt billows around him like there's a wind I'm not privy to. Not for the first time, I wonder if he functions within an entirely different weather system from me.

'Were you really playing football in a button-up?' I ask.

'I didn't *plan* to, someone just had a ball and I joined in. But how do you even pee in that thing anyway?' Finn's eyes roam over my jumpsuit, looking for an exit. 'I don't understand it.'

'With immense difficulty,' I sigh. 'And you don't need to understand it. It's for the female gaze only.'

'You can just call us lesbians, you know,' Josie quips, which makes both Finn and me snort.

Another familiar figure appears behind Finn, crisps in one arm, bottles clinking in the bag on his opposite shoulder. 'Room for one more?'

Never one to turn down sustenance, I motion for Julien to find a free spot on the blanket. He drops a water bottle into the gap between Finn's legs, which makes him jump. Good. I was beginning to worry he's incapable of being bothered by anything.

Once fresh introductions have been made and Julien's deposited their drinks and snacks, we all shift into a circle around the blanket like we're worshipping at a makeshift shrine of G&T cans, Kettle chips and Tesco sweet chilli hummus.

'Please don't tell me you're one of those men who takes his top off in public,' I say to Finn, who's fanning himself with his own collar. The only evidence of the heat on him is the damp hair sticking to the back of his neck.

'Absolutely not,' he replies, opening a can with deft fingers. I'm sure the disappointment I feel is because he picked the elderflower G&T I had my eye on, not because of his answer.

'I am, though.' Julien lifts the bottom of his shirt, watch glinting, and I look approvingly, my horizontal position putting me at eye level with his abs. He has a habit of looking like he's shooting an advert for luxury jewellery everywhere he goes.

'Put that away,' Finn says with a grin, setting his can on the blanket and leaning back on his palms. Then he glances back at his friend's stomach, tilting his head and adding, 'Okay, but I get it.'

Thankfully, Julien reins in the obnoxiousness and doesn't actually remove his clothing, but it's enough for us to settle into an easy flow of conversation.

'What's next on your bucket list?' Alina asks.

'I usually let Ava take charge, but maybe you can help pick the next thing.' Finn hands her his phone, forever comfortable giving his life away to someone else.

While Alina's scrolling, Finn takes another sip of his drink. Still wishing I'd grabbed that last elderflower instead, I watch his throat move as he swallows, and analyse the veins on the hand that grips the sweating can. His eyes drop to mine and it makes me feel like I've been caught doing something I shouldn't. He holds my gaze for a beat before silently setting the can next to me and diving back into the pile to find a new one for himself.

'Oh!' Alina exclaims, interrupting my ogling. 'Outdoor swimming?'

Finn's nose wrinkles as he takes his phone back. 'I dunno, for that one I was thinking of just taking the train to the coast somewhere. I assumed Ava wouldn't wanna join in with something like that.'

I'm thankful I've spent our entire friendship demonstrating a lack of desire to partake in any activity that the average person may constitute as exercise. And yet, a voice that sounds suspiciously like my own says, 'Have you been to any of the lidos?'

'The what-nows?' Finn asks, his arm brushing mine as he moves from his seated position to lie on his stomach next to me.

'The lidos. You know.'

'Repeating it doesn't make me understand it, Ava,' he replies patiently, eyes zeroing in on the grass graveyard I'm creating at the edge of the blanket.

'They're outdoor swimming pools,' Josie offers. 'London has a few.'

Finn looks up in surprise. 'London has outdoor pools?'

'I believe that's what Josie just said, yes,' I reply.

'Huh.' He is, as expected, unrattled. 'Then let's go.'

'We can't "just go",' I explain. 'It's a whole mission; making sure you're there before the rush, especially on hot days.' I've never actually been to any of them, but I've heard Josie and Alina talk about it.

'I've always wanted to go,' Julien says, grabbing a crisp from the centre of our picnic shrine.

'Then let's do it! Next Saturday, Finn, if you're free?' Josie's buzzing. I, on the other hand, am suddenly regretting bringing the lidos up.

'I'm free. Julien, are you?'

'Me too. Ava?'

I grunt in agreement.

'Brockwell Lido is closer but Tooting is way better,' Alina says, sifting through our stash to find another can to pass to Josie.

'Tooting it is, then,' Finn says with a nod. 'Toot toot.'

'Don't do that,' I mutter.

We're all still eating and drinking our way through our stash when I remember I have something for Finn.

'There. All corrected.' I place the stack of his printed presentation and handouts between us on the blanket as the others chat amongst themselves. 'When I used to help Max with his homework he always found it easiest to read from yellow paper. I know you said you weren't sure if you were dyslexic too, but I figured I'd try a few colours for you just in case it helps.'

'You printed all of this for me?' His eyes are bright as he leans closer to grab the pile.

It's only when he starts flipping through the thick wad of pages that I realise I may have gone slightly overboard at the printing shop, and embarrassment threatens to take over. 'It was nothing. We're one of approximately seven millennial households in the UK that has a printer.' Josie's head snaps up from her conversation with Alina and Julien, and she opens her mouth to refute my lie but I scramble to my feet before she can say anything. 'Does anyone want an ice cream? I'm gonna get us ice cream.'

'I'll come,' Finn says, starting to get up too.

'I'll be fine. Ninety-nines for everyone alright? And a Calippo for you, Alina?' I don't even wait to hear the replies before I grab my purse and scurry away from the group towards the ice cream van that I know is waiting by the entrance of the park.

As I stride across the grass my eyes are almost closed with how much I have to squint against the brightness.

'Ava,' Finn calls, catching me up easily. 'Can you stop for a sec?' I slow down and he hands me the sunglasses I left on the blanket, which I reconcile with my face immediately. 'The pages you printed for me. Even if it was no effort, I really appreciate it.' He steps forward and lifts my glasses so he can look directly into my eyes for a second. 'Thank you.'

# 25

## I am, in a word, whipped

### FINN

SOMEHOW, EVEN THOUGH THE entirety of South London congregates on Clapham Common on sunny days, I didn't expect to see Ava here. As much as I'd intended to avoid her until Monday, the second I saw her it felt like stepping into the shade on a hot day. Which, incidentally, is exactly what I did. Maybe that wasn't as poetic as it sounded in my head.

I try not to look at her while her attention is on the menu board as we stand in line for the ice cream truck, but I can't help it. Her lips are slightly pouted as always, her chest flushed from the heat, and her hair's piled into an uncharacteristic bun, with wispy waves stuck to the back of her neck. I understand why that guy she hooked up with wrote poetry about her. I've understood for a while, if we're being honest.

'What do you think they're talking about?' she asks, nodding her head back the way we came. If she caught me looking, she doesn't show it.

I consider lying but decide against it. 'Whether we're secretly sleeping together.'

She nods slowly. 'What do you think their conclusion is?'

'They think we have. Well, Julien does, at least. I'm almost certain he doesn't believe me.'

I can't see her eyes behind her sunglasses and for a second regret giving them to her. She reveals more in them than anywhere else on her face. 'Why not?'

*Because I slip your name into conversation so often even I'm bored listening to myself speak.* 'Because we spend so much time together,' is what comes out instead.

'That's all?' We step forward a few paces in line and she unties her hair and restyles it, the way she often does when she's thinking.

'No, that's not all.' The heat's loosened the truth from my tongue, and I give her the smallest amount of it that won't scare her away. 'Because you're very much my type, as Julien is well aware.'

The sun goes behind a cloud and she slides her glasses up onto her head, revealing open curiosity in the slight widening of her eyes. 'And what's your type?'

What's my type? Smart, confident, beautiful. Probably too smart and confident and beautiful to stay interested in someone like me for long. That's not self-deprecation; it's just the way it is. I know who I am, and however much she holds back, I'd like to think I know her pretty well too.

'Brash, kind of rude, perpetually toes the line between tolerating me and wanting to shove me off a bridge.' She chuckles softly and it makes me want to pull out a full laugh; one of her rare, unapologetic ones that opens up her whole face. 'Oh, and bangs. Historically, I have always had a thing for bangs.'

There it is; the laugh that releases whatever burden she holds close at all other times. I almost don't want to taint the sound with my own, but I can't help it, so I let my laugh blend with hers; two instruments in a symphony.

A smile still tugs at her mouth when she stops, and she's quiet for a few moments. 'Didn't realise ten centimetres of hair could have such an effect on someone.'

'You have no idea.' I mean it as a joke, but the truth is, every tiny piece of her has an effect on me, and I'm too needy to walk away.

---

The following weekend Julien and I head to Tooting Lido a little earlier than the others. A rectangular gem of blue amidst the green of the common, with changing huts in vibrant primary colours lining one length of it, it's still early enough that we're not yet packed like sardines in the water. But with the morning sunlight beginning to blaze, it won't be long before crowds start to spill into the pool.

Julien's spent the better part of an hour trying to beat my lap times, and while I respect his dedication to failure, I'm glad when he swims to the edge to take a breather at last, leaving me floating somewhere in the middle of the pool. Which is where I am when I spot Josie and Alina approaching from the huts, Josie holding the crook of Alina's arm as they walk. From behind them, Ava appears.

I'm used to seeing her in her work clothes; dark t-shirt, jeans, an apron. I'm used to seeing her in regular clothes now too; usually a skirt or dress that hints at what's beneath but doesn't give anything away. I'm not used to *this*.

Not this much skin; slightly sunburnt below her neck, limbs dotted with bruises she no doubt has no recollection of getting.

Not the entire length of her legs where the black swimsuit cuts high up her hips.

Not the way the material hugs every curve and dip of her body, how it alerts me to the fullness at her chest, her stomach, her thighs. Fullness that makes my hands feel suddenly empty.

The person swimming past me looks at me in concern when I let out a groan of distress. And so, like the grown man I am, I swim to the other end of the pool before she notices me. I take my time with it, focusing on every move, every breath, and in doing so come to the conclusion that this lido trip was an awful idea. I'm like a horny teenager who's never seen a woman before.

By the time I reach the far end of the pool, I grab onto the edge and inhale deeply. Then, like a mirage or a nightmare, I hear her.

'Morning, Finn.'

I look up to find Ava's blue eyes sparkling brighter than the sun-flecked water, a smile casting its magic over her face as she perches on the edge. I pull myself up to sit next to her, which may be a terrible decision, but I'm losing my mind not being close to her.

Her gaze slides down my bare torso, neither subtly nor brazenly, and I manage to ignore the hammering of my heart to say coolly, 'Hey bud. My eyes are up here.' Ironic, coming from me, because it's taking every atom of restraint not to move mine from her face. She laughs, and I feel like I've won. 'Why are you so chipper this morning, Ava Monroe?'

She moves her legs in the water, taking her time to answer. 'I feel like I'm at a crossroads.'

'What kind of crossroads?' I watch her kick, hoping her ankles are a safe enough body part to look at.

'Seeing Josie finalise stuff for her exhibition, watching you go for a job you really want, knowing Max is thriving; it's made me feel like I should start making changes.'

She looks towards the far end of the pool as she continues, 'First of all, I'm going to stop hooking up with men I don't care about.' She juts her chin out and looks me in the eye, like she's worried I'm going to berate her. 'I'm not ashamed. But I don't think it's helping my mental health anymore. They filled a void for a while, and now they don't. I want to meet someone and try something simple. Something that doesn't leave my head in chaos.' Her eyes flicker to my mouth for a split second and I feel my jaw go tight.

'Sounds smart,' I get out.

'But more than anything,' she knocks me with her shoulder, a rare moment of physical contact, and my skin tingles where hers touched it, 'I want to keep spending time with the people I actually care about. My family, my friends.'

There it is, that word. Friends. Because I'm leaving. And as much as I think she also feels that little *something* pulling us together, maybe it looks different for her than it does for me.

'Chums,' I say at last, harking back to one of our first conversations on the day we made our weird, tenuous agreement to be friends. 'I don't think I've ever said that word in my life.'

I don't know if she remembers. The innocuous conversations that mean so much to me probably don't mean anything to her.

'There's a reason for that,' she says with a grin, just like that first day, and my heart expands in my chest.

Without warning, she pushes me in the pool, and I grab her arms at the last second to drag her in too, and we both emerge from the water a spluttering, laughing mess.

'This is fucking freezing,' she says through a shiver. Goosebumps peppering her skin, half her hair fallen out of her ponytail and her teeth chattering like some kind of deranged marionette, I realise with terrifying certainty that no one could ever come close to her. She calls back to me as she starts to swim away, 'Race you to the others?'

I let her win. I want her to win.

---

We float in a loose circle for a while—Josie and Alina holding the pool's edge while Julien, Ava and I tread water—until Julien says what we're all thinking and suggests we grab some food. The pool's busier now, which means Ava's hands keep brushing against my skin under the water by accident and I have to consciously try to not react.

'Another bucket list item crossed off,' she says, hair floating around her on the surface of the water as Alina climbs the ladder first.

'Is there a deadline?' Josie asks, hand sliding along the wall before getting out too.

'Whenever I leave,' I reply, and Ava shoots me a look I don't understand, and then, almost imperceptibly, shakes her head. I change tack, 'The list is never-ending though, so who knows if I'll ever finish it. I might do something with my dad when he comes to visit.'

Ava's head snaps towards mine. 'Your dad's coming?'

Finally, after tons of rescheduling and endless chats with his assistant, we've decided on a date. I'd been stuck to my phone for weeks waiting for updates, so the moment I received the text saying it had all been confirmed, a weight was lifted.

'Yeah, didn't I tell you? It took forever, but we've finally planned something for a few weeks' time.' I look up at Alina and Josie at the side of the pool to explain, 'He's great, but he lives in the US so I don't get to see him very often.'

For weeks now, San Francisco's held complicated feelings. I can't wait to get to know a whole new city, to try the food, see my dad more regularly and find out all his recommendations. Usually by this point in the process I'd have already researched restaurants and activities for my first few weeks, but I haven't planned anything yet. Maybe it's the fact I don't know for sure yet if I'm going, so I'm reluctant to get too enthusiastic in case it doesn't work out.

But in the meantime, the excitement I have to show London to my dad bubbles through me, and my nerves are simmering to near-boiling at the prospect of telling him I might be joining him in San Francisco soon. But that's normal, isn't it? Everyone wants to impress their dad, wants him to tell his friends about you, to tell you he's proud.

'What are your plans?' Ava asks, playing with the hair tie at her wrist as Julien ascends the ladder next.

'We're gonna be together for the whole day, which we never do, so I've got a few options depending on what he's up for. I'm gonna meet him at his hotel in Knightsbridge in the morning, then we'll go somewhere bougie for brunch—he has expensive tastes—and then, because he's really into this very specific type of antique, I was thinking of taking him to a few shops and dealerships.'

By now it's just Ava and me left in the pool, and she nods towards the ladder to tell me to go first. I don't trust myself to be a normal human with her climbing the ladder in front of me, so I heave myself up the rungs ahead of her.

I continue while Ava pulls herself up, 'I've made a reservation at this steak restaurant in Soho that he mentioned. I mean, I'm not a massive fan of steak but I'm sure there'll be something on the menu I'll enjoy. His assistant told me he was here a couple of months ago and tried to go but it was fully booked.'

'Did you know he'd been in London recently?' Julien asks quietly.

When I shake my head, the exact same expression flashes across his and Ava's faces, and I can't tell if it's pity or annoyance. They've misunderstood, so I scramble to explain, 'No, it's fine, I was busy anyway. But it's why I've been trying so hard to get this visit sorted.'

Ava clears her throat and says, 'Sounds like fun.'

It will be, and hopefully, with Ava's feedback on my presentation, my interview will go smoothly next week, and by the time I see my dad I'll have positive news for him. My chest hums from the anticipation of following in his footsteps.

# 26

## wish me luck, and some sanity would be nice too

### FINN

I'M BARELY INSIDE THE shop, still holding the door open for another customer when I hear, 'Finn, I need your expertise.'

'Good morning Ava. I've had a great week, thanks for asking.'

'Fine. What have you been up to?' I open my mouth to respond but she interjects with, 'Actually, I don't care.' My lips come together with a quiet pop as I approach the counter. 'I need you to teach me how to be charming.'

'I can't imagine why you'd need me to do that.'

Her eyes narrow into slits. 'I've been doing some soul-searching—'

'I didn't know you had one of those.'

'Has anyone ever told you it's rude to interrupt?' We settle into our spots; her behind the till, me perusing the snacks. '*Anyway,* I was thinking that if I want to start dating with intention—Google says that's what it's called—I need to work on being more agreeable.'

She pauses her spiel for a second to take a breath and it gives me enough time to ask, 'Can I get three flat whites, please, to drink in?'

She rolls her eyes, because really, how dare I order a drink? 'I can't be *me* for this hypothetical love interest. I need to be nicer. Warmer.'

'Ah, changing yourself for a man. That always works out.'

She aggressively tamps coffee grounds in response. 'This is actually the part where you say "oh no, Ava, you're already super nice and warm".'

'But we both know that would be a bold-faced lie.' I grab three packets of wafers and slide them onto the counter. 'You don't need to sand off your edges. Someone out there will be into the whole prickly thing you've got going on.'

'Right, well, I disagree. I need your tips on how to—' she moves her hands around in front of her, searching for the words '—embrace my natural charm.'

Her *natural charm*. Ava has the natural charm of one of those spiders that shoots needles from its body. 'Why can't Josie teach you? She's literally a professional speaker.'

'She's busy,' she says, pouring milk into a jug.

'And I'm not?'

'I'm not convinced you even have a job. All I ever see you do is drink coffee, move your notebook from one side of your laptop to the other, and periodically get up to flirt with our middle-aged customers.'

'The elderly customers too, in my defence.'

'That's not a defence. Have you ever completed a piece of work in here?' She starts steaming the milk and, as always, I marvel at how it's one of the rare activities she can execute non-clumsily.

'Sorry boss, I didn't realise you were keeping tabs on me.' In the hope she won't hear me over the machine, I add under my breath, 'It's not my fault this place is distracting.'

She turns off the steam and knocks the jug against the counter, swirling it in place. 'Why do you work here if it distracts you?'

Now is not the time for that conversation. I rub my jaw and reply, 'I thought this was about you and the desire to unleash your latent charisma.'

'It is,' she says. 'Just tell me how to be charming. Use your super-alpha-male, manly, masculine knowledge—'

'Don't love how many adjectives you used there.'

'—To help me figure out the perfect level of softness to make this guy I'm going out with like me in the right way. Not in, like, a purely sexual way.' She widens her eyes to emphasise the last part.

'Hold on, I'm lost. You want the guy you're dating to *not* be attracted to you in that way?'

'Yeah. No. I don't know. I haven't had much experience dating for any reasons other than sex.' She lowers her voice so that customers won't overhear, although frankly I doubt this conversation would be the most scandalous thing Belinda's ever heard. 'I want him to view me kind of how you do.'

Because I never view her the way I know I shouldn't. Right. I really can't tell if I'm a fantastic actor or if she's just horrifically unobservant. Both could be true. 'You want him to treat you like a human, essentially?'

'Yes, Finn.' She has the audacity to look at me like I'm the stupid one for not understanding her non-problem. 'I'm going on a date tomorrow with this guy who likes climbing, or bouldering, or whatever the fuck it's called, and he seems very nice.' She spits out the word "nice" like it's a live grenade. 'And I really want to try and get a second date. He feels like the kind of guy who'd be easy to date. Easygoing, interesting, *nice*. Believe it or not, I have never been asked on a second date with a guy I'm actually interested in. The only ones who've asked to see me again have been utterly unhinged or, like, eighteen.'

I'm not sure I want to know about the latter. 'I'm sorry, but I'm not going to tell you to change who you are.' She rolls her eyes before setting the last mug on the counter. 'Look, you've obviously already decided what you're doing. But I think you should be yourself.'

Ava looks at me incredulously. 'That's a terrible idea.'

'Okay, see? You don't want my advice.' I think about anything real I can give her. 'I guess, for me, I like it when someone shows an interest in something I enjoy. So the fact you're going climbing should put you in his good books. Then for the next date—because that is definitely happening, if you want it to—pick something *you* want to do instead. Something you're excited for.'

'Thanks. And how's it going for you?' The words dart out of her. 'With Alex. Have you been on any more dates?'

'Why do you wanna know?'

'I'm nosy, I guess.' She shifts on her feet. 'You were having a good time together at the restaurant, and I've seen you glued to your phone recently. I put two and two together. Figured you might've seen her again. Call it curiosity.'

'You're curious. That's the only reason?' Her cheeks turn slightly pink but she doesn't say anything. I wonder if she'll ever admit it. 'If I were to tell you that I've been on my phone a lot trying to plan things with my dad, and that I met up with Alex that evening because she's in marketing too and her mum thought she might be interested in taking over my contract when I leave, would that satisfy your curiosity?'

It's only when I finish my sentence that I remember I'd intended to keep the truth of that meeting to myself. So much for my morbid enjoyment of Ava's reaction to thinking I was on a date. Turns out lying isn't for me, even if it's only by omission.

Ava's trying to hold back her bewilderment when a pair of hands grabs my shoulders. I recognise Julien from his cologne alone. He smells expensive. 'Getting a pep talk from Ava before the big interview?'

Rory appears from behind him, perpetually looking both lost and dishevelled.

'Shit, that's today?' Ava asks, mask back on, running my drinks and snacks through the till at an unbelievable discount. She's definitely gonna get in trouble for that with her manager. 'Why didn't you tell me?'

'Must've slipped my mind,' I say with a shrug. In reality, the prospect of this new job and next stage of my life buzzes through my brain constantly; more responsibility, more opportunity, more new things to try. But when I stand in front of Ava listening to her complain about her ridiculous issues, the new job is barely a hum in the background. I don't want to sully the time we have with it, for some reason. 'Julien and Rory are here to help quiz me and listen to my pitch.'

Rory grabs a packet with a noise of unconstrained glee and Ava watches him clutch it like Gollum and his Ring. She meets my eye and says, 'That's my requirement. Someone who looks at me the way Rory looks at biscuits.'

'You don't think anyone looks at you like that?' Julien asks, a smile teasing the corners of his mouth.

'Full transparency, I don't actually know much about your job,' Rory says as he peels the packet open. 'Whenever you talk about SEO I zone out. I'm here because I wanted a coffee, and Julien said he might need reinforcements to keep you away from Av—'

'Let's sit,' I say, a surprised chuckle bursting out of me. As we take our places at a table in the corner, I sweep a few sugar granules off the table into a napkin and look at both Julien and Rory to say, 'Thanks for that, you two.'

'No worries,' Rory says, crumbs flying everywhere as he chomps on a biscuit. 'Wait, for what?'

---

The sounds of the coffee shop are a soothing soundtrack to my afternoon of interview prep, and Ava has been covertly administering sustenance in the form of free drinks and snacks for the past few hours.

At one point, she places a cup on my table and says, 'This is decaf. Because, you know, your bowels.' Romance isn't dead, folks.

As it nears four o'clock, I glance away from my laptop to see her running her hands through her loose hair, lifting it into a makeshift ponytail and then dropping it onto her shoulders. She touches her wrist and frowns.

'By the till,' I say, stretching my arms above my head with a grunt as I peer at my laptop one last time.

'What?' she asks, distractedly reaching for the missing band around her wrist again.

'Your hair tie. It's to the left of the till.'

She finds it where I said it was, secures her ponytail again, and pulls the ends apart to tighten it. I pretend I can't feel her eyes on me as I pack up my stuff.

Her voice is calm when she starts to speak. 'You're gonna smash it. You're good at what you do. At least, I assume you are. I don't actually know. But there's no way they won't hire you. You are,' she pauses, taking the time to choose her words, 'to my great distress, extremely likeable.'

I raise an eyebrow as I turn to face her. 'Are you flirting with me?'

I can't help it. This is the game we've played for months; teasing that goes nowhere, incessant back-and-forth. The longer it goes on, the more I know how much I'll miss it.

'As always, you have decided to make this conversation about how much everyone fancies you, which is not only false, but also untrue and incorrect.' She tries to keep a straight face but a grin spills over her expression the way moonlight brightens the dark. 'But it's true. They'll love you. So go, and good luck.'

'Good luck to you too, with your date.' We have such different plans for the next twenty-four hours, but both of them could culminate in something new. In opposite directions.

'Not as important.' We walk to the door together and she darts in front to open it for me. 'Don't let my lateness rub off on you.'

I stop inches away from her in the doorway, close enough that I can smell the vanilla in her perfume. My mouth opens to start a sentence my brain hasn't quite figured out how to finish yet. 'You're…'

'I'm what?' She leans against the door, a ghost of a smile on her face, watching me spin out of control behind the eyes.

*Impossible,* I think. Impossible to know, impossible to want, impossible to have.

'You're needed in the back.' I swallow and nod towards the counter. 'Dylan's been trying to get your attention.'

She's not the only one.

# 27

## what's the least sexy sport and why is it bouldering?

### AVA

*We'll get on if you're active, adventurous and outdoorsy.*

I am not active, adventurous or outdoorsy. This has never been something of particular significance in my life, until I got in the habit of lying.

When the automatic doors open from the changing room at Brixton Leisure Centre, I'm treated to a solid mass of sensory overload; the smell of both stale and fresh sweat, the air warmer and muggier than I'd like, and dubstep pounding through the speakers, punctuated by squeaks and bangs as people scamper up walls and drop onto mats.

'Ava, over here!' a booming voice yells from the far side of the room, at a clarity and volume I can only express as "musical theatre".

Every man from his mid-twenties onwards has his kryptonite; some physical activity to base his entire personality around. For Jacob-from-Hinge, it's climbing. For a multitude of reasons this is not a particularly sexy sport; the bendy shoes, the scurrying movement, the little tippy tap at the top of the wall.

I watch Jacob perform the aforementioned tippy tap, ugly shoes providing him with ample grip. I swallow. *Be nice.* When he catches my eye and grins from the top of the wall like a pirate atop his mast, I'm comforted to find he has a nice smile. I make my way over and reach him just as he touches the ground.

'So good to meet you, thanks for coming,' he says, bending down to lean in for a quick, sweaty hug that I pretend isn't gross.

'Thanks for inviting me!' I respond, channelling my most easygoing self. His dark blonde hair is half tied back in a messy bun and I mentally run through a checklist to make sure he is as he seemed online. Sweaty physical contact aside, so far so good. Now it's on me to be, well, not me.

'This wasn't exactly my plan for us this morning, but I was asked last-minute to teach a beginners' class to a group of summer school kids. But I'm really glad you're here—it'll be good to have another adult here to help show the students how it all works.'

'No worries,' I say. There are, in fact, plenty of worries. 'I've, uh, injured my ankle a bit though, by the way. It's fine, mostly, but I just won't be able to do anything super intense.'

If I were smart, I'd have said it was my wrist. But I am, demonstrably, not smart.

'Oh, that sucks,' his expression is comically sad. 'Just do as much as you're comfortable with. And we can head to the café after, if you'd like, to chat properly?'

'Sounds good,' I say with an uncharacteristic thumbs up. I realise I may now need to limp slightly for this whole session. Thumbs *down.*

He claps his hands together and addresses the group of teenagers milling around us.

'Alright everyone, it's time to climb!' I wonder if he's going to rhyme for the whole session. 'Climbing is about care, coordination and concentration.' Apparently he does alliteration too. A GCSE English paper come to life. 'My friend Ava is here to help today in an unofficial capacity, so if I'm busy and you have questions, just ask her.'

I spend the next fifty minutes roaming the room, refilling my water bottle, tapping the wall and doing nondescript stretches that I hope make me look professional. I successfully avoid answering any questions from the youths and make it to almost the very end of the session before being pulled onto the wall. Predictably, it does not go well. I blame my "hurt ankle".

By the end of the hour I'm a sweaty mess. No one else is as much of a sweaty mess as I am, but then, no one else has the upper-body strength of a worm. I make a mental note to stop lying. Or, like, to do it a little less, at least.

Most of the students have left by the time I muster the energy to approach Jacob. He's talking to some fellow climbers, and his face lights up when he sees me. I wait for the others to turn away before I say anything.

'You were amazing.' The compliment catches in my mouth on its way out. I try again. 'Honestly, I'm *so* jealous. But I'm gonna go grab my stuff from the changing room—meet you in the café in ten minutes?'

'Absolutely. Man, I was so busy I didn't even get a chance to watch you climb.' The cartoonish sad face returns. 'Next time, for sure.'

'For sure,' I agree, walking away.

As sweat trickles down my back, I realise I definitely need to rinse off, so I collect a towel from the dispenser and head towards the showers. I laboriously remove every layer stuck to my sweaty skin, before shoving them into my tote bag hanging on its hook. As the water runs over me in my tiny stall and I try not to gag every time my skin touches the freezing tiles, I think about Jacob. He seems friendly, polite and *sweet*. And so far, I think I've done an incredible impersonation of someone who is also friendly, polite and sweet.

I'm too distracted by my own smugness to pay much attention to the obnoxiously loud noise that starts up from the main changing area. They should really fix that. If it were a real alarm, it'd be blasting through the shower room too.

But then the alarm begins to blare in the shower area too, and a voice yells, 'Showers off, everyone out, this is an emergency fire evacuation!'

*Shit*. I frantically turn off the water and a million thoughts speed across my brain. Is it a real fire? Do I have time to get dressed? I can't leave the building in a fucking *towel*. I go to grab my leggings but they're caught in my bag and half-drop onto the wet floor, and frankly, putting them on requires a level of dexterity I barely possess when my skin is dry, let alone now.

The same voice shouts again, and fuck it, I refuse to die at a leisure centre.

I shove my feet into my Converse like they're flip-flops, grab my bag, and in what is possibly my worst nightmare come true, reenter the main changing area clad in nothing but a towel. I'm clearly not the only person who was caught unawares; people in various states of undress stumble out of the door, wincing against the endless blare of the fire alarm.

Luck is not on my side, because at the precise moment I step out of the changing room into the corridor, a flummoxed but impossibly familiar male voice says, 'What the fuck?'

Finn is, I'm surprised to note, clutching a towel around his waist, dripping with water like he also just escaped the shower, wet hair sending rivulets down his bare chest. I avert my eyes and we stand still in the hallway as the flow of people exiting our respective changing rooms eddies around us. How is it possible that this man shows up everywhere I am? Can't a woman participate in a fire drill half naked in peace?

A lady in a hi-vis jacket who must be the source of the prior yelling starts up again, 'Keep moving and *do not* block the doorways.'

I shake my head furiously and tighten my towel, which now feels far too small, silently following the flow of people to the closest fire exit. I'm relieved to find it opens onto a quiet side street away from the prying eyes of the general public. I join a few others sitting on a low wall on the opposite side of the street and Finn stands in front of me, droplets still glistening on his skin. The August sun beats down on us and I have to squint when I look up at him. Wordlessly, he steps to the side to block the light from my face.

When my retinas stop burning, I let them settle on the sight in front of me. Sun-kissed shoulders, those arms that easily lifted him out of the water to sit next to me at the lido, the shape of his torso that seems to *ask* my gaze to draw downwards.

'I can take the towel off, if you'd like.' My head snaps up to meet his eyes. They're playful like they always are, but behind them, something smoulders. It's fine. He's an attractive man, and I'm allowed to look. But that doesn't mean I want him to catch me doing it.

'Are you flexing?' I counter, trying to keep my eyes level.

One corner of his mouth raises in a smirk. 'Might be.'

I don't think it's the fire drill that's sent adrenaline beating its thunderous drum through my body. Somehow, even though I'm more covered up than I was at the pool, I feel like I'm showing every possible inch of skin. It's at this point that I realise I should've just risked putting my sweaty clothes back on. How likely was I to burn alive in the shower, of all places?

'This is the worst day of my life,' I groan. Josie's going to *die* when I tell her.

'I don't know,' he says smoothly. 'I'm having a great time.'

In an attempt to reroute my thoughts, my brain switches gears and I remember our last conversation. 'Wait, how was your interview? I meant to text you about it.'

'Honestly?' A lock of hair flops onto his forehead and he pushes it back. 'I don't wanna jinx anything, but they as good as told me I had it. There are some formalities they need to go through first but I'll find out for certain within the next two weeks.'

Finn's rarely bashful, but when he unsuccessfully tries to push down a smile, pride crashes through my chest. But there's something else I can't place too. I push it aside to say, 'Told you you'd smash it.'

I shuffle to the left to make space on the wall, tapping the empty spot for him to sit, but he shakes his head and stays where he is, continuing to block the sun for me.

'It feels like everything's falling into place, and with my dad coming to visit soon I'll be able to tell him about this new job.' He wrings his hands. 'I'm thinking maybe it could bring us closer.'

'You really want to make him proud.' If I had a son like Finn, I'd be proud simply by default. Not many people glow so bright that it makes you believe you could step out of the shadows and see the road ahead with their light.

'I guess.' He looks away and shrugs, and a few droplets glide down his arms from his shoulders. He blinks a few times and then meets my eye again, clarity sharpening his focus. 'What are you even doing here, anyway? I thought the gym was against your personal beliefs.'

'It is.' I send my mind back to just twenty minutes ago, but it feels like I'm wading through sludge trying to remember the reason I came. 'I'm here for the date I mentioned to you yesterday. Jacob the climber.'

'Hmm.' He gestures to the swelling crowd around us, the fire alarm still blasting in the distance. 'There must've been quite the spark.'

'I was *minutes* away from meeting him for coffee.' I tuck my hair behind my ears. 'We hardly spoke while we climbed. My polite and agreeable act was a waste.'

A muscle jumps in his jaw. 'I told you, you don't need to be someone you're not. Soft and polite and gentle isn't going to work.'

'And I told *you* I want something easy and uncomplicated. No drama.' What I don't say is that I'm not even sure I deserve anything more than that. 'I want to see what I'm capable of if I loosen up a little. And in this instance, loosening up means faking it till I make it. Who knows, if I act this way long enough, maybe I'll become sweet Ava permanently.'

I end the sentence with a grin, but it's like someone's taken a drawstring and tightened Finn's entire body. His forehead crumples, his mouth pinches, and his shoulders hunch as he looks down at me.

'Stop doing that,' he says in a low voice. 'Everything about you is exactly as it should be. I'm sure of it.'

His sudden intensity throws me off. It pushes and pulls at the same time; blasting me into space while the g-force pins me down and presses in from all sides. I don't like the way the tension closes up his features, so I let the moment tug between us, flexing and stretching and tugging until it settles.

'Okay,' I say with a nod.

'Okay,' he repeats, a small smile loosening the lines on his face. As the smile spreads, I grow too, a flower bud tasting the start of spring. It seems unfair that he can do this to me while all I ever do is bring the clouds to him.

After far too heavy a silence, I break eye contact to look around us and am suddenly aware again of the fact we're out on the street wearing nothing but towels. 'This whole thing is absurd,' I say at last.

I'm not sure what to do with myself, so I start digging through my bag.

'Sure you didn't orchestrate it to get out of climbing?'

'If I had, I probably wouldn't have set it up to go off while my naked body was writhing around a shower cubicle.' I glance up just in time to see a vaguely pained expression cross his face before he clears his throat and returns to nonchalance. Before I can unpack that, I spot something I'd completely forgotten about in my haste to leave the changing room. 'Oh my god. I have a dress.'

One expression after the other flicks across his face like an old stop-motion animation. Confusion, amusement, fondness, repeat. Every single one of them makes my heart hurt, just a little bit. I can only hope that wearing real clothes will stifle the tingling on my skin any time he looks my way.

'You're gonna leave me to be the only towel-clad person in this duo?'

'Sorry,' I say, tugging out the midi dress I'd stashed at the bottom of my bag. I've never had a baby, but I imagine this moment is akin to a first-time parent looking at their newborn. 'I'd offer it to you, but I have a sickening feeling you'd look better in it than I do.'

'You're probably right.' He runs a hand through his hair, the strands reflecting more red in the sunlight. 'I think the toga thing is working for me at the moment anyway.'

I risk another glance at his torso. Yeah, I'd say it's working for him.

Focus, Ava. You are here for your nice, easy date with a man who's staying in London and doesn't muddle every thought in your brain.

So, making sure I'm stable on the wall, I position my arms in the sleeves of the dress and try to squeeze my head through the neck hole.

I should've seen it coming. Just as my head catches in the opening, my towel slips. I don't even have a chance to gasp before Finn's standing between my legs, grasping the dress in an effort to help pull it down. For a brief second I'm concerned he might've seen something he shouldn't have, but I'm not exactly in a position to *ask* him about it.

My hand clutches at the towel in a desperate attempt to preserve a modicum of modesty, but the more I twist, the more I seem to get stuck in the dress.

'Just stay still,' he says in a measured voice, warm hands brushing against my skin, careful and commanding. I have to remind myself to breathe. Because I'm panicked. Not because I like the way his hands feel.

When my head finally makes contact with the outside world again, the first thing I see is the underside of his clenched jaw and the hard movement of his throat as he swallows. I wonder why he's so tense. But I am, for all intents and purposes, straddling the poor man; two measly layers of fabric between us. Which is why, when he moves closer to pull the rest of my dress down and his lower half presses flush against me, I instantly understand the jaw clench.

As soon as I'm covered, he leaps back like I've electrocuted him, and in a moment of what can only be described as pure comedy, his own towel starts to unravel. I yelp, he yelps, people turn to look at us, and tears well in my eyes at the sheer chaos of the situation.

'Fuck,' he mutters, sitting next to me on the wall at last. My eyes shift to the right and we both notice his predicament at exactly the same moment, and he frantically grabs my free towel and sets it on his lap. He puts his head in his hands and after a few seconds his muffled voice says, 'That was—'

'Absolutely disastrous,' I finish, and delirious tears start to stream down my cheeks as silent laughter rolls through me.

Still with his head in his hands, Finn's shoulders start to shake too. 'I'm *mortified*.'

Every pained laugh I hear from him elicits more tears from me, and I bump my side against his. He's as solid as ever. 'Thought you didn't get embarrassed?'

'I can say with confidence,' he turns his head to peek at me through the cage of his fingers, 'that you're the only one who gets this reaction out of me.'

I wipe a tear from my cheek and try to pick up my heart from where it's dropped to somewhere below my stomach. 'It was equally embarrassing for the both of us. I'll never mention it again if you don't?'

'Deal.' He reaches a hand out to shake mine but his towel shifts again and he shakes his head and mumbles, 'Nope, not doing that.'

We sit there for a while, my mind spinning as the final chuckles leak out of me, until Finn lifts his head from his hands and shoots me a smile that feels like a secret. He opens his mouth to say something, but then—

'Ava!' a voice calls, and I spot Jacob jogging towards us. *Jacob*. Who I'm meant to be on part two of my date with right this second. I wave meekly. 'I'm so glad I found you, I left my phone inside and didn't know how to contact you. You still up for the café?'

'Absolutely.' I ramp up the enthusiasm, eyes wide.

He glances over at Finn. 'Oh, hey. I've seen you around before, right?'

'Yeah, I swim here a few days a week,' he replies, fully recovered. 'I'm Finn. And you're Jacob? I know Ava from work. She was really excited to meet you.'

Jacob laughs, and it doesn't make me feel like a flower opening up in the spring, but it's still a nice enough sound.

'Cool. I hope we can actually hang out properly now.' He glances at my dress and adds, 'You look nice.'

The sun must dip behind the clouds for a moment, because the briefest shadow passes over Finn's face.

Our friend in the hi-vis jacket shouts above the din, 'Everyone, you can go back inside! Everything's safe—this was just a drill. Please move in single file and,' her narrowed eyes find Finn and me, 'do not block the entryways.'

'I'm gonna quickly say hi to these guys, and then we can head back in,' Jacob says, before jogging over to a group of people a few metres away.

'I might stay out here for a bit longer.' Finn watches a pigeon with ratty wings and a mangled foot hop along the pavement. 'Make friends with the locals.' Just as I start to get off the wall, he touches my arm with the lightest possible contact. It still burns, somehow. 'Hey. Be yourself for him. Please.'

He looks at me, and I might be clothed now, but the way his eyes bore into mine, I may as well be naked.

'Maybe. I'll see you next week.' I adjust my dress, fixing the neckline that's skewed to one side. 'Fully clothed, I hope.'

He makes a strangled sound that I assume is a yes.

After a trip to the bathroom where I added all necessary layers of underwear, I find myself sitting in the leisure centre's café with Jacob; all fluorescent lights and vinyl tabletops and polystyrene cups I feel guilty about using.

'If you didn't want to have this coffee with me, you could've just said.' Jacob nurses a green tea in his Keep Cup with a smile. 'After everything you've told me about yourself, I should've known that going on a date where we stay still the whole time wasn't going to be your vibe.'

'Actually, uh, I have a confession to make.' I take a deep breath. 'Funny story. To be honest, I'm not into climbing. I'd never even tried it until today. I was worried you'd turn me down if I mentioned it.'

I brace myself for his response.

'That's so sweet, Ava.' *Sweet.* That's a first. He sips his tea and reaches out to grab the hand that's not clutching my coffee, his gaze intense. 'You wanted to impress me?'

'Something like that. Sorry I lied about it.'

'Seriously, no worries. Guess this means I'll just have to teach you.' It's not exactly what I expected, but it's better than him being annoyed. 'Right. Where were we?'

Jacob tells me about a climb he did in Switzerland that changed his life, and I *ooh* and *aah* in all the right places, my customer-service experience coming in handy. He talks about the Alpine camp they stayed at, shows me photos of the views from the top of the mountain, describes the avalanche his group only just missed, and by all accounts, it's an interesting story.

But all I can think about is the fact that the unflappable Finn O'Callaghan isn't quite so unflappable after all.

# 28

## I can read you like a fucking book

A V A

JACOB CONVINCED ME TO join him for a second date at the climbing wall under the guise of it being a "do-over". With my newly adopted mantra to be more amenable, I agreed. And to be perfectly, divinely honest? I hated it just as much as I expected to. But Jacob thinks I'm charming and hasn't stopped talking about the "little white lie" I told him to get him to like me.

This is, so far, a success. I don't feel like my head is imploding when I'm around him. I don't feel nauseating butterflies in my stomach when he looks at me. Aside from the effort of pretending I'm nicer than I actually am, it's easy. Uncomplicated.

But today, maybe I'll hear a little less about climbing and a little more about, well, anything. Because at last, it's my turn to decide what we do. I drop him a text to confirm what time we're meeting, and, for probably the first time ever, Finn finds me smiling to myself at work.

'You're in a good mood,' he accuses, his own face lighting up when he sees me.

'Just excited for my date with Jacob later,' I reply. His smile falters for a fraction of a second, but it's back before I even blink. 'I remembered you suggesting we alternate between activities both of us are interested in. I've wanted to go pottery painting for ages, so I found a deal on Groupon for a class.'

'I'm sure it'll be fun,' he says, leaning against the counter. 'I, for one, am impossibly excited to see you do karaoke at the party tomorrow.'

'I will not be doing karaoke,' I argue, starting a coffee for him without finding out what he wants.

He cocks his head. 'We'll see.'

This party's been hovering in the background for months, and I'm almost surprised it's come at last. Things have changed since Josie first told me about it. One of those things is standing in front of me, the other is at the other end of a text. 'I'm considering inviting Jacob too.'

Finn blinks a few times and then takes his glasses off to clean them, not looking at me as he says, 'You want him to meet your friends and family so soon?'

'Not specifically. But Josie is a good judge of character, so she'll be able to tell me if anything seems weird about him.' Finn's expression is inscrutable and I sigh. 'When did we both get so busy? I used to have plans, like, once a week.'

My phone buzzes with a text, and from the sheer bulk of it, I know the kind of message it's going to be before I read a single word.

> Hi Ava, thought I'd send you a text explaining what's going on in my head at the moment. I won't be able to make the class tonight. It's not really my thing and I just don't think I'd enjoy it. I also think we should stop seeing each other. I've found your constant texts pretty overwhelming and, sorry if this is big-headed to say, but I think we're looking for different things. I should've called it off the moment I found out you'd made so much

> effort to get a date with me. Sorry it's not
> better news. PS stay rad, sweetheart.

Finn notices the drop of my jaw and I wordlessly hand him my phone. I watch the emotions roll across his face until he murmurs, 'Stay rad?'

'Really, that's what you got from all that?'

'He's an idiot,' he says simply, giving my phone back.

'Aren't you going to say "I told you so"?' I pour milk into a jug and steam it angrily. Which is to say, I scowl while I do it and hit the jug five times on the counter when I'm done. 'You told me not to pretend to be someone else, and here I am. Rejected by a man who told me to "stay rad, sweetheart".'

'Well, before I decide, are you upset about it?'

I pour milk into the mug as I take stock of my feelings. Kind of embarrassed about being dumped, slightly ashamed for putting on an act, and more than a little annoyed, because what did he mean by "constant texts"? I sent two one-line messages in a row. And maybe, just maybe, part of me is relieved. But upset?

'No, not really.'

'Then yes, I told you so.' I get the urge to ruin his latte art in response. His fingers tap the edge of the counter and he says, 'You deserve someone who pays attention, Ava. It's not difficult. You were playing a part, which was stupid, *as I said*, but if he was really paying attention he would've noticed. Because, no offence, but you're not as good an actor as you think.'

'Excuse me? I am a woman of mystery.'

'Don't even try that.' His fingers stop tapping and his warm eyes hold me captive, suspended in time for just a moment. 'I can read you like a fucking book.'

What's that supposed to mean? My heart pounds in my ears but I'm saved from any further confusion by another customer coming to the till. As soon as she's gone, my shoulders sag. Despite everything, I was actually looking forward to this evening. I scroll through my emails and groan when I see those fateful words: *non-refundable ticket*.

At my groan a quizzical expression crosses Finn's face, so I explain my predicament. 'I booked the non-refundable option for the class because I'm a cheapskate, so now I'm going to lose money.'

He looks me square in the eyes and says. 'Only if you don't go. So I'll come with you instead.'

'You don't need to do that.'

'You were really excited five minutes ago. Do you or do you not want to try pottery painting?'

I shrug, and he waits for a verbal response. Eventually, I say, 'Yes. I do.'

'Then it's settled. Besides,' he takes his phone out and his fingers fly across the keyboard, 'it's on my bucket list.'

He turns the screen to face me, and at the bottom of the list I read:

*Go pottery painting with Ava when a man who wears bendy shoes is a prick.*

---

We make it to the converted warehouse with moments to spare, after I'd got distracted trying to do eyeliner in City Roast's bathroom and Finn's restless phone-checking informed me he was getting antsy about being late. Somewhere along a labyrinthine corridor is our classroom, and there are two tables available; one right at the front, the other at the back. We head to the back because while I'm keen, I'm not *that* keen.

Just as we fold onto the plastic chairs, our instructor shakes a tambourine. I assume this is to get our attention, but she also strikes me as the kind of person who spontaneously plays the tambourine, so I'm not sure.

'Welcome, artists. My name is Rosetta and I'll be overseeing you today.' Her voice is almost hypnotic, and the quiet murmurs around us dull as everyone turns to listen to her. She looks exactly how you'd expect a pottery painting teacher to look; bedecked in jewellery that glints and chimes with every movement and wearing more layers than I'd imagine is comfortable in this August heat. 'In this class you'll be painting two items; a coaster, along with either a plant pot or trinket dish. Your coasters are on the table already, and I'll come around soon to find out what second item you'd like. You have an array of paints and utensils to choose from, so dive into the very recesses of your imagination and find out what your soul wants to share.'

'What does your soul want to share?' Finn whispers, nudging his knee against mine under the table.

I peer at the paints on our table to see what we've got. 'Some kind of retro pattern, probably?'

Rosetta finishes her explanation and with one last sweep of a supersized chiffon sleeve, she leaves us to it.

On our table we have a pile of paints, brushes and sponges, along with two ceramic coasters and two aprons. Finn rolls up his sleeves, one of which falls down almost immediately.

'If I'd known I was gonna be painting today I would've worn short sleeves.'

'Sorry for not telling you in advance I was going to be cancelled on,' I say drily, finishing tying my apron.

He stops rummaging through the paints to look at me. 'Are you really okay about that?'

'Thought you could read me like a fucking book,' I reply, one eyebrow quirked.

'That wasn't an answer,' he counters.

I go to grab the black paint from his hand while he's distracted but he swats me away. I take my hair out of its ponytail and relax as the tension leaves my scalp. 'I'm fine. I knew him for, like, two weeks; he didn't exactly change my life. But I'm just annoyed, I guess. That I lied to myself. That I pretended it could ever become something more than it was.'

He seems to turn his words over in his head before answering. 'Why were you so adamant he shouldn't see who you really are? Don't get me wrong, I think you dodged a bullet, but what makes you so sure that he, or someone else in the future, could never be interested in the real you?'

He squeezes black paint onto our palette and slides it towards me.

'Because,' I dip into the paint and start brushing it onto my coaster, 'how many people have you ever met who've said "oh yeah, my dream woman is cold, emotionless and incapable of love"?'

He doesn't respond for a while. I'm not sure if he even heard me.

'I don't think you're any of those things,' he says quietly. It's not until he's painted his entire coaster yellow that he speaks again, cautiously advancing through the words like he's walking an unfamiliar path; testing out each step before putting his full weight on it. 'I think you know most of that is a front, and it's easier for you to pretend you don't care, to believe you can't love anyone and they can't love you, because you're so scared of putting your heart into something and it going wrong.'

Well, what do you know? Maybe he can read me like a book.

Something fundamental shifts in slow motion inside me, my heart decelerating to a heavy thud.

'Why the long faces?' Rosetta's smooth voice comes from behind us. 'Pondering life's big questions?'

'Exactly that,' Finn says easily, and when I finally look up from my painting I catch him shooting Rosetta a smile.

'I'm here to find out whether you'd prefer a plant pot or a trinket dish.'

Finn opts for a plant pot but I have too many thoughts buffeting around my head to decide anything. 'Finn, you choose for me.'

'Nope.' He leans back in his chair and locks his eyes on mine, and the jolt it sends through me is enough to jumpstart my heart. 'You know what you want.'

Do I?

'Fine,' I mutter. I remember Rosetta's waiting for an answer and add, 'The trinket dish, please.'

With unparalleled glee, I learn that Finn is bad at painting. Like, really bad. Worse than he was at latte art.

He squints at the rim of his plant pot like he might find some answers there. 'I'll give it to my mum for Christmas.'

'I'm so sorry to tell you this, but I don't think even a mother's love could save that.'

'You're supposed to be encouraging,' he says, attempting to cover up a mistake with more paint and just making it worse.

'I am encouraging. Encouraging you to never try this again.'

Meanwhile, I'm pleased with my coaster, and while the trinket dish isn't perfect, it's not bad. I've painted it with blues and silvers like the night sky, and I tried to add a moon shape in the middle with thick enough paint for Josie to be able to feel it.

'That smug expression is unbecoming, Ava Monroe.'

I look at his coaster and snort, and I'm adding another flower to my own when a thought comes to me. 'Imagine Jacob in this class. Why did I think he should come?'

'He'd probably have scaled a wall by now.' He gestures with a paintbrush. 'He'd be up there in the rafters lurking like a little bat.'

The image forces a spluttering laugh out of me. 'He missed out.'

'He really did,' Finn says with a hum. 'Specifically, he missed out on seeing you with paint on your face.'

'I have paint on my face?'

He leans forward with his brush and swipes once along my jaw. 'Yeah.'

'You've watched too many rom-coms,' I tell him, shaking my head, because I know how this is meant to go. And yet, I can't help myself. I grab my brush and draw a line of blue on his left cheekbone, just below his glasses.

His smile splits open a trench in my heart, and for the first time, I want to put seeds down to see what could grow there if I nurtured it.

As we continue painting our masterpieces, every so often one of us will take a swipe at the other with their brush. We develop unspoken rules; we have to alternate streaks, we can't hit the same spot twice, and we need a different colour every time. It's ridiculous, but I've come to realise that this is often the case when it comes to Finn and me.

After a particularly successful attempt, he looks at me and says, 'Red's a good colour on you. You should wear it more often.'

When Rosetta comes to check up on us and heaves a sigh at our paint-splattered faces, it sends us into a fit of laughter.

'I feel like I've been told off at school,' Finn says between laughs, the sound seeping through my skin.

Once Rosetta's made it to the front of the room, she shakes her tambourine again to get everyone's attention. 'You have five minutes left, everyone, so start finishing up.'

I use my phone as a mirror to start cleaning my face while Finn does the same with his, and we're quiet for a while as we concentrate, sharing a pot of clean water, our legs angled towards each other under the table. I glance over at him at one point, and somehow, even with bright yellow across his forehead, his eyes are the brightest thing on his face.

'How's my face?' he asks after a few minutes, leaning forward and sending me a lopsided smile that makes my heart do a little flip. Just a tiny one.

'Paintless,' I reply. I look back at my phone and move my head around to get all the angles. I think I'm all clear too. 'What about mine?'

He licks his lips and I feel like he's about to say something else, but in the end he just says, 'You missed a spot.'

'Where?' I contort my neck some more but can't see anything.

He clears his throat. 'Can I?'

I nod and he picks up a fresh tissue before dipping it into the water. We swivel in our seats until we're facing each other, his legs either side of mine. He peels a few strands of hair from where they've stuck to the paint just under my jaw, before moving all of it to the opposite shoulder.

Every movement is gentle and considered, like he's handling something delicate. I close my eyes, because I'm too aware of him, and I'm worried about what he might see if he looks too close.

He takes my chin with his left hand, softly moving my head to the side so he has better access to the paint. There's no chance he can't tell my skin is heating everywhere he's touching me, can't feel my erratic pulse thumping like it's trying to make an escape.

When I open my eyes, I find his own, pupils wide, sweeping across my face like he's committing every feature to memory. If my heart did a tiny flip before, now it's winning gold at the Olympics, twirling and leaping around my chest. His voice is barely a whisper. 'Perfect.'

There's a loud clap and we jump apart. Rosetta yells, 'Alright everyone, please finish what you're doing. Leave your pieces on your table—since this is an express session, they'll be ready for you to pick up tomorrow after they've been fired in the kiln. All the information is on the pamphlets. Let me know if there's anything else you need from me. Thank you so much for coming!'

There's a chorus of *thank you*s and a low buzz as people pack their stuff away.

'Finn,' I begin, not looking at him. 'I don't want to be scared.' I scratch at a line on my coaster. 'But I want something that makes sense.'

He waits for me to meet his eyes. I can feel him searching for something in mine. 'What about this doesn't make sense, Ava?' Maybe he doesn't find what he's looking for, because when Rosetta drops a tub of paintbrushes up front, he glances over and says, 'I'm gonna see if she needs any help.'

He's removed his apron and has shot out of his seat before I've even registered what he said.

By the time my heart has eased back into a medically appropriate rhythm, I've removed my apron and tidied the table as best I can, but when I look around I realise Finn is nowhere to be seen. I make my way up to the front, where Rosetta is packing things into boxes.

'Hi, I was wondering if you've seen my friend, the one I was, uh, painting with,' I finish weakly.

She floats past me in a swish of fabric and says, 'Ah yes, the young man has been helping me carry some things to the storeroom. I usually have an assistant but she couldn't make it tonight, and my wrists just can't handle carrying things nowadays. Arthritis. Can't even do much painting anymore.'

'Oh,' I say, taken aback.

'Be a dear and take these to the storeroom too, would you?'

Before I can either accept or protest, she places a cardboard box in my arms and perches another two on top, where they wobble precariously.

'Where is the storeroom, exactly?'

'Take a right out of this door, walk all the way to the end of the corridor, then take a left, keep walking until you reach the painting of Jesus on rollerblades, and then the storeroom is through the door next to the sculpture of mushrooms wearing hats. Just put the boxes anywhere they'll fit.' As I head out of the room, narrowly avoiding knocking the top box off the pile, I just about hear her say, 'And make sure to keep the door wedged open—the handle's a bit temperamental.'

Right, end, left, rollerblading Jesus, stylish mushrooms. Got it.

# 29

## 3, 2, 1, game over

### AVA

My boxes aren't particularly heavy, but I'm relieved when I finally find the storeroom. The door's propped open with a plastic tub and Finn looks up from his crouched position as I approach.

'I wondered where you'd disappeared to,' I say, slightly out of breath as I step over the tub, almost tripping on it as I do. 'Thought you'd run away.'

Finn smiles but it doesn't quite reach his eyes. He stands up and relieves me of the top two boxes from my pile. 'Just got roped into helping Rosetta.'

The narrow room is lit with a single fluorescent strip, lined with overflowing shelves, boxes precariously stacked at the far end and various tubs of craft supplies piled on the floor. I look around for somewhere to put my final box.

'Did she tell you she has arthritis?' I say. 'That's so fucked, to be an artist who can't paint anymore. The universe was a dick with that.'

'It's shit,' he agrees, squeezing one of the smaller boxes into a gap on a shelf. 'The universe is a dick about a lot of things.'

I'm about to say something when I hear a strange noise I can't place. We both realise what it is at the exact same moment. The plastic tub holding the door open slides forward with a crunch into the storeroom and the door closes with a loud slam. Finn leaps forward to try the handle but it's too late.

'I'm so sorry,' I say. 'I must've nudged it when I was coming in.'

He tries the handle again and when it doesn't budge he lets out a low, '*Fuck*.'

'You're not claustrophobic are you?' I ask, nervous I've unintentionally made him live out his greatest fear.

'No,' he says, forehead against the door.

'I'm sure Rosetta will be here soon to save us,' I say, attempting to lighten the atmosphere that suddenly feels incredibly taut. 'Our knight in chiffon armour.' He turns around and slides down the door to the floor, arms resting on his bent legs, knees bobbing in agitation. 'Are you sure you're not claustrophobic? You don't have to be all macho and pretend. It's just me.'

'Just you,' he repeats with a quiet, disbelieving laugh. 'You're not "just" anything. I wanted to head home, that's all.'

'Oh. Right.' I swallow and turn away so he can't see the hurt on my face. I thought we'd been having a good time. We've been laughing all evening. It's been easy.

'Hey, that's not what I meant,' he says softly, standing up again.

'It's fine.' My voice is too breezy as I move to the end of the room and feign interest in a pot of buttons. 'I'm sure you have things to do that don't involve me.'

He leans against the shelving unit. 'Not really, no.' I move along to analyse another shelf, this one filled with miniature animal figurines, and he continues, 'That's kind of the problem.'

'How is that a problem?' I chance a glance at him.

His brows draw together. 'Because we spend all this time together, but every day it gets harder and harder for me to...' He doesn't finish his sentence, instead saying, 'When I said I wanted to go home, what I meant was that being near you sometimes drives me crazy, and going home would be a lot easier than desperately trying to keep my thoughts to myself while stuck in a closet with you.'

I ignore the warning bells in my head, focusing on turning a tiny clay horse around in my hand. 'What kind of thoughts?'

He runs a hand through his hair and then rests it on the back of his neck, bowing his head as he expels a long breath. When he looks at me again, there's a fever in his eyes. 'I've realised I don't even want to spend time with people if they're not you. No one compares.'

'Why?'

He rubs a hand along his jaw with a frown. 'What do you mean?'

'I mean,' I put the figurine back on the shelf and don't look at him when I continue, 'I don't understand why you'd want to spend time with me.'

The noise that comes out of him is pure frustration. 'Because you're smart and loyal and mean and kind of weird, but somehow even those words don't feel quite right, and because a smile from you is worth a hundred from anyone else, and because all of that—' I go to interrupt him but he puts a hand up to stop me, stepping forward as he does. 'No, please let me say this. I think for some ridiculous reason you think I couldn't possibly like you, but I do. I really like you, okay? Not just as a friend. Because friends don't think about friends the way I think about you.' When he speaks again, his voice is more desperate than I've ever heard it, pulling at something deep inside me. 'I'm sorry if that messes up this whole thing we've had where we pretend there's nothing going on here. Where you pretend you don't like me and I pretend the air isn't on fucking fire when you're standing too close. But it's how I feel.'

The walls are drawing in with every breath I take. I shake my head. 'It's so messy.'

'Fuck, I'm sorry. I know there's a high chance I'm leaving soon. I wanted to be your friend and only your friend, because that's what both of us needed. I tried not to feel like this. And then I tried to ignore it. But now it's too late, because it feels like my entire life revolves around you. Like you're the centre of everything.' Heat burns through my lungs, through my veins, and something within me thaws in response to his words. His voice is strained when he continues, 'Every decision I make I think of you. Every single happy moment from the last few months has been with you. Every time anything happens I want to share it with you.' His chest rises and falls with the force of his admission, and his voice is quieter now. 'And I really don't know what to do with myself when you act like you don't feel something too, because it's written all over your face.'

'You can't know that,' I whisper. His words sit between us, and the air is sticky honey, coating every square millimetre of my skin until all I hear is the buzzing of bees in my head. 'You don't know me. Not fully.'

'Really? I know that when you're concentrating you take your ponytail out and redo it over and over. I know that you would go beyond the ends of the earth for the people you care about. And Ava,' he moves closer and my back meets the sharp edges of the shelving unit, 'I know that your breath catches when I'm this close to you. So tell me I'm imagining it. Tell me this is all in my head.'

Heat pools beneath my skin with every word and for a few moments all I can concentrate on is remembering to breathe. He's one step away now, the light above our head flickering like it too feels the electric charge between us.

'Finn,' I whisper, but there's no fight in it. Only fear. Because one wrong exhale and the fragile illusion we've crafted these past few months will shatter. 'We know how this ends.'

'Maybe.' He wades through the heaviness to take his final step, until the only space left between us is that barren no-man's land between two sides of one decision. 'Maybe not.'

As though I might break if he moves too quickly, his hands find their way to my face, the pads of his thumbs slowly passing over my lips, fingers gently weaving into my hair. But he leaves the final move to me.

I wonder if I'm even in control anymore. Because there's something hopeless about this. Something inevitable.

*You know what you want.*

I move my head until there's nothing at all between us, not uncertainty or indecision or fear, and my lips brush against his. That featherlight touch alone sends my nervous system into a frenzy. He dips back in, testing the waters, swallowing the sigh I breathe into his mouth. It's even better the second time. The moment he pulls back an inch I know I've never been so desperate for someone in my life, so I knit my hands into his hair and tug him back against me, *finally*.

My lips part for him as his do for me, and it's not sweet, or graceful, or soft. It's months of desperate almosts and not-nows culminating in a greedy frenzy that sends me reeling with every touch. My heart's running rampant in my chest as the kisses deepen, and I feel his mouth everywhere; my jaw, my throat, my collarbone, but I pull at his hair to bring his lips back to mine, because somehow I miss them being there already. *More*, I want more.

One of his hands holds the side of my neck while the other acquaints itself with every line of my body, pausing at my lower back and pulling me flush against him. That hand slides under the hem of my t-shirt and clutches at the softness of my hips and waist forcefully enough that I'm sure it'll leave a mark, but I welcome it with raspy exhales, because it's proof this is really happening, that I haven't floated away into nothingness like my brain is telling me I have.

The unyielding shelves creak against my back, forcing me even closer to him, the solidity of his body pressed against mine; broad shoulders, strong arms, stomach muscles that tighten when I slide my hand under his shirt and hit the skin just above his waistband. His teeth graze my neck as his hands continue their tour of my body, until the one at my waist slides down to my thigh, pulling my leg up to hook around his hip. I let out a whimper when I feel he's exactly where I want him, and he pushes forward and takes my lips again with half a groan as I roll my hips towards him. This isn't going to happen again. It can't. But I'm not going to deny myself the vision of Finn against me the way he is right now, so I clutch him tighter and kiss him harder.

I try to decipher the thoughts swirling around my head, but then Finn's lips find my collarbone, or his breath hits my ear, or his hands drag down my lower back, down, down, and in the end I realise I don't need words when he's telling me everything I need to know without them.

Because Finn kisses like a man who wants to learn. To understand every sharp exhale, every slow sigh, every movement of my hips, and somehow he already knows that whenever he brings his lips to my throat, I push against him, hands dragging through his hair, clutching at his shoulders, his arms, running along his jaw, all the hard parts of him making way for the soft parts of me.

'*Fuck*, Ava,' he murmurs, kissing up my throat, leaving one hand at the base of my neck while the other slides up my waist to splay against my ribs, then down to the curve of my ass, then back up, like he can't decide what he wants to do.

'Don't talk,' I grit out.

He laughs against my ear, and even within this frenzy there's a warmth to him that I know I could never emulate. It occurs to me that we should swap; it's strange for someone so gentle to have a body so solid, while I'm here with this iron fortress of a heart, housed in a body that's nothing but jelly.

But then, maybe that's why it feels so good to be this close. Maybe we're what the other is missing.

I can believe he's what I'm missing when I hold his jaw and angle his face towards mine and he kisses me so intensely I feel like I'm transcending the need for oxygen. Because I don't want to do something so mundane as *breathe* right now, not when his tongue is in my mouth and sending shivers down my spine.

I can really believe he's what I'm missing when he pulls my leg tighter around him and I rock against him to appease some of the heaviness pooling between my thighs, and I'm certain I've never been so furiously needy before, coming undone just being this close to him.

And then I wonder about what else could come undone, and my hands are at the top button of his shirt, and I'm clumsy and slow and perhaps in the end that's my saving grace, because it's at this moment that the storeroom door opens with a thunderous bang.

We spring apart and I'm so disoriented I forget where I am or why I'm here.

Rosetta stands in the doorway with a knowing look on her face. 'Realised you two hadn't come back and thought you might've had a mishap with the door. Sorry about that. Hope you weren't too bored in here.' There's a glint in her eye and I smile weakly, sure my hair is a mess, my face is flushed, sure that even if I looked perfectly normal, she'd be able to feel the suffocating tension in the room.

Finn faces away from the door, breathing deeply, eyes up to the ceiling, adjusting his trousers as subtly as he can manage. I have to make an effort to look away from him.

I clear my throat before I reply. 'Thanks for rescuing us. Thought we might have to set up camp for the night.'

'I'm sure you'd have found ways to entertain yourselves.'

# 30

## 'I'm not going to do karaoke' and other lies I tell myself

### AVA

I WOULDN'T SAY JOSIE'S events management style is dictatorial, but I wouldn't *not* say it either. She's had me running errands and setting up for the party all day, and I've been so busy I've not had the chance to think about what happened last night. She's even roped Max into helping, who arrived earlier this afternoon, enlisting him to hang fairy lights as our resident walking ladder.

Now, as I'm scouring my wardrobe, is the first opportunity I've had to let my brain wander. I cannot for the life of me figure out what to wear, which definitely has nothing to do with the fact Finn is coming.

I more or less ran away from him when Rosetta let us out, intent on putting as much distance between us as I could, as soon as I could. I was concerned about what might happen if I'd stayed with him. Because he was right. There *was* something between us. Some tension we needed to quash. Now it's out of our system, it never needs to happen again and we can get on with our lives.

I mean, I can try, at least. My brain decides this is the moment to remind me that Finn O'Callaghan's kisses are utterly obscene.

I tug a top off a hanger with a groan. Okay, I'll just try to get through this evening. That's all. Baby steps. No need for any weirdness while my two favourite people (who I will never, *ever* tell about any of this) are here too. I refuse to let Finn send everything into chaos.

I'd half expected him to text me about it, but so far there's been nothing. Maybe he's not even coming to the party anymore. I might be safe. But I also want him here. I think. Fuck, I don't know. See? Chaos, and the party hasn't even started yet.

The sound of Max and Alina laughing in the living room makes me smile, and then there's a knock at my door, followed by Josie barging into my room with the subtlety of a bull in a china shop trilling, 'Today's the day!'

She stands expectantly in front of me, a glass of Prosecco in each hand. I take one of them gratefully, relishing the fizz on my tongue.

'It is,' I say noncommittally. Then I analyse her face and say, 'You've got a tiny bit of mascara flecked under your left eye, hold on.'

I hand her a cotton bud and she wipes it away as I go back to rummaging through my wardrobe. We had this routine when we were at uni; she'd knock at my door, I'd check her makeup, and then we'd do whatever our eighteen-year-old selves were in the mood for, which mostly revolved around me agreeing to join whatever new hobby she'd decided to start.

'You don't seem excited. I thought you might *finally* be looking forward to this.' She perches on my bed, which is bestrewn with proof of my sartorial indecision. She, on the other hand, looks immaculate, with an emerald silk blouse tucked into a darker green mini skirt.

'My get-up-and-go appears to have got up and gone.'

'I'm not sure your get-up-and-go ever got up and came,' she points out, pulling an uncomfortable-looking pair of denim dungarees from under her.

'Well, exactly.' I sigh. 'I don't know what to wear.'

'The nineties dress,' she exclaims. 'The one from the charity shop that I forced you to buy? We can be matching in green.'

'Josephine, you are the answer to all my prayers.' She shrugs and sips her Prosecco, and I unhook two hangers that have got tangled up in each other as I ask, 'Are you all packed for your trip?'

Tomorrow, Josie and Alina are going away for a few days visiting Josie's family, and I can't tell if it's admirable or insane to do this the day after a party.

'I think so,' she says, finishing her glass just as Alina calls for her help from the other room. 'My services are required elsewhere. But Ava,' she brushes invisible dust off her skirt, 'just relax tonight. And have fun.'

She sweeps out of my room in a cloud of floral perfume, and I eventually find the dress pooled at the bottom of my wardrobe, fallen off its hanger.

---

The low hum of music through the wall is regularly punctuated by hoots of laughter and the sound of the front door opening and closing. I've only just finished getting myself sorted, mostly due to a chaotic experience styling my fringe that made me seriously consider just chopping it off.

My too-low mirror taunts me, and I stand far away to get as much of myself in the reflection as possible. The dress is a forest green, and as close as I'll ever get to a colour found in the rainbow. It's tight across most of my body, clinging to every dip and bump in the way the world thinks I should be insecure about, thin straps holding it up over my shoulders. I fluff up my hair, smooth the material over my hips and step out into the party.

People are milling about in the living area, sprawled across the sofa and armchair clutching drinks, or sitting at the wooden chairs around our dining table. Rudy's clearly enjoying the attention he's getting while he's off duty, moving around to find new people to receive pets from. The crowd is mostly made up of Josie and Alina's peers from the art and museum circuit. I recognise a few of them from Instagram photos and shoot a smile at two of Josie's author friends who I met once at a pub in Tooting. Interspersed amongst them, Josie's playing hostess offering drinks, Alina never far behind, and Max is cracking up at the end of the breakfast bar as he talks to a curly-haired man in a burnt-orange shirt with his back to me. But I recognise that back. The last time I saw it was in a messy storeroom.

As if he feels my eyes on him, Finn turns around, and in that moment I don't know if I'm relieved or terrified he's here. I still can't quite believe I acted on impulse last night. I don't *do* things like that.

'Late to your own party,' he says as he approaches, stopping a foot away and leaning against the archway that separates the living area from the bedrooms.

'Technically, it's Josie's party. I'm just her sous-host.'

I don't miss how he drags his gaze down my body and back up again. But then, I'm not sure he wants me to. 'You look—'

'Don't finish that sentence,' I cut in. 'Let's not do that here.'

When he meets my eyes again he says, 'I went back to the warehouse and collected our pottery. I just gave your pieces to Josie and she stashed them away somewhere. But,' for the first time I notice he has something in his hands, 'I figured that since this is a housewarming I should bring you an actual gift.' He gives it to me and I can't stop the stupid smile from spreading across my face. The ugly plant pot he painted yesterday is now home to a tiny, spiky cactus. 'Apparently these things are almost unkillable.'

'Sounds like a challenge,' I say, peering again at the terrible artwork. It somehow looks worse than yesterday.

He grins again. 'If anyone can do it, you can.'

I laugh and take the plant to my room, depositing it on my chest of drawers and hurrying back to Finn before he gets any ideas about following me. 'I'll cherish it forever. But also, calling this a housewarming was just a ruse to get people to come. We've lived here for the better part of a year.'

'In that case, give me the pot back.'

'Absolutely not. I'm giving it to Josie to put in her exhibition.'

His laugh unfurls, and I do too, and then I can sense what's coming next. He takes the smallest step towards me to ask, 'Are we gonna talk about it?'

'No,' I say simply, and I can practically feel his eyes rolling at my refusal as I brush past him, inadvertently swirling his cologne around me as I do. I make myself an Aperol Spritz while one of Alina's friends grabs a can from the fridge, and Finn waits for them to move out of earshot before speaking again.

'I don't understand.'

'There's nothing to understand.' I take my glass and walk past him once more, but he catches me by the wrist so that I can't help but face him, and the air thickens enough to make it difficult for me to talk. I keep my voice as level as I can. 'It was just a kiss.'

He shakes his head with a short laugh and leans in, voice rough against my ear. 'I was there, Ava. No it wasn't.'

He lets go and I walk away, pretending the thunderous pounding of blood in my ears isn't drowning out the conversation I join.

# A COLLISION OF STARS

I glance over at the sofa, where Finn and Max are howling with laughter. Finn lifts his shirt to clean his glasses of tears and the second I see that innocuous strip of stomach I'm launched back in time to last night, to the feel of him under my hands. I avert my gaze and try to pay attention to the conversation, where Alina's bashfully talking through some of the pieces of her art that we have on our walls.

As her friends move closer to one of the frames, Alina steps towards me, her tone suspicious. 'Ava,' she says slowly. 'What exactly is going on between you and Finn?'

'There's tension, right?' Josie asks, appearing out of nowhere—a magnet for gossip—and passing her girlfriend a drink.

'Nothing is going on.'

Finn raises his drink to his mouth and looks my way, holding my gaze for a beat too long. I bring my own glass to my lips but find there's only ice left. He smirks and turns back to Max.

'Right,' Alina says. 'Because all you're doing is looking at each other and I'm blushing.'

'I don't know what you're talking about.'

'Mate, are you good for a beer?' Max asks Finn as he heads towards the kitchen for a refill, where Julien and Rory are talking with one of Josie's work friends. My tipsy brain notices he's still not putting his weight on his leg fully, just like the last time I saw him.

I push past everyone to sit on the newly vacated sofa.

'Behave yourself,' I say to Finn, no preamble.

He laughs and I hate what it does to my insides. 'You're the one acting weird tonight.'

I can't even deny it. 'Just be normal.'

'As addressed. I *am* being normal.'

'No, you're looking at me like,' I brandish my glass, 'I don't know, like you want to devour me.'

'Funny,' he murmurs, so low it's more of a feeling than a sound. His tongue flicks across his lips and when his gaze moves over me, it turns my blood to syrup. 'Because that's exactly what I want to do.'

The entire bottom half of my body melts like wax to a flame, and I shift on the sofa in the hope that I might solidify back into the shape of a stable human. Max laughs in the kitchen with one of Josie's friends and it draws me back into the room.

Finn raises his eyebrows and then leans back against the cushions, looking over my shoulder for a moment. 'I think I'm in love with your brother.'

I bite back a smile. Finn doesn't even know half of what makes Max so incredible. 'Not the first time I've heard those words come out of a friend's mouth, funnily enough.'

'Is it fair that he's tall, funny *and* cool?'

'Adjectives that describe only my brother, and definitely not me at all, not even a little bit.'

'You, Ava Monroe,' he tucks a strand of hair behind my ear, fingertips lingering for a fraction of a second at my neck, 'evade description.'

There it is again, my heartbeat finding a home somewhere between my legs. I inhale deeply and ask, 'What were you two talking about, anyway?'

'Everywhere I've lived, the places we've both been, where we wanna travel to next. I'm pretty sure I watched some of his videos before I ever met you, actually.' He watches me swirl ice around my glass. 'Maybe that's why I like him. I feel like I'm in the presence of a celebrity.'

'What am I, a piece of dirt?' He sighs at my petulance, but his smile is fond when I continue, 'You're right though. Max is something special.'

The party buzzes around us but here in this pocket of space, everything is still. He studies me, choosing his words carefully. 'Did you know everything on this planet is made of stardust? You, me, this couch. All of it. But I think it's often easy to forget that.' His gaze sends static shocks tingling across my skin. 'I never forget that you come from the stars, Ava.'

My voice is quiet. 'You have to stop saying things like that.'

Max reappears and flops down into the space between us, jerking me backwards. 'Saying things like what?'

'Nothing,' Finn and I say in unison.

'Are you bullying my sister?' For a split second, I can tell Finn thinks he's serious, but then Max shrugs and adds, 'Was hoping to join in. It's one of my favourite pastimes.'

'I think you probably already know who the bully is in this relationship,' Finn says under his breath, taking a beer from Max, who barks out a laugh. A laugh threatens to escape me too, for an entirely different reason.

Max sits forward to talk to someone on the opposite side of the coffee table and I lean towards Finn behind him to whisper, 'You don't have to pretend to like beer around him. Just ask for something else if you want it.'

'I like beer,' he says unconvincingly, taking a swig from his bottle and just about hiding a grimace.

Max sits up straight before looking around the room like he's searching for something. 'Okay, I was told there'd be karaoke. Why is no one singing?'

Finn catches my eye again and says, 'See? I knew I liked him.'

'Before we do, I have a question.' Max shoots me a grin, mischief in his eyes, and I can tell what he's going to ask because we've been playing this game since we were old enough to drink. 'My sweet, sweet sister, what time is it?'

I release a noise that's probably a laugh but could easily be a sob. 'I think it's shots o'clock.'

Josie does, of course, coax me into performing with her. And once Max's shots are involved, I need even less persuasion.

I open my eyes as I release my hand from an air grab, successfully ending a particularly emotional ballad that really shows off my range. My range is, arguably, extremely small, but I've shown it off nonetheless. Someone whistles from the kitchen, Rory applauds from the sofa like he's front row at the O2, and Finn lets out a choked sound from the dining table before dropping his head in his hands.

Alina and her friend get up to sing Dolly Parton and I pull out the chair next to Finn. After a couple of moments, he looks up at me, eyes watering, and I wonder if I should offer him a tissue.

'Oh my *god*,' he says at last, the final word breaking the fragile remnants of his resolve and sending him into a fit of laughter. 'That was life-changing. In entirely the worst way. Like, genuinely, I fully understand why you didn't want me to come to the party now.'

I flip him off, which only makes him laugh harder. 'Fuck off, I don't see you hitting those notes either.'

'Tell me,' Finn looks at me again, laughter escaping from him in sharp bursts as he tries in vain to recover his composure, 'when you encounter a melody, would you say that you typically consider it a concrete set of rules to follow, or more just a vague suggestion?' Max passes us on his way to the bathroom and Finn asks him, 'Did you hear that?'

'That's one of her better ones, unfortunately. You're forgetting we were raised in the same household.'

'This,' I point between the two of them and shake my head, 'is not happening. You're not allowed to gang up on me. I just bared my soul. Have some respect.'

'Maybe you should have some respect for my eardrums,' Max says, scooting away before I have the chance to deliver my scathing retort.

Finn watches me with a smile on his face and it sends my pulse skittering. But then the buzzer goes and I glance at the door to see who's arrived.

'It's Dylan,' I say, and the pair of us stand up, though neither of us steps away yet. 'I invited her last minute. She wasn't sure she'd be able to come because she had something with her boyfriend.'

'Hey, after all that, you didn't even need to make up a fake friend from work for this party.' He points his thumb towards the door and starts to turn. 'I guess I'll see myself out.'

I rest my hand on his bicep instinctively, the muscle hard beneath the fabric. 'I do need you. As a fake friend. Or a real friend. Or,' I let go of his arm and shake the thought from my head, 'something.'

He turns back to face me, inches between us, and I remember what it was like to be even closer to him than this. What it was like to feel him, to taste him. And there by my dining table, what little control I thought I had plunges out of my grasp like smoke between my fingers.

'At this stage, Ava,' I'm convinced he's about to mention how he can see my heart ricocheting around my ribcage like a balloon with its air let out. But all he does is trace the lightest pattern on my hand with his fingertips and say, 'I'll be anything you want me to be.'

As Max, Josie and Finn perform an enthusiastic cover of *Take A Chance On Me* by ABBA to raucous cheers from everyone in the flat, a heat descends on me, and I wonder if anyone else can feel it too.

The warmth that coats my skin isn't sticky humidity like that day at the Barbican, or the biting burn of the midday sun on Clapham Common, but a fizzing haze that melts the frozen fortress around my heart, sending it floating away as steam.

It feels like time's playing on my side for once. Like it's saying, *don't worry, I'm saving this one for you.* I'm sure that someday, when I go to look back on this night through the sepia-tinted lens of nostalgia, these time-warped memories will have settled deep into the recesses of my mind. But I'll bring them out and dust them off and see them for what they were: bold and bright and packed to the brim with the arrogant invincibility of youth.

Is this what I've been holding back from? People and places and new experiences, risking it all in the reckless hope of having more moments like this?

When Finn catches my eye as he sings into the microphone he's sharing with Max, that smile so big it pushes up into the creases of his eyes, a laugh floods out of me, and then the warmth turns to light and the whole room is aglow.

*I could take a chance on you*, I think. *I could take a chance on all of it.*

# 31

## I'm not okay (not even a little)

### FINN

I HAVE NO IDEA how I've successfully been in Ava's presence for multiple hours without doing anything stupid, but it's getting more difficult by the minute.

First, she came out of her room in that green dress and I had maybe the world's least family-friendly thoughts. Then she sang some horrific renditions on karaoke and *somehow* that still sent every one of my internal organs careening into the abyss. Now, she's on the floor with Dylan talking about their terrible manager, cheeks pink, long legs stretched out in front of her, absentmindedly petting a curled-up Rudy.

'Colin!' Max yells from the kitchen, pulling me out of my reverie. Who the hell is Colin?

I'm surprised when Ava's voice replies, 'What?'

'Help me get these glasses.'

'I just sat down,' she grumbles.

'But I can't reach them,' he says with a grin, as if he isn't, like, six-five. I can't help that my eyes cling to her every move; the extraordinarily ungraceful way she gets up, how she pulls her hair up into a ponytail with the scrunchie on her wrist, how she tugs her dress down over her hips and—

'You good?' Dylan asks with a chuckle, quiet but observant as ever.

She knows, I know, I'm pretty sure everyone in this room knows, because despite how desperately I've been trying to play it cool in front of her, I have a neon sign flashing above my head saying *SOS! Ava Monroe makes me feel a lot of things!*

I don't even bother denying it. I just laugh along with her and say, 'Not really.'

---

I'm chatting with one of Alina's friends by the time Ava returns from her conversation with Max, her eyes bright.

'Ava, have you met Sage?'

I gesture towards the silver-haired person at the far end of the sofa, who replies, 'We met before at Alina's birthday, I'm pretty sure.'

Ava hands me one of the two glasses she's carrying, and I'm grateful because I didn't even realise I'd finished my last drink. 'We did—you were wearing those Lucy & Yaks I wanted.'

'Well, did you know they work at the Natural History Museum? With the dinosaurs.' I grab her forearm to reiterate, 'The *dinosaurs*, Ava.' I expect her to sit in the space between Sage and me, but she chooses the smaller gap between me and the armrest instead. 'I asked them to tell me if any job comes up. I repeat: I will do anything. I will fold leaflets, I will hand out headsets, I will sweep the floor beneath the fossils.'

'I promise I'll keep you posted,' Sage says with a chuckle, though I'm sure it's just to get me to shut up.

I don't want to move away from Ava but I'm concerned she doesn't have enough space, so I shuffle the tiniest distance to the side. I'm surprised when she moves in the same direction.

'Who's playing Articulate?' someone yells from the dining table. 'We're starting in five minutes!'

There's a chorus of *yes*es and *let me get a drink*s and people start moving around, including Sage, who heads to the kitchen.

I'm extremely conscious of how close Ava is. I inexplicably do that pre-teen move of stretching my arm across the back of the sofa, my hand hanging somewhere near her ear. She lets out a quiet snort when she notices, and then we put our drinks to our mouths in perfect unison and she laughs again, and everything in me wants to pull her against me, feel her soft warmth, breathe in her vanilla perfume and shampoo and whatever pheromone she gives off that turns me into something not unlike a caveman. But the woman's like a cat; you have to let her come to you.

She inches closer, and then her head is on my shoulder, and I don't know if she's just sleepy and drunk and in need of comfort, but I'll give it if she wants it. Whatever the reason, I'm thankful we're facing away from the rest of the party, because Julien would rip into me for the rest of time if he could see the expression on my face right now.

'What did Max want to talk to you about?' I ask, one hand clutching my glass at my lap, the other tracing circles on her bare shoulder and feeling her skin fleck with goosebumps at my touch.

'Oh,' she says, lifting her head. I miss the weight of it the second she sits up. 'He was telling me how he's been offered this amazing work opportunity for next year. He seems excited. More excited than I've seen him in a while, actually. He really deserves it.'

She looks over at him, mid-conversation in the kitchen with Julien and some of the people from Josie's gallery, and smiles to herself.

'I like seeing how much you love your brother.'

'Is that weird?' She meets my gaze, blue eyes blinking slowly, tipsily, smile still rippling across her face. 'Don't you love your siblings?'

'Of course. But I've always been kind of jealous of them.' I don't let myself think too hard about how true that is. 'It felt like they were bound together somehow. I bet it's the same for you and Max.'

Something passes across her expression but it's gone before I can place it. I don't want to bring the mood down, so I don't mention that there's something almost mournful in the way Ava looks at Max too, like she loves him so much it makes her sad, like she wishes he were here when he's already standing right in front of her.

'I do love him. A lot.' As if his ears are burning, Max's head whips around and his eyes narrow into slits as he sees us sitting so close. He doesn't strike me as the possessive brother type, but you never know, so I shift away slightly. Ava rolls her eyes and he smiles, breaking the façade. He puts his thumb and index finger to his mouth a few times, asking if we want to go out and smoke, and Ava shakes her head. As a small group of them leaves, she adds, 'Although I wish he didn't smoke weed.'

'Ava, where are you?' Josie calls from the dining table. 'I need you on my team!'

'Can't we play over here?' Ava asks.

And with that, everyone agrees there's more space by the sofa, so we set up Articulate on the coffee table and settle into our positions around it. I offer up my spot but no one takes it, and Ava slides down to sit on the floor between my feet, leaning against the sofa.

'By the way, you're not on my team,' she says lightly, patting my knee. 'I don't want you distracting me.'

After Josie's first turn—which proves she and Ava must have some secret code, because the latter guesses the right answers with single-word clues almost every time—I lean into Ava's ear.

'I didn't know Articulate cards had braille on them.'

'They don't.' She looks up at me and smiles, one of those unrepentant ones that knock me out for a second. 'Josie once mentioned she wished she could play, so Alina got them made for her birthday last year.'

Okay, that's romantic. They're cute.

At least, they're cute until it's Alina's team's turn and Josie hurls outrageous insults and distractions her way to get her to lose.

'The first president of the United States! Who was it?'

'Denzel Washington!' Rory frantically guesses, and we descend into hysterics that only worsen when he asks, 'Was that wrong?'

The game is pandemonium, and as the night goes on the volume and drunkenness increase in parallel, with about half the group continuing to take it seriously, and the other half either finding new ways to cheat or doing their own thing entirely. I'm convinced Ava and Josie's neighbours must hate them, until I'm informed that the person who just handed me a shot of sambuca lives next door.

'We're heading back out for a smoke, do you guys wanna come?' Max sets his hands on my shoulders from behind the sofa but directs his question mostly at Ava.

She waves a hand to say no and in the process knocks a drink off the table, missing Sage but entirely covering herself. I can tell it's going to happen before it does, but my own reflexes have been dulled by aforementioned sambuca, so I'm not much help.

'Oh my god, I'm so sorry,' Sage says.

'It's fine, it wasn't your fault,' Ava replies easily, swaying a little as she gets up, using my knees as support. 'I wanted to get changed anyway.'

She heads to her room and I join in with my team's round. But then everyone gets into an argument about whether "cricket" should be accepted as an answer when the real answer was "cricketer", so I take it as an opportunity to get up to go to the bathroom. Someone's in there already, so I knock at Ava's bedroom door and wait for her to answer.

When she opens it, she's no longer in the green dress. Instead, she's wearing a baggy t-shirt over a pair of extremely short shorts.

She catches my eyes dropping to her thighs and says, 'I didn't think about whether this outfit was appropriate for polite company.'

'Since when have you cared about being polite?' I lean against the doorframe in what I hope she sees as a sexy way, and not the reality, which is that it's helpful to have something to support my own weight. I can't tell yet if I'm more drunk on her presence or the alcohol.

I cock my head, drinking in the sight of her, feeling every bit of it rush to my head and my heart and somewhere extremely inconvenient. Her hair is loose from its ponytail and she plays with the ends before moving to her dresser, poking through a drawer.

'You can come in, you know.' She pulls out another pair of shorts, squinting at them and then shoving them back in the drawer without folding.

I step over the threshold and take everything in. There's a gallery wall above her bed, mostly prints and song lyrics, plus a few photos. I spot pictures of people who I guess are her parents, a photo of her with Josie, her and Max as kids, both dark-haired and big-eyed in matching outfits, and another with Max where his hair is buzzed and he's on crutches.

Shouts emanate from the living room. Clearly they're still on cricketgate.

There's a mass of clothes on the bed, and she looks back at me sheepishly. 'Sorry it's so messy.'

'I would expect nothing less.'

She eyes me intently and it makes me feel naked, so I check out the rest of the room to avoid having to look at her. Finally, I reach the bookcase, analysing its contents. But when I turn around to ask her something, she's midway through getting changed, peeling her shorts off at the ankles. My eyes draw to the curves of her body, the black lace of her underwear, and my insides set off on a one-way trip to chaos. Instinctively, I push her bedroom door closed so that no one in the other room will see, before looking back at the bookshelf.

'Finn,' she says from behind me, much closer than I expect. 'You can turn around.'

'Are you sure?' I don't trust her. I don't trust *me*.

She lets out a low laugh and saves me from making the decision by pulling me around by the hand. I meet her gaze now, clear and purposeful, and I get the distinct impression both of us have sobered up.

Ava's eyes always make me feel like I'm in a house of mirrors; bending the light and tricking me into thinking I can escape, until I remember that I'm trapped, entirely at her mercy until she says I can leave.

She plays with the collar of my shirt and says, 'There are people on the other side of this wall.'

'There are,' I agree, mouth dry, aware in every millimetre of my body just how little material there is between us. 'They might wonder where we've got to.'

'I think they'll be distracted for a while.'

I stay perfectly still as she runs her hands down my chest, her touch setting my skin on fire through the fabric. 'I really hope so.'

'To be perfectly honest,' she says into my neck, and I close my eyes as her lips brush the skin there. 'I probably won't need very long.'

I don't know if it's a laugh or groan that comes out of me, but it's made worse when one of her hands makes a lazy trail downwards, stopping just above where I crave her touch most.

I have to use up every morsel of restraint to pull back and look in her eyes to ask, 'Are you sure you want to do this?'

'It felt like *you* were pretty sure last night.' She links both hands behind my neck, setting off goosebumps across my skin. 'And a few hours ago, didn't you say you wanted to— what was it? Devour me?'

'I was feeling extremely overwhelmed by the sight of you in that dress.'

'I'm not wearing the dress anymore.'

'No,' I say, swallowing hard. 'You're not.'

'Are you still overwhelmed?'

My hands fist the hem of her t-shirt, lifting the material higher up her thighs, and her chest heaves when the tips of my fingers brush the band at her hips. 'I'm only a man, Ava.'

She moves forward with a smirk and my breath catches at the press of her against me. 'I'm hurt. A physiological response—is that all I am to you?'

'You and I both know you'd run a mile if I told you what you really are to me.' My voice is quiet, a stark contrast to the way every cell in my body is screaming at me at eardrum-splitting levels. 'But listen to me. I asked if you were sure you wanted to do this.'

There's a pause before she responds. It might be half a second, it might be a whole minute, but I wait, until my new favourite word tumbles out of her on an exhale. 'Yes.'

The sibilance of it hasn't even left the air before I take her face in my hands and crush my lips to hers with the same urgency from last night. I don't think I'll ever be able to kiss her and not feel like I'm starving and she's my first meal in years.

She sighs against me, and when my teeth drag against her bottom lip I realise I've never wanted to learn a language so badly in my life. I wish we had more than a few frantic minutes. I want to relish the softness of her; find out if my theory is correct, if our bodies have been purpose-built for each other, for fitting in the gaps we both leave behind.

This time, she smiles into my mouth, and when it turns into a breathy laugh I almost die right there. She knows she's got me wrapped around her finger. Knows I crave her attention and affection and touch so much, I'd do anything for it. Knows if she said to jump, I'd only ask how high.

'I could live right here forever,' I say, mouth moving across her skin. Lips, jaw, cheeks, neck, nose, there'll never be enough seconds in the day for the amount of her I want to get to know. 'I'm serious. This is all I need.' She tilts her head so I can run my mouth up the length of her throat. My voice drops to a whisper. 'You're a fucking constellation.'

'So dramatic,' she murmurs.

A low chuckle spills out of me. 'I'm trying to be romantic.'

'You're being corny,' she says, voice hoarse as her nails dig into my shoulders through my shirt to pull me closer.

I spin us to pin her against the bookcase, and when I push my hips forward and her eyes close briefly, I know she feels all of me, the way I feel all of her. I've never thought about the convenience of us being a similar height before, but it suddenly makes complete sense; the way every part of us perfectly aligns, the way all I need to do is shift my weight slightly and there's friction right where she likes it, right where I need it.

'If you didn't want corny,' I say, hands moving under her t-shirt, gliding over her stomach, her waist, resting just below her bra, 'you shouldn't have started kissing someone who thinks the sun shines out of your ass.'

She pulls away and takes off her shirt before I have a chance to blink, and she's so beautiful I almost don't want to look, but I do, of course, because finally she's given me permission, and it elicits a noise I don't fully recognise from my mouth, sending blood roaring through my body.

'In that case, maybe I should've stuck with Jacob,' she muses. I freeze and she laughs at my expression. 'It's not good etiquette to mention another man right now, is it?'

My lips move back to her neck, and I listen for every hitch of her breath to guide me.

'It wasn't good etiquette when that man said you looked *nice*. Nice is for chain restaurants.' She sighs as I work my way down to the flushed skin of her chest. 'And supermarket flowers.' I move her chin so I can look at her, ocean eyes churning; hungry and desperate, hunting for a victim to drag into the waves. But my whole life, I've never been able to resist the water. 'It's not for this.'

# 32

## is this what it feels like to believe in a higher power?

### AVA

'God,' he says, voice a rasp as he presses me against the bookshelf, urgently kissing along my jaw, down my throat, across my chest, all while his hand finds its way between my thighs.

'I didn't know you believed in that kind of thing.' My breath catches when his fingers drag across the lace in a slow, precise rhythm.

His darkened eyes bore into mine as he increases the pressure, and then he leans closer, warm breath fanning across my face. 'I'll get on my knees, Ava.' His lips brush the shell of my ear. 'But it won't be for God.'

A shiver runs through me and all I can say is a breathy, 'Prove it.'

I don't let him decide what to do next, instead threading my fingers through his hair and pushing his head downward, and his quiet laugh fizzes across my skin. My entire body pulls taut as he presses his lips against my chest, down my stomach, until he's on his knees, dragging his mouth from one bare hip to the other.

And then he loops two of his fingers into my underwear and pulls it to the side, and I guess now he has proof of how much I want him, because he releases a throaty sound before making contact with his tongue, immediately working some kind of magic with careful, practised strokes that send me into a squirming, heavy-bellied stupor.

'You're still wearing all your clothes,' I accuse, somehow getting the words out despite the havoc he's wreaking between my legs.

'One of us has to have some decorum around here.' He pulls me closer and one of my hands digs into his hair to keep his head in place, to keep that heat bubbling beneath the surface. 'Is this okay?'

'Very okay,' I manage, and his eyes wrinkle at the sides when he glances up, never breaking the steady contact of his mouth against me. He must have the codes to every pleasure centre in my brain; each swipe of his fingers and glide of his tongue a password that unlocks the parts of me that feel like chaos and bliss and delirium all in one.

He lifts my right leg to hook it over his shoulder, angling me towards him, and a whimper escapes me as he buries his head further between my thighs, the damp heat of his tongue making me writhe.

When he slides a finger inside me, I clench around him and whisper, 'One more.'

Immediately, he adds a second finger, and my whole body shakes with every movement he makes. When I roll my hips into him he makes a low noise that consequently makes *me* make a noise, and I laugh to myself, because this feels like some weird, unholy echo chamber.

Somehow, people are still yelling in the other room, and I thank whatever higher power exists that everyone is drunk and apparently extremely competitive about Articulate, because the sounds that spill out of me are absolutely not for public consumption. They weren't meant to be for Finn's consumption either, but it's hard to remember that when my brain is getting more nebulous with every passing second.

Yet, despite all he's doing right, I don't want to be patient. Not after how long I've needed this.

I detach myself to stretch an arm to my bedside table, fumble with something in the drawer, and practically launch the purple object at his head in my eagerness for him to have it. I manage to get out a ragged, 'This'll be faster.'

'You know best,' he murmurs. Before I know it he's pressed the button and lit the fuse, and where each sensation was warm and fuzzy before, now everything is pure electricity, and I can't focus on anything but letting the pressure expand within me.

Still on his knees, he peppers me with delicate kisses while his hands are occupied, pressing his lips against my stomach, my hips, my thighs, and it's so intimate for such a frenetic moment that it takes my breath away.

He pulls back and his voice is thick when he says, 'Look at me.'

Heavy lids part to find his eyes, the echoes of a laugh forever etched into the skin around them. Briefly, my ecstasy-addled brain wonders what it would be like to see this face on a pillow next to mine every morning. But the heavy feeling beneath my stomach is building to a crescendo, threatening to launch me out into the atmosphere, and the thought drifts away.

'*Supernova*!' someone shouts from the other room.

'*Asteroid*!'

Finn's mouth takes over at the last second, his tongue bringing me over the finish line, and then I'm floating up, up and out, vainly grabbing at anything to tether me to this spot, to keep me from disappearing. I'm grateful when, from the depths of oblivion, I feel strong hands holding me, his steady presence bringing me down to Earth.

'*Meteor*!'

*That's me*, I think. A shooting star burning up in the atmosphere, scorching a trail through the sky. At least if I make impact, I'll go out with a bang.

---

I lean against Finn, breathing heavily, one hand on his shoulder and the other knotted into his hair, until I hear Josie's voice call out from the other room and it shocks me back to the very real, very inappropriate present. 'Ava, it's our turn next, are you coming?'

Finn looks up at me and I notice red crescent-shaped marks on his skin where the neckline of his shirt has shifted. He whispers, 'Are you coming, Ava? Or did you alre—'

'Shut *up*,' I hiss. I push off against the bookcase as he gets to his feet, handing me the t-shirt I discarded a few minutes ago. I shove it over my head and open my door a crack to yell, 'I'll be one minute!'

I close it and when I turn back around I catch Finn twirling the toy in his hand with a grin. I grab it from him with a quiet squawk and hide it under my duvet, brain too much of a puddle to deal with it right now.

'I'm gonna go to the bathroom. I just remembered I got up to pee forever ago.' He pushes his sleeves further up his arms, entirely too pleased with himself. 'Got sidetracked.'

I make the mistake of looking down. By the time my eyes find their way back up to his face, he's looking at me with one of those obscene half smiles of his. I swallow hard and ask, 'You don't want, uh, any help with that?'

'Pissing? I can probably manage.' I try to glare at him but my mind is still fuzzy and, infuriatingly, it probably comes out more like heart-eyes instead. I step into new shorts that are a perfectly adequate length, and then Finn catches me by the arm, sliding a scrunchie from my dresser onto my wrist. 'Because I have no doubt your brain is gonna be going a million miles an hour and you'll be spending the rest of tonight relentlessly tying and untying your ponytail.'

It suddenly occurs to me how much of a mess I must look, so I step away, craning my neck to look in the mirror. While I'm smoothing my hair, I catch his eye in the reflection to say, 'I'm sorry this was, you know, one-sided.'

'I'm not.' He folds his arms as he leans against my chest of drawers and I don't know if it's his smug expression, the smouldering heat in his eyes, or the way his biceps push against his sleeves in this position, but I have to tamp down every urge that's begging me to go for round two. 'You can help next time.'

'What makes you so sure there's going to be a next time?'

'The same reason I knew there would be a first time.'

The self-satisfied smirk on his face makes me want to scream, so I stand up straight and leave him in my bedroom without another look. When I settle back into my seat on the living room floor after downing a glass of water in the kitchen and then giving in and pouring myself a rosé, Josie whispers something in Alina's ear. I pretend not to notice.

'Have you seen Finn?' Rory asks. 'Did he go downstairs to smoke with the others?'

'Dunno. There's a light on in the bathroom, though.' For some reason I don't want people to suspect anything, so I add, 'Maybe he's taking a shit.'

# 33

## and just like that, the universe makes its opinion clear

### AVA

Blazing sunlight fills my room thanks to the curtains I accidentally left open last night, waking me far earlier than I'd hoped. My heart feels simultaneously lethargic and supersonic, like it's preparing for something I'm as yet unaware of. But then, it's probably just hangxiety. After ten silent minutes staring at the ceiling, I conclude that I am in dire need of a tea.

Max is wrapped in his duvet so tightly on the sofa bed I can't tell which end his head's at. When we were kids I'd always wake to see him swaddled like this, so I take a photo and send it to Mum, who replies almost immediately. I can see her now; sitting in her armchair by the window, glasses perched on the end of her nose but somehow not actually using them when she peers at her screen, typing out her message exclusively with her index finger.

> Lovely, so glad he's resting. But isn't it too warm for a duvet? And why is he on the sofa bed? He should have the proper mattress.
> Xxx

I'd do anything for the boy, but I draw a line at letting him claim my mattress with his giant, sweaty man-child body. While the kettle boils—I'm hoping Max's ability to sleep through a hurricane hasn't changed—I think over the events of last night. With Finn.

Finn, Finn, Finn.

My head spins, and I don't think it's because of our neighbour's budget alcohol.

When Finn returned from the bathroom, he sat in his spot on the sofa and I positioned myself between his knees on the floor, and nothing else happened. He may have murmured something wildly inappropriate in my ear under the guise of leaning forward to grab his drink from the coffee table. And I may have retaliated by using his legs as support when I stood up to get a drink, holding his thighs slightly higher than necessary. But for the rest of the evening I kept my hands to myself, and so did he. When we said goodbye, we hugged for less than a second, and it was almost comical how chaste it was.

What's he doing right now? Is he waiting for a text from me the way I'm waiting for one from him? What would I even say if I sent one? *Hey bud, thanks for last night, it was fun. I reckon I'll spend the rest of my life comparing every other man's mouth to yours though, lol. Anyway, see you on Tuesday!*

But last night is only the tip of the iceberg. Everything from the past couple of months sends me reeling. He's leaving. Isn't he? Some selfish part of my brain hopes he won't get that job in San Francisco. What will happen if he does? What will happen if he *doesn't*?

Thoughtful, considerate Finn, telling me things that make me believe I might be made of magic. Things that make me think there could be something worth wanting, some joy at the end of the tunnel to run towards. That make me think I could try. I've never considered it before, but a seed of possibility grows roots and I wonder what it would look like to let the light in.

'Are you making drinks or did you just rouse me from my slumber for no reason?' a gravelly voice asks from the sofa, and I realise the kettle stopped boiling ages ago.

'Sorry, I didn't mean to wake you.' I grab a second mug from the cupboard and make both of us a drink. 'You're usually dead to the world when you sleep.'

I bring our mugs over to the coffee table—tea for me, coffee for Max—and, for fear of unleashing Josie's wrath, find coasters for both. Max gets my new one from pottery class.

He must be sweating, but he pulls the duvet tighter around himself as he raises to a half-seated position with a grunt. 'I haven't been sleeping great recently. Got some stuff on my mind.' He catches my concern and adds, 'I've been prescribed sleeping pills. But I knew I'd be drinking and smoking last night so I didn't bring any.'

I perch on the end of the bed. 'You should be careful with all that.'

'I am careful,' he says, the barest hint of annoyance in his voice. 'Hence, me not mixing them.'

'Is there anything you want to talk about?'

I remember how excited he was to tell me about his work opportunity last night. It lifted me too, let me know the world is still turning, still tipped in his favour the way it always should've been. Looking back with sober eyes, I wonder if his excitement was a little too frantic, too skittish.

Instead of answering my question, Max says, 'Let's have something to eat.' Right on cue, his stomach gurgles, and he mumbles, 'Who the fuck brought sambuca? And why?'

Between Max, Josie, Alina and me, the flat is spotless by eleven. Josie's on dishwasher duty, Alina sorts out the recycling, Max cleans up any spillages, and I wander around with a bin bag collecting rubbish.

Once we've fuelled ourselves with coffee and a fry-up, I feel considerably more human. Inexplicably, Alina has the energy to go for a run, and I simultaneously envy and fear her. By the time she returns, Josie's ready with her bags and the pair of them head off to Josie's parents'. So an hour later, it's just Max and me wallowing at either end of the sofa under the duvet with a sitcom on that neither of us is paying much attention to, instead scrolling on our phones and occasionally letting out a short puff of air through our nostrils in place of an actual laugh.

I draw my phone closer to my face, even though I know Max couldn't give less of a shit about what he sees on my screen. I test the waters with something entirely innocuous.

> have fun with your dad tomorrow!!!!!

God, never in my life have I used five exclamation marks in one go. Max glances up and catches the vaguely disgusted grimace on my face, and a quizzical expression briefly crosses his own before he shrugs and goes back to his phone.

> Thanks, I'm so excited

> !!!!!

He's *mocking* me. Dots appear and disappear on the screen as he types and deletes, and then a message comes through.

> At the risk of sounding like a broken record, we should talk about it

> I've never met someone so frustratingly into open lines of communication

You should know by now that talking is one of my favourite activities

> thought you might've been avoiding me

> giving me a taste of my own medicine and ghosting me after we hooked up

I wouldn't do that

> I would though

I am aware

Which is why I waited for you to text first

Didn't wanna scare you off

I do know you, believe it or not

I feel a smile replacing the grimace and try to hold it back in case Max looks up again. Because really, Finn's right. I didn't mean to let him get to know me, he just strong-armed his way in, the way I strong-armed him into being my fake friend that day in the coffee shop with Josie at the start of summer.

> Can we talk in person rather than over text?

> I'm with Max today and don't know when he's leaving
>
> we can meet tomorrow evening?

> I'll let you know when I'm finished with my dad and you can come over if you want

He sends me his address and my thumbs hover over my screen while I debate the merits of sending a flirtatious text I might come to regret. I tap "send" before I lose my nerve.

> is this an excuse to get me alone again?

> Well, yes, but not like that at all, I promise
>
> There's something else I want to talk to you about

I don't know whether to feel offended by this. He wouldn't want me alone again *like that?*

> Shit that made it sound like being alone with you is something I wouldn't want
>
> I absolutely would
>
> Like, a lot
>
> But I need to discuss something with you and it might change things

Also while we're here I'd like to confirm

I don't just like you for reasons pertaining to what happened last night

I mean I assumed that was obvious

I'm surprised you haven't sent me away for being annoying yet

I am infinitely glad you haven't

But I'd understand if you did

Agh why can't I speak normally

I feel like I'm devolving

Is this too much am I being too eager

It's too much isn't it

Nooooope

Feel free to respond at any moment

...

????????

> Oh my fucking god Ava
>
> Please reply and put me out of my misery
>
> Help
>
> Goodbye

I try to imagine him typing these messages out, hair getting more dishevelled with every run of his hands through it, and my heart flutters at the image. I've never wanted chaos, but if it looks like this, maybe I wouldn't mind it.

> I'll see you tomorrow evening, Finn

After a particularly robotic, canned laugh from the TV, Max turns to me. 'You and Finn are a thing, right?'

I burrow under the duvet with a grunt and shove my phone between the sofa cushions for fear he can somehow read the texts from his spot. 'Can we please not pretend we're the kind of siblings to talk about this sort of thing?'

'Fine, fine,' he says through a laugh, wiggling in the duvet cocoon and touching me with a single, repugnant foot, which makes me gag.

As I squirm away, my brain drifts to the party and I dimly remember something. 'Did you get to speak to Dylan, by the way? The tall woman who showed up halfway through?'

His forehead creases as he tries to remember. 'I think I did. Blue jeans? Amazing a—' He clears his throat when he remembers who he's talking to. 'Eyes. Amazing eyes?'

'Subtle.' He bites down a guilty grin and I continue, 'But yes. She's very pretty.'

'Wasn't she called Ellen? Why did I keep calling her Ellen?'

'Because she was probably too nice to correct you. She works at the shop with me but wants to go travelling at some point. I meant to introduce you two properly but I completely forgot.'

He raises his eyebrows and says under his breath, 'I wonder why.'

'Sorry, what was that?' I cup my hand to my ear.

'I said, I totally understand why your mind would be elsewhere, because you were extremely busy having weirdly intense eye contact with Finn in front of everybody and thinking no one would notice.'

I'm now impossibly glad Max was out in the courtyard towards the end of the night. 'What happened to not talking about our love lives?'

'Oh, so you admit it's your love life?'

'I'm not entertaining this.' I take as much of the duvet as I can but he yanks it back.

'Whatever. I liked him. So if you *were* a thing, it'd be nice. I feel like you've been happier recently.' He echoes what Josie said to me a few weeks ago. Has Finn's presence really affected me that much? 'And if he's around, maybe it'll be easier for you to take my news.'

I stop tugging the duvet, my stomach dropping with my hands. 'What news?'

I immediately want to tear off the duvet, tear off my skin, because the room is suddenly fifty degrees hotter and panic boils in my chest.

Max plays with the label on a cushion. 'It's fine, it's not a big deal. Not as big of a deal as last time, anyway.'

Hope grows like weeds between the cracks of a pavement. All it takes is the tiniest amount of light, and then it sprouts, unruly. But it's only ever one misstep away from being trampled on.

'Max. What's not a big deal?'

My heart pounds in my ears and I know what he's going to say before he says it. Still, the words drag me under.

'At my most recent scan the doctors found something concerning. They think the cancer's come back just next to the original site. On my hip socket, this time.'

And just like that, the shutters go down, the windows are boarded up, and any hope of letting the sunlight in is snuffed out. Because this is the only thing that matters. The darkness that's lived in the pit of my stomach for years rears its head, finally given the fuel it needs to do some damage.

A million questions run through my mind like they're on ticker tape, but I start with the most important. 'Are you okay?'

He heaves a sigh, a smile I don't believe pulling at his mouth. It's not been that long since the first time, but he looks so much older now. He's lived so much more. Lived through so much more.

'I will be. It might be a false alarm anyway. It might be nothing.' He doesn't need to say *but it's probably not*. I hear it anyway. 'I always knew it was a possibility. The hip replacement should've been enough to stop it returning, but that was never a given. Guess it couldn't stay away.' He attempts the kind of joke we haven't used in years, the ones we pushed between us in our delirious, fear-driven panic, the ones our parents could never laugh at because it hurt too much. 'I'm irresistible, apparently. Which I completely understand.'

I nod slowly, trying not to let him see what's going on behind my eyes. 'When do you find out more information?'

'I had a bunch of tests last week—'

'I could've come with you.'

'You didn't need to. Seriously,' he nudges me under the duvet, 'it's not like this thing is new to me. I go for scans and tests all the time anyway. I should find out the results soon, and if it's what they think it is, they'll probably put me on a course of radiotherapy and specifically target the spot on my pelvis.'

'No chemo? Or surgery?' I ask, my fingers curling in on themselves, nails digging into my palm as the memory of what happened last time takes over my vision in high definition. My body tingles like I'm coming down with something, and my skin feels like it doesn't quite fit anymore.

Max understands why I'm asking. Of course he does. 'It's unlikely. So don't panic.'

'I'm not panicking,' I say instantly, ironing out my features. While Max is in front of me, I can't let him see the truth. My only job is to be here. No distractions.

'I had a hunch something was wrong a little while ago but didn't want to admit it,' he mumbles. 'My leg's been feeling weird. I assumed it was my hip starting to play up because I've been doing too much physical activity. It's always been a bit more sensitive to pain ever since everything happened. But I knew I had a scan coming up anyway, so I waited.'

'Max,' I chastise softly. Why didn't he push for an earlier appointment? How could he be so careless with his health, knowing what's at stake?

He shrugs and suddenly he looks five years old. 'I know I'm an idiot. I get it. Trust me, I've heard it all from Mum and Dad.' He catches my expression. 'I told them the other day but I wanted to tell you in person. And I wanted to have fun last night. I wanted to be normal for a bit longer, before it fucks things up again.'

This is what he struggled with last time. Depending on people, bearing their pity, disrupting the vibrant life he loves so much. An inconvenience as much as it was a nightmare.

I squeeze him and it all comes back to me; everything I've spent years trying to forget. The fear that kept me awake every night. The dread any time Dad's contact info appeared on my phone screen, knowing he was calling with more bad news. Having to consciously avoid the bandage-wrapped PICC line in Max's arm whenever I hugged him, how he looked in the hospital bed with his life in the metallic hands of machines, the way my heart has never quite healed from that one terrible day.

I shake my head to clear the image, to banish the fog to the corners of my vision until I'm alone. If he wants to feel normal, that's what I'll give him. 'What do you need me to do?'

'Can you not tell anyone?' he asks, voice quiet. 'I mean, you can tell Josie, and Finn I guess, if you're together, but the more people who know, the more real it is. It feels like I'm jinxing it or something. I dunno. It sounds stupid, but I just want to pretend, for now. If that's okay.'

My heart grows ten sizes. I know better than anyone how it feels to want to put your faith into something bigger than yourself, to ask it for help even if you're not sure you believe it can. Jinxes and wishes and prayers never felt more real to me than the last time he was sick. 'It doesn't sound stupid. Whatever you want, I'll do it.'

We continue watching our generically funny sitcom, and by the time he packs up his stuff to leave, it's only the hug that lasts a few seconds longer than normal that alerts me to what must really be going on in his head.

'Can you promise me something else, Col? Don't worry until you need to worry. I know that's easier said than done. But until then, please just,' he squints like he's reading the words in the air, 'be normal.'

'I promise,' I say, my head beginning to throb as it unpacks the boxes I'd long since shoved to the back of my brain.

'I've been dreading telling people, but not you. I can always count on you to be okay. You're the only person in my life who doesn't give those stupid trite platitudes that make me want to throw up.'

'*God gives his hardest battles to his toughest soldiers*,' I say, dropping my voice to make it sound more dramatic, which sends his eyes rolling. I bump against him. 'You're alright, as far as brothers go.'

He scrunches his nose in distaste, adjusting the bag strap on his shoulder. 'That was alarmingly close to sentimental, for you.'

'You're alright, as far as brothers go, but I'd drop you the second a better option came along?'

He grins and says, 'Much better.'

We both know he'd still be my favourite, though. And I'd do anything for him; even act like I'm not shitting myself too.

# 34

## excuse my French, but everything's going to shit

### AVA

I DON'T SNOOZE MY alarm for work like I usually do. I've already been awake for an hour. Or longer, I don't know. I'd crawled into bed after Max left and lay there for hours with the fading daylight, tears burning my cheeks, muscle memory dragging the old fears back to the forefront of my mind and sending me into a fitful sleep.

In moments of quiet, when there's nothing to keep me occupied, images blast across my brain in high definition. An empty chair at the dinner table. Family-sized bags of spicy Doritos left in the cupboard because he's the only one who ever eats them. A Christmas stocking that'll never be filled. Songs I'll never play again because I'll have no one to sing them with. Our special language going extinct, every connection between us disappearing in a puff of smoke. No matter how hard I try to keep them at bay, it's like they survive on my fear, consuming it until it consumes me.

And so, I drag myself out of bed and find the energy to make myself look presentable, covering any evidence of my restless night with makeup. The last thing I need is for customers to ask if I'm okay.

Go through the motions and keep it together. This is what's expected of me. I won't show the fear sweeping through me, or the guilt snaking over my shoulders. Guilt for being okay, guilt for not being okay, guilt for even thinking about my own fear when I see it so clearly in Max's eyes. When Josie comes back, I'll tell her, but I won't taint her time with her parents with this news. For now, I'll handle it alone.

Because no one else needs to know about the fog seeping under doorways, blocking up any of the fissures that had just started to let the light in. I can't help but notice that the moment I thought I was safe, the scales tipped back exactly the way I'd hoped they wouldn't.

It doesn't matter that this time feels different. Doesn't matter that we never have to experience the gut-wrenching panic for the first time again. Doesn't matter that this time, I wasn't alone in my uni bedroom when I found out, sitting on a rickety desk chair as I feverishly Googled everything I could and regretted it, repeating that cycle again and again until I knew every piece of literature, every variable, every study, every statistic off by heart. Until I realised my parents' fears had frozen them in place and my family was breaking and they needed me home. Going to Tesco, making sure everyone ate, filling up the car with petrol. I was there to keep things moving, reliably stoic and levelheaded.

And I was glad I went home in the end, anyway, because I was there when things got better, and I was there when it all went terribly, impossibly wrong.

No, this time is a dull ache, an opening of old wounds that were poorly stitched together in the first place, and a reminder there's too much to lose.

The mundanity of my routine when I step into City Roast comforts me. Lights, till, coffee machine, dishwasher, stock. I've spent years perfecting this, relying on predictability to keep myself protected. So, by the time the first customer walks through the door, everything is as it should be. I am exactly where I should be. I function for the rest of the morning on autopilot, spouting small talk where needed, cleaning surfaces that aren't dirty, and making drinks exactly how the regulars like them.

'Did you have a good weekend?' they ask.

'It was pretty uneventful,' I reply.

They don't know me well enough to detect the lie, and I'm glad.

When Dylan arrives fifteen minutes early, she gets on with her work, reliable and consistent and somehow detecting my need for space by choosing every task far away from me. Eventually, when we're both behind the counter, I turn to her, ready to at least pretend my brain isn't in tatters.

'I'm sorry we didn't get to hang out much on Saturday. Did you have fun?' We form a mini assembly line; me passing her clean mugs from the dishwasher while she neatly stacks them on the coffee machine.

'Yeah. I don't go to parties often, especially without my boyfriend, so it was nice to get out of the house. I liked your friends.' She grins. 'Is Finn in? I thought he'd be here by now. He's usually glued to your side.'

I'm grateful I have a bit longer before I see him. I know what I need to do when I see him this evening, and I don't particularly want to do it. We need to stamp this out. Keep it strictly platonic until he leaves. I'm not ignorant enough to think I could cut him out completely; he practically lives at the shop. And I'm selfish too; selfish enough to keep him close, to make the most of the way he makes me feel a little brighter, a little lighter.

But whatever this *thing* was, it can't happen. I don't have the brain capacity right now for anything other than putting one foot in front of the other and keeping this simple. A quiet, mean part of my brain tells me that maybe if I hadn't been so distracted with him, I would've paid more attention to Max and pushed him to get checked out sooner.

'Uh, no, he's seeing family today.' I swallow. 'I assume he'll be in tomorrow.'

'I see you're both still in the weekend spirit,' Carl's grating voice hits my eardrums. 'But come on, back to work now. Nadia is back in today, so I want this place to be perfect.'

Dylan's eyes widen and she scurries away, still afraid of his authority in a way that I'm not.

I pull out a folder from below the till. For months now, I've been keeping track of our deliveries, noting down when each tin of coffee beans or box of crisps goes out of date so we'll have a record of everything and can push sales on soon-to-expire items. Not that Carl knows I do this. I set up this system less for the purposes of saving the shop money and more for the fact this job makes me feel braindead and the task keeps my mind occupied. But we're killing two birds with one stone.

The irony is not lost on me that I try to be frugal with the shop's expenses here but continue to stuff my face with stolen KitKats and give away free drinks to Finn.

'What's this?' Carl asks, disconcertingly close as I make a latte. He watches my every move with uncharacteristic attention. He never stays behind the counter—presumably for fear of being dragged into doing actual customer-facing work—and his presence distracts me enough that I don't immediately notice who enters the shop behind Nadia. It's only when I hear the soft laugh he shares with her that I realise who it is.

Carl grabs the folder and greets his guest, calling out an order over his shoulder as he leads Nadia to his table.

'Morning, Ava Monroe,' Finn says, his voice and movements slow, like he's approaching a wild animal.

'Finn,' I say curtly. I thought I'd have more time to psych myself up to talk to him. I drop my eyes, worried about what he might see on my face. And yet, despite everything, it's a little easier to breathe having him nearby.

He waits for me to finish making Nadia and Carl's drinks and Dylan takes them over to them on my behalf, probably detecting my need to talk to Finn alone. I continue to avoid eye contact to ask, 'What are you doing here? I thought you were seeing your dad.'

He takes his glasses off to clean them, and I take the opportunity to look at him properly. He's less rumpled than I'm used to; shirt ironed, hair almost too neat, stubble as short as I've ever seen it. He looks younger than usual. My heart squeezes at the sight, at the effort he's made.

'He's had to push it back, I'm meeting him for lunch in a bit.' He looks through his glasses to check for smears and replaces them on his nose. 'But we need to talk. There's something I wan— are you okay?'

His affable tone switches instantly, the question shooting out of him like a bullet. Concerned eyes roam my face and I know he's noticed everything I've tried to cover with makeup and a fake smile.

'I'm fine.' I really need to come up with a word that doesn't sound like a lie. I hunt for a way to distract him. 'We can't have this conversation while I'm at work.'

*This conversation* being that we need to address what happened on the weekend.

*This conversation* being that I need to tell him I can't do anything else. I can't *be* anyone else.

His fingertips brush against mine where I'm resting my hand on the counter, and he dips his head to say, 'Please?'

I wish the touch of his skin against mine didn't simultaneously ground me in comfort and send my heart cartwheeling. It's this kind of complication I can't handle right now. But I need to rip off the plaster.

'Dylan,' I call her name, already untying my apron. 'I'm going for lunch.'

---

I don't know if either of us outwardly suggested it, but we find ourselves back at the rooftop we went to months ago. This time, we have iced coffees instead of wine. This time, we aren't strangers.

'Is this awkward?' he asks eventually, after a few minutes sitting on the bench in silence, the incessant noise of cars down below barely covering my racing pulse. 'I'm never awkward around you.'

'Then let's get it out of the way. Let's talk.' I'm a coward, because I say, 'You go first.'

He nods and brings his cup to his lap. 'Okay. I need you to listen to all of it before you say anything. I think we should talk about what happened on Saturday. But I need to say something else first. I heard back about the San Francisco job yesterday.'

'On a Sunday?' I try to keep my voice even. 'The legendary American work-life balance.'

He shrugs. 'Yeah. I found out I didn't get the one I applied for—'

'Really?' My heart forgets a beat or two, discordant and stuttering.

Finn's knee starts to bounce as he continues, 'There's more. I didn't get that job because they've decided to hire internally. But it turns out someone else in the company left unexpectedly and they need a replacement ASAP. They were impressed by my interviews and really liked me and think I could bring good things to the team, so they've offered that position to me instead. It's better pay, more opportunity for progression. They somehow found out who my dad is, even though I have my mum's last name, and I think that swayed them. I have big shoes to fill.' He swallows and watches my face as he says, 'They offered me a job that starts in three weeks.'

*Oh.* I let out a weak, 'Congratulations.'

'I haven't accepted it yet.' A siren passes below.

'You should.' My voice sounds like it's coming from someone else. Wasn't this what I was hoping for? There I was, looking for a way to tell him that whatever was brewing between us couldn't work, and here he is, with exactly the kind of opportunity he was looking for, but better. Serendipity.

A dent forms between his brows. 'I should?'

'This is what you wanted, isn't it?' I need to read the signs. Max's news reminded me why I can't take risks. Finn's news is showing me a way to send him away with minimal hurt. The universe wants me to stay on the path of least resistance, and I'm going to listen.

'It *was*.' He seems to be looking for something in my expression. He doesn't find it. 'But recently I've felt less sure.'

'You were sure when you applied.'

'That was before... everything.'

I don't know how to tell him that the portcullis has dropped, the drawbridge is up, and the fortress is as closed as it'll ever be. What comes out is, 'This is the real world. You don't just drop your whole life plan because you had one good night with a woman.'

'One good night?' He clenches his jaw, the lack of stubble drawing my attention to the muscle there.

I wave a hand dismissively. 'Fine, two if we count the night before.'

'Stop.' His voice reverberates through me, dangerously low, and the command sets off goosebumps along my skin. He meets my eyes, and if my gaze is steel, his is a blazing furnace. 'Don't act like what happened this weekend is all we are. As if it doesn't feel like we've been laying the foundations for something, even if we don't know what it is. Lie to yourself all you want, but not to me. Not about this.'

There's a beat of silence, then two, before he speaks again. 'Now is the first time in a long while that I've wanted to see what could happen if I try.'

It's not enough just to want and be wanted. I need to be able to give back, and I can't. 'You know what would happen? We'd fuck it up. You think we'd be able to start and maintain that kind of relationship over the phone? You think you'd be able to do long-distance again? You think I'd be able to give you everything you need?'

He shakes his head, and I think it's less to disagree, more to shake the thoughts loose. 'You're still assuming I'm taking the job.'

'You're taking the job, Finn.' Exasperation coats every word. 'You want to prove yourself. And that's okay. This was your goal. You say I'm lying to myself, but so are you. You wanted a new job in a new city, and then this one shows up, better than you even imagined.' *Maybe one that's enough to impress your dad*, I silently add.

'Come with me,' he says in a bout of desperation, eyes wide, hands raking through his hair and reverting it to the messy curls I'm used to.

Anger pulses through me. 'I'm sure my life seems small in comparison to yours, but I can't uproot it. I'm needed here. I *want* to be here.' As if to remind me of what's at stake if I take any more risks, the familiar shadows skulk at the edges of my brain. I set my jaw too, lifting my chin. 'You have a habit of investing too much of your heart into people who can't give you any of their own.'

He flinches like I've struck him and I regret it immediately. But instead of hitting me back with a deserved cutting response, his eyes dart between mine and he asks, 'Is there something else going on with you?'

*I can read you like a fucking book.*

He's going to know if I lie. But I haven't survived this long by being vulnerable. In the end, I go for something in between. 'Do you remember what you said to me the other day? You said you'd be whatever I wanted you to be. Did you mean that?'

I see the earnest man I met on that very first evening. 'Of course.'

'Well, I could really do with a friend right now. Like we were meant to be from the start.' For half a minute all I pay attention to is the steady rise and fall of his chest. Eventually, the tension between us goes slack, marking his resignation in parallel with mine. My voice is level when I speak again. 'I'm sorry for what I said. I like that you put your heart into things.'

*I wish I could do that too.* I watch the bob of his Adam's apple as he swallows.

'That's okay. And I didn't mean to make it seem like I thought your life was small or insignificant when I said you should come with me. So I'm sorry too. I was just,' he sighs like he's releasing an entire summer's worth of stress, 'clutching at straws. I like your life. I like being in it. I guess that's what I was trying to say.'

'I like you being in it too. But you'll do well in San Francisco. You've wanted this for years.' I let my knee touch his, tentative. He looks down and I wonder if he'll pull away, but he presses his leg against mine in response.

'Yeah, I have.' His resolve sets in, and he sits up a little straighter. 'So I'll accept the offer.'

'And we'll complete your bucket list like we planned. No stone left unturned.' I sip my watery coffee, the ice almost completely melted by now.

He lifts his cup and taps it against mine in a toast. 'No stone left unturned.'

His phone pings with a calendar notification and he looks across at me guiltily for a fraction of a second. But there's a renewed excitement to the lift of his shoulders, to the tilt of his eyes, like he's only just remembered what his plan is for today.

'Go and see your dad. Tell him about San Francisco.' When he catches my eye and smiles softly it feels like a truce. Like maybe we really can go back to how we were, if we try. If we pretend.

# 35

## the healing powers of pizza and more

## AVA

'What do you mean he's *leaving*?' Josie flings crumbs everywhere as she anxiously snaps her pizza crusts.

'Can you stop manhandling those? I thought we had an unspoken agreement that I get to eat your crusts.' I'm sure Il Pulcinella is warded by magic, because I feel better just being here. Though it could just be the dough balls.

She slides the plate in my direction before lifting her glass, furiously slurping through her straw. After I've brushed her crumbs to the floor, she says, 'Well? I think I must've misheard. Because it sounded a lot like you said Finn is moving to San Francisco in less than three weeks.'

I take a crust fragment and dip it in garlic butter. 'Nope, you heard correctly.' *Crunch.* 'I always knew it was going to happen, just wasn't sure when.'

For once I don't know what's going on in her head, but I can tell it's turbulent in there. She blinks once, twice, three times before she speaks again. 'And you're completely fine with that?'

*Crunch.* 'I am. With everything going on with Max, it feels like good timing that he won't be around to add to the chaos. I have enough on my plate.'

'This is terrible news,' she says, leaning an elbow on the table and cupping her face in her hand. Her expression is tortured, which I feel is a bit much considering she's only met the man a handful of times.

'I didn't realise he'd made such an impact on your life.'

'I'm not talking about *my life*,' she hisses. She taps her fingers against her face, releasing the same distressed noises she makes when she's trying to reach something on a high shelf. For a woman who's never been speechless in her life, this inability to find the right words feels monumental. 'I'm talking about the fact you so clearly like him. Does he know how you feel?'

'I'll miss him, but I'll be fine.' I ignore most of what she said. Inside, it feels like my heart's being controlled by a puppeteer, not quite within my control.

Finn leaving is the best move for so many reasons. He wants new opportunities, new experiences, new connections, and I know, however hard we pretend, that he wants more than I could ever give. I also know that he'd never ask that of me, despite how much he deserves it. He can get that *more* somewhere else, and I can stay here, living a quiet, chaos-free life where nothing is at risk. And we can be friends, just like we agreed.

'Ava, you really need to work on expressing your emotions.'

'No, I really don't. Can't express them if they're not there.' Any time I've shared emotions in the past, it's left me feeling hollow and raw. Locking them away keeps them safe. I have so much going on in my head worrying about Max; the last thing I need is to try to untangle the complicated feelings I have for Finn too.

I'd expected him to glide into the shop today on his invisible jet stream and tell me all about his afternoon with his dad, but he didn't come. This was good for my productivity, but bad for my feeling that our time is dwindling. He doesn't seem like the type to have his pride hurt over me essentially friendzoning him, but then, he is still a man.

'We've decided we need to try to complete his London bucket list before he leaves.' I want his final weeks here to be *fun*. I want to give him a good send-off. Especially knowing Max specifically requested continuing as normal until there's more news.

Eventually she sighs, and it feels like resignation. 'What's left on the list?'

I start reading out the remaining items from my phone, until one of them sparks an idea. 'Hey, do you think you could put me in contact with Sage?'

By midday the next day I still haven't heard from Finn. He's an unhinged person who keeps his read receipts on, so I know he's seen my texts, but so far he hasn't responded. I accidentally pour half an Americano over my hand while I'm distracted and the customer I'm serving steps back in alarm.

'Happens all the time,' I tell him flatly, my barista skin immune to pretty much anything. My lack of reaction seems to scare him, and by the time he's left the counter with a new drink and an expression of wide-eyed alarm, I've already opened my text thread with Finn, my last two messages read but unanswered.

> how did it go with your dad?

> are you coming into the office?

Ava of a few months ago would've cringed at seeming so eager, but current Ava just wants to make the most of these next few weeks. Finn usually replies before I've even finished retrospectively checking my message for spelling mistakes and I can't figure out why he's staying quiet now. Is he really this wounded from our conversation the other day? I was sure we'd come to an agreement when I said goodbye to him on the rooftop. And his excitement to see his dad was palpable, brightening his eyes and making him restless on his feet.

Max still hasn't heard back about his test results and I need some distraction in the form of a curly-haired man with a million passports. Because while I can go through the motions and keep busy at work, as soon as I'm home with nothing to do, the worry percolates, dripping into every corner of my brain and filling it up until I feel like I'm drowning.

Hours later, just as I'm leaving work, I finally get a response from Finn, but it's the single blandest text I've ever received from him.

> Feeling weird today, was working from home

I ruminate over his absence while I'm on the Tube. I ruminate so hard, in fact, that when the doors open at Stockwell, I stay seated. And then when the line ends at Brixton, I get off. He has less than three weeks left here; there's no way I'm letting him mope for the entirety of it.

Finn lives in a Victorian terrace on a residential road in Brixton, not far from the leisure centre, and when I press the intercom, his tired voice comes through. 'Hello?'

'Hey.' It strikes me as odd that I'm the one imposing on his space today. 'It's me.'

He's wary when he meets me in the doorway, looking starkly different from the other day. Where the last time I saw him he was perfectly coiffed, now he's gone the other way, scruff darkening his jaw and neck, hair dishevelled, unkempt in a white t-shirt and black sweatpants. Yet the inherent pull of his still draws me in, and I cross my arms so my hands won't do something stupid like reach out and touch his face.

'What are you doing here?' His voice is coarse, like it's the first time he's spoken in a while.

'Nice to see you too. You were texting weirdly and I wanted to make sure you hadn't been abducted by aliens.'

'I'm not in the mood,' he says, fingers running through messy hair. His eyes skim my face like he's trying to piece a puzzle together. I didn't cry as much last night, so the bags under my eyes probably aren't as prominent today, but his eyebrows draw together and I can tell he's noticed again that something is still off. This man needs to stop being so perceptive. It makes pretending to be okay far more difficult than it needs to be.

I barge past him and into the foyer, the movement of air whipping up his now-familiar scent. I rest an elbow on the banister and ask, 'What floor are you on?'

He continues to analyse my face and while his frown doesn't budge, eventually he closes the front door and says, 'Follow me.'

He motions towards an open door when we reach the second floor. I step inside the flat and it's not what I expected at all. It's all chrome appliances, grey walls and sharp lines, out of place in a building with the potential for so much character. Out of place for someone as vibrant as Finn, too.

As if he can read my thoughts, he says quietly, 'My landlord has an aversion to fun, apparently. Do you want a drink?' When we walk to the perfectly tidy living room, glasses of water in hand, he asks, 'What exactly were you intending to do if I had been abducted by aliens?'

'I'm still not sure you haven't been. Jury's out.'

I wince when we drop down onto opposite ends of the sofa and the leather doesn't give, and I wait for him to start talking. For once, the man doesn't say a word. Shit, maybe the aliens did get to him. 'If you're not gonna talk about how you've been sulking in this flat for days, I'll start. You're coming with me on a bucket list item on Friday. I cannot express the effort I've gone to and I refuse to waste it. It's for entirely selfish reasons.'

'Ava,' he says gently. 'I'm not feeling up for it.'

Part of me wants to yell at him for wasting time, another part wants to yell at him for being so weird when there are much bigger problems to despair over than whether some cold, commitment-phobe of a woman can change.

Maybe I just want to yell, come to think of it.

'Well, get up for it. It'll be fun. Stop sulking about being permanently relegated to the friendzone.'

This seems to jolt him out of his stupor, and his eyes widen as he says, 'God, I'm not moping about that. I agree it's the smartest move right now.' He shakes his head, curls shifting with the movement. 'You didn't friendzone me. That makes it sound like only being your friend is a demotion, somehow. As if it's not my favourite thing to be.'

His words embed in my heart like an ice pick trying to breach the surface, and I have to clear my throat in the hope of dislodging them.

'So what are you brooding about?' The seconds pass and he still doesn't respond, and I'm beginning to ache for his easy demeanour.

'Is this how you felt a few months ago, trying to get me to loosen up? God, I don't envy you. This is tedious as fuck.'

He breathes out sharply through his nose. I think it might be a laugh. After a few moments, he admits quietly, 'Any time you opened up, it wasn't long before you closed yourself off again. So all I could do was try again, over and over. Like Sisyphus pushing that fucking boulder up a hill.'

'Great workout though,' I hedge, monitoring his posture. I poke his arm, solid with muscle. 'Probably why you're so hench now.' He laughs with actual sound this time, and I know I've got him. I swivel on the sofa to face him, bringing one leg up under me. 'There's only space for one angst-ridden emo in this room. Tell me why you haven't been in the shop to annoy me since last week.'

He flops against the back of the sofa with a grimace and finally starts to talk, the words coming out rough, like they're scraping his throat as he pushes them out. 'I'd been planning this day with my dad for ages. Had the whole day organised. His assistant messaged me early in the morning to let me know he had a last-minute meeting, so we rescheduled everything for the afternoon instead. After I left you, I showed up at his hotel like we'd agreed, and then I waited. And waited. I know he doesn't like being nagged so I didn't want to text him, but eventually I did.' He looks up at the ceiling. 'And it turned out he'd completely forgotten about the rescheduling and was already out and about with a woman. I couldn't figure it out if she was a client or someone else. It doesn't matter, he just forgot.' Anger writhes along my skin seeing how Finn's dad makes him feel so small. 'He told me to come to the bar they were at, and by the time I showed up he was already a little drunk. I told him about my new job, but I dunno, I've never been able to read him very well. He was kind of apathetic about it. Maybe even annoyed I'm gonna be working at the same company as him.'

With a long exhale, he leans forward onto his elbows, still looking straight ahead. 'I was about to call my mum to tell her about it before you came, but then one of the twins needed her for something so she asked to reschedule.' He squints as he adds, 'Happens a lot. They'll always take priority.'

'Finn.' It's all I can think to say, but I inject it with as much sympathy as I can.

'I think I'm just bummed nothing went how I'd planned it with my dad.' He turns his head to give the smallest closed-mouth smile, like it doesn't matter. But it does, and I hate seeing him so dejected.

'You know he doesn't deserve you, right?' I don't mean to say it, but it spills out of me unfettered, splashing around us like waves against a boat.

His tone is defensive when he replies. 'He's just really busy. It's hard to make time for me.'

*No it isn't*, I think. *You're very easy to make time for.*

'Okay.' I can't make him resent his dad, and I don't want to. But I'm worried the realisation will hit him one day, that he'll see the lack of effort clearly and it'll break his heart. But I get it, wanting to believe something so strongly you get tunnel vision. 'I'm sorry you didn't get to spend as much time with him as you wanted. And I'm sorry for him too, because he missed out on spending time with you.' At his widened eyes I laugh, and something close to a real smile touches his face when he hears it. 'I'm making the most of being corny because you only have a few more weeks to make fun of me for it.'

He analyses me, resting a hand on the cushion between us. 'I will come back, you know. To visit.'

I don't know if that's true. Not if this job is perfect for him, if he falls in love with San Francisco, if he finds someone else to listen to his endless fun facts and flower-blooming laugh. But I don't say that. Instead, with the same halfhearted smile he just gave me, I reply, 'I know you will.'

The universe has sent me too many signs to ignore, but it doesn't make it any easier to stomach. There's too much in my head to make space for anything else. I can't have everything. I don't *deserve* everything. That much I've learnt.

'I should go,' I say, rising to my feet. 'I promised Josie I'd spend the evening with her. I just wanted to check you were alive.'

We head to the door, and as always, Finn opens it for me. And then my heart breaks a little, because it hits me that maybe it's not only politeness that makes him do this. Maybe it's the fact that his whole life, people have shown him he's not worth a second glance. Not worth their time. He can be cheated on and forgotten about and left to fend for himself at a school across the world, and the only person who cares is him. And maybe, subconsciously, he hopes that if he helps every stranger and holds every door, someone will think about him. Someone will value him, if only for a moment.

I pause in the doorway and my voice is steady when I say, 'I'm glad I know you, Finn. And I'm glad you're okay.'

His throat works while his eyes warm to melted chocolate. I'm sure I'm about to liquefy too. Then his jaw clenches and he pulls me roughly to him, wrapping his arms around me so tightly I bet that if a natural disaster struck right now, we'd still be standing at the end of it, rooted to the ground and intertwined like this.

One hand clutches my waist while the other slides up to the back of my head, fingers knitting into my hair and pressing my face against his shoulder. My own arms tighten around him, and I keep my eyes shut so that I can focus on his steady presence; the thrum of his heart in his chest, the worn fabric of his t-shirt, the comforting smell of him.

He doesn't know that smoke has filled my head ever since Max told me his news, that I've been lying awake for the past few nights with thoughts churning through my mind like silt dislodging from a riverbed; murky and muddy and moving too fast to ever settle. But with his arms around me, the current slows. It doesn't stop, but it doesn't drag me under either. I might be able to take a breath.

When we eventually pull apart, I pretend he hasn't left open wounds everywhere we were touching.

# 36

## we're what killed the dinosaurs

### FINN

I MEET AVA OUTSIDE South Kensington Tube station at six-thirty. Well, no, I arrive at six-thirty as planned and she shows up eight minutes later, but it's better than I expected. As soon as she comes into view I have to smooth my features so she won't see me react. I've been expending a lot of energy trying to keep our relationship platonic. The part of me that's desperately trying to forget everything that happened between us last weekend has been constantly warring with the part that replays it on repeat at extremely inopportune moments.

Her hair's tied back in her usual ponytail and she's wearing clothes that lead me to believe she's either going camping or on a hike, but I know her well enough by now to know we are doing neither of these things. She gave me instructions to wear comfy clothes too and I've obliged, although I'd imagine seeing me in my sweatpants doesn't make her heart stutter the way mine does at the sight of her in hers.

I pull her in for a hug. It's self-serving, sure, but she relaxes against me too. When I pull away her shoulders inch up again like she's on edge. It's subtle, but I notice. She's been like this for a few days now and I can't figure out why.

'What's in the bag?' I nod towards the giant backpack she's wearing. Maybe distracting her will make her feel more at ease.

'Do you really want to know?' She removes the bag from her shoulders and positions it against the wall as she opens it to show me the contents.

My head shoots up. 'Sorry, is that my *underwear*?'

'I got Julien to take stuff from your room when he was over the other day without you noticing.' She's extremely cavalier for someone admitting to aiding and abetting undergarment theft.

'Is it, like, a fetish or something? I didn't accidentally put *sex club* on the list, did I?'

'No, Finlay, it is not a fetish. If you'll notice, he also stole a hoodie and a t-shirt.'

'I'm gonna be honest, that hasn't eased my concern. All I'm getting at the moment is kleptomaniac.'

She tightens the drawstring and closes the bag, before lifting it and looping the straps over my shoulders for me to carry it instead. A grin flashes across her face, like she believes she's tricked me into being her pack mule. In reality I'd probably carry *her* if she asked me to.

I have to remind myself this agreement is what's best. I wasn't lying when I told Ava that being her friend is my favourite thing. I like who I am when I'm with her, and I'll take any variation of her if it means we can keep spending time together before I leave.

'Let's walk,' she says, and I follow her along the pavement. 'All will be revealed. You trust me, don't you?'

'You know my answer.'

Her expression's coy as we wander along paved streets for a couple of minutes, and I sneak glances to capture as much of her as I can; the way her ponytail swings as she walks, the slight upturn of her nose, how she keeps tugging the sleeves of her hoodie down. Just as I come to the conclusion that whoever decided to call them the apples of your cheeks must've been using Ava as their source material, we arrive at our destination. It's an ornate building I recognise, with four pillars holding up the stone façade.

'Here we are,' she says with a flourish. 'The Natural History Museum.'

I think back to my list. *See the dinosaurs.* She grins, her whole face hopeful, and I peer at the entrance. 'Is it open late tonight?'

'Better,' she leads me towards a sign near the door, which says *A Night at the Museum*. She watches my face to gauge my reaction. 'It's this event they do every so often where they invite guests to eat and drink at the museum until late and then sleep in the main hall under the massive dinosaur skeleton. I got in contact with Sage from the party because I remembered they work here, and they managed to get us tickets. I thought you'd like it. Especially after your intense week.'

I don't know why, but there's a lump in my throat, and it stops me from speaking. Her eyes flick between mine and the longer I don't say anything, the more the excitement fades from her face. She scrabbles for a caveat. 'But if you're not interested, we can just go inside to look at the fossils and then leave in an hour or whatever, that's fine too.'

'Ava, no,' I grab her arm and the lump finally shifts. 'This is perfect. What the fuck?'

Relief floods back into her expression and I let her smile soak into me.

'Let's go and see if our names are on the guest list. If not then this is going to be *extremely* embarrassing.'

Sage pulled through; we're let in with no further questions and I get to see what else is in the bag. Ava's planned it all; there are two sleeping bags—turns out Alina's an avid camper—along with mini toiletries and inflatable pillows. We set the bag in a storeroom with everyone else's stuff so we won't have to lug it around the museum with us.

'You can take your pillow with you on the plane,' she says as we step back into the main area.

I'm trying not to think about the move. It's coming together quicker than I have time to process. I don't need to wait for a visa like I have in the past—thanks for that American passport, Dad—and I've got a few apartment viewings lined up in my first week. There's that familiar buzz at the prospect of starting afresh, though I know saying goodbye to this part of my life is going to be harder than usual. But for now, I'm here.

We spend the evening wandering through the exhibits, which is code for: I show Ava the fossils I like and she pretends she's interested. We spot Sage in one of the galleries and I talk their ear off about armoured dinosaurs while Ava watches like we're speaking a different language. There's a sit-down meal at around eight, and then the bar opens and I'm kind of obsessed with the fact people are getting drunk at the Natural History Museum. Just what the dinosaurs would've wanted.

Neither of us is drinking tonight. I'm glad we both get to experience this with a clear head. Plus, there's a quiz we do moderately well on, and I'm certain if we were drunk it would've been a whole other story.

At the end of a science show, while I'm peppering a palaeontologist with approximately fifty questions, Ava pulls away and spends a few minutes on her phone, frantically texting, periodically drawing her fingertips up to her mouth like she's trying to pull out the words to send. When I catch her eye and mouth *are you okay?* she smiles and nods, but I can tell she doesn't mean it. Her real smile makes my stomach drop—this one just twists it.

She rejoins the group with that insincere smile, acting like she's listening and pointedly ignoring every concerned glance I send her way. Then we head back to the galleries, slower this time, taking in the artefacts we didn't notice on our first round. The more we roam, the tighter Ava's eyebrows pull together, and I know she's not here with me anymore.

I wonder if she just needs some time alone, so we're quiet for a while, and I reluctantly let her drift away as we wander.

'Hey, look. Send a photo of this to your brother,' I say at last, pointing at a plaque that reads *Maxakalisaurus: sauropod, herbivore*. 'Did you know there's a dinosaur called the *Avaceratops* too? I might petition for them to place both sets of fossils together, in honour of you two.'

It's a terrible joke, but it feels like a disproportionate response when her eyes well. If there's one thing I know about Ava, it's that she is not a crier. I step in front of her. 'What's wrong?'

'Nothing.' She says it immediately and I don't believe her. My hand moves down to her wrist and I pull her to a corner of the gallery that's free of people, behind a glass case of ammonites.

'Ava, please. What's really going on? There's something bothering you.'

She slides down the wall to the floor and I try to give her space by sitting against the other wall. For a few moments, we listen to the quiet murmur of people at the other end of the room, our legs outstretched on the floor, feet almost touching.

She scrunches her nose as she thinks, and I hold my breath while I wait for her response. 'Do you remember ages ago I told you that Max was in hospital a few years back?' She lets out a long exhale. 'He's ill again. It wasn't confirmed until today.'

A few more people enter the gallery, either studiously analysing the plaques or drunkenly giggling at some of the funnier names, but they steer clear of us.

'How are you feeling?'

I ask the question, but her emotions sit across her whole body; the sadness pulling her shoulders in, anxiousness in the twist of her mouth, and something else in her eyes. Guilt?

She frowns like it's a stupid question and picks at a loose thread on her trousers. 'It's knocked me. Because he seemed okay, you know? And he will be again.' She nods decisively. 'But it's brought back some memories I've spent a long time trying to push down. It took me a while to get out of that space the first time, and now I can feel myself going back.' She sighs. 'It's never been fair that I'm healthy and he's not. Sometimes it feels like... It feels like anything that's happened to him could've happened to me, if the tiniest thing were different. Like maybe it *should've* been me.'

Trying to ignore the way my heart is shattering at what she just said, I shuffle over to sit next to her, hoping that my proximity is as healing to her as hers is to me. 'You can't think like that.'

She doesn't respond, only continues to tug that loose thread.

More people enter the gallery, stumbling around the corner of the central glass case and running away with drunken giggles when they spot us on the floor. Their carelessness sends a flare of uncharacteristic anger through me. When the group leaves I murmur, 'It must've been a shock.'

'It was last time. It was hard to even process while it was happening. We just had to deal with it day by day. I think if it were a more common type of cancer, maybe it wouldn't have felt quite so scary because I would've heard about more people who'd survived it. But then, it's not like there's ever a *good* type to have. It's always terrible.' She looks straight ahead, breathing shallow, fingernails curling into her palm. I take her hand, sliding my fingers under hers to unfurl them, reminding her that she's on solid ground, and I'm with her. 'I can't really explain the feeling of watching him when it happened. It's this weird, prolonged sense of grief. Like, a preemptive mourning. It was draining. Constantly fighting against the what-ifs. What if this doesn't work? What if this is the last version of him I see?' The words snag in the air, bulky and difficult to see past, and I feel her tense.

'Hey. You don't have to talk about it if you don't want to.'

'I think...' She looks down at our hands like she's only just noticed she's been drawing circles on mine with her thumb and slowly, she says, 'I do want to.'

'Okay.'

She inches closer, pressing the side of her body against me, and I desperately hope that, at the very least, I can absorb some of her sadness by osmosis. Her throat bobs as she swallows. 'Last time, he responded really well to treatment and was getting better. He had chemotherapy first, which got rid of most of the cancer, and then was set to have what they call limb-saving surgery. After the initial shock wore off and we realised he was improving, it felt like things were looking up. Max got very good at making *awful* jokes. Our parents never laughed at them, but it was our way of coping, I guess.'

Briefly, she smiles like she's nostalgic somehow, and then sadness contorts her features into something I don't recognise. 'He was healing from chemo, waiting out the weeks until surgery, when he took a turn for the worse. Because the twisted thing about chemotherapy is that while it kills all the bad cells, it gets rid of the good ones too. And when Max didn't have enough good ones to fight an infection, the infection triggered sepsis. So he was in the ICU, hooked up to a ventilator, and he seemed so out of reach.' Her voice cracks on the last word.

'I dropped out of uni not long before he got the initial infection. I'd been going home a lot anyway, but I realised I needed to be with everyone. I didn't even tell Josie why at the time. I thought that if I didn't talk about it, it wasn't real. I distanced myself from the few friends I'd made at uni. It was only because Josie's so relentless and wouldn't stop messaging me that we managed to keep up the friendship afterwards.

'My parents and I were staying at a hotel by the hospital and I'd lie in bed every night praying to gods I didn't believe in, wondering what kind of deal I could strike to make Max better. Then I worried that by thinking about those horrible what-ifs in the first place, I was putting negative energy out into the universe and would end up manifesting them into existence. So I tried the best I could to stamp the fear out.

'Some mornings I'd wake up and realise my face was wet, so I'd dry my cheeks and go next door to my parents' room and be the one who didn't cry, because they were already going through so much. I can't imagine how it feels to watch your child deteriorate, knowing it's entirely out of your hands.'

'He's your brother, Ava,' I say, brushing a tear from her cheek. 'You were entitled to be upset too.'

She shrugs, and I realise there's not much I dislike about Ava, but I despise how she deflects, how she discounts her own feelings.

'One night we got a call from the hospital. There's only one reason hospital staff call you in the middle of the night, so we got there straight away. And he was just so *small*. So fragile. So unlike him.

'And I probably just imagined it as some twin telepathy thing, but I swear I felt the moment he slipped away. It was like a tug on a piece of rope, like he'd stumbled off a cliff. Then the heart monitor made that terrible sound, and the doctors came in and I knew I was right. I knew it because it felt like my own heart had been torn open. Like he'd grabbed at it for purchase as he fell, and took a piece with him over the edge.

'I'd thought those misdirected prayers I'd been sending out were loud before. But as we were bundled out of the room, they were deafening. *What do I have to promise to get him to stay? I'll do anything. Take anything you want from me, take me instead if you have to, just please, give him back.*'

Tears trail down her face as she continues to look blankly ahead, and I blink the moisture away from my own eyes.

'When we were kids he used to joke that the minutes I was out in the world and he wasn't were the loneliest moments of his life. But that's not true anymore. It was that night in the ICU. Knowing he was on the other side of us. In the dark.' She sniffs and pauses before she speaks. 'Then somehow, they managed to restart his heart, and he came back. Reckless and stubborn until the end. But you don't forget that type of sadness. It lives and breathes with him.' She lifts our linked hands to her face and wipes more tears away.

'It was touch and go for a while. He took such a long time to heal. It really took a toll on him, and he still had to have his surgery, heal some more, and do physio after that. But in the end he was okay. And I guess I've always felt like I've never had the right to be sad about it because he got better. Because he came back.'

'You have the right,' I say. 'You spent months in this state of anxiety and dread and then the worst thing happened, and then you still had to live through more of that fear while he healed. There's no way that wouldn't affect a person. Especially not when you're as close as the two of you.'

'So many people aren't as lucky. We got him back.'

'Your family is lucky to have you too, you know.' She ignores me, and I'm willing to repeat it over and over until she admits it's true. 'They are. If I can see it, so can they. You try so hard to hold your emotions back, but you feel so much for the people you love. It's a wonder they don't collapse under the weight of it.'

'I don't think it matters. If saving someone were as simple as sending out love and tear-stained pleas, no one would die.' She swallows hard and continues, 'So even though I knew in my heart that it was medicine and sheer coincidence that brought him back, on the off chance it wasn't, I couldn't risk it. I kept my life small and quiet, hoping the universe wouldn't hear and remember I owe it something. But slowly, I started to let the happiness in. Started to think it was safe to relax. And now, here we are. It's happened again.' She grits her teeth and mutters, 'And I hate that I'm scared and upset when Max is the one who has to go through it all. I'm *ashamed* of it.' Her chest heaves when she stops, and mine tightens at the sight.

'They're not mutually exclusive. You can be sad for both you and him.'

She blinks a few times and says, 'Maybe.'

There's enough space between her tears now that they dry on her cheeks.

'Not *maybe*. Definitely. You're allowed to feel, Ava. I'm not a therapist, but I know they'd tell you the same.' I run my thumb over the soft skin at her wrist and hope she doesn't recoil against what I'm about to suggest. 'I can't tell you what to do, but if it helped telling me everything, it could be even more helpful telling a professional. Someone who you can be sure won't say the wrong thing.'

She turns her head, looking at me for the first time since she started talking, and the intensity of it shatters my heart into a thousand pieces.

'You never say the wrong thing. I don't know how you do it. It's like you live in my brain.'

*It feels like you live in mine too*, I want to say.

But I don't. Instead, I let her rest her head on my shoulder and breathe.

---

I don't know how long we sit like that. As the minutes pass, I'm sure I see some of the weight roll off her, grey smoke uncoiling and dissipating, until eventually her head is light enough to lift off my shoulder and face me. Her voice is croaky when she asks, 'Be honest, how puffy are my eyes?'

She's trying to bring back a sense of normality, so that's what I'll give her.

'They look fine if you just,' I gingerly put my hand over them, 'cover them up.'

Even in her laugh's weakened state, the sound of it fills my chest.

'I'm glad I told you all of this,' she says. 'I thought I'd be okay with keeping it quiet, but I realised I didn't want you to leave and not know what was going on.'

'Thank you for trusting me. I'm really sorry I can't be here to help out, somehow. Now feels like the time to have people around you who—' I swallow the word down and continue, 'People who care about you.'

She nods, and I want nothing more than to be able to take away the memories that hurt her and stomp down the fears that plague her. But I don't have that power.

'I'll have Josie nearby this time. I won't be by myself.'

'She'll be a good support for you.'

'She will. And maybe it'll be easier than last time. I've been through it before; I know what to expect. I think I'll deal with it better this time around.' She heaves a sigh as someone yells to their friend from the other end of the room. 'Fuck, this was meant to be a fun evening. I'm sorry for crying.'

'Ava.' I peel a few strands of hair away from her cheek, her dried tears acting like glue. 'Don't ever apologise for that.'

'Okay.' She peers at the doorway. 'Come on, let's look around some more. You only get to sleep under the dinosaurs once.'

'Unless you're Sage.' I stand and stretch my legs with a groan, offering Ava my hands to help her up.

---

'Finn,' Ava's voice comes from the floor next to me in a stage whisper. I turn in my sleeping bag to face her. 'Do you think anyone's going to try to get it on beneath Dippy the Diplodocus?'

Everyone's chatting in low voices and hushed giggles as they set up their sleeping mats around us, and it feels a lot like we're at a primary-school sleepover. But looming over us is a full dinosaur skeleton, its shadow casting funny shapes over Ava's face; her eyes still slightly swollen.

'You know what they say, Ava. There's no aphrodisiac quite like sauropod fossils.'

'You're telling me.' She kicks her leg out towards me in her sleeping bag and I twist away to avoid it. 'But you *are* wearing grey sweatpants. Everyone knows men wear grey sweatpants when they want to get slutty.'

A laugh jolts out of me and I tuck my arms deep in my bag, tugging a cord to pull the hood tight around my face so that all she can see are my eyes and nose. 'No funny business over here.'

'The funny business is you using the phrase "funny business".' She stretches across and loosens the hood from my face, and I feel the accidental graze of her fingertips against my skin long after she's settled back onto her mat. For a while, all I hear is a series of rustles as she wiggles around. With a grunt, she says, 'I just want you to know, I am outrageously uncomfortable right now.'

'I can be the big spoon if that'd help?' I look over at her just in time to catch her rolling her eyes, just about visible in the dim light.

'You and I both know you'd be the little spoon.'

I lean back against my pillow, eyes on the vaulted ceiling. 'Goodnight Ava.'

'Goodnight Finn.'

'And goodnight Dippy.'

She laughs and whispers, 'Goodnight Dippy.'

It's the last thing I hear before I fall asleep.

In my dreams, I wonder if the dinosaurs knew what they were in for when that asteroid hurtled towards them on its one-way course to ruin.

Maybe they did. Maybe they welcomed it.

# 37

## plaid pyjamas and dino-snores
### AVA

It's a confusing thing, to want time to still and speed all at once. There's the part of me that wants to savour these last days with Finn, and the part of me that hopes they pass in a single second so Max can get started on his treatment sooner.

On Max's end, he's been up to London a couple of times for various tests in preparation for the radiotherapy that'll start in a few weeks. In line with my promise for normality, we don't talk about the elephant in the room, and he even joins Finn, Josie and me at Somerset House for the last of their summer movie sessions; a showing of *Legally Blonde* in the courtyard. Not quite under the stars, but I know they're out there, through the smog.

One evening Finn and I go to a Never After gig at Brixton Academy with Dylan, and as we stand at the back with our two-pint cups of cider and overpriced merch, I question what possessed me to have spent my teen years queueing for hours to be near the front at shows when there's just so much more room at the back to dance. Or, specifically, to watch Finn dance. Terribly.

Another day we see a play at The Globe and I wonder if Elizabethan theatregoers also felt like their feet were falling off after standing for three hours watching *Titus Andronicus*, or if they had stronger extremities than I do.

We walk along the canals in Little Venice with Josie and Rudy, trek up Primrose Hill to admire the view, and see the deer in Richmond Park (there's lots of walking, incidentally, but I don't mind it).

And so, the days pass by exactly as I thought they would; jam-packed with moments so vibrant they'll be branded onto my memory forever.

On his penultimate day, Finn has leaving drinks at a pub in Clapham, and Josie comes along too. I hold the door open for her as she tells me about her week.

'We've finalised some of the tech for the big piece in the exhibition and I cannot *wait* for you to see it.' Rudy leads her to the beer garden out back. September's mild temperatures mean we can still sit outside, although this might be the last time we get to do it this year. It feels like a fitting end to summer. 'But oh my god, I'm exhausted. I intend to do absolutely *nothing* this weekend. I'm locking myself in the flat. If you find me wedged between the sofa cushions, do not attempt to move me.'

'Noted.' I spot Julien and Rory already seated at one of the tables at the back under the vine-draped pergola, heads bowed, knees touching. Rory waves us over and I slide onto the bench directly opposite an empty spot, the table wobbling as I do. 'You both good for drinks?'

'The man of the hour has already ordered,' Julien says, nodding towards the doorway, through which Finn is coming with a tray of drinks, including an Aperol Spritz for me and a G&T for Josie.

'You're an angel,' Josie says. Her eyes light up when she sips her drink. 'And you got it with cucumber!'

'I distinctly remember you going off on a whole rant at the party about cucumber being underrated in G&Ts,' he points out. 'Thought you might kill me if I came back with lime.'

She grins, and my heart aches seeing the two of them interact.

'What's your plan for tomorrow?' I ask. We've been so busy that we haven't really discussed the logistics of saying goodbye. Or rather, I haven't wanted to think about it. I was hoping to meet for a coffee tomorrow before he goes.

'The two of us are having brunch like real millennials,' Julien answers, the sunlight reflecting off his watch as he swigs his beer.

'After that I'll head down to Heathrow to check into a hotel. Flight's the next morning.' Finn clears his throat, dropping his gaze as soon as my eyes meet his. 'And then I'll be gone.'

'Just like that,' Josie says slowly.

'You managed to sort out the room, I take it?' Rory asks, his neck craning as he watches a member of staff pass by with some chips. The smell alone is enough to make my stomach rumble.

But I don't think Finn's mentioned anything about a room, so I ask, 'What's that about?'

'I need to stay in a hotel tomorrow night because my tenancy's over, and Julien's family's visiting so I can't crash at his.' Golden hour casts long shadows across the table, but the glow lands on Finn like a spotlight, bringing out the auburn in his hair, warming his skin tone. 'The reservation for the room I initially booked didn't go through, so now I'm looking for one that doesn't cost, like, eight hundred pounds for the night.'

'You should just stay at ours,' Josie says. She's acting casual, but something in the set of her shoulders tells me she's feeling anything but. 'You can sleep on the sofa bed. I'm at Alina's this weekend so Rudy and I will be out of your way.'

What happened to "I'm locking myself in the flat"? She looks at Finn, expectant.

'Oh, uh, I don't mind paying for the hotel,' Finn says. 'I was exaggerating about it being eight hundred pounds.'

Josie turns to me now. 'You don't mind having some company, right, Ava?'

Maybe it'd be nice to hang out at the flat tomorrow instead of go out for coffee. And he's probably exhausted after bucket list-ing and packing. 'Yeah, no worries. You can stay at ours.'

'Cool,' he says, and I can't quite figure out his expression. 'Thanks. I promise I'll be quiet in the morning when I leave. You won't even know I'm gone.'

And with that, the plan is in motion. I realise I'm just delaying the inevitable, but I find I can relax a little, knowing I don't have to say goodbye just yet. We sit at our rickety table for hours, chatting and drinking, and when Julien and Finn spend half an hour trying to one-up each other with embarrassing stories from their childhood, I laugh so hard my stomach hurts. Then Josie gets involved airing our ridiculous moments in uni halls and I saturate a napkin dabbing at my eyes.

The sun's long gone by the time we start saying our goodbyes, and there's a pain pulsing at my temple from too much laughter and too many Aperol Spritzes.

Finn hugs Rory, slapping him on the back and saying, 'Look after Julien, okay?'

'Always,' Rory replies. 'Come back and visit.'

'I will.' Finn smiles and then looks down at Rudy, clenching his fists to hold back from petting him. 'Bye Rudy.'

'He says he'll miss you. And I will too, so come here.' Josie goes in for a hug. He whispers something in her ear and she smiles as she replies, 'Of course.'

Julien and I don't get the heartfelt goodbyes from him because we're seeing him tomorrow, but I still make the most of our embrace, however brief, inhaling his comforting smell, the scent of a swimming pool never quite fading from his skin.

'How are you getting back?' I ask, the last one out of the door he's holding for all of us.

'I think I'm gonna walk home. Might look at the stars.' His eyes flash to mine. 'Or aeroplanes, maybe.'

Under the streetlight, I study him; messy hair, open face, warm and patient and earnest. 'Did your wish ever come true? The one you made that night?'

He puts his hands in his pockets and looks directly at me too. 'I'm not sure yet.'

---

When the intercom buzzes the next day, sometime in the early evening, I let Finn up. He's lugging two massive suitcases behind him, a rucksack slung across one shoulder, a Tesco bag on the other arm. He's unusually dishevelled, with wonky glasses and hair askew. I take one look at him and cover my mouth to catch the laugh before it leaks out.

'Did you take the stairs?' I ask, completely bewildered. 'Why not the lift?'

He follows my gaze to the metal doors in the hallway and lets out a tearless sob. 'For fun. I saw it and I thought, "nah, not today".' He drags the cases in behind him and closes the door.

'Did you not get the lift up last time?'

'I'm gonna be honest, I don't even remember how I got here last time. I was a little preoccupied.' It was the night after we kissed. The night we ended up doing a lot more than kiss. I let the memory fizzle out when I realise he's still talking. 'I wasn't even sure if you'd let me in that night.'

I reach forward to pull one of the suitcases further into the flat. 'Well, at least you made it today.'

'Barely,' he mutters, following me into the kitchen and leaning against the counter like he always does at City Roast. Always *did*, I correct myself.

'Do you want a drink?' I pull out glasses from the dishwasher and inspect them for any grossness. 'We still have some stuff left over from the party. There's wine, rum, the shitty sambuca—'

He crosses his arms, eyes twinkling. 'Does not-shitty sambuca exist?'

'Unsure. But what do you want? Water? Tea? Coffee? Milk?'

I'm not quite Josie when it comes to hosting, and his laughter lines deepen at my aggressive hospitality. 'Did you really just suggest milk?'

'Oat or cow's.'

'Ava, I'm not drinking a glass of *milk*.' He blinks as he thinks through the onslaught of options and proceeds to take a completely different approach. 'No squash?'

'If you're being facetious,' I dig around one of the cupboards and pull out a bottle of orange and pineapple, 'it's not working. I live for squash.'

'I was being serious,' he says through a laugh. 'I remembered they don't have it in the US and I wanna fill my quota before I leave.' We take our drinks to the sofa and he says, 'I have something for you.'

'I have a gift for you too. But you go first.'

'Okay wait, no, it's not actually exciting.' He empties the contents of his Tesco bag onto the coffee table, following it with something akin to jazz hands. It's multiple family packs of crisps and popcorn and, inexplicably, a handful of carrots.

'God, you know how to treat a woman.' I rake my hands through the loot.

'Sorry, that was ridiculously underwhelming. I just didn't wanna waste the food I had in my cupboards.'

I burst out laughing at his grimace and open one of the packets, crossing my legs under me on the sofa. 'There is no gift I enjoy more than salt and vinegar crisps, and I mean that with my whole heart.'

'Well, now I wish I'd brought more.' He leans in and takes a handful. Once he's finished eating, he adds, 'Think of me every time you see them from now on.'

*I'll be thinking about you more often than that, I'm sure of it.*

My clothes suddenly feel like they're too tight and I leap to my feet again, Finn glancing over at me in surprise. 'I'm gonna put my pyjamas on. If you eat all those without me I'll kick you out.'

When I come back to the living room Finn's rooting through his rucksack. 'I'm gonna put mine on too.' He puts on an American accent and says, 'Slumber party?'

'Please never, ever do that again.'

He laughs to himself all the way to the bathroom.

I wait for him to come back, the gift I'd grabbed from my room for him now tucked behind my back on the sofa. By the time I hear the bathroom door open, I've made an impressive dent in the snacks. I look up as he comes closer and have to immediately avert my eyes, narrowly avoiding choking on a crisp in the process. In theory, plaid pyjama trousers should be wholesome. Somehow, on Finn they border on obscene.

One corner of his mouth lifts infinitesimally but he doesn't say anything straight away. He eyes the packet I'm clutching. 'Don't worry about saving any for me.'

'Wasn't going to,' I say, crunching my way through a few more crisps and keeping my eyes on his face.

'I assume you've noticed my shirt. Got it at the museum.'

I hadn't noticed, actually. I was otherwise occupied. He stands in front of me in the kind of emotionless pose of a kid waking their parents to tell them they had a bad dream, wearing a ridiculous blue t-shirt that reads *I survived a night with the dino-snores.*

'Firstly, I have no recollection of you making that purchase and *absolutely* would have talked you out of it had I known.' I tilt my head back like I'm praying to the heavens, but I can't help the laugh that spills out of and over me. It turns his deadpan expression into a grin. 'Secondly, and most importantly, why are you like this?'

'I'm like this because I have minimal shame.' He stretches, all faux-awkwardness gone from his posture, dropping back onto his spot on the sofa. 'Hey, so I know I should be like *oh no, Ava, you shouldn't have got me anything,* but the suspense is killing me. What did you get me?'

'Give me your phone. Wait, no, unlock it first.'

'You're very commanding.' He does what I say anyway. He usually does.

I catch a flash of his lockscreen and my heart pangs when I realise he's changed it to one of the photos we took under the archway at the Barbican. That was before I really knew him. Before he really knew me.

'Now close your eyes,' I say, clearing my throat. I place two items in his hands and he opens his eyes. He looks at the larger item first; a pack of hazelnut wafers. One of those sunshine smiles spreads across his face, and I repeat his words back to him, 'Think of me when you eat them.'

He shakes his head with a small chuckle. 'I'm not gonna eat them.'

'You don't want a reminder of me?' I say it with a laugh, but when he meets my eye he says what I kept to myself just a few minutes ago.

'I'm gonna be reminded of you all the time anyway.' He blinks a few times and looks at the second item, turning the plastic over in his hand. 'What's this?'

I slide along the sofa until I'm pressed against his side. 'I removed Mateo's name from his badge when he left the coffee shop and added yours instead. As proof of your last bucket list item.' I show him his phone and the final point on the list stares at us, waiting to be crossed off. *Become a regular.* 'Finlay O'Callaghan, I hereby declare you a regular.'

A sad smile tugs at his mouth and he nods at his phone. 'Will you do the honours?'

The act itself is kind of anticlimactic; I press the tick mark and then it's over. But seeing the whole list in front of us is unexpectedly heavy. For a while we both stare at it, at all the items we've completed. A scrapbook, of sorts, of the summer. I feel the sway of the boat bar, smell the plants at the Barbican Conservatory, taste the bagel from that shop on Brick Lane. It's all here, on this note in Finn's phone.

'Can you believe this whole thing started because I wanted to run away from a dickhead in a pub? It feels like forever ago.'

'I'm glad he was a dickhead,' he says simply. 'But I think I would've found a way to hang out with you anyway.'

I often feel like I got caught up in Finn's orbit. All those times I've tried to close myself off, be alone, wallow, and he's pulled me towards him instinctively; easy and warm and safe. But when he says things like this I wonder if maybe he got caught up in mine too; two lonely satellites tumbling through the cosmos, some gravitational pull drawing us together.

I don't know how to say what I want to say without making it the sentimental goodbye I was hoping to avoid. But in the end, I lean into it. 'I think I've had more fun in these last few months than I have in years.' I push my arm against his. 'And it's because of you. So thank you.'

Uncertainty creases his forehead. 'Am I making the right decision?'

'There's no such thing as the right decision. It's just a decision.' Everything in me wants to avoid eye contact, but I fix my gaze onto him. 'You make it, you nurture it, and eventually you find out what it grows up to be.'

'Then why does it feel wrong?'

'It's a big change.' I analyse him; messy curls, ridiculous t-shirt, eyes like velvety espresso, curious and playful and thoughtful all at once. 'Are you excited for this job?'

'Yes.'

'And are you ready to explore a new place?'

He sighs, scratching his jaw. 'Yeah.'

'So what's stopping you?'

The silence stretches between us into something physical. It presses against my lungs, an ocean opening its jaws. His voice is low when he says, 'I think you know.'

I let the next wave of quiet roll over me before I speak again. 'You can't pin your happiness on someone else.' The words surprise me. Because really, haven't I been doing the same? I gain momentum, remembering what Josie said ages ago about how she and Alina take the time to work on themselves individually so they can become better for each other. 'It feels good, but it's not healthy. And it's not the right time. I think we both have things to prove. I need to know I'm okay. That I'm not broken.'

He curls an arm around me and pulls me to him, his face in my hair as he murmurs, 'You're not broken.'

'I have to confirm that for myself.' I relax into the security of his hold and give him some of the truth I've been unpicking over the past few weeks. 'Being around you made me forget, but it didn't get rid of the stuff in my brain, underneath. That's still there.'

His chin rests on top of my head and I feel him nod, feel the urgent, anxious pace of his heartbeat. 'I want you to feel better. More than anything.'

'And I want you to feel settled. You won't be satisfied until you've proven to yourself that you can do this job.'

'I just hope I'm good enough for it.'

You will be. But you have to give this decision the attention it deserves,' I say, closing my eyes and imagining a world where I can spend more time tucked against Finn like this. 'A couple of months ago, San Francisco was all you were talking about. Maybe it'll become your favourite place you've ever lived.'

I don't say I'll visit, because it feels too close to a lie, and because he might do what he's always done and cut contact completely with his old life as soon as he settles in his new home. There's no way of knowing.

His pulse slows and finally, he gives a long, low sigh. 'A decision is a decision. I've got a new job and I'll make friends, and it'll be fun.' It feels like a mantra.

'It'll be fun. And you're excited,' I remind him. That's when the idea comes to me. 'Let's make a San Francisco bucket list. Tonight.'

As we scroll through pages and pages of tourist websites and travel blogs, I could almost forget he's leaving. We get sucked into bizarre Reddit threads and read *Am I the asshole?* posts aloud like they're slam poetry, making our way through a good chunk of Finn's secondhand snacks in the process.

It's still fairly early when he notices the time; the sky a dusty violet, wisps of clouds only just visible through the living room window. But this man is not me, and I watch him do the maths to make sure he can get enough sleep. 'I don't really want to sleep yet, but I probably should finish getting ready for bed.'

I join him in the bathroom and we stand next to each other at the mirror as we brush our teeth, taking part in that silent contest you do in other people's company where you spend far longer brushing than you normally would. I don't know how many minutes it's been by the time he caves.

'Jesus,' he says after he's spat out the toothpaste and rinsed it away. 'I thought I was gonna end up having to swallow that.'

'It wasn't a competition,' I say through my toothbrush, the words garbled. 'I won though.'

'Where's your spare bedding? I'll set up the sofa.' I point towards the airing cupboard as I spit out my toothpaste and he says, 'I hope I'm not being a stereotypical man here, but I can't see anything.'

I wipe my mouth and go to the cupboard, sure I'm going to find our spare set right in front of me. But he's right, it's not there. And I know I washed it after Max used it recently. I open Josie's bedroom door and there, in the corner, is a pile of bedding. Grabbing my phone from its spot on the side of the sink, I see a text on my home screen from Josie from over an hour ago that I must've missed.

> just remembered that rudes peed on the spare bedding so it needs to be washed, sorry!!!

As far as I'm aware, Rudy hasn't had an accident since he was a puppy, but I don't think too much about it after that. I spin around and Finn's running a hand through his hair, still squinting into the cupboard like the sheets might materialise if he looks hard enough.

'Sorry, Josie's used it recently so it's dirty.' I wish we still had the sleeping bags from the museum, but Alina took them back already.

'I can just sleep without a sheet or anything, it's fine.' He closes the cupboard door and I can feel the warmth coming off him, he's that close.

'No.' I step back and make a decision, determined to be a good host for his last night. 'You can sleep in my room and I'll sleep in Josie's. I washed my bedding a couple of days ago. I'm not gross, I promise.'

'If you're sure you don't mind me stealing your bedroom?' he asks.

Without warning, my mind flashes back to the one other time Finn was in my room, and maybe his does too, because his face contorts and he looks up at the ceiling, slightly pained.

My voice is breezy when I say, 'I'm sure. All good. Do you want some water?' I catch sight of the clock as I head to the kitchen and my heart pangs with the realisation. He's leaving. Soon. Fuck.

While I'd personally be happy with a glass of London's finest chalky tap water, I use Josie's filtered water from the fridge this time. In these last few moments we have together, it feels like every decision I make is important. Finn takes his glass from my outstretched hand and leans against the counter in the corner, his left arm braced against the worktop as his right holds the glass to his lips. His stance is relaxed, but his knuckles on the hand against the counter are bone white.

That's how we stand for a while, wordlessly sipping, like the longer we make our waters last, the longer we can pretend he's not getting on a plane tomorrow and flying thousands of miles away. I'm distracted enough by the thought that I'm surprised when I hit the bottom of my cup. I stare at it for a while, as if there's a solution to soothing my clamorous thoughts to be found there.

I'm dimly aware that the sirens that usually screech at all times of day seem to have quietened. It's like we're trapped inside during a snowstorm; the outside world muffled and distant while we're suspended in time and space in this corner of my kitchen, the air between us heavy and singing with static.

'So,' I begin, breaking the silence by placing my empty glass on the counter. I wince when it hits the granite. 'The London bucket list is officially complete.'

Finn inspects me over the rim of his glass and says quietly, 'No stone left unturned.'

'No stone left unturned,' I agree, eyes locked on his, aware of the determined set of his jaw.

I don't move a muscle. All I hear is the sound of the clock and the roaring of my own heartbeat. Everything else in the flat seems to be holding its breath.

He finishes his water like it's a shot. Maybe he wishes it was.

And then he delicately places his glass in the sink, takes a single step forward, and says, 'Apart from one.'

# 38

## impatience is a virtue

### AVA

He closes the distance between us like he's trying not to disturb the air; his breathing steady, no sudden movements, intention painted across every pane of his face. When we're only a couple of inches apart, his eyes dart frantically between mine; the only giveaway there's something erratic taking place below the surface.

My hands find their way into his hair and he brings his forehead against mine. I taste the mint from our toothpaste on the air as we breathe each other in, lips almost touching, nothing but our resolve separating us now.

'Ava,' he murmurs. He wraps my name in velvet and I want to curl up in the softness of it.

Finally, when it feels like my entire body is aching, our lips meet, the softness of his a stark contrast against the scratchiness of his stubble, and my brain short-circuits as it tries to make sense of what's happening. He teases my mouth open with his tongue and I let him in, my hands snaking into the hair at the nape of his neck.

This is different. This isn't the frenzied moments we've had before. This is slow, deliberate. It doesn't escape my notice that it should be the most urgent time of all.

He kisses like he's been away for a decade, like he's telling me ten years' worth of stories with every minuscule shift in position. Or maybe it's the opposite. Maybe he's storing up these seconds like they're the life source that'll sustain him over the coming months.

The realisation hits me like a punch to the gut. I wish I were ready for Finn the way he wants. I wish we were right for each other, at the right time. Because I want to know his sleepy morning kisses and sweet welcome-home kisses and heavy-eyed carnal kisses. I want him instantly, slowly, all at once, bit by bit, now, tomorrow, always. But somehow, all we have left is tonight.

'Can we pretend we have more time?' My voice comes out as a whisper against his lips.

'I don't know what you're talking about,' he says, planting delicate kisses along my jaw. 'We have all the time in the world.'

With the languid pace of his tongue and the slow trail of his hands down my body, I almost believe him.

When one hand makes its gentle way down my spine, resting at my lower back, it's too chaste and I'm too eager, so in the least subtle message in history, I grip his wrist and move his hand to my ass, and he may be in the midst of attempting some kind of Regency-era gentlemanship, but his fingertips still dig into the softness there.

'I meant the time thing on, like, a larger scale,' I say, tugging him closer by the hair. 'I didn't mean I wanted it to take an hour to get all our clothes off.'

His laugh rumbles through me and it sets off an avalanche, all coherent thought cascading down a hillside and into the valley below. Incidentally, *below* is where a lot of feelings are surging at the moment.

'You're rushing me.' His lips press against my collarbone. 'I've wanted to do this for a long time. *Slowly*.' He emphasises the last word by dragging his mouth up my neck, breath sending waves of heat radiating across my skin until it settles between my thighs.

'I've wanted it for longer,' I admit, though truthfully I can't pinpoint the exact moment I started aching for him like this.

'I let you think you're right about a lot of things, Ava Monroe,' the nip of his teeth against my skin sends a current through me, 'but I'm willing to fight you on this one.'

My hands run along his shoulders and down his chest to the hem of the stupid dinosaur top. 'As hot as this is...' He pulls it over his head in one smooth motion and I briefly wonder if other people are as turned on by mundane things like that as I am, or if I'm just preternaturally horny. 'Why do you ever wear a shirt?' I ask into his mouth, grazing his torso with my fingers and leaving a goosebump trail in my wake.

'Why do *you* ever wear a shirt?' He tugs mine off in another movement that, yes, also gets me going, and dips his lips to where my neck meets my shoulders as he mutters, 'It's sickening.'

'I can make it worse,' I say. Maybe I can convince him to speed things up. I unhook my bra, and when he looks at me, lids heavy, pupils blown out, I think I might finally have the upper hand. I take the moment of distraction to press against him, and he lets out a groan as our chests touch.

We must be part of the same circuit, because electricity conducts through every point our skin connects, and any time we pull apart the energy crackles, desperate for somewhere to go.

'You're going to be the death of me,' he rasps, long fingers skimming my sides. All the usual warmth of his voice has burnt away, leaving nothing but texture in its husk.

'I know.' As gentle as he's trying to be, one part of his body spoils the game. I run my hands up his hips, then along his waistband. 'Did you wear these on purpose?'

'They're no grey sweatpants,' he manages, mostly succeeding at maintaining eye contact while my fingers find the taut skin of his stomach, muscles flexing against my touch.

'And yet, you're still getting slutty.'

He laughs despite himself, and I watch his face change as one of my hands moves lower, as I apply the softest pressure over the fabric. His attempts at staying composed are admirable, but when I take hold of him through his trousers and begin to move my hand slowly, purposefully, his eyes blaze and his jaw tightens.

He grabs my wrist just as he lets out a quiet *fuck*. The kitchen counter presses into my lower back as he leans in to kiss me again, and more want gathers between my legs every second.

'Take these off,' I say, my hands making their way back to his waistband.

He ignores my request and moves his lips up my throat, lapse in composure all but forgotten, and his ease sends me reeling. I've never been willing to get on my knees and beg for a man before, but at this point, my morals are out the window.

'Always so bossy,' he replies, punctuating each word with a kiss.

I let my fingers tangle in his hair. 'I like to be in control.'

'I know you do. But can I tell you a secret?' He takes my chin in his hand, angling my ear to his mouth, and whispers, 'So do I.'

The sound travels down my entire body, and I can barely think straight when he finds a new target. Two new targets, in fact. I squirm as his tongue drags, as his lips close over me, and it takes everything in me to force the next words out. 'I have a question.'

'I'm listening,' he says, although the way he's using his mouth and hands feels like something that would require a lot of concentration. At least, it's definitely taking me a lot of concentration to talk through it.

'What do you call your penis?'

'Are you asking if I've given it a nickname?' To his credit, he doesn't stop what he's doing, and his words buzz against the skin of my chest.

My hands run along his neck and shoulders, so sharp from the endless hours he spends in the pool. 'I mean, how do you refer to it?'

'Why have you chosen,' he grazes my nipple with his teeth and it takes everything in me to keep from whimpering, 'this moment in time to ask?'

'The wrong answer might make me want to stop.'

He pulls back, and the quirk of his utterly self-confident smirk tells me he knows there's nothing on this planet that would make me want to stop right now. Then he kisses my forehead and sighs, and the sound is half affectionate, half long-suffering. 'My dick?' He catches the relief on my face. 'That's the right answer?'

'Correct. Not cock. Never cock.' I kiss him, satisfied with his response, and the subject in question presses between my legs with every movement.

'Of course not.' His teeth pull at my bottom lip. 'On a completely unrelated note, your dirty talk needs some work.'

'You don't need me to talk dirty.'

'No,' he says into the space between our mouths. 'I don't. But you're a strange woman sometimes, I hope you know that.'

Not strange enough to scare him away though, I notice, because it's then that he discovers a sense of urgency. Breaths come faster, tongues push deeper, hands grip harder, and the force of all of it pushes me backwards out of the kitchen.

'We've waited this long,' he mumbles against me as we stumble into my room. 'I wasn't going to let this happen on a counter next to the fucking crumpets.'

'But crumpets are sexy,' I say, my calves hitting the mattress. 'All those—'

'I swear to god, if you say "holes", I'm gonna leave.' I fall onto the bed and his arms cage me in. 'And we all know the sexiest bread is focaccia, anyway. So let's move on.'

A laugh spills out of me and his eyes light up in response, before he moves me further up the bed until I'm leaning against the pillows, half naked and buzzing with anticipation.

'Beautiful,' he mutters, so quietly I think he might not have meant to say it out loud. But then he meets my gaze and says it directly to me, his voice clear. 'You're beautiful, Ava.'

The sardonic part of my brain wants to tell him to stop using that mouth for words when he could be doing other things with it, but truthfully, he's setting off fireworks either way.

He moves back down to my breasts, tongue and teeth skimming the skin there while I scrape my nails along his scalp, his neck, his shoulders. Meanwhile, his hands snake to the waistband of my shorts, stopping at my thighs and stomach and ass on the way down, digging into the flesh like he's not convinced it's real.

He grips the fabric at my hips. 'Can I?'

Taking my nod as his cue to continue, he pulls my shorts and underwear off tantalisingly slowly, kissing along the inside of my thighs, my knees, my calves, all the while moving further away from where I want him, taking my restraint with him as he goes.

As the world's current most impatient woman, I move my own hand between my legs, and a gasp escapes me at the contact, drawing Finn's heavy gaze first to my fingers, then up to my face. I don't break eye contact as I touch myself, enjoying the way he swallows, the way he fidgets slightly to relieve the pressure in his trousers, the way he takes short, sharp breaths through parted lips as if he's the one doing any of the work right now.

For a few wordless moments more he watches and listens, and then he's kneeling between my legs, gently taking my hand away and tracking the movement as I bring it up to my mouth. When I suck my own fingers clean, I swear he looks at me like I'm some kind of god. It makes sense, because there on his knees, he could be a disciple praying at an altar.

But then he pushes my legs further apart and drops his head between my thighs, and I wonder if he's the Devil instead.

'This isn't fair on you,' I say, ignoring my increasing breathlessness as he cups my ass to angle me closer to his mouth, as his fingers work in tandem in all the right places. 'I got all the fun last time.'

'Believe me,' a hand presses me against the bed by the stomach while his tongue almost sends me into orbit with one deliberate stroke, 'I'm having fun.'

t doesn't take long before my hips take on a mind of their own, jerking forward to meet him, warmth spreading through me until the sparks ignite into an inferno that sets every nerve ending ablaze. My back arches as I grab at his hair and the sheets, dimly aware I'm crying out, so blissfully absent I don't even know where I am, or if the fire will ever go out.

Once my contented body has burnt down to embers, I pull him onto me and register every inch; the strong line of his shoulders, the firm muscle at his back, the urgent thump of our hearts beating in time like the Doomsday Clock.

My hands tug at his hair as his lips find their way back to mine, and we move back into a heady rhythm of tongues and sighs and gentle movements that satisfy me for maybe twenty seconds, before the desperation hits me again and I remember how much more I want to do.

'Do you trust me?' I ask, meeting molten eyes.

An incredulous laugh tips out of him, and for the first time since we met, he replies, 'Not at all.'

I push him onto his back and make my way down his body until I'm kneeling between his legs. He leans against the pillows, one arm folded behind his head while he watches my hands trail down his broad chest, past the dusting of dark hair below his belly button, until they're at the top of those godforsaken pyjama bottoms.

'Can I?' I repeat his question to me.

'Please,' he says through another laugh.

Then he's naked too, and I finally wrap my fingers around him, skin to skin, relishing the feel of this unchartered territory and the reaction it elicits from the man underneath me. I move my hand slowly at first, watching each rise and fall of his chest, listening for every deep sound he makes.

When I bend down to taste him, eyes meeting his just as I make contact, his head lolls backwards and he lets out a string of expletives that go straight to my ego.

'Ava.' He says my name like it's water in a drought, and he drinks it up, and I drink him up too, completely inebriated on the way he reacts to every pump of my fist, every glide of my tongue.

Leaning forward to scoop my hair back with one hand and hold it in his fist, he murmurs, 'I've always liked your hair in a ponytail.'

I hum in response, and when his eyes drop to mine again, I think he might ascend there and then.

As a man who, generally speaking, cannot shut up, I could've predicted him to be vocal. But I didn't expect to enjoy the words that spill out of him as much as I do; the violent praising of my mouth, my body, even my "illogical cynicism" at one point, which is a new one for the bedroom but, well, it does the job.

'You know,' I release him from my mouth with a quiet pop, 'dicks are objectively kind of hideous, but yours could be a lot worse.'

'I'm really gonna miss that way with words,' he says hoarsely, lightly tugging my ponytail with one hand while the other roams my body, sending shivers reverberating across my skin like ripples in a pond.

'Is it the only thing you're going to miss?' I run my tongue upwards and the noise that comes out of him is almost primal.

After a few more laboured breaths he lets go of my hair and reaches towards me, pulling my face back to his and tasting himself on my tongue, making the weight below my stomach ache even more than I thought possible.

I lift my legs over his hips to straddle him, aware of how painfully close we are, how my insides feel like a maze of tripwires just one mistake away from detonation.

'I want this. But do you want to keep going?' he asks, running his hands up my sides and resting them in the dip of my waist.

'Obviously,' I rasp, unsure how exactly I could make my intentions any clearer at this second. 'I thought you were smart.'

I rest a hand on his torso to steady myself as I stretch across him to dig through my bedside table.

'There's nothing stupid about consent,' he replies smoothly, tearing open the foil packet and, because he is Finn O'Callaghan, handing me the wrapper to throw in the bin while he rolls the condom on.

'You sound,' I lean forward to kiss him, tasting toothpaste and lust and that unnameable thing that's been building between us for months, 'like a sex education video they'd show in schools.'

And then I put both hands on his chest and sink onto him, and I don't think there's any universe where this happens and I don't make a borderline-embarrassing noise at the feel of his body so profoundly interlocked with mine. His thumbs dig into the creases between my thighs and hips as I shift position, slowly easing him out and back in, setting a pace where every movement is torturously drawn out.

His grip on my hips tightens with each passing moment as he guides me onto him, a vein straining in his neck as he watches me. I'm certain no one's ever looked at me like this before. The usual playful ease in his eyes is now blistering lava instead, and it sears into my skin every time his gaze moves over me. I'm probably being selfish, because what I'm doing has to feel better for me than it does for him, but nothing in his body language tells me I should stop. It's only when I'm teetering on the edge that he slips a hand between my legs, moving his thumb in response to my quickening pace and shortening gasps. Then, that familiar warmth spills over me like bottled sunlight tipped from my head to my toes, and all I can do is ride it out until I'm a shuddering, boneless wreck against his chest.

I press against him while I attempt to regain control of my breathing; my face tucked into his neck, mouth somewhere near his Adam's apple. I hear the soft click of his glasses as he sets them on the nightstand, and feel his quiet voice vibrate down his throat when he says, 'My turn.'

Before I know what's happening he's turned us over again, hands landing on either side of my head. He doesn't move other than to brush my cheekbone with his thumb, and the longer he stays like that, the more eager I get.

'What are you waiting for?' I ask. 'Do you want me to say please?'

He chuckles, a huff of air pulsing between us. 'No, I don't want you to say please.' My lips come apart to meet his and his tongue makes a lazy journey towards mine, curls tickling my face as he moves. 'We're just friends, aren't we?'

I reach between my legs to position him. 'I'm not feeling very friendly right now.'

'Good.' He kisses along my jaw to my lips and then pulls back, and I watch his focus change as he pushes inside me again. 'Me neither.'

He moves against me painstakingly slowly, never quite giving me all of him the way I want, and it turns me into a writhing mess.

'Come *on*,' I beg, clutching his arms and shoulders, feeling the muscles move under his skin, willing him to go faster.

By the clench of his jaw I know he wants it too, but there's a familiarity to the way he's taunting me. The mischief in his eyes grows with every needy whine I let out, and I realise he's handling me the way he always does; with aggravating patience and a smirk.

The heat of his mouth drags up my throat and he asks, 'What do you need from me?'

'I need you to stop fucking around.'

He laughs, and it appeases a little of the mess in my head. 'Wrong answer.'

'You already know what I need,' I say, shifting position, trying to generate some friction.

'Probably,' he replies, nose nudging my jaw. 'But I want you to tell me.'

The truth rises to the surface when his gaze meets mine. 'I need however much you're willing to give me.'

It's quiet for a few moments, just our ragged breathing breaking the silence.

'I'd give you everything, Ava,' he whispers at last.

There's a flicker of sadness in his eyes, but I don't want that, not now, not when we're doing this.

So I wrap my legs around his back and dig my heels in, pushing my hips towards his as hard as I can. The new angle forces out a low noise from deep in his throat, and that's all it takes for him to drive into me harder and faster at last; my entire body rocking with the force of it, mattress springs complaining with every movement, moans I can't control tumbling from my lips.

I wind my fingers into the mess of his hair and pull his face towards mine, trying to catch his kiss in the chaos and missing his lips almost every time. I refuse to forget what he feels like, sounds like, looks like in this moment; fierce eyes, sweat forming at his hairline, words spilling out of him that might be curses or compliments or both, melded together into a kind of furious reverence.

A sharp gasp escapes me when he hits a certain spot, and he slows instantly, chest heaving. 'Are you okay?'

I lift my hips to meet his in response and he pushes into me again, forcing the headboard against the wall with a thud. Then he drops onto his forearms, and even when we're pressed together like this, I still wish we could be closer, somehow.

We move against each other with increasing urgency and I know he needs me as much as I need him, because just before my world erupts, he breathes, 'You.'

And I get it.

You holding the door open for me, you bringing me into the sunlight, you waiting for me to burst into colour and sound before you let yourself unravel too. You, me, two ends of the same thread unspooling as one.

*You, you, you.*

Finn's fingers draw lazy circles on my hip as we face each other in the dark, the gap in the curtains casting a cool strip of moonlight over his face.

'I don't think I've ever liked anyone as much as I like you.' He kisses my forehead and lets out a sigh before he continues. 'You don't have to feel the same. But I had to say it.'

His honesty spears my heart. My own emotions are too tangled up to unpick while he's still here. I feel the weight of time on our shoulders, and the right words stick in my throat. Instead, what comes out is, 'You've always been very patient with me.'

'Should I not have been?'

His eyebrows draw together and I reach a hand out to smooth his forehead. 'I'm not sure I deserve it.'

'I wanted to know you, Ava. Every version. However long it would take. For months,' his fingers trail past my waist, up to my shoulder, dusting my skin with sparks, 'I've had to pretend the sound of your laugh doesn't make me want to fucking *skip*. Had to pretend watching your face light up while you do really bad karaoke doesn't take all the oxygen out of the room. Pretend being near you doesn't make me feel like I'm in the presence of a star exploding. It's suffocating.'

'Sounds painful,' I offer weakly, stupidly. Right now, enveloped in silver moonlight, I'm an imposter in someone else's life; a person who lets herself receive forehead kisses and comparisons to the stars.

'I'm sorry if I keep saying things that are too intense. I just...' His hand moves to cradle my face. 'I wanted you to know. That's all.'

'I'm sorry for being the world's worst compliment receiver.' I turn my head to kiss his palm. I want to live in this feeling. In this possibility. 'And I'm really sorry this hasn't worked out the way we might've wanted it to.'

'Me too,' he says softly. Then he presses his lips against my shoulder and his breath tickles my skin as he laughs. 'We're apologising too much. What's something you aren't sorry for?'

I let the question sit between us. There's so much I could say, but even the thought of it weighs on my chest. 'I'm not sorry for lying to Josie about you being my friend.'

He tilts my chin up and our lips meet, and I wonder how much he knows I'm holding in. How deeply I wish I could be as open as he deserves. How painfully my heart wrenches, knowing that might never happen.

But tonight isn't about never. It's not even about tomorrow. So we kiss further, deeper, limbs intertwining, hands and mouths dragging across skin, and we have unhurried, lazy sex in our own bubble, where time doesn't pass and people don't leave.

---

By the time I wake, there's no imprint on the pillow next to me. I squint against the light spilling through the split in the curtains, groggy but well rested. There's something twisted about the fact it's the best night's sleep I've had since Max told me his news.

When I sit up to hunt for my phone, I spot a blue t-shirt folded up on my dresser. I know I shouldn't do it, I know I should try to make things easier for myself, but I put it on, relishing the way it smells like him. Tomorrow, I'll figure out what London looks like without him. Today, I'll let myself miss him.

My phone tells me it's just past midday, and aside from the usual meaningless notifications, there are two texts from Finn.

**I'm sorry I didn't say goodbye, it felt too final**

I check the time stamp and find that the second one was sent two hours later.

> I promise I'll come back

Despite the walls, despite the defences, Finn worked his way in. He found the soft spots and made a home there. Now, a torn-off piece of my heart is currently miles above the Atlantic, and I feel it like a phantom limb as time and distance stretches between us. No stone left unturned, but plenty left unsaid.

# 39

## give yourself a try

### AVA

Max's treatment is all that occupies my mind for the next few weeks. He stays in our flat on Monday to Friday so that he can go to his specialist hospital in London, and on days where I'm on the late shift at work I accompany him. When he goes back to our family home on the weekends, I can't tell if he dreads being coddled by our parents or secretly looks forward to the comfort of it.

After the first week he's tired and loses his appetite, and I do my best to provide alternative sustenance in the form of nostalgic TV shows and a playlist of emo music from 2006. It doesn't give him energy and it doesn't bring his appetite back, but it keeps his spirits up, which is all I can ask for.

I'm struck by how different this time around is. Beneath his perfectly warranted fear and fatigue is an undercurrent of annoyance. Annoyed this thing just won't leave him alone, annoyed he's had to put a stopper in his plans, annoyed he's pretending he's fine just to avoid having to tell other people what's happening and experience their wide-eyed condolences.

Slowly but surely, we start making those dreadful jokes again. When other people overhear, their discomfort is so tangible it's almost funnier than the joke itself.

'Kind of unfair that you get to spend ages off work when you actually enjoy your job,' I say one morning as we make our way up the wide steps in front of the hospital. 'Where's my month off?'

'You know the stats nowadays,' he says tonelessly. 'One in two, Col. It's only a matter of time.'

I choke on a laugh, and when he shoots me the kind of troublemaking grin from our childhood, I let the hope trickle in, hope that this will be the last time he has to do this, hope that we'll never have to use these terrible jokes to cope again.

Those familiar fears from last time worm their way through the cracks too, attaching to the hope like a parasite, but I know to expect them, and it means I can meet those feelings halfway instead of letting them bowl me over. They still ache, and I'm still scared, but I don't feel the pain quite so acutely as before.

---

I take the day off work for his last radiotherapy session, accompanying him to the hospital and then going into a coffee shop to buy us drinks and doughnuts while I wait for him to finish. In line with his wishes to keep everything quiet, when Dylan asks if I'm doing anything fun on my day off, all I tell her is that I'm spending time with my brother.

Under the soulless fluorescent lights of the waiting room, my phone pings. Adrenaline surges through me but leaves as quickly as it arrives, like the tide pulling water from the shore. It's just a notification from Uber reminding me how long it's been since I used the app.

Finn and I texted back and forth at first. He let me know when he landed in San Francisco, I shared a funny customer story, he sent a photo of his shitty hotel coffee. We tried to keep up our constant texts like before, but it hurt, picturing him on the other end of the phone, so close but so far, imagining that half-smile tugging at his face as he typed. We FaceTimed a few times too, and it just made his physical absence even more glaring.

On Max's first day of treatment he asked me to wish him luck, and then he checked in a few more times after that, but since my reply to his text a few days ago where he told me he'd found an apartment, it's been radio silence. And the more days that pass, the more I think I'm grateful our texts have waned. It makes the break a little easier.

I knew this might happen, but the recently softened part of me still hoped it wouldn't. He's busy starting a whole new life, exactly as he warned me he would, right when we first met. He was always going to leave, and I was always going to stay. Sitting by my phone waiting for a reply isn't going to undo that.

When Max appears through the doors, all thoughts of Finn disappear, and I unfold myself from the chair with a creak of plastic to greet him. My heart twinges as if it can detect the missing part of it that he took over the edge all those years ago, like it's a magnet trying to tug its pieces back.

'It's done,' he says with a satisfied sigh, stretching his neck and pulling himself up to his full height. He's always tall, always takes up space, but today he feels larger than life.

'Do you get to ring the bell?' Despite the faintly acerbic hospital smell lingering on my brother, when I pull him into a hug, beneath it all is the familiar lemony smell of him.

'Didn't want to. It feels like tempting fate.' He releases me and squints slightly as he looks down. 'I know that's ridiculous. Maybe I'll come back to ring it if I'm still cancer-free in five years. Maybe I'll just have a party.'

I'll celebrate anything he wants, whenever he wants. I grab my tote bag from its spot on the linoleum and we step through the automatic doors out into the October air.

I've been so focused on getting through this month that it's only when we enter Regent's Park that I realise the leaves are starting to turn. We wind along the gravel paths, coffee in hand, and I inhale the beginnings of autumn; delicious golds and ambers and calls for cosy nights in.

Max sprawls across the first empty bench we come upon and says, 'After I've slept for about two weeks straight, I can't wait to be out exploring again. London's great, but I still can't believe you live here full time. It's just... a lot.'

Tiredness leeches into the lines of his face, but adrenaline and relief bring the light back to his eyes in a way that makes me so giddy I could float.

'I think that's why I like it.' I watch a child run away from his mother, who lifts him in the air to joyful squeals when she catches up. 'There are always so many people around that you can trick yourself into thinking you're not lonely or bored.'

I fight the urge to move Max's cup from its precarious position when he rests it between us on the bench. He links his now-free hands behind his neck and pulls down to stretch out the muscles. 'I can't imagine choosing somewhere permanent to live. It still feels pointless getting my own place when I'm constantly on the go. Well, I mean, not *constantly*.' He grimaces and points at his hip. 'Not when the big guy comes to visit.'

'Uncle Neil stays over that often?'

He flings forward and barks out a laugh, and in a move I definitely foresaw, his cup starts to tilt, spilling some of his Americano onto the hem of his plaid shirt before he has the chance to grab it. Unbothered, he says, 'One day I'll move out of Mum and Dad's. One day.'

'You know they'll just follow you.' I open up the box of doughnuts and pick a cartoon-looking one with pink icing and sprinkles. 'They hate you travelling already. Stresses them out having you so far away.'

'Ugh. You have it so easy. You could fuck off to the Gobi Desert and all they'd do is ask you to send them a postcard.' His features instantly pull in on themselves as he tries to backtrack in a fluster. 'Wait, I didn't mean they don't care about you. I just mean they don't try to wrap you in cotton wool.'

'It's fine. You're right.' I finish my doughnut and brush the crumbs from my lap. 'I do have it easy.'

I'm not just talking about Mum and Dad being overbearing though.

An unreadable expression crosses his face. 'Can I ask you a question?' He sets his coffee down again but doesn't wait for me to confirm. 'Would you swap places with me, if you could?'

'Yes.' My answer is immediate. I'd take the pain from him in an instant.

'I thought so.' He nods to himself. 'I wouldn't, though. Swap places. Sometimes I imagine being in your shoes and it sends me spiralling.'

*Spiralling* is one way of putting it. *Freefalling into the abyss* is another. Those sleepless nights imagining life without him will probably hit me when I least expect it for the rest of my days, try as I might to push them aside. 'It's nothing in comparison to what you've had to go through.'

He releases a frustrated grunt. 'I'm not gonna lie to you and say I don't desperately wish it never happened. Or that it won't affect me for the rest of my life. But being the one to experience it firsthand turns me into an active participant, at the very least. Watching it must make you feel helpless.'

I've always admired Max's ability to see other people's perspectives. He's wrong about this, though. 'All I've done is stand next to you and worry.'

'Exactly. That's painful too. Especially after what happened last time. One person's experience doesn't cancel out another. You need to stop thinking your feelings aren't valid, Col.' His eyebrows draw together, and he looks so disapproving that it throws me for a second. 'I'm serious, it's getting annoying.'

Finn said something similar at the museum, without the irritation. I look at Max; messy hair that never sits right, the remnants of sunburnt freckles across the bridge of his nose. Somehow he manages to be strong and soft, where I've let it harden me. 'I should be comforting you.'

He lets out another groan. 'This is what I mean. I get enough pity, I don't need it from you too. I shouldn't have told you last month that I rely on you to be a certain way. I didn't mean I rely on you to be stoic. I just meant that I appreciate that even though you might want to baby me, you don't.'

I pull my denim jacket tighter around me as a breeze rustles the trees, and take a few breaths.

'I *do* feel sorry for you, though. And sad for you. That's the truth. But mostly...' I exhale slowly, letting the truth coagulate into a sentence. 'I feel guilty.'

'Shit, why?' He scratches his arm and looks at me with a frown. 'It's not your fault I got this instead of you. It's just the way it is.'

'But it's not fair.'

'*Obviously* it's not fair. But nothing's fair.'

In some ways, Max is still the same little boy I grew up with. But it's moments like these when I see the man he grew into; still reckless, still incapable of sitting still, but someone who can't help but take life exactly as it comes, problems and all. I envy it.

He narrows his eyes and continues, 'I think your guilt is getting in your way. I've seen you hold back for years from really living and I've never said anything about it because I haven't wanted to believe it, but that's what you're doing, isn't it? Maybe you don't feel like you deserve good things, or you're scared they're going to be taken from you, so you never even try?'

I fiddle with my buttons just for something to do, and he gives me a knowing look that punctures the flimsy protection I'd draped over everything I've been trying to hide.

'That's bullshit, Ava, I'm sorry. Because if you live like that, then it means this disease has stolen from both of us. And that's such a waste. Such a huge waste.' He takes a doughnut from the box and adds, 'And just really fucking stupid.'

'*You're* really fucking stupid,' I mumble, like I'm five. But he's not stupid at all, because he's got me all figured out. As much as I've tried to hide it, he's been seeing everything all along. 'I'm sorry, Max.'

'For what?' It's like looking in a mirror when he's annoyed. I don't know what that says about my natural expression.

The words swell in my chest, itching to escape. 'I thought I was handling it. It's not your fault, I need you to know that. I've never wanted you to feel like you've—I don't know—burdened me somehow. Not when you've had to go through even worse.'

'Feelings, Ava. We've been over this. You have them. Let them exist.' He sounds irritated, but he musses my hair briefly with his doughnut-free hand.

I wriggle out of his grasp. 'You're right about all of it. I think I've been using this mentality as a safety blanket, or a scapegoat. I could always blame this weird logic I've built that says everything's going to be taken from me if I try. So when I started loosening my grip on that mentality and the rug was pulled out from under me, with you, and everything else,' my mind flashes to Finn, so willing to tell me how he felt, whether I reciprocated or not, 'it felt like vindication. Proof I was right all along that I shouldn't try.'

'Don't you think it's become a bit of a self-fulfilling prophecy? Things can't be taken from you, because you never let yourself fully have them in the first place. But that's setting yourself up for failure every time. At least when you take a chance, you only fail *sometimes*. It's a better success rate than never trying at all. Surely that risk is worth the reward.' His gaze is discerning when he says, 'Especially when the reward could be something really special.'

I sip my coffee, lukewarm by now, and we watch a mini leaf tornado spiral past us. 'I don't know how you see things so clearly. My mind's a mess.'

He hasn't completely finished chewing by the time he speaks again. If Dad were here he'd be shooting daggers. 'I'm not sure I do, but I'm trying. And I'm better than I used to be.' My mind flits back to a few years ago, when it felt like all we could do was watch him self-destruct from the sidelines. 'I've bulldozed my way through five and a half therapists.'

'What's the half?' I can't tell if he's guilty or amused. With Max, the two usually come as a package deal. 'You know what? Never mind.'

'The fact is, there's a high likelihood this thing is a ticking time bomb,' he says simply. 'But if I let it consume me—and believe me, it's crossed my mind—I'd be wasting so much fucking *energy*. So much time. Time I may or may not have. So I have to just... do things in spite of it. *Because* of it. I have to keep moving, have to keep living for right now.' There's a flash of sadness in his eyes, but it's gone by the time I blink. He tears the rest of his doughnut in two and pops one of the pieces in his mouth. 'If you want, I can give you all the tips on how to pretend you're not dying. It's liberating.'

'Aren't you scared?'

'Of course I'm scared.' It's the first time his voice wavers. 'But I'm alive, too. So that'll have to do for now.'

'That'll do,' I repeat in a whisper. Because it's more than enough.

'When you think about it, I might be the luckiest person on Earth.' He stretches his legs out towards the path and starts listing items on his fingers. 'The statistical probability of any human existing is so low to begin with. Factor in the fact I'm a twin, which is even less likely, add the fact I get this one-in-a-million cancer—'

'Four million.' Those sleepless nights on Google weren't for nothing.

'Of course you researched it. I get this one-in-four-million type of cancer, and then I fucking *die,* like, fully out, gone, took a trip to the pearly gates, was promptly denied entry, et cetera. And somehow I'm still here? I don't think many people could say they have that kind of luck.'

When I was younger, I always believed I was lucky to be part of our family. To get on with both parents, to have a best friend for a brother, to have our weird nicknames and stupid traditions and ridiculous inside jokes. Then, when everything happened and we got Max back, I was sure of it. But it always felt like an abstract kind of luck. Hearing

Max lay it out like this so quantitatively sends me spiralling in a good way, up and out towards the stars.

'You're lucky,' I concede. 'And I'm lucky by default to know you.'

'You and everyone else in my life, Colin,' he drawls. Whenever he says things like this, I'm reminded that if I didn't know him beneath the bravado, I'd almost definitely find him insufferable.

He yawns and it's enough to make me check the time and ask, 'Lucky enough to make it to Waterloo in time for your train?'

I show him my screen and he shoves an entire doughnut in his mouth with a garbled, 'Shit,' and we scramble to grab all our stuff.

'Why,' I gasp, promptly approaching oxygen deprivation as we speed-walk to the Tube, 'did our parents not instil in us the importance of punctuality?'

'I have no idea,' he replies easily, stupidly long legs taking him further than mine without even trying. 'Keep up, you gnome.'

We make it to Waterloo just as the conductor blows the whistle to announce the train doors are closing, and we yell hurried goodbyes as Max darts through the barriers. Someone's bag is caught in a door further up the train, so all the doors reopen for five seconds. In that tiny pocket of time, he manages to step on. Maybe he really is the luckiest person on the planet.

---

I settle on the sofa next to Josie, grabbing the other end of her blanket to drape across my knees, the pair of us refusing to admit defeat and turn the heating on even though we wake up to condensation on the windows every morning by now. We've left *Twilight* playing on the TV in the same way some people listen to classical music while they relax.

She peels back the lid of the tub of olives I picked up on my way home and pops one in her mouth, doing a little happy wiggle of her shoulders. 'How was today's session?'

'Easier than last week, but I'm still getting used to,' I wave a hand around my head, 'diving deep. I need to practise.'

Every Wednesday evening, I make my way to a plant-filled office on Clapham High Street to talk to a woman called Anita, who sits and listens and has the vaguely uncanny ability to get me to talk without saying a word herself.

And every Wednesday night I come home feeling like my brain's been scooped out of my skull with a spoon. But by the next day, I always feel a little lighter.

'Not to be soppy,' she clears her throat, 'but I'm proud of you.'

It took me longer than it should've to bite the bullet. I spent so many years telling myself that nothing in my mind was as bad as it is for some people, that even putting myself on the NHS waiting list would be taking up space from someone like Max. But after talking to him, I knew what had to be done. I have a duty to myself to listen to my brain and unearth what it's trying to tamp down.

'Thanks.' It takes everything not to squirm under it, but still I add, 'And thank you for the recommendation. Even though she's expensive.'

The answer was right in front of me, so obvious I felt stupid for not seeing it sooner. I'd been saving money all this time paying hardly any rent, building savings with no clear goal. I had all this stagnant money to use, and figured it was time to invest in myself with a private therapist. I'm a long way from where I want to be, but I'm on my way. I'm better than I was.

Maybe when my mind's more settled I can start using my savings for fun things. I could join Max on one of his trips, or visit Josie on tour.

Or I could go to San Francisco. As much as I want to move forward, I miss Finn. It'd be impossible not to.

'Oh!' Josie jolts me out of my daydream, setting her pot on the coffee table and swapping it for her tea. 'Invites have been sent out for the exhibition opening, so check your email, you should have a ticket. Clear your calendar.'

'I can't wait.' She's been working on this for so long, and excitement hums through me thinking about what her team has put so many hours into. 'Don't think there's much danger of me having clashing plans, though.'

My social life has dwindled after my hectic, vibrant summer, save for the occasional drink with Josie or Dylan at the pub. But it's been good to spend some time working on myself. I've been alone before, but never spent the time really putting any effort into making myself better.

'You need to make the most of having normal human working hours. Now you've got your shiny new job and don't have to wake up before some people have even gone to sleep.'

It was strange; the minute I decided it was okay to give myself a try, change came flooding in, as if it had been piling up against the door, just waiting for me to open up.

Not long after Max's treatment ended, or, alternatively, not long after he called me out on being a little bitch, one day I went into work and Nadia from head office was sitting with Carl. She pulled me aside and informed me she was looking for an assistant. She'd gauged from our earlier conversations that dealing with customers was not my favourite thing to do, and had remembered how I was always on top of stock and payments and doing things for the shop outside of my jurisdiction. I'd never really thought about it before, but I guess I was more efficient and organised than I'd realised. (Despite the blatant KitKat theft, which I so far have kept to myself.)

And so, I've spent the last month as her assistant, which has mostly consisted of setting up meetings, planning training sessions for new employees, and joining her on site visits at other branches. It's not customer-facing, I get to wear my own clothes, and my new boss is possibly more deadpan than me, so it's working for now. Sometimes, the fear creeps in, fear I'll never be truly fulfilled. But I'm not shackled to the monotony of the shop's routine. Leaving was at least a step in the right direction. I took the step. I've been taking lots of these steps, recently. That has to count for something.

Josie's holding her mug with one hand, scrolling her phone with another, when she asks, 'Do you want a plus-one?'

As soon as his scans came back clear, Max jumped back into his normal life with that aggressive intensity of his, and he's away in Germany at the moment. I briefly consider asking Dylan, but ultimately I say, 'Nope. Just me.'

She drops her phone in her lap and tilts her head to consider me. 'You should talk to him. Don't you think it's been long enough?'

I don't pretend not to know who she's talking about. Everything else in my life is slowly coming together, but Finn's the one piece I haven't quite figured out what to do with yet. I've been trying to be gentle with myself. I don't regret telling him to leave. Because he needed to, and because I wasn't ready. I wouldn't have been good for him. But I do regret that I didn't sort myself out sooner.

'One day I will. But he's busy starting afresh. I don't want to interrupt his life.'

Now, his absence ebbs like a yellowing bruise. Hardly painful anymore, but sometimes I poke the tenderness just to be sure it's real.

'Like he interrupted yours?' Her eyes twinkle. Finn disrupted my life like a bulldozer in a library.

In reality, I've drafted and deleted more texts than I can count. But I don't want to drop in with a text. I have to let him live. He inadvertently set off a chain reaction and I have to continue reaping the benefits of that so that I can make my life better, too.

But here, tucked under the blanket next to Josie, I'm overcome by a wave of gratitude for her. She's been here for me this whole time, quietly supporting me, even when she thought my decisions were stupid. And they were, objectively, stupid.

'I don't think I've ever thanked you,' I say at last.

'For what?' She blows her tea and the steam wafts around her face.

'For being so understanding over the past few years while I've been getting myself together. And for trying to help me get out there. Even though I was bad at listening.'

'Finn was the one who really got you out of your shell.'

I smile at the mention of his name but shake my head. 'Well, today I'm thanking you. For staying with me inside my shell.'

'It was *extremely* cramped in there.'

'Thank god you're only about two feet tall.'

'Would've been a disaster if I'd been a giant like you.' She shifts position, knocking a cushion to the floor. 'But you don't need to thank me. You're my best friend. And you were there for me when I was going through it when we were at uni.'

'You had a perfectly good reason to be in a dark place. I was just,' I search for the word, 'repressed, probably.'

'Emotionally selective,' she amends, setting her mug back on the coffee table and feeling for the dropped cushion. 'I don't take it for granted, you know. The fact that you care about me. I doubt Max ever has, either, or Finn, or anyone else in your little circle.' She sets the cushion on her lap. 'I don't even think you realise that you take people under your wing. You did it with me, you've done it with Dylan, you'll probably do it again to someone else. You make it seem like you don't care, but you do. You just do it quietly.'

The blanket rustles as I shift position. 'Thank you for saying that.' I exhale with a shudder. 'I hate that these conversations only make me a *little* nauseous now. My reputation will be in tatters if anyone finds out.'

'Your secret's safe with me, my delicate little flower.' Then, tucking her hair behind her ear, she leans forward to ask, 'Are you happy, Ava?'

I fiddle with the label on the blanket, trying to quieten the part of my brain telling me to stop talking about my feelings. Despite any loose ends, any missing pieces, for the first time in a long while, my brain is calm. It's granted me a contentment I'd forgotten I could feel.

I'm not being dragged along with the current, life happening around me without my permission anymore. I'm not clinging to moments of joy like they're a life raft. They exist in spite of the stormy seas. I'm finally swimming.

Eventually, the words spill out, and I'm surprised by the truth of them. 'I am.'

# 40

## seasons change

### AVA

I'M A FERVENT BELIEVER that coats are for bitches, but I do immediately regret not wearing a jacket when I step outside in nothing but a decidedly thin strapless red dress that Josie forced me to buy for the opening. Luckily, my Uber drops me right outside the building, and I make it inside without doing any permanent damage to my extremities.

When I duck into the foyer, there's a massive poster saying *Access to Art: As It Lives & Breathes*. I show my ticket to the attendant and they let me into the gallery, where people are milling about with glasses of Prosecco and nonchalantly analysing the art.

I don't think I've ever been anywhere so clearly signposted, and that's art in and of itself. Tactile lines snake along the floor, winding around the room, each one taking a different route around the exhibition. Every exhibit's plaque has braille explanations beneath the written text, while some have buttons that produce an audio explanation when you press them, along with a QR code, so people can take in the information at their own pace on their phones if they want. I text Josie to let her know I'm here and receive a "yay" in all caps in return, although I can't see her amidst the swell of people yet. I spot Alina on the other side of the room in a navy velvet pantsuit, and she gives me a wave, busy talking to some people about one of the sculptures.

Miraculously, I've made it on time, which means I get to listen to Josie's Prosecco-fuelled speech, which results in the BSL interpreter next to her having to bite down their laugh the longer she rambles. She pulls it together enough to deliver a coherent end to the speech, putting down her glass so she can gesticulate at peak performance.

'Before I go and finish off another bottle, I just want to echo what everyone else has said. Thank you to all the artists who've contributed their craft, to all the people who took part in our research and helped us figure out how to make this work, and to everyone who was willing to take a chance on this idea. For anyone watching the live stream, or who can't make it to the gallery for whatever reason, we've just published our virtual tour online. It's free to access, but we welcome donations.'

I look around me at what Josie helped create, at the people she brought together, and I want to nudge the person next to me and whisper, 'That's my best friend, by the way.'

'We're here for a couple of months,' she continues, 'so if you enjoy it, please tell your friends. And if there's anything you think we could improve on, we're always open to suggestions. Thank you so much for coming, please grab a glass, and have a wonderful evening.'

The whole place is a sensory masterpiece. I wander towards a piece called *Tangible Sound,* which looks unremarkable at first; a square marked on the floor with what looks like a tall speaker at each corner. Each pillar is lined with different coloured lights, casting overlapping technicolour shadows onto the floor, but when I step into the square, that's when the magic happens. I realise my body's interrupting sound waves, and when I move, the pillars generate this dreamy, otherworldly sound, like I'm under the sea.

Another piece is a sculpture that's partly solid, while other parts move and shift under your touch, and something about it is familiar. When I press the button on the plaque to listen to the explanation, I learn Alina's one of the collaborators.

I catch Josie just as she finishes a particularly effusive conversation with a few peers, waving her giant fluted sleeves around so aggressively I'm willing to bet she'll whack herself in the face with them at some point tonight.

'This is amazing,' I say, as I approach, and when she turns to me, I don't think I've ever seen her look more alive; cheeks flushed, eyes bright.

'Have you looked around it all yet? What's the verdict? Tell me all your thoughts.' She tugs her dress down—green, obviously, because she's Josie—from where it's shifted in her exuberant speech-giving. 'Unless they're bad thoughts, in which case, please lie like you've never lied before.'

'I don't need to lie,' I say. 'The sound square is my favourite so far. I felt like a mer—'

'Mermaid, right? I've been saying that this whole time but everyone else says it has space vibes instead. But have you checked out *Seasons Change* yet?' She gestures towards the back of the room, where a line of people snakes around a huge circular structure, a timer flashing outside the door.

'No, wait, is that the one you had the idea for?'

'You have to go in. Although,' she drops her voice, 'wait for the queue to go down. I personally think it's better when there are only a few people in there. It feels more immersive.'

'Got it.' I make a note to keep an eye on the line. 'Josie, you're a force, you know that?'

'I know,' she says in a hum. 'But thank you for reminding me.'

---

It takes a while for the queue to go down outside the circular room. The door opens and a few stragglers spill out, eyes wide, raving to each other about how cool it was. When the five-minute timer above the door starts counting back down to zero again, I head towards it.

I don't know what to expect. The plaque outside the door simply says:

*Time passes, life goes on, seasons change. Take a moment to breathe.*

The room is dark when I step in, but I use those raised lines on the floor to help find my way. There's some seating around the edges, but I choose the backless bench in the centre of the room. I sit facing away from the door, ready to take a moment to breathe, as instructed. The walls curve around me in a circle and when I notice the faint hum buzzing at the far end of my range of hearing and a hazy light emanating all around me, I realise the entire wall is a screen, as if I'm enclosed within a TV.

By chance, I'm the only one in here, and I can't work out if it's eerie or soothing to be surrounded by nothing more than my thoughts and the dark. So when someone comes into the room and sits behind me on the bench just before the countdown hits zero, I'm the tiniest bit relieved.

Suddenly the room lights up and we're surrounded by images of spring; unfurling buds, tiny farm animals, dew drops gliding down blades of grass. Then come the sounds of wind chimes, chicks cracking out of their eggs, the low bleating of sheep. Even the tone of the light seems to match the kind of sunshine you get on spring mornings; hesitant but hopeful. There's a gentle breeze, and is that the smell of rain? The person behind inhales too, shifting on the bench as they do.

I breathe in deeper, relishing that earthy richness, until I smell flowers, and then my brain takes half a second to register scents that seem out of place.

A musky cologne. Swimming pools.

*Oh.*

'Would you say we met in spring or summer?' The voice comes from behind me. It's quiet enough that I could almost convince myself it's not him, if not for the fact that no one else's voice makes me feel like a flower blossoming under the sun.

I stay focused on the wall and let my heart skip a few more beats before I reply. 'Late spring.' An exhale rattles through me as that petrichor breeze drifts between us. 'The season for new beginnings.'

'I think you're right,' Finn says quietly. It takes everything in me not to turn around. The chirping of birds fills the silence before he asks, 'Are you doing okay?'

'I'm good.' It feels too small a word to encapsulate how much I feel I've changed over the past few months. 'Are you?'

'I am.'

There's a cacophony in my head just having him near me again, drowning out the sounds from the speakers. 'What are you doing here?'

'Ava.' Just hearing my name from his mouth sends adrenaline crashing through my bloodstream, and I spin around, heart somehow breaking and expanding and jumping off a cliff all at once when I see him, careful eyes fixed on me as he says, 'I told you I'd come back.'

We're both analysing each other, dissecting the changes we've missed. He's wearing a suit for the occasion and I'd be lying if I said it didn't make my breath hitch. His glasses are the same, but his new haircut has tightened his curls. I wonder if he notices I've had my hair cut too, that my fringe is shorter than it used to be. His eyes flit to my forehead. Of course he notices.

Imperceptibly, the season changes around us, and now we're in summer, seagulls cawing, the smell of freshly cut grass permeating the air, golden hour sun illuminating the room just like on the night we walked to the boat bar, and I'm melted ice cream under Finn's gaze.

'I didn't believe you,' I say. What I mean is *I didn't want to hope*.

'I know,' he murmurs, a crease deepening between his brows. 'And I didn't help things with how bad I've been at staying in contact. I just...'

'Finn, it's fine. I get it.' I offer him a small smile. 'You were busy.'

'No, I wasn't.' He tears his eyes from my face and looks down at my hand on the bench. 'I've spent years staying in contact with my family through texts and FaceTime. It's normal to me. But fuck, I've never found it so difficult to accept before, that the only way to see you would be on a screen. I'd see things I wanted to tell you about, stuff I thought you'd like, and I'd type out a text, but I'd overthink and never send it. I thought maybe if I stopped trying then I could get you out of my head. But it didn't work. You were always in my head.'

His expression twists with guilt. 'And now I keep thinking I should've stayed and supported you while Max was sick. That was the one thing I could've done, as your friend.'

'You were on the other side of the world and you still checked in when you could. That was enough. I didn't expect you to upend your whole life's plan for me. Don't beat yourself up about it.' I know better than anyone what happens when guilt festers for too long, the way it blisters your insides and causes more damage than the thing you initially felt guilty about. 'I told you to go. You needed to go. I needed it too, I think.'

'Are you doing okay, really? Is Max?'

'Yes. To all of it.' There's a smile on his face at my confirmation, but his eyes are still guarded. 'I promise, Finn. I'm in a good place.'

'Good. I'm glad.' He goes to push his sleeves up out of habit but remembers he's wearing a blazer and tugs at the cuffs instead. 'Jesus, I really fucked it. I took that job for all the wrong reasons. I think you realised before I did.'

'You wanted to prove yourself. There's nothing wrong with that.'

His curls bounce with a shake of his head. 'But it wasn't about me. Not really. Can I tell you what I've learnt?' I nod and he swallows before starting to explain, 'As a kid, I knew my mum loved me, and I knew my stepdad did too, but when they got their perfect new family I felt like the odd one out. It felt like the twins were more important to my mum, somehow, and that's why she only stopped moving us around so much when they came along. That's always been in the back of my mind. Even in therapy over the years I was pretty good at avoiding telling them anything about it. I never let myself say these thoughts aloud because I didn't want my mum to feel bad; because I knew how much she'd sacrificed to give me all the opportunities I had.' He sighs and says quietly, 'But at least she tried. And keeps trying. We had a long discussion recently and since then we've been really trying to stick to our weekly calls. Turns out I need attention. Who knew?' His weak chuckle makes me want to pull him to me and never let go.

'Has it helped?'

'I think so.' Another deep breath, and I can tell it takes a lot for him to say what's coming next. 'All I remember is the rose-tinted version of my childhood with my dad. I always felt like he was the odd one out of the family too, like me. It didn't register that he did that to himself.

He was the one who left. But I thought if I could prove myself to him, become more like him, he'd see me as an equal and I wouldn't be so lonely.'

His voice is level when he continues, 'You said once that my dad didn't deserve me, and I hated hearing it. I hated it because I've spent years trying to earn crumbs of his attention. But you planted this seed in my mind that he should be better. That I deserve better from him. These past few months, every time he rescheduled a meet-up or dismissed some achievement I told him about, that seed grew and I realised he's not worth it. And that I can't control the way he is.'

'Him being a bad dad to you isn't your fault.'

'I know that now. But somehow I projected this onto you. Onto everyone. I'd got into the habit of feeling like I needed to try to earn people's affection. But you're not the dad I was seeking approval from, you're not the mum who I thought didn't care, and you're not the ex who made me feel small.' I see him; eager, earnest Finn, and I see the shadows of all the people who've taken advantage of his openness, of the people who've tried to extinguish his light. 'You've always made me a better version of myself without even trying. Any time you laughed, or opened up to me, it felt like you were telling me I was worthy. Like I was enough.'

'You *are* enough,' I say. 'And everyone sees it. Your dad should be begging at the door for you to be in his life, but he's not, and that's his loss. You're incredible, Finn. If I need to tell you every day until you believe it, I will.'

I'm dimly aware of autumn arriving around us; images of fireworks and pumpkins, the sound of leaves crunching, the smell of bonfire in the air.

I keep going. 'Just existing near you made me remember how to be happy. I feel like I'm finally giving myself a chance, and it started with you.'

'You did that yourself.'

'But I couldn't have done it without you. One of the new things I've been working on is being more honest about my feelings. Making sure I communicate them. I just...' I shake my head as I try to collect my thoughts, and Finn looks down at my fidgeting hands on the bench, sliding his own over them and squeezing. 'It was like I was living on autopilot for so long. And then you arrived and you coaxed me out and I started to turn into someone I liked. Someone who participates in their life. You set that in motion, and I'll never be able to thank you enough for it. I'm so sorry I didn't tell you all this earlier. How important you are to me. Do you know how special it is, that you help people bloom?'

Maybe now I can take steps forward on my own, but I needed the initial nudge. I won't deny how much Finn contributed to getting me out of the dark. If he's the sun, I must be the moon. Sometimes you need a little help to glow.

His warm eyes settle on mine and I feel my throat tightening when I speak again. 'Sometimes, you meet someone and they change everything. That was you, for me. You changed everything.'

He lets out a sound somewhere between a sob and a laugh, and I close the distance and pull him into a hug, his chin settling in the crook of my neck like we're two clichéd puzzle pieces that fit together in a way they never could with other people. Because I might not speak four languages, but I understand Finn O'Callaghan. This man is not unlovable. He's not someone to ignore, to replace, to abandon. He's a fireplace burning in a cabin, warmth amidst the barren cold. He is, without a doubt, someone to come back to.

I lean back just enough to see the firelight flicker across his face, casting shadows over his cheekbones. His smile spreads like the low, sultry light of sunset, and the only way I can think to appease the swell of emotion threatening to surge out of me is to squeeze him harder. I settle into the familiarity of his shape, feeling the heat of his hands at my back, breathing him in and relishing the fact he's here, exactly where he should be.

Fireworks burst across the screen and colour dances between us, over us, around us. Then the light fades and all I know is the feel of his hands sliding up to cup my face. I hold his wrists to keep them there as we look at each other, my chest somehow filled with rocks and air, weighing me down and lifting me up at the same time.

His thumbs brush across my cheekbones when he speaks again, our chests rising and falling in sync. 'All those years I spent looking for reasons to run away, I didn't realise I was being pulled towards something. The place I belonged. Somewhere that felt like home. Then I came here, and suddenly it all made sense. It's you, Ava.' His voice is perfectly clear, like he's sat with this thought for a while and knows exactly how to say it. 'Before you, I didn't know home could be a person.'

We're still just as opposite as we were on the first day we met, but when his lips find mine in the dark, I'm certain no one has ever belonged with anyone more than he belongs with me.

My hands drag through his hair, graze his jaw, run along his shoulders, and his do the same to me, and I know we're trying to ground ourselves here in this place, in this moment, on this planet, because everything about us feels otherworldly. Maybe it always has. It hits me that we never were those lonely satellites spinning out of control in the cosmos. We've always been two stars, bound for monumental collision.

We stay like that for so long that the season shifts to winter around us. Christmas lights, snowflakes, gingerbread. When we eventually pull apart, he's still rubbing slow circles on my back and peppering my face with kisses like he's trying to make up for lost time.

'You got a new shirt,' I whisper, arms looped around his neck, inhaling everything I've missed over the past few months.

His mouth curls up when he says, 'You got a new dress.'

He runs a hand down my hip and I'm about to close the distance between us again when the door opens and light from the gallery spills in. We both squint against the onslaught, then Finn plants one last kiss on my temple and stands, reaching out a hand to pull me up.

I keep hold of his hand once I'm upright, testing out the feeling of it in mine as we walk towards the door, and his smile is barely contained when he realises I'm not letting go.

We step out into the gallery and are almost bowled over by a tiny redhead and her dog.

'I was so close to locking you in there,' Josie says, slurring slightly but clearly delighted. 'But I thought that might've been a bit much.'

'Also against health and safety regulations,' Alina adds helpfully.

'Did you two know about this?' I ask, catching the suspicious glances dancing between everyone.

'Josie invited me months ago when I was still here, but I never RSVPed,' Finn explains. 'As soon as I realised I'd be in London today I asked if she could put me on the guest list last minute.'

'He's actually my plus-one,' Josie offers smugly, tucking her hair behind her ears before losing her balance and bumping into Alina, who surreptitiously curves an arm around her waist to help out.

'Thank you both so much for coming.' Alina's eyebrows pull together in earnest. 'I think we're gonna head back to mine. As soon as we find some water for this one.'

'I'm just resting my eyes,' Josie says.

Finn and I head to the exit after we've all said our goodbyes, and that's when I realise we haven't really addressed what's going to happen next.

'You didn't technically answer my question,' I say. We still have far too much ground to cover, and I don't even know how long he's here in London. I need to cram in as much time as possible. 'What *exactly* are you doing here, right now?'

'Shit, I didn't even get around to that.' He runs a hand through his hair and then his eyes pass over me, sending heat smoking across my skin. 'I was busy.'

'We should talk about it.' He catches the way I've stolen his line and smiles. For a second I falter, but then out spills the easiest question in the world. 'Will you go out with me?'

'Like, on a date?' He pauses just before the doorway, stepping aside to let me go through first.

I take his shoulders and gently push him through, following behind into the winter air, where our breath comes out in wispy puffs. 'Yeah. Tonight.'

---

I don't often feel small, but there's something to be said about being wrapped in Finn's blazer, its weight trapping the warmth he left behind. Unfortunately, his chivalry has left him freezing in the December night, so we end up in a kebab shop only a few doors down from the gallery to avoid imminent hypothermia. I appreciate the gesture nonetheless.

So, under the ugly fluorescent lighting of Dave's Kebabs Dulwich, Finn and I share a massive portion of chips, and we talk.

'I connected with Sage on LinkedIn a couple of months ago, and they messaged me recently to let me know there was a marketing manager role going at the Natural History Museum.' He dips a chip in the ketchup at the edge of the carton. 'I applied and got an interview. The guys said I could do my interview virtually, but I wanted an excuse to come back here.'

My own chip freezes midway to my mouth. 'And? Did you get it?'

'I don't know yet. It was this afternoon. That's technically why I'm in London. But I've already made a decision.' He cleans the salt from his hands on his trousers. 'I handed in my notice before I left. I told my manager I'd stay and work through the rest of my probation, or until they find a replacement. But whether I get the museum job or not, I'm coming back. Permanently.'

I let the hope in, and it comes out as a breathy, 'Really?'

'Really. This city just works for me. All of it.' He studies me. 'Some parts more than others.'

It's unfair someone can look this good under the lights of a kebab shop, but here sits Finn O'Callaghan; sleeves rolled up, tie discarded on the table, and a teasing grin that creases the corners of his eyes.

I drop my gaze, feeling my own smile threaten to do some serious damage to my cheek muscles. 'I have news too,' I say at last, giving him my hands to look at. His eyebrows draw together in confusion but he tilts my hands this way and that, clearly unsure what he's supposed to be looking at. 'No coffee grounds, no burns. No more City Roast. I'm working as an assistant to one of the executives at their head office. I get to wear my own clothes, I don't have to wake up at the asscrack of dawn, and I don't have to make much small talk. I know it's an *incredibly* low bar, but at least I'm finally over it.'

'Ava, that's amazing.' He places my hands on the table but keeps holding them, trailing delicate swirls over my skin. But after a few moments, guilt leeches into his expression. 'Sorry, I have a confession. I already knew you had a new job because I stalked you on LinkedIn the other day.'

'I really didn't know you were such a fiend for LinkedIn. This is your second mention of it in two minutes. Is this a new thing for you?'

A grin pulls up one side of his mouth, and god, I've missed this back-and-forth, the way nothing I say ever seems to get under his skin.

'It's not, I promise.'

'Are you one of those people who posts really dramatic status updates about how powerful it is to wake up at five-thirty and hustle for fifteen hours a day until you die?'

'God, no. I post those on Facebook.' I lift one of my hands from under his to grab a chip, making sure the other one stays interlocked with his. 'But in all seriousness, I didn't want to congratulate you on fucking *LinkedIn*, of all places. And more importantly, it would've shown I'd been stalking you, and I wasn't sure if I wanted you to know that yet. So this is me saying I'm really happy for you, and I hope this is the start of you finding something you love.' He rests his chin on his fist, eyeing me across the table. 'Although, I was kind of banking on you providing me with regular free coffee again upon my return, so if that's not on the cards anymore then I might just not move back.'

I pull the carton away from him as he reaches for another chip. 'Even *I* don't get endless free coffee anymore, so frankly, you're even further down the priority list.'

'Fuck,' he groans. 'The coffee in America is shit, you know.'

'Are you sure you just haven't found a good place yet?'

He purses his lips and nods. 'Highly likely, but I'm sticking with this opinion until proven otherwise. Some people use cream instead of milk, Ava. Not to be dramatic, but that makes me wanna die.'

'Not to be dramatic,' I repeat, sliding the tray back in his direction.

'It's gross,' he says with a chuckle, squeezing my knees between his under the table. When he looks up at me, he cocks his head. 'We don't have to decide yet what we're going to be—if it's anything at all, no pressure, I'm not expecting anything, I know this is a lot all at once—and whatever happens, I know we should take it slow, but I just—'

My eyebrows move higher and higher up my forehead with every second of his spiel. 'So many words to be saying so little.'

'If you'd let me *finish*, you infuriating woman. You're making me nervous. I want to tell you that, as much as I have, in the past, enjoyed, you know,' he waves a hand ambiguously, 'the other parts of our relationship—'

I snort. 'The other parts?'

'Ava Monroe, you know what parts I mean.' He knocks my knee with his in some sort of reproach, but there's a glint in his eye. 'I really enjoyed them. Couldn't rate them more highly, actually. Fuck, now I sound weird. Don't look at me like that.' A laugh ripples out of me as he unravels before my eyes. 'More than all that, I do just really enjoy being your friend. So if that's how we end up, that's perfect.'

'I like being your friend too.' I don't know what the future holds for us, but this time, I want to let myself hope. I lean across the table and wait for him to do the same. 'But if you've come all this way to friendzone me, I'm sending you back to California.'

He lets out a soft laugh, and the sound of it warms me the way it always has. His hand moves to cradle my jaw just as I weave my fingers into his hair, and I know it's not just Finn who's back where he should be. When our lips meet, it feels like coming home and coming undone all at once.

The part of my brain responsible for feeling shame registers that it's probably a good thing there's a whole table between us, because apparently I'm someone who does public displays of affection now. But then, Finn's changed me in lots of ways, bigger and smaller than this.

He smiles into the kiss before pulling back to look at me for a moment, eyes crinkled at the sides. His thumb swipes along my cheekbone and then he dips back in, murmuring against my mouth, 'I told you you'd like me.'

# epilogue
## AVA

### six months later

'Welcome home!' a chorus of voices greets us as we walk through the door, rumpled and sleep-deprived and suitcase-laden, Finn's hand warm at my back.

Through the chaos—has someone thrown confetti?—I see Max, a head taller than everyone else, and his eyes light up when he sees us. 'Oh my god, I've missed you so much.'

He barges past Josie and Alina, making a beeline for me. And then he bypasses me completely and embraces Finn instead, as if they didn't see each other only a few weeks ago. They hold each other's heads in that vaguely homoerotic way sportsmen do during a pre-match pep talk, and I accept the possibility I am now second place to both of them. But honestly? I understand.

Finn pulls me over by the arm and I find myself squeezed between them, and while I'm concerned about my rapidly depleting oxygen supply, affection for these two men spills out of every crevice of my little guarded heart.

'I don't mean to be rude,' I say after a while, my voice muffled. 'But I do value the use of my lungs.'

'Don't worry, I missed you too, Col,' Max says, squeezing me once more as Finn steps backwards to give me some room. Then he drops his voice and adds, 'Just not as much as him.'

I finally wrest myself from their hold and head to Josie, who holds a glass containing some unknown liquid out to me and says, 'You have to tell us *everything*.'

I register the fact our vase-stroke-cocktail-carafe is out on the kitchen counter, which strikes me with The Fear. Largely because it's barely midday, and I slept for approximately eight minutes on the flight.

'We decided to celebrate your return,' Josie says. 'It's not every day you come home from your first holiday in ten years.'

'It is, in fact, only every ten years,' Alina offers.

'Want a beer, Finn?' Max calls out, already at the fridge.

'I think I'll have some of Josie's cocktail actually.'

I catch Finn's eye and mouth *well done,* and his responding grin goes straight to my chest.

We move to the living area, and I sit on the floor between Finn's feet while we tell everyone about our trip. This mostly consists of me letting Finn tell stories with his huge hand gestures and unrelenting enthusiasm while I lean my head against his knee and interject when he goes off track. Which is, unsurprisingly, fairly often.

They hear about the ten days we spent in San Francisco working through the bucket list we scrabbled together one evening all those months ago; how I spent a solid four days complaining about how hilly it was, how we found good coffee in multiple places (turns out Finn just wasn't very good at looking), how we wandered around Fisherman's Wharf and ate overpriced seafood at more than one of the tourist-trap waterfront restaurants. How I'd never seen joy on someone's face quite like on Finn's when he saw the sea lions, how he'd never seen such unadulterated regret as on mine while the wind whipped us across the Golden Gate Bridge.

'I'm not usually a city boy, but I might put it on my list,' Max says, procuring Doritos out of nowhere and inhaling half the packet before I get the chance to put my hand in. 'But I'm already booked up for most of the year.'

'That trip you booked ages ago is finally almost here, right?' I ask.

'Yeah, but the friend who I'm meant to be bringing as my plus-one is making noises about dropping out.' He grabs another handful of crisps and adds, 'But whatever, I'll go alone if I have to.'

Most people wouldn't know Max has gone through anything out of the ordinary, but I do, and we both have the scars to prove it. Those scars remind me how precious it is to love someone so hard your heart's already broken from missing them, even when they're still right in front of you.

Alina elbows Josie. 'Tell them your news.'

'Oh,' she says, pulling her hair up into the claw clip previously attached to her skirt. 'You're looking at the new senior curator for Dulwich Arthouse.'

We celebrate with her deadly cocktail concoction and talk about the plans for the next few days. Finn's back at work at the museum on Monday, but I've still got another day off. I've been tentatively looking at going into some sort of teaching or training job, but nothing's set in stone yet, so I'm intending to use my day off to do some more research. Realistically, I'm no closer to figuring out what I want to do than I was a year ago, but at least now I'm willing to get up and try. That alone is progress I won't take for granted.

Eventually, Max has to leave to catch his train, and the second he's out the door Alina snorts and says, 'There is no way that man is getting a train. He's definitely going to meet a woman.'

'Let him live his slutty little life,' Finn says, pulling me up from the floor to sit next to him on the sofa. 'He deserves it.'

'You know that's my brother you're talking about, right?' I push my side against his chest in a way that's meant to be indignant, but ends with his arms wrapping around me and drawing me against him.

'What? I said he deserved it.'

I laugh under my breath, because even after all this time, I still don't want him to know I think he's funny.

We have a slow afternoon trying to beat the jet lag by doing laundry (Finn), making food with actual nutrients (also Finn) and watching Homes Under the Hammer (me). Somehow, we make it to five in the evening before crashing, and Alina and Josie go out to dinner, leaving us alone in the flat, curled up on the sofa, as if we haven't just spent the entirety of a trip together.

'They love you, you know,' I say, finally showered and comfy in a well-worn blue dinosaur t-shirt.

It's one of those long summer evenings where the sun's still high in the sky and you can almost convince yourself you still have the whole day left. Or at least, you can when you haven't been awake for almost twenty-four hours.

'Yeah?' He pulls me closer and kisses my hair, and I close my eyes and let myself be that person I wasn't sure I could be.

'Everyone loves you.'

'Everyone?' His palm rests on my hip, fingertips pressing lightly into my skin.

Loving someone means giving them a piece of your heart for safekeeping, knowing they'll take care of the fragments while you're struggling to look after the pieces yourself.

I look up at him, into that face with the laughter lines and the warm eyes and the mouth always milliseconds away from opening into a smile. 'I don't think I ever had a choice.'

I find Finn in my room an hour or so later, freshly showered and messy-haired, changing the sheets for me.

'Are you staying here tonight?' I ask from the doorway.

He gives the duvet a thrash before it drifts down onto the bed, where he smooths it out as best he can. Then he looks up, his eyes shining the way they always do. 'Do you want me to? I thought you might wanna spend some time alone after being stuck with me non-stop for ten days.'

'I want you to.'

'Then of course I'll stay.' He joins me in the doorway, leaning against the frame in that stupid easy way of his, one hand already sliding up my neck to cup my jaw, fingers weaving into my hair. 'For you, Ava Monroe, every time.'

I know he will. And I will too, because it's not nearly as complicated as it seems. It's bucket lists and board games. It's changing the bedding for me because I once drunkenly mentioned it's my least favourite chore. It's dark jokes in darker times, and it's *Twilight* reruns and terrible karaoke and aeroplane wishes and hazelnut wafers snuck home from work. It's not being fully okay yet, but it's the brilliant, blazing hope that one day you will be. It's laughing loudly and living fully and leaving trails of stardust in your wake.

Like sunlight, love finds its way in through the cracks regardless.

Might as well open the door.

# acknowledgements

I've never been particularly good at being effusive or earnest (gosh, I wonder where Ava's personality came from?), but I'm going to try my best with these acknowledgements. Get ready for the most long-winded thank you spiel ever.

First of all, this book wouldn't be what it is without my early readers. Thank you to my alphas, who read the messy, unedited first ten chapters and gave invaluable feedback: Emo (I will never use your real name, it is what it is), Ernie (I will never use your real name either, whoops!), Georgia and Natalie. Sorry you had to experience the chaos of a first draft; I will not do that to you again.

The next thank you goes to my iconic team of beta readers, whose comments were as helpful as they were funny, who killed me with their unhinged messages, and who filled out my absolute beast of a feedback form with no complaints. So, thank you to: Aly, Ashleigh, Evie, Georgia (again), Harriet, Marie, Natalie (also again!), Niamh and Sarah (who, as the first person to finish *ACOS* in full, got first dibs on Finn. You'll have to fight her for him). A special thank you to my fellow Georgia, who joined me on endless chai latte-fuelled writing dates at Caffè Nero, helped talk through plot points and listened to me go on about these characters, and who, for a long while, probably knew more about this story than anyone else.

Thank you to my ARC readers for taking a chance on a debut indie author. I really appreciate your enthusiasm and early support, and hope you enjoyed the story as much as I enjoyed writing it. An extra dollop of a thank you to any early reader (and internet resource, but that feels a bit less personal to include here) who offered me any advice pre-publication on writing characters who come from communities different from mine.

It feels presumptuous to write this before the book is published, because who knows, maybe no one will read *ACOS* from here on out, but here I am, preemptively thanking you, my reader. Whether you come across this book on publication day or ten years from now, if you read so much as a page, it means more than you know.

Next, thank you to everyone on booksta who sent me excited words of support every time I posted a sneak peek. But mostly, thank you for not unfollowing me when I wouldn't shut up about writing this thing, especially if you're on my close friends list and had to listen to me ramble on about it for a year and a half. I appreciate it.

Speaking of friends from booksta, thank you to the angel that is Meg Jones, for not only offering me writing and indie publishing advice, but also for spending hours formatting my book for me and not getting annoyed at my constant requests to change things.

My words wouldn't exist without my favourite authors, from romance to fantasy, YA to adult, and everything in between. But in particular, thank you to all the romance authors who continue to forge ahead in a genre that doesn't always get the respect it deserves.

While a handful of music artists pushed me through those late-night writing and editing sessions, I feel I need to offer a special shoutout to Neck Deep, for inadvertently inspiring this book's title with one of their lyrics. I can only hope my storytelling is half as good as my favourite musicians' someday.

I'm not going to name my friends individually because I simply cannot, but you know who you are. Thank you for being around either on the other end of a phone or in real life. Thanks for the laughs, the chats, and for always going feral at gigs with me.

Finally, thank you to my family. I don't know if I want my relatives to read this book, but if you're here then I fear it's far too late. Please do not talk to me about certain scenes, ever. Many thanks! I have the best family in the world (sorry to anyone reading this who disagrees, but you are, unfortunately, wrong), so to anyone who's part of it, thank you.

To my parents, thanks for always being there, for letting us figure things out as we go, and for somehow raising four kids who all actually like each other.

Dan, Loz and Soph, thank you for the inspiration behind Ava and Max; the nicknames, the lols, the songs, the weird language, the bunk bed with teeth marks in the wood (@ Lauren), etc. But most importantly, thanks for making fun of my stationery obsession as a child. Who's laughing now?

On a serious note, it'd be remiss of me not to think about how different these past few years could have been if certain things hadn't happened the way they did. *A Collision of Stars* itself wouldn't even exist the way it does. So, this may be a weird thing to include in the acknowledgements of a romance novel, but last, but by no means least, I want to say thank you to the scientists of the world for developing the kinds of treatments that save people like Max, and my brilliant, brilliant sister.

This story was my baby for so long, but now it's all of yours too, and that's as scary as it is exciting. I hope it makes you laugh, swoon a little, and maybe even shed a tear or two (I'm a sadist, sue me!). I hope Ava and Finn and all the gang bury their way into your heart the way they did mine. I hope you give yourself grace, and I hope you see the beauty in opening up and taking those leaps. It's something I'm working on too, but my little ink children have taught me to try.

So here's to more leaps, more stories, and even more trying.

# about the author

**Georgia Stone** is a London-based contemporary romance author. She writes love stories that she hopes make people swoon, laugh out loud, and angstily clutch their chests in equal measure, with plenty of banter and a type of humour that is likely only funny to a very small subset of people. As a longtime daydreaming connoisseur, she very much appreciates that being a fiction author is essentially just a socially acceptable way of having imaginary friends.

When she's not reading or writing, you can usually find Georgia partaking in DIY projects in her ridiculously colourful flat, spending far too much time feeding TikTok's algorithm, and acting borderline-unhinged at gigs with her friends. And if you want to chat/yell/sob in her direction, you can head to @georgiastonewrites on Instagram. She's embarrassingly attached to her phone, so she'll almost definitely be around.

Printed in Great Britain
by Amazon